A
Whisper of
PEACE

Books by
Kim Vogel Sawyer

FROM BETHANY HOUSE PUBLISHERS

A
Whisper of
PEACE

Kim Vogel
A Novel by
Sawyer

BETHANY HOUSE PUBLISHERS
a division of Baker Publishing Group
Minneapolis, Minnesota

Cover design by Brand Navigation
Cover photography by Steve Gardner, PixelWorks Studio, Inc.

Published by Bethany House Publishers
11400 Hampshire Avenue South
Bloomington, Minnesota 55438
www.bethanyhouse.com

Bethany House Publishers is a division of
Baker Publishing Group, Grand Rapids, Michigan

Printed in the United States of America

ISBN 978–0–7642–0785–3 Trade Paper
ISBN 978–0–7642–0920–8 Hard Cover

Library of Congress Cataloging-in-Publication Data
Sawyer, Kim Vogel.
    A whisper of peace / Kim Vogel Sawyer.
        p.   cm.
    ISBN 978-0-7642-0920-8 (hardcover : alk. paper) — ISBN 978-0-
7642-0785-3 (pbk.)
    1. Missionaries—Fiction. 2. Racially mixed people—Fiction. 3.
Athapascan Indians—Fiction. 4. Alaska—History—19th century—
Fiction. I. Title.
PS3619.A97W48 2011
813'.6—dc22   2011025212

Scripture quotations are from the King James Version of the Bible.

11   12   13   14   15   16   17   7   6   5   4   3   2   1

For *Don*,
who walks with me through
sunshine and shadow.

"Thy righteousness is like the great mountains . . .
How excellent is thy lovingkindness, O God!
therefore the children of men put their trust
under the shadow of thy wings."

Psalm 36:6a, 8 (KJV)

Chapter One

Not once in all of her twenty-one years had Lizzie Dawson seen a moose behind her cabin. The dogs' noise always kept wild game at bay. Even squirrels—brazen, chattering creatures—avoided her small plot of ground. She couldn't imagine a timid moose possessing the courage to come near the team of dogs. Yet there one stood, unconcernedly nibbling at the pin cherry shrub a mere twenty feet from her open back door, its proud antlers glowing pink in the morning light.

Lizzie hid behind the doorjamb and absorbed the peaceful scene so unexpectedly displayed before her. The soft *crunch-crunch* of the moose's teeth on the pin cherry's tender tips joined the wind's whisper in the aspens—a delicate melody. Silvery bands of light crept between branches, gilding the moose's tawny hump. It was a young moose. No evidence of fights marred its hide. She'd seen the damage the animals caused one another with their sharp, slashing hooves and antlers.

An unblemished hide . . . Lizzie's heart skipped a beat. Surely this moose had come to her as an offering! *Let the dogs stay sleeping.* The wish winged from her heart as she tiptoed to the corner where her bow and arrows waited. A rifle was easier, but the bow and arrow was silent—she wouldn't frighten the animal away by cocking a noisy lever.

She returned to the doorway and stood in the shielding slice of shadow. Her elbow high, she slowly drew back the gut bowstring. The string released a faint whine as it stretched, and she cringed. But the big animal didn't even flare a nostril in concern. She held the hand-carved bow securely, her left arm extended as straight as her father's rifle barrel. The arrow's feather fletching brushed her jaw, but she ignored the slight tickle and kept her gaze on her target.

Magpies began to call from the treetops. The dogs would awaken soon—she needed to shoot before she squandered the gift. But she wouldn't release the arrow yet. As her mother had taught her, she offered a brief prayer. *Thank you, brother moose, for giving your life that I might live.* She clenched her jaw and released the string.

The high-pitched *twang* brought the moose's head up. The arrow whirred across the short clearing and its tip penetrated the animal's neck. The moose dropped, a few pale green leaves still caught in its lip.

Birds lifted in frantic flight from the trees, squawking in protest as joyful barks exploded from the dog pen between the sheltering aspens. Lizzie stepped into the yard and whistled—one sharp, shrill blast. The dogs ceased the clamorous barking, but they continued to whine and leap against the chicken-wire enclosure in excitement. Lizzie set the bow aside and crossed the mossy yard, her moccasin-covered feet nearly silent on the cushiony bed of deep green. Sorrow pierced her as she gazed down at the magnificent animal. Death always saddened her. But she pushed the emotion aside. She would celebrate this kill. This gift.

Quickly, the routine so familiar she could perform the actions without conscious thought, she removed her knife from the sheath she always wore on her belt and bled the moose to prevent the meat from spoiling. *Thank you, thank you,* her thoughts sang. How fortunate that the animal had come in the early hours—before the dogs awakened and frightened it away. How fortunate that it had ventured near during the first days of nearly endless sun, when she could work late into the night and still be able to see to skin it, prepare the meat for the smokehouse, and boil the bones for future use. Everything about the kill felt miraculous.

She turned toward the cabin to retrieve her skinning knife, but her gaze drifted to the pen where the dogs lined the fence, their tongues lolling, mouths smiling, tails wagging. Lizzie chuckled softly. The carcass could wait a few minutes while she greeted her companions. As she neared the enclosure, they leapt, bouncing off the wire fence and springing over one another's backs in eagerness.

Lizzie reached for her favorites first. George and Martha served as the lead dogs for her sled. The two worked in accord with each other. And with her. The pair had been her father's, which made her love them all the more. Surely there were no two finer dogs in all of the Yukon. She wove her fingers in their thick ruffs, and they wriggled around, their identical black-and-white snouts nuzzling her palms. She scratched them beneath their chins, laughing when they tipped their heads for more.

The other dogs swarmed her, nudging George and Martha

out of the way. Lizzie tried to pet each one by turn, but slowly they drifted away, sniffing the air and panting. They whined again, but from deep in their throats, and Lizzie knew the breeze had carried the moose's scent to their keen noses. She hoped her dogs were the only animals that had picked up the scent of the kill. She had no desire to fight a grizzly for her moose. But she'd do it if she had to—she needed the meat as well as the hide. If she had to fight, the dogs would help. Their faithfulness to her knew no end.

"I must go to work now," she told the dogs. "Be good, and you will have fresh meat for your dinner today."

The dogs, as if able to understand, leapt in circles, their white teeth biting at the air in happiness. Still laughing softly, Lizzie hurried to the cabin to retrieve her skinning knife. Just before slicing the blade through the moose's thick shoulder, she paused and allowed herself a moment to admire the smooth, flawless hide—the biggest miracle of all. Gratitude filled her. If everything went well, the gift of this moose's hide might make reconciliation with her grandparents possible.

And once peace existed between *Vitsiy* and *Vitse* and herself, she'd finally have the freedom to leave this place and join Voss Dawson. *Thank you, moose.*

∽

Clay Selby strapped the wooden accordion case onto his back, shrugging to adjust the bulky weight on his spine. He turned to his stepsister, Vivian. The weeks of travel had taken their toll. She looked ready to wilt. He'd tried to convince her to stay behind with their parents—if she found the Kiowa reservation on the Oklahoma plains formidable, living in a village in the Alaskan wilderness would certainly be difficult for her to endure. But she'd insisted she could be of use in opening the mission school.

Now she sagged against the railing that lined the paddleboat's deck, bedraggled and with dark circles under her eyes. She caught him looking at her. With a jolt, she stood upright and curved her lips into a weary smile. "Almost there." Despite her brave posture, her voice wavered.

Clay hoped she'd make it. He'd have more than enough to do, getting the school started. If he had to mollycoddle Vivian, too . . . *"Give her a chance, son,"* his father had said. *"She's an intelligent girl, and you will need a partner for this ministry. You can't do it all yourself."* Clay offered Vivian a smile and echoed, "Almost there."

Other passengers pushed past them, nearly sending Clay onto his nose. He planted the soles of his boots and held his footing, curling a protective arm around Vivian's waist. He waited until everyone else reached the paddleboat's gangplank before grabbing the handle of their large carpetbag. "Let's go."

Vivian lifted the smaller valise, and together they fell behind the line of rowdy men whose eager voices proclaimed their intentions to get rich in the goldfields. Clay also hoped for riches, but of a completely different kind.

Holding Vivian's elbow, he stepped off the paddleboat. His gaze searched up and down the riverbank. He'd been told he'd have no trouble hiring a canoe to take them upriver past Fort Yukon. But with so many people milling in impatient confusion, he wasn't able to determine which men were hiring canoes and which were offering them for use.

He contemplated elbowing his way through the crowd to the riverbank, where he would be able to secure a canoe. The sooner he and Vivian reached their destination, the sooner he could begin God's work. But after having witnessed several skirmishes between rough travelers on the paddleboat—one of which resulted in a knife fight—he decided a little patience might be warranted. No sense in scaring

Vivian out of her wits—or in putting her in harm's way. The Gwich'in village wasn't going anywhere.

As if reading his mind, Vivian said, "Let's sit and give things a chance to calm."

He followed her to the end of the dock. She sank onto the rough wood, placed the valise near her feet, and began smoothing the wrinkled skirt of her traveling dress. Clay thought it a fruitless pastime, but he wouldn't say so. He plopped beside her, the accordion case making him clumsy. She shot him a little smile of amusement and he shrugged, then turned his attention to his surroundings.

Clouds had rolled in with the afternoon, painting the ramshackle town a dismal gray. A cool, damp breeze whisked across the water and chilled him. Back home, mid-May brought occasional rain showers, but the sun shone brightly, warming the land and those who occupied it. Looking up at the nickel-plated sky, Clay experienced a jolt of homesickness for Oklahoma's endless canopy of clear blue. Yet at the same time, excitement filled him.

Finally, after years of dreaming, he had the chance to begin his own ministry. Vivian would handle the housekeeping and teaching the native children to read and write, and he would preach. Thanks to his father's diligent training, he felt confident he'd be able to win the souls of the villagers. As a wave of impatience filled him, he twitched on his perch, willing the crowd to clear so he could locate a canoe and complete his monthlong journey. He craned his neck, searching the shoreline for an available vessel.

"Hey, mister . . . lady."

Clay turned at the voice. A scruffy boy, perhaps ten years old, stood so close his dirty bare toes bumped against Clay's boots.

"You need totin'?"

Clay looked the boy up and down. He couldn't imagine this scrawny child possessing the strength to paddle a canoe loaded with both passengers and belongings upriver. But maybe, if the boy gave him the use of a vessel, Clay could paddle it himself. He posed a question of his own. "You have a canoe available?"

The boy pointed. "My pa does. He'll tote you, if you need it. Dollar apiece."

Clay had been warned prices were high in Alaska, thanks to successful gold hunters, but he wasn't a miner. He was just a missionary, and he couldn't spare two dollars for a canoe ride. "I can pay two bits apiece."

A frown furrowed the boy's forehead. He inched backward, shaking his head. "Won't do it for less'n six bits apiece. I'm sure o' that."

Clay sighed. He heaved to his feet, angling his shoulders to center the squeeze box on his back. "All right, then. Six bits each."

The boy held out his hand. Clay removed the coin purse he wore on a cord beneath his shirt and withdrew a round silver dollar and two twenty-five-cent pieces. With a grin, the boy curled his fist around the coins. He spun and darted through the crowd.

Vivian bounced up. "We'd better hurry, Clay."

With the bulky box on his back, a heavy carpetbag in one hand and Vivian's elbow in the other—he didn't dare let loose of her or she might get swallowed by the crowd—Clay wasn't able to move as quickly as the wiry, unfettered youngster. He lost sight of the boy when a group of miners surged around them, blocking their pathway. Just when he'd decided he'd been bilked out of a dollar and fifty cents, he heard a shout.

"Mister! Mister, over here!"

Clay pulled Vivian close to his side and wriggled his way past the men. He spotted the boy about ten yards upriver. A short, heavily whiskered man with his fists on his hips stood beside the boy. Clay took in the man's untucked flannel shirt, baggy dungarees jammed into laceless boots, and low-tugged, misshapen hat. He didn't seem the savory sort. Clay hesitated. Pa had always told him to trust his instincts. Even though it meant forfeiting the money he'd given the boy, he wondered if he should turn around and look for another canoe owner.

Before he could move, the man clumped toward him, his bootheels dragging through the mud. The youngster scuttled along behind his pa. "Boy says you an' your woman need totin'. Where to?"

A foul odor emanated from the man, making it difficult for Clay to draw a breath. He pretended to cough into his fist, then kept his hand in place to protect his nose. "I need to reach Gwichyaa Saa. Are you familiar with the village?"

"Yup, done some tradin' with the siwashes."

Vivian sucked in a disapproving breath, but Clay took care not to bristle at the man's use of the derogatory term—no sense in alienating the man. He'd let his work with the native Alaskans prove his lack of scorn.

"You here for tradin'?" The man's curious gaze swept from their feet to their faces. "You don't look like no traders."

Vivian tucked a stray strand of red-gold hair behind her ear, lifting her chin in a regal manner. Clay smoothed his hand over his jacket's front. Over their weeks of travel, his father's hand-me-down wool suit and Vivian's dark green muslin dress had become rumpled and dusty, but their attire didn't compare to the clothes worn by the canoe owner. Clay wondered if the man's clothes—or the man himself—had seen soap and water since last spring. "We aren't traders."

The man shrugged. "So . . . ya want totin' or not?"

Clay glanced along the shoreline. No other empty canoes waited. If they didn't take this one, they might not be able to leave until tomorrow. Which meant they'd need to pay for a night's lodging. He turned back to the man. "If you're willing."

"Can get there an' back in about four hours, so it'll only cost ya a dollar—the lady's free." The man's grimy hand shot out, palm up.

"I already paid your boy a dollar and four bits for the both of us."

Fury filled the man's face. He whirled around, his fist raised.

The boy cowered. "I'm sorry, Pa! Just tryin' to get a good deal for ya!"

The man shook the boy by the neck of his scruffy shirt. "Gimme the money." Whimpering, the boy obeyed. The man cuffed the boy's ear, and the youngster slinked away. Shaking his head, the man pressed the two smaller coins into Clay's hand. "Never let it be said Chauncy Burke cheated a white woman." He took the valise from Vivian and scuffed toward the canoe. "Let's get movin'."

Clay's boots stuck in the soggy ground as he crossed to the craft, which appeared to be constructed of wooden ribs framed with animal hide. Burke tossed Vivian's valise into the canoe and then grabbed Clay's carpetbag and did the same. Clay held his breath as the bags smacked into the canoe's bottom. But they didn't break through, so Clay took comfort that the canoe could support them.

Chauncy Burke reached to pluck the box from Clay's back, but Clay pulled away. "I'll get it." The man frowned, and Clay added, "It's fragile."

Burke offered a brusque nod. He turned to the boy, who

hunkered on the bank. "Get on home." He flipped the remaining coin through the air, and the boy caught it. "Buy a hambone to flavor the beans—I expect a good meal when I get back."

Without a word, the boy dashed away. Burke faced Clay and Vivian again. He appeared surprised to see them standing on the bank. "Git yourself an' your woman in, mister." A grin climbed his cheek, his gaze grazing over Vivian. "'Less you're needin' a hand."

Clay quickly lowered his accordion box into the canoe, wincing as the boat sank several inches with the weight. *Lord, grant us safe passage, please.* He'd offered the same prayer before boarding each train, stagecoach, and riverboat between here and Oklahoma, but it had never been as heartfelt as in that moment. He took Vivian's hand and helped her settle in the canoe's belly. Then, gingerly, he stepped in. The vessel sank another few inches, but water didn't pour over the sides. Relieved, Clay sat next to Vivian and leaned against the accordion box.

Burke clambered in, causing the canoe to rock, and Clay grabbed the edge with one hand and Vivian with the other. Burke grinned as he plopped down, seeming to take delight in making the narrow boat shift to and fro. Then he swung a long wooden paddle into position. "All right, here we go—to Gwichyaa Saa." He stroked the paddle through the green-blue water and the canoe glided away from the bank.

Chapter Two

S
o if you ain't tradin', what'cha carryin' around that big wooden box for?"

They had ridden in silence for nearly half an hour. Vivian dozed, her head bobbing on Clay's shoulder, but Clay had used the time to scrutinize the landscape of their new home. Rugged beauty greeted him from every angle, but he'd seen little that reminded him of Oklahoma—not that he'd expected to. But he'd searched anyway. Even one field bearing stalks of tassled corn would ease some of his homesickness and perhaps help put Vivian at ease.

He shifted his gaze from the grassy bank lined with spindly pine trees to Chauncy Burke. "The box holds my accordion."

Burke puckered his brow. He sliced the water with the paddle and flipped it to the opposite side of the canoe, sprinkling Vivian and Clay in the process. "Accordy-what?"

Clay tugged Vivian closer to his side and leaned more fully against the box as more water spritzed from the paddle's blade when Burke traded sides again. "Accordion—a musical instrument." When the man's expression didn't clear, he added, "It has a piano keyboard and a squeezebox, and when you pump air through it and press the keys, it makes musical sounds. Like an organ."

Burke's eyes widened, his hands pausing midswipe. "That so? An organ you carry around on your back?"

Clay nodded.

"Ain't that somethin' . . ."

Clay agreed. He loved playing his accordion. The children on the reservation where Clay's father and stepmother served had loved listening to it. He hoped the Gwich'in children would be as fascinated as the Kiowa children in Oklahoma had been. It would give him a means of befriending them.

"But what'cha doin' way out here with an organ? Need to stay in town, where there's saloons. Lotta music-playin' goes on there day an' night—oughtta keep ya good an' busy."

A saloon? To prevent the man from seeing distaste in his eyes, Clay tilted his head and admired the dark green tips of the trees against the gray background of sky. "I've got use for it in the Gwich'in village—playing hymns. I plan to hold church services."

A derisive snort blasted from Burke's nose. He gave the water a vicious swipe with the paddle. "Church? For the siwashes? Mister, that's a plumb waste o' good time. They ain't gonna be interested in no church service. I'm for certain-sure those poker-faced heathens don't even have souls." He looked Clay up and down. "'Pears to me you an' yer woman're folks o' quality. Folks such as you shouldn't waller low enough to spend time with the likes o' them."

Clay had encountered this negative mindset toward natives many times before. Even though it irritated him, his father had taught him to overcome evil with good. "Mr. Burke, have you considered how much Jesus lowered Himself to leave Heaven and spend time with us on earth? Should we do any less than He did?"

Burke set his jaw in a stubborn angle and didn't answer.

Clay continued, "I believe all men—white, yellow, red, or black—are precious in the sight of God. And I intend to tell the Gwich'in people how much He loves them."

Burke grunted, but to Clay's relief, he dropped the argument. They coasted along, the swish of the paddle in the water and the wind's whisper through the pines the only intrusions. As they rounded a bend in the river, a thrashing sound along the bank stirred Vivian from her nap. She sat up and craned her neck, seeking the source of the sound. Clay looked, too, and spotted a shaggy, hump-backed animal with enormous antlers sloshing through the shallow water. Vivian gasped as the creature lowered its nose to some green, stringy plants floating on the surface. The great animal lifted a string of the green and stared back at the canoe while munching.

Vivian spun her wide-eyed look on Clay. "Is that a deer?"

Clay whistled softly through his teeth. "If so, Alaska has the biggest deer I've ever seen."

Burke coughed out a laugh. "Deer? Lady, that's a moose." He gave the paddle a few brisk strokes, carrying them away from the oversized creature. "Ornery things. Look clumsy, but they can move faster'n you'd think. Might wanna steer clear of 'em. 'Specially the mamas when they're nursin' a calf. More cantankerous than a woman who's—" His face flooded with color. "Beggin' your pardon, ma'am. Mostly men in Alaska, ya know, so a fella forgets how to act when a white lady's present."

Clay assumed the man found no reason to mind his tongue when in the presence of the native women.

Burke flicked a glance at Clay. "Didn't mean to offend your woman, mister."

During their weeks of travel, most of the people they

had encountered assumed he and Vivian were husband and wife. Although it had twinged his conscience to allow the misconception to go unchallenged, he'd decided silence was wiser. The shortage of white women made Vivian a target for unwanted attention. His stepmother would never forgive him if he allowed unpleasantness to befall her only child.

Vivian continued to peer back over her shoulder, even though the animal was now hidden from sight. "A moose." Her tone held amazement. "I've heard about moose, of course, but hearing about them doesn't hold a candle to seeing one so close."

Clay nodded, imagining the damage the rack of antlers might cause a man. He told Burke, "We'll steer clear. Thanks for the warning."

"Also wanna be careful 'bout approachin' a bear. Got lots of 'em around here."

Vivian clamped her hand over Clay's knee.

Clay gave her cold fingers a reassuring pat. "We have bears in Oklahoma Territory, too." Although he'd never seen a live one, he'd seen their hides displayed at a trading post near their reservation.

"That so?" Burke raised his brows, as if he didn't believe Clay; then his forehead crinkled. "Well, then, you know they're more dangerous than the moose. A feller shouldn't never catch one by surprise."

Vivian leaned forward slightly. "And how do you avoid surprising a bear?"

"Make sure he knows you're there." Burke's tone took on a wise edge. "Crunch some leaves under your feet, whistle . . . talk to yerself." The man continued a steady stroke-stroke with the paddle as he talked. "Thing is, them critters ain't gonna want to come face-to-face with you. They'll hide if they know you're there. But if you come upon 'em an' take 'em by surprise, their instinct is to attack." Burke chuckled. "Seein' as how most bears outweigh a stout man by a good two hunnerd pounds, even a fool can figure out it won't be much of a contest."

Clay's mouth went dry. "Yes . . . yes, I see your point."

"But you oughtta be all right, mister." A smirk climbed the man's grizzled cheek. "One of 'em snarlin' monsters comes after you, just hold yer ground an' whack 'em with that big ol' wooden box." He laughed and sliced the water with a firm stroke. "Then run."

An hour later, Burke ran the canoe's nose onto another mossy bank. Plopping the paddle on the floor of the canoe, he grinned at Clay. "Well, here's where we part ways."

Vivian stared at the man. "Here? But . . . there's no village."

Pine trees stretched skyward behind a curving riverbank lined with thick brush. There were no signs of human life anywhere. Burke obviously hadn't approved of Clay's reason for coming to the Alaska Territory, but was the man contrary enough to leave him and Vivian stranded in the woods miles from any town?

Burke laughed. "You think them siwashes're gonna make it easy for ya? No, sir. They build their log houses in clearings with lots o' trees surroundin' 'em. But you can find 'em—'bout a two-mile walk northeast o' here."

Worry created a tingle of awareness across Clay's scalp. On the Oklahoma prairie, he possessed a sense of direction, but in this land of woods, mountains, and sunshine that lasted far into the night, he had no way of determining direction. "Um . . . which way is northeast?"

Burke grunted low in his throat. He pointed. "Thataway. You can keep yourself on track by lookin' at where the moss grows on the trees—always on the north."

Clay tucked the bit of information away for future use.

"All right, then." He shouldered his accordion and grabbed the carpetbag. Balancing his belongings, he stepped onto the soggy riverbank. Vivian clambered out behind him without assistance. Her skirt dipped into the water, and she released a little huff of irritation as she shook water from the heavy folds of fabric.

Clay lifted the valise from the canoe's bottom and handed it to Vivian. "Mr. Burke, do you hire your canoe regularly?"

The man scratched his head. "Onliest way I make a livin'. Give up on gold huntin'—too many others stickin' their pans in the creeks, an' less'n half of 'em findin' color. Ruther earn my keep in more certain ways."

Praying he wouldn't regret his request, Clay said, "Within the next few days, we should receive several crates of supplies from home. We had them shipped, but they didn't reach Alaska at the same time we did." Clay hoped their precious belongings hadn't been lost. Or stolen. "Would you watch for them and then transport them to this location when they've arrived?"

Burke's eyes flew wide. "Bring 'em here? You gonna just sit an' wait for 'em?"

Clay hadn't yet processed how he'd retrieve their items. Maybe he could enlist a couple of young Athabascans from the village to come check the bank on a daily basis.

Burke added, "Don't mind committin' to bringin' 'em. It'll cost you the fare of one passenger, an' I can't make no guarantees they'll still be a-sittin' here when you come lookin'. Once I drop 'em off, my part's done—I won't be held accountable for no losses."

Even though all the assurances were on Burke's side rather than his, Clay had little choice but to agree. He reached for his coin purse and withdrew another silver dollar. "Thank you. And thank you for the ride."

Burke quickly pocketed the coin and then gave Clay's hand a firm shake. "Good luck to ya, mister. You too, lady." He hunkered into the canoe and took up the paddle again, chuckling the whole time. "I'm thinkin' you're gonna need it." With a push of the paddle's blade against the bank, he returned the canoe to the middle of the river. He glided away, leaving Clay and Vivian standing in the wilderness alone.

∞

Lizzie crossed to the smokehouse, pulling the small travois bearing the last of the moose's meat behind her. Her body ached from the long hours of work, but every sore muscle was well worth it. The meat would feed her and the dogs for weeks. She glanced into the dogs' pen and couldn't stop a smile from growing. They lay in small groups, sound asleep, their bellies distended from their hearty meal of fresh meat. Her father would no doubt berate her for indulging them so extravagantly—it wasn't winter when they would work off the extra fat by pulling her sled—but her father wasn't here and she could do as she pleased. And it pleased her to give her companions a treat.

After hanging the last of the cuts of meat from the sturdy log rafters, she banked the fire, then closed the door securely and leaned the travois against the smokehouse wall. That task completed, she set her attention to the moose's hide. As much as she'd wanted to work on it immediately after removing it from the animal, she'd understood the importance of preparing the meat first. So she'd sprinkled the flesh side heavily with salt, folded it gently in half, and left it lying beneath the bushes where the sun wouldn't be able to reach it.

She pulled it from its shaded shelter and shook it out. Two shiny, black-shelled beetles fell from the fold, and she hissed in displeasure. Flopping the hide flat, she examined it closely. She found no places where the insects had chewed—the salt had served its purpose in discouraging them. Releasing a breath of relief, she carried the hide to the rear of her cabin, where a canvas canopy protected her father's stretching frame from even the tiniest ray of sunlight.

While lacing the hide into the willow frame, the image of another pair of hands haunted her memories. Broad hands, the pointer finger on the left one bent at the second knuckle from a childhood accident, blunt fingernails cut so short no dirt could gather underneath. Her father's hands. She shook her head hard, dispelling the image. But even then, other memories nibbled at the corners of her mind, all snippets of time during the carefree years when Pa was here and Mama was alive. When Pa left, the happiness drained from this place, which must mean Pa had been their source of happiness.

So why did remembering him never make her happy?

Lizzie's vision clouded. Clicking her tongue against her teeth in irritation, she swept the distorting tears away. Hadn't she learned long ago dwelling on the past only made her melancholy? Yet she relied on lessons from the past as she laced the hide onto the frame and stretched it as tightly as the skin would allow. She'd removed most of the meat already, but she retrieved a scraping tool made from bone and used it to carefully carve away all remnants of fat and tissue.

As she worked, her father's voice echoed in her head: *"Don't press too hard, Lizzie, or you'll poke holes and ruin the hide. Firm pressure, back and forth, like buttering a slice of bread— that's the proper way to flesh a hide."* Her head tilted slightly, she examined the clean-scraped area. Would her father be proud of how well she'd learned to follow his teachings?

In her cabin's small loft, piles of furs—beaver, otter, badger, fox, wolf, and caribou—gave mute evidence of her ability to hunt, trap, and prepare hides. The stacks rose high enough to brush against the rafters, the accumulation of several years' work. Although the furs would fetch a tidy sum at the trading post, she didn't intend to sell all of them. A few—the finest ones—would be used to adorn Vitse's moosehide coat. She'd thought of it so often, she could picture the coat embellished with foxtail fringing, a thick badger ruff, and delicate forget-me-nots formed of dyed porcupine quill beads circling the hem.

Her hands began to tremble, and she stepped away from the hide lest an errant slice of the bone cut too deep. Pressing one hand to her chest, she willed herself to calm. But her heart pounded fast and hard beneath her palm. How long had she dreamed of the day she would present this very special peace gift to her grandmother? The idea had sprung to life the day she'd put Mama in the ground—four long years ago.

Lizzie experienced a sharp pang of grief. Despite the passage of time, she thought of her mother every day. And she continued to mourn. Clenching her fists, she drew in deep breaths that cleared her tumbled thoughts and slowed her racing pulse. Determinedly, she lifted the bone scraper, her plan unfolding without effort: Complete preparation on the moose's hide; construct the coat; offer it to her grandmother and fulfill Mama's dying request; sell the accumulated furs; take the money and—

Raucous barking brought her thoughts to an abrupt halt. She dropped the bone and spun toward the dog pen, her senses alert for danger. But no bear or two-legged predator lurked in her yard. She crossed to the pen and whistled, bringing the dogs under control. Martha propped her front feet on the wire fence and nosed Lizzie's hand, a soft whine escaping her throat. The other dogs all looked toward the trees, their fur bristling, some of them baring their teeth.

Lizzie angled her ear toward the woods, listening intently. What had caused their unrest? A sound—an enchanting one—carried from the thick stand of trees east of her cabin and delighted her ears. In a way it reminded her of wind in the pine trees, rising and falling in a lovely melody, yet the sound was deeper. Richer.

Martha whined again, and Lizzie hushed her with a hand on the dog's ruff. "Down." She stepped away from the pen, inexplicably drawn toward the alluring music. But her feet stopped, her body tense. She needed to finish the hide so she could construct Grandmother's coat. With a sigh, she turned toward the frame.

The music rose in volume, the tune turning light and cheerful.

She'd waited four years—she could wait another few minutes. Curiosity sent her skipping toward the sound. She would discover the source of the music, and then she would return to work.

Chapter Three

Lizzie moved on stealthy feet, her ears tuned to the unique melody. She'd heard a similar sound drifting from a roadside tavern when she had accompanied her father into White Horse years ago. She'd wanted to peek through the door and find out what created such a glorious sound, but her father had hurried her right past the rickety building. Now, however, no one would stop her. She'd finally know the source.

The music increased in volume, telling Lizzie it was near. She angled her body to align with an aspen trunk and peered around the tree, alert and watchful. Her diligence found reward a few moments later when two people emerged from the brush. The first one—a man about her age—pumped what appeared to be bellows attached to a dark-stained wooden box. At the same time, he ran the fingers of his other hand along a row of white teeth. Music poured from the box. Entranced, Lizzie forgot herself and stepped from behind the tree.

The man came to a startled halt, the last note slowly wheezing into nothing. He swung one arm outward, as if to hold back the woman following him, but she peeked around his shoulder. When her eyes met Lizzie's, she released a little gasp and clutched the man's arm with a very white, very thin hand.

For as long as Lizzie could remember, white folks had poured into Alaska Territory to seek their fortunes. These two didn't look like they would last long. Dressed in fine clothes similar to ones designed for the paper dolls Pa had given her for Christmas one year when she was small, they stood out like a single stalk of purple lupine in a meadow of yellow aster. They didn't even have the sense to put their bundles on a travois and allow dogs to do the work. The woman bowed beneath the weight of a bag strapped to her back, and the man's face glowed red while moisture dotted his forehead. The wooden case on his back must tax his strength.

But she didn't care about the people as much as the music-making box. She pointed. "What is that?"

The man's brows rose. "You speak English?"

What a ridiculous question. Hadn't she just spoken in English? Lizzie pointed again, jabbing her finger with emphasis toward the box.

He patted the instrument. "This?"

Lizzie nodded.

A smile curved the man's lips. The wary expression he'd donned when Lizzie stepped from behind the tree disappeared. "It's a piano accordion. It plays music."

Lizzie slashed her hand through the air, dismissing his last statement. She had surmised its purpose. "How does it work?" She moved forward two small steps, maintaining enough distance that she could escape if need be. He seemed harmless and was well weighted with encumbrances—he wouldn't be able to give chase easily—but she should be cautious. Both Mama and Pa had emphasized that some white men couldn't be trusted.

The man flashed a smile, but his woman held back, uncertainty lining her features. "When you force air through the bellows and then you push on the keys, it—" He shrugged. "Here. I'll show you." He began pumping the box in and out, creating a low hum. Then his fingers moved along the row of keys. A lovely melody floated over the hum. Lizzie stared, amazed that something so awkward looking could create such beautiful sounds.

The man stilled his hands, and the accordion sighed into silence. "Would you like to try?"

Lizzie's fingers itched to touch the shiny white rectangles and create a pleasing melody. She closed the distance between them. He pumped the accordion, and Lizzie pressed three side-by-side keys. A sour note blared. She jumped back.

The man laughed softly, his teeth as straight and white as the row of keys on the instrument. "Try pushing one key at a time."

Lizzie gazed with longing at the accordion, but she shook her head. Obviously only white people could coax beauty from the ungainly box. Only white people could do a lot of things. Saddened, she backed away.

The man's smile didn't dim. "I am Clay Selby, and this is Vivian." He held his hand toward the woman, who gave a quick nod of greeting. "What's your name?"

"Lu'qul Gitth'ihgi."

"White Feather," Clay Selby translated. "It's a beautiful name."

Surprised by his knowledge of the Athabascan language, Lizzie blurted, "But I'm called Lizzie." She clamped her lips together, aghast to divulge something so personal to strangers.

Clay Selby caught the woman's elbow and drew her to his side. "Vivian and I are here to start a mission school in Gwichyaa Saa." His smile grew broader, his eyes crinkling in the corners the way Pa's had when he laughed. He was handsome like Pa, too, with thick brown hair that curled over his ears and collar and a square-jawed face toasted tan from the sun. "We're going to teach the children to read and write in the English language."

Lizzie's stomach twisted into a knot. She'd been right— this man was up to no good. She inched backward.

"Are you from Gwichyaa Saa?"

"No." Lizzie moved another few feet, keeping her eyes trained on the white man named Clay Selby.

"Are we near it?"

She couldn't lie—her mother had taught her to be honest—but she pushed the reply through clenched teeth. "Yes."

"What's the name of your village?"

Pain stabbed so fiercely her body jolted. "I don't have a village." She whirled and darted between the trees, quick as a jackrabbit escaping a fox. The man with the musical box called after her, but she ignored him and raced for home.

⁂

"Well . . ." Vivian stared after the retreating native woman. "What an interesting encounter."

Clay berated himself, remembering the way Lu'qul Gitth'ihgi had tensed when he asked the name of her village. He'd pushed too hard too fast and inadvertently inflicted discomfort. His pa wouldn't have scared away one of his prospective converts. Clay needed to rein in his enthusiasm if he hoped to establish relationships with the Gwich'in people.

"She startled me when she stepped out of the trees." Vivian shivered. "So quiet . . . sneaky, almost. Who knows how long she'd been watching us before she made herself known?" She glanced around, as if seeking other natives in the bushes. "Unnerving . . ."

Clay shook his head. "We might have heard her if I hadn't been playing the accordion." He slipped to one knee and allowed the box on his back to slide free. Bits of dry leaves drifted upward, making him sneeze.

Vivian frowned as he plucked the carpetbag from the accordion's case and placed the instrument inside. "You aren't going to keep playing? But what about bears?"

At Vivian's request, he'd played the accordion since they left the canoe. He wasn't sure he appreciated being asked to use his music to scare away wild animals, but it had given his uneasy stepsister a measure of assurance. He closed the latch on the case and heaved the box onto his shoulders. "We're close to the village—the native woman said so." He bit down on his lower lip, sympathy for the woman called Lizzie welling in his chest. If she didn't have a village, how did she survive? He added, "It's unlikely we'll encounter a bear if humans are nearby." Clay pushed to his feet and staggered a bit finding his balance on his tired legs.

Vivian shook her head, peering in the direction the woman had disappeared. "I hope the next Gwich'in we meet is friendlier than she was."

Clay chuckled. Catching the handle on the carpetbag, he set off again. "Didn't Pa tell you the people might have difficulty accepting us at first? Unfortunately, many of the white people who intrude on native lands don't treat the Indians well." Was that why she'd run? Had someone mistreated her in the past?

Vivian huffed along beside him, stirring up dried pine needles and decaying leaves with her skirts. "But the Indians at the reservation talked to me—to all of us. They treated our family as if we were part of the tribe."

"They were used to us there, Viv." Vivian couldn't know how hard Pa had worked to earn the trust of the Kiowa people. After Pa and Vivian's mother had wed, they'd sent the girl to live with an aunt and uncle in the East rather than subject her to the harshness of reservation life. She'd returned to Oklahoma a little over a year ago at her mother's request, but she'd never really settled in at the reservation. Why she'd begged so hard to be allowed to accompany Clay to Alaska, he couldn't begin to fathom. Did she think living on the frontier would be less stressful? If so, she was in for some rude surprises.

Clay paused and examined the telling moss climbing a tree trunk. He adjusted his steps accordingly. "By the time you moved in with us, Pa and Ma had worked for several years to establish relationships with the Kiowa. So they accepted you as a part of our family without question. It will take some effort to gain a connection with the Gwich'in people." He frowned, voicing the same warning he'd given her before they'd left the reservation. "Setting up the mission school won't be like hosting a tea party. It'll take a lot of work and—"

She held up her hand. "I know, Clay, I know. I'll do whatever it takes." She squared her shoulders and heaved a mighty sigh. "Contrary to my mother's opinion, I'm not a hothouse pansy in need of constant cosseting. I'll do my fair share of the work."

Clay suspected Vivian didn't have an inkling what her fair share of the work would encompass, despite Pa's lectures and her mother's warnings. But Vivian could be as stubborn as a mule when she wanted to be, and he was too tired to argue. So he trudged onward, forcing his weary legs to carry him the rest of the way.

Chauncy Burke had said a two-mile walk, but slogging through the woods made it difficult to determine how much distance they'd covered. He hoped they'd reach Gwichyaa

Saa soon. His arms ached from the weight of the accordion, and his back ached from the weight of the carpetbag. Vivian dragged her feet. She wouldn't hold up much longer. He didn't fancy spending the night in the woods without any kind of shelter.

A delicate sigh left Vivian's throat, and Clay braced himself for a complaint. But she said, "I thought when that Gwich'in girl stepped out of the trees, we'd found the village. But—" She came to a sudden halt, her eyes flying wide.

Clay stopped, frowning in concern. "What's wrong?"

"I just realized . . ." She took a couple of gulping breaths. "The girl in the woods—I assumed she was native. But her eyes . . . did you notice?"

Clay crunched his forehead, trying to picture the girl in his mind. He recalled moccasins, a buckskin tunic and leggings, dark braids hanging alongside her serious, brown-skinned face. A pretty face. "What about her eyes?"

"They were *blue*, Clay." Vivian shook her head, her tangled hair sweeping across her dirty cheek. "Have you ever seen a native with blue eyes?"

All of the Kiowa on the reservation had brown eyes. "No, I haven't."

"It certainly raises questions, doesn't it?" Vivian adjusted the straps holding the valise on her back and started walking again. Clay fell into step with her as Vivian continued in a pensive tone. "She said she wasn't part of a village and took off as if bees pursued her. Could it be she's merely pretending to be a Gwich'in?"

"Why would she do that?"

"Maybe so the natives will make better trades with her? Or maybe to escape the law?"

Clay resisted laughing. Vivian had an overly active imagination. At least she was moving at a good pace again, her tiredness apparently forgotten. "I suppose anything is possible. All kinds of people have made their way into Alaska in the past few years."

Vivian went on as if Clay hadn't spoken. "Or maybe she *is* Gwich'in, but she was exiled because of her eye color."

Clay sent Vivian a startled look. She fell silent, seemingly out of ideas. But Clay's brain ticked through possible reasons for a young native woman to live separated from the protection of a village. Her blue eyes could mean she wasn't native at all. But more likely, she was of mixed heritage. He couldn't imagine the Gwich'in rejecting a member of their tribe over something as insignificant as eye color. Why blame a child for something outside of her control? But perhaps she'd done something else—something against tribal law—to earn eviction.

The sound of voices reached his ears. Vivian stumbled to a stop, her gaze searching ahead. She sent him a questioning glance, and he nodded. "I hear it, too. It must be the village." He pushed aside his musings about the blue-eyed woman and curled his hand around Vivian's elbow. "Come—let's go meet the people we've come to serve."

And once we're settled, I'll explore how to minister to the woman in the woods.

Chapter Four

L izzie burst into the clearing behind her cabin, her lungs burning from her race through the trees. The dogs awakened, barking in surprise, but when they recognized her, they immediately calmed. She stumbled to the pen and reached over the top of the wire enclosure. Martha rose on two legs, offering a gentle whine while nuzzling her owner's hand. Lizzie ran her fingers through the dog's thick ruff. The warm contact soothed her, and her gasping breaths slowly returned to normal.

"There was a white man in the woods . . . and his wife." Lizzie spoke into the dog's floppy ear, her voice raspy. "They are going to Gwichyaa Saa to teach the children white men's ways." An ache rose in her breast. "They'll confuse the children, make them uncertain of who they are. I know all too well . . . white and red, they don't mix. What should I do?" Martha gazed at Lizzie attentively, her mouth open in a tongue-lolling grin. But she offered no advice.

Lizzie stroked the dog's head, her mind seeking a way to prevent Clay and Vivian Selby from harming the children in the village. Her gaze turned toward the peak of Denali, the High One, the place her mother had sought when in need of answers or support. Mama had believed the tallest mountain looked over her and offered strength and wisdom. But today, like so many other days, the peak was blanketed by gray clouds. Neither the dogs nor the mountain could offer assistance.

Defeated, she whirled away from the pen, but Martha's pleading whine drew her back. Opening the gate a few inches, she allowed Martha to slip through. The other dogs stormed the gate, eager to be released as well, but she ordered, "Stay!" They whimpered in complaint but obediently retreated.

"Come, Martha." With the dog trotting happily at her side, Lizzie returned to the lean-to where the moose hide waited. Martha flopped onto her stomach and rested her head on her paws. Her eyes—one brown like Mama, one blue like Pa—followed Lizzie as she picked up the scraping tool.

"I'm not going to worry about Clay Selby and his woman. Why should I care if they change things in the village? The villagers don't care about me." Lizzie forced a flippant tone, but deep down, the truth of her statement stung. Gliding the scraper along the hide, she continued talking to the attentive dog. "I've never had a place with them. They rejected Mama the moment she chose to marry Voss Dawson, and they've never accepted me. So let the white man and his woman do whatever they wish."

Yet she couldn't deny the worry that gnawed at the fringes of her heart. The children in the village were accepted, were content. Why should white people be allowed to destroy their peaceful existence? Her hands trembled. She sank to her haunches, tossing aside the scraper and reaching for Martha. The dog rose up to meet her, and Lizzie buried her face in the dog's neck. "Oh, Martha, why must things change?"

Despite her efforts to hold them at bay, buried memories

from long ago awakened. How she'd loved the happy sup-
pers in their little cabin, with Mama serving steaming bowls
of fresh stew or slabs of succulent salmon while Pa teased
and laughed. Behind her closed lids, she could easily envision Pa sitting in the yard at dusk, the stem of his beautifully carved pipe caught between his teeth. Lizzie would
snuggle on his lap, giggling when his beard tickled her
cheek. If she imagined hard enough, she could still catch
the sweet aroma of his tobacco. Lizzie also conjured Mama's
smile—the smile that disappeared the day Pa returned to
the white man's world.

Tears stung, and she sniffed fiercely. Crying wouldn't
bring Mama back, and it wouldn't make Pa change his mind
about taking them with him. He'd said Mama wouldn't fit in
his world—that it would be cruel to make her try. "You're an
Athabascan, Yellow Flower. Your skills of moccasin making
and salmon drying aren't well respected in San Francisco.
You'd feel out of place in my city. Your home is here, with
your people."

Pa's deep voice echoed in Lizzie's memory, competing with
the heartrending sounds of deep distress that had poured
from her gentle mother's lips. But Pa had turned away from
Mama's tears, tugged Lizzie's braid, and said, "Take care of
your mama. Be strong for her. She needs you."

Lizzie pulled back and cupped the dog's face in her hands.
"Until Mama's dying day, I did what Pa asked of me. I
hunted and trapped and fished so my mother would be
clothed and fed. When Mama sang mourning songs in Pa's
memory, I offered words of comfort. When Mama knelt
and prayed to the High One, I knelt beside her and prayed
to Denali, too." Her voice caught as she recalled her most
fervent prayer—*Bring my father back to us.* But the mountain
never replied.

Lizzie gulped twice. "I tended to Mama's every need, Martha, except one. But I'll do it now, in her memory."

Martha whined and swiped Lizzie's chin with her warm tongue. Lizzie hugged the dog, squeezing her eyes tight, her lips quivering with the effort of holding back her tears. On Mama's dying day, she'd extracted a promise from Lizzie: "Make peace with your grandparents for me so I can rest without regret. Then leave this place, my daughter. You're more white than Athabascan—you belong in your father's world."

Four years after her mother's death, Lizzie still puzzled over Mama's strange statement. How could she be more white than Athabascan when she'd lived her entire life a few hundred yards from the village of Gwichyaa Saa? She knew all she needed to know to be an Athabascan—canoe building, salmon trapping, fur skinning, and garment making. But while the books Papa left behind taught her geography and history, they didn't tell her how to be a white woman. Mama's words made no sense. Regardless, Lizzie would fulfill the promise that had given Mama a splash of joy before she crossed into the spirit world.

She whisked away her tears and pushed to her feet. Martha whined and wriggled, bumping her head against Lizzie's hip. Lizzie absently petted the dog as she mused aloud, "A special gift—a lovely coat made by my own hands—will convince my grandmother of my mother's desire to reconcile. I cannot leave without peace restored between my grandparents and my mother." Her hand fell idle, and Martha sat on her haunches, her bushy tail gently sweeping back and forth.

Picking up the scraper, Lizzie returned to work, her lip caught between her teeth in concentration. How long to complete the coat—four months? She flipped her hand in dismissal. Probably six. By then, the snows would return. She gave a nod, sealing the time in her plans. The days of snow would be the right time to gift Vitse with a warm coat. The right time to load her travois with her cache of furs, hitch the dogs, and mush to Fairbanks.

She'd sell the furs and the dogs and use the money for transport to California—to her father. Her heart caught when she considered the loss of the dogs. They provided a service, but more importantly, they were her companions. Her only companions.

Her gaze drifted to the pen where the dogs gathered, some stretched out in sleep, others sitting up, peering with bright, adoring eyes in her direction. She examined each by turn—George, Andrew, Martin, John, Abigail, Thomas, Dolly, William, and Zachary. Pa had allowed her to name them, and she'd given them names of American leaders, straight from the history book he'd left behind. Her chest tightened in agony at the thought of handing them to another owner.

She reached again for Martha. She curled her arms around the dog's thick neck and kissed the top of her head. Martha returned her affection with several wet kisses. Lizzie laughed, but the sound ended with a strangled sob. "I won't sell you to just anyone," she promised, sealing the vow in her heart. "I'll specially choose your new owners—only those who will treat you kindly."

Just as she finished speaking, a dog's bark sounded from a distance. Martha didn't react, so Lizzie knew the bark carried from one of the village dogs rather than from an unfamiliar team. Was the animal warning the village of Clay and Vivian Selby's approach?

An image of the two white people flooded her mind. It was evident from their appearance and speech that they were familiar with the ways of white men. Of refined white men, like Pa. And they'd come to teach the children white men's ways. Thoughts rolled through her mind so rapidly she had difficulty grasping them before one faded to another. She must go to her father, yet she had no knowledge of the white men's world. The white people came to teach . . . so might they be willing to teach Lizzie how to be white?

Her fingers tightened on Martha's ruff. She pushed the idea away. The white people were teaching in the village. And she wasn't welcome there. The white man and woman would be of no use to her. Burying her face again in the dog's muscular neck, Lizzie murmured, "I can't stay here, yet I don't fit anywhere else. What should I do?"

∽

Vivian stood a few feet away from the partially constructed school, her hands clasped at her throat, and peered over the building's log ribs. Clay straddled the center roof beam, deftly strapping a cross beam in place with a length of rope. He whistled while he worked, and a group of native children clustered near Vivian. Their giggles and excited exclamations contrasted with the fear that wiggled through her heart.

A silent prayer winged upward: *Keep him safe.* She'd been useless in the face of past disasters. If her stepbrother tumbled from his perch and was hurt or killed, what would she do? She cupped her hands beside her mouth and called over the children's chatter, "Are you nearly finished up there, Clay?"

He grinned and waved, swinging his feet in a careless manner that sent shivers of fear down Vivian's spine. "Two more beams to tie, then I'll start layering on the pine boughs we collected to hold the sod roof. See if the children will help you drag the boughs close to the school, where they'll be easier for me to retrieve." He began scooting his way toward the next crosspiece.

Vivian, unwilling to witness his topple, spun to face the children. Using her limited Athabascan speech—thankfully, it was similar enough to the Kiowa language she needn't be mute before the natives—and many hand gestures, she eventually communicated her wishes for the children's assistance. They scampered eagerly toward the pile of boughs, their laughter ringing. Vivian wished she could summon as much enthusiasm as Clay and the children displayed. Where did Clay find his energy?

In this land of long days and short nights, he worked more hours than he had in Oklahoma. He'd accomplished a great deal in their first three weeks in the village. Of course, he'd had help. After the village leaders decided knowledge of the English language in both spoken and written word would benefit the tribe, they'd offered assistance in constructing the mission school. Several Athabascan men had helped fell trees and transport the logs to the village. Others had erected huts—mere eight-foot-square shelters of twigs and bark—to serve as temporary homes for Clay and Vivian.

But for every hour others contributed to the mission, Clay contributed two. He expected her to work twice as hard as anyone, also. That's why she'd come—to be his helper. Mother had said Vivian would be his Timothy, referring to the young man who'd accompanied the biblical missionary Paul on his journeys. Oh, how Vivian wanted to be useful . . . but exhaustion plagued her, and her feet dragged as heavily as the pine bough she tugged across the ground.

By the time she and the children had transferred a third of the boughs to the shelter, Clay had finished his overhead task and climbed down, using the logs that formed the walls as a ladder. With no mud chinking filling the gaps, the building resembled a huge bird cage. But Vivian had no doubt by the time Clay finished, it would be a lovely school. Her stepbrother's abilities far exceeded her own. To waylay feelings of incompetence, she reminded herself that her turn to be most useful would come when the school was finally complete. She would *teach*. And she would teach *well*, thus proving her value.

Clay threw his hands wide, indicating the pile of boughs, and beamed at the children. In Athabascan, he praised their fine work. They'd lived with the villagers less than a month, but Clay had picked up much of their vocabulary. The little ones danced in excitement, their round brown faces alight with pleasure. Then Clay turned to her. "I'm going to re-ward them with a song on the accordion. Keep bringing in branches while I play, would you?"

Vivian wished she could sit and listen—to catch her breath and enjoy a cup of cool water from the stream that ran alongside the peaceful village. But she doubted Timothy ever disregarded Paul's instruction, so she carted the pine boughs, one by one, and placed them next to the opening that would eventually hold a sturdy door while Clay played a lively tune and the children clapped along. Women and older men, drawn by the music, gathered near and created a barricade between the school and the pile of boughs. Al-though she'd intended to keep working, she stood on the outer rim of the circle and listened to Clay make music with the piano box. Was there nothing Clay couldn't do?

She didn't want to be jealous of her stepbrother, but no matter how hard she tried, the bitter emotion wove its fin-gers through her middle. From the moment Clay's father married her mother, Clay, three years older than Vivian, had assumed a position of importance in their family. Clay was strong and brave. He wasn't afraid of spiders. He wasn't afraid of *anything*. He could climb trees and chop wood and swing himself onto a horse's back without clambering onto fence rails for a boost. When his father gave an order, his obedience was immediate and cheerful. He'd never let someone die, and there was never cause to send him away for his sins.

"Viv?"

Tangled up in thought, Vivian almost missed Clay's query. She jolted and pushed her way through the gathered natives to reach Clay's side, eager to escape the rush of guilt her inner reflections had brought to the surface. "Yes?"

"Hand out some of the shortbread cookies. I think everyone would enjoy a treat."

Vivian hesitated, nibbling her dry lower lip. She'd hoped the shortbread cookies Mother had made from Aunt Vesta's recipe would last a long time, giving her a little taste of home when she felt lonely. If she gave even just one to each of the people in the circle, the supply would be nearly depleted.

"Vivian . . ." Clay's tone took on a hint of impatience.

Vivian nodded. "Of course." She flashed a smile to the group of Gwich'ins and asked them, in a jumbled mix of Athabascan and English, to wait for her return. Then she dashed to the little hut where she slept and retrieved the tin container of cookies. She popped the lid and held the open tin toward the natives. They reached eagerly, and when all had cleared away, happily munching, only a few crumbs remained in the bottom. Vivian pressed the lid into place, determined not to cry and shame herself or Clay.

Clay ambled to her side and watched as the natives wandered back to their own duties. "We're making progress, Viv. They wouldn't have eaten your food if they didn't trust you."

His words should have cheered her—after all, she wanted to be accepted here—but she couldn't help mourning the loss of the small piece of home. She forced her quavering lips into a smile. "I'm g-glad they enjoyed the c-cookies." She ducked her head, abashed by her stutter and the sudden sting of tears. Why couldn't she be strong like Clay?

Clay cupped her shoulders and turned her to face him. "What's wrong?" He sounded genuinely concerned.

Vivian swallowed twice, bringing the irksome tears under control. "It's silly. It's just . . . they ate all the cookies, and the cookies reminded me of Boston and Aunt Vesta." The reason sounded ridiculous even to her own ears. She jerked free of Clay's loose hold and headed for her hut. "I'll put the tin away and then—"

Clay jogged to her side and caught her arm. She stiffened, prepared to be scolded for behaving childishly over something as insignificant as a tin of shortbread cookies. But when she looked into Clay's face, she glimpsed compassion and a hint of remorse.

"I should've asked if you wanted to share. The cookies weren't mine to give." He sighed, his gaze drifting from their side-by-side huts to the large, half-completed school building at the edge of the village. "I want to do good here, Viv—to give everything I've got so I can begin ministering." Impatience flashed in his eyes. "Just getting the school built . . . it's taking so long."

He grit his teeth, releasing a little growl. "I'm eager to follow my father's footsteps, to stand in a pulpit and preach life-changing truths." He faced her again, his expression softening. The gentleness in his eyes reminded her of her stepfather. "But I was wrong to expect you to give all. I didn't realize the cookies meant so much to you."

He meant to comfort her—she recognized his sincerity—yet his words stung. Whether he realized it or not, he'd just accused her of selfishness. She blinked away the last vestige of tears. "I want to give all, too." Her voice tightened with conviction. "I'm probably just . . . tired." As if to prove her statement, her shoulders slumped. But she couldn't be sure if weariness or defeat weighed her down.

"Me too. We've worked hard." Clay slipped his hands into his trouser pockets, his gaze drifting to the log building. "But doesn't it feel good to have so much accomplished?"

Most of the accomplishments were his, but Vivian nodded.

"Tomorrow's Sunday—our day of rest. We'll enjoy it, hmm?"

Clay always honored the Lord's day, the way they had in Oklahoma, even though so much work awaited. Vivian sighed. "That sounds lovely."

He grinned. "We can read the Bible together, like we've been doing, but I think I'll play some hymns on the accordion this time. And we can sing. The villagers will probably come listen—they're so curious about everything we do. It'll be their first church service, even if they don't recognize it as such."

"Then maybe . . ." She paused for a moment, gathering her courage. "If the villagers will join us, should I prepare a larger meal? So we can . . . share?"

She expected him to praise her for her thoughtfulness, but instead he laughed. "They might've enjoyed the cookies Ma baked for you, Viv, but I think we might scare them off with your cooking."

Vivian's chest panged. Chauncy Burke had kept his promise to deliver their supplies to the river's bank. A trio of Athabascan youths had willingly used their dogs and travoises to cart the crates to the village. But having pots, pans, and canned foods hadn't transformed her into a suitable homemaker. She hung her head. "I know my cooking pales in comparison to Mother's. But she's had many years of practice. And Mother has a cookstove. It isn't easy to cook over an open fire, Clay."

She cringed. Although she'd spoken truthfully, her reasons sounded like excuses, and excuses were for the weak.

He patted her shoulder. "I know you're trying." He chuckled, leaning down to catch her eye. "I don't reckon you learned open-pit cooking at Miss Roberts' finishing school, huh?"

Despite herself, Vivian released a soft giggle. Miss Roberts would be appalled if she saw Vivian right now with her broken, dirt-rimmed fingernails, filthy dress, and hair askew. "I certainly didn't."

"Maybe you could ask one of the Gwich'in women to teach you," Clay suggested. But then he shook his head. "Never mind. They probably wouldn't be willing. They tend to protect themselves . . . not that we should blame them."

Vivian knew many white people didn't treat the natives well. The Gwich'in had good reason not to trust Clay and her. She hoped she could win their trust before she wasted all of their precious food stores learning to cook—or before she starved Clay. She shuddered at the thought. Bearing the responsibility for the death of one person she loved was more than enough.

"I'll learn, Clay, I promise." She turned and scurried into her hut. She sank onto the pile of pine needles covered by a wool blanket that served as her bed and closed her eyes, her heart pounding. She *would* learn. She would be a good missionary. She would save souls. She *had* to. It was the only way she could redeem her past sins.

Chapter Five

Lizzie groaned as she rolled out of her rope bed Sunday morning. She pushed her feet into her well-worn hand-sewn moccasins and shuffled to the window to peer out at the already bright day. Birdsong rang from the treetops, and the dewy ground glistened beneath the sun's golden rays. No sign of the drizzle that sometimes accompanied the beginning of summer. She sighed in appreciation for the beautiful day.

Her gaze wandered to the dog pen, and she released a soft giggle. The dogs were sitting up, their attentive faces aimed toward the cabin door as if they wondered why she hadn't yet emerged. She smiled, grateful they hadn't barked to rouse her. She'd slept hard and well last night—her first good sleep in weeks. She'd needed it after her hard work preparing the moose hide, its meat, and her garden plot.

She yawned. Now that the seeds were safely in the ground, assuring her physical needs would be met, she could put her hands to work on Vitse's coat. The moose hide had lain waiting, ignored, for too long. But today she could begin its construction. Her heart pounded in eagerness. A dog whined, reminding her the animals needed tending.

She snagged the water bucket from its spot on the half-log bench beside the back door and headed outside. The sun's brightness proved deceptive when she stepped into a damp, chill morning. She'd left her fur cloak on its peg and she considered retrieving it, but the dogs were already yipping and leaping against the fence in eagerness for their breakfast. She could ignore her discomfort long enough to feed and water her faithful companions.

Swinging the bucket, she headed to the burbling creek. A rose finch swooped from its perch, its red plumage a bold splash of color against the green backdrops of pines. "Did you see that?" Lizzie gasped in delight, then sobered. Who was there to respond to her query? Sadness fell over her as she bent to fill her bucket. She glimpsed her reflection in the water—a solemn face, empty eyes. She straightened and headed toward the cabin, moving as quickly as possible without spilling the water.

She filled the dogs' water cans and then retrieved dried salmon for their breakfast, hardly mindful of their enthusiastic yips of pleasure. Even after living on her own for so long, the loneliness still took her by surprise at times. When she, Mama, and Pa all lived here, she hadn't missed other people—her parents had served as friends and playmates as well as teachers and providers. But as much as she loved her dogs, they couldn't replace the need for human companionship.

"If I join Pa in San Francisco, I'll never be lonely again," she whispered to the dogs. Busy eating, none of them so much as looked up. Swallowing a sad sigh, she left the pen and fetched another bucket of water for her own use before returning to the cabin. She slipped inside and sat on the edge of the bed, the cheer of the first morning minutes forgotten. "I miss you, Mama . . ."

With thoughts of her mother, another longing rose.

Sundays had been special days before Pa left—his one rare day of no work. They played games such as checkers, crokinole, or a matching game using a worn deck of cards. Mama always prepared an extra-special meal from the recipe book Pa had brought from his California home rather than cooking her traditional Athabascan foods. Pa loved sweets— any sweets—and Mama favored him with as many as she could bake in their tiny rusted cookstove. Lizzie's mouth watered, recalling Pa's favorite treat.

Eager to grasp just one small piece of the happiness she once possessed, Lizzie dashed to the apple crate she used as a bookcase and pulled out the battered cookbook containing American recipes. She turned the pages with great care, and she let out a happy gasp when she came to a page with a turned-down corner. Setting the book aside, she hurried to her storage tins. Flour, sugar, baking powder, lard . . . She had everything she needed. Her mouth began watering in anticipation. The day suddenly seemed much brighter.

✐

Clay placed his accordion into the case and closed the lid. As soon as he buckled the case, sealing the instrument away, the villagers rose from their squatted positions and ambled toward their own huts. He winked at Vivian. He'd been right—the moment he'd begun to play, they'd gathered around, drawn by the music. When the mission school was completed, he'd add Bible-reading and a short sermon to the accordion playing. The natives were so fascinated by the accordion, surely they'd be willing to hear everything he had to share once he was ready to begin services.

Vivian tugged her skirts aside and pushed to her feet. "It must be noon. My stomach is growling. Should we eat?"

Clay managed to hide a grimace. Vivian, despite her best

efforts, still hadn't managed to conquer the challenge of cooking over an open flame. Everything was either underdone or charred. But he'd eat whatever she fixed. He needed food to keep up his strength to finish building the school. "Sure." He slapped his belly and forced his lips into an eager smile. "What're we having?"

"Stew." She scurried across the cleared ground to her hut.

Clay followed and peeked into the pot that held their dinner. A thick grayish broth burped up lumps of potatoes, carrots, and—judging by the smell—some kind of fish. Clay's appetite fled. Vivian approached with two tin bowls and a ladle. Spoon handles poked out of her apron pocket. She pressed the bowls into his hands and dipped the ladle into the stew. Steam rose as she lifted a scoopful and filled one bowl. She scooped a serving for the second bowl then dropped the ladle into the pot.

She looked at the felled log where they'd sat to eat all of their meals so far, and she pursed her lips. "I wish we at least had a decent table and chairs at which to sit."

Clay stared at the bowls' unappetizing contents, his nose twitching at the strong fishy odor rising with the steam. "Would that help the food taste better?" He hadn't intended to voice the thought, and he instantly regretted his slip of the tongue.

Vivian snatched up her skirts and stormed to the hut. She gave the blanket that covered the opening a fierce toss and disappeared. If there had been a solid wood door to slam, Clay felt certain his ears would be ringing. He heard a couple of deep chuckles, and he glanced over his shoulder to find two native men watching. Clay's cheeks burned with humiliation. He set down the bowls and scurried to Vivian's hut.

"Viv, can I come in?" He kept his voice low, aware of listening ears.

"No. Go away."

Another rumble of chuckles from the men behind him squared his shoulders. Even though he knew he'd face Vivian's ire, he said, "I'm coming in." He pushed the blanket aside and stepped into the hut. With a blanket guarding the door and no windows to allow in light, murky gray shrouded the small room. Only a few thin bands of sunlight sneaked between tiny cracks in the walls and ceiling. He blinked a few times before making out Vivian's stiff form in the opposite corner.

She folded her arms over her chest and glared at him. "I told you to go away."

Clay took two steps into the room, nearly closing the gap between them. A scuffling noise came from outside the hut, and Clay knew the men had drawn near, eager to hear his exchange with Vivian. He wanted to be gentle with her, as his father had directed before they'd left home, but would the men think him weak and therefore lose respect for him? Inwardly praying for his stepsister's cooperation, he said, "I heard what you said. But my going away won't change anything."

Her chin jerked upward, her lips forming a grim line of irritation. Before she could form a retort, he leaned forward and whispered, "We can't talk here—let's take a walk in the woods where we'll have privacy."

Mutterings and another chuckle sounded from outside. Vivian's gaze zipped to the doorway, then returned to Clay. She gave a brusque nod and moved past him to push the blanket aside. The two Gwich'in men jumped back in surprise. Clay hurried after Vivian, with the men's chortles ringing in his ears. He waited until they were well away from the village before he grabbed her arm and drew her to a halt.

"Vivian, I'm sorry. I shouldn't have said what I did." Her

expression remained stony. He sighed. "I know you're trying. Maybe we should see about having a stove shipped to us here in the village."

Her lips twisted in derision. "A stove takes up room, Clay. I hardly have the space to turn around in my little hut without bumping my elbow on something."

She was right—their huts, although they provided shelter, were much too confined to accommodate even a small cooking stove. Eventually, after they'd established themselves well with the natives, he hoped to build each of them a large log cabin, but it might be a full year before he had the time to spare. "What if we put it in the mission school? And I could build a work counter where we could pull up a couple of stools and take our meals."

Hope flared in her eyes. "Truly? That would be lovely. Even such a small measure of civility would—" Her head jerked sharply toward the west, her eyes widening.

Clay's heart gave a jolt, and he looked in the same direction, fully expecting to see a bear or some other predator advancing. What else could have brought about such a strong reaction? But only trees, shrubs, and ferns greeted his eyes. He looked at her again. "Viv, what—?"

She sniffed the air, her face lighting. "Do you smell that?"

A delightful aroma found his nostrils. Saliva pooled under his tongue and his stomach rolled over in longing. He swallowed. Vivian took off. "Where are you going?"

She paused midstep and shot him an impatient look. "I want to know where it's coming from."

"But—"

"Do we have work to do today?"

"No. This is our day of rest."

A smile burst across her face. "Then let's go!" She shot toward the trees.

The delightful aroma enticing his senses, Clay decided not to argue. He trotted after her.

∽

Lizzie used a mitten made of rabbit fur to protect her hand as she removed the tray of cookies from the stove's belly. Just as her fingers grasped the blackened tray, her dogs began a raucous chorus. She slid the tray to the top of the stove, slammed the door, and ran to the window. The dogs leapt against the fence, teeth bared, their angry barks mingling with snarls.

A chill attacked her frame. Wild animals rarely ventured near enough to stir the dogs' fury, but the occasional hunter, gold seeker, or trapper entered her clearing. Not all of them were good-hearted. She grabbed Pa's rifle from its pegs on the wall and charged out the back door, the barrel aimed in the same direction the dogs faced. "Hush!" At her command, the barking ceased, but the dogs continued to snarl and growl low in their throats, straining against the fence. Lizzie called, "Who's there?"

The brush rustled, and two people emerged, both with white, wary faces. The same two people Lizzie had encountered a few weeks ago. The tip of the rifle barrel wavered as Lizzie considered lowering her weapon. But she'd better wait until she knew their intentions. She cocked the rifle, squinting. "What do you want here?"

The man—Clay Selby, Lizzie recalled—held up both hands. His gaze zinged back and forth between her rifle and the bristling dogs. "We don't mean any harm. We . . ." He licked his lips, showing his nervousness. "Vivian smelled something good, and—"

His woman darted in front of him. "Are you baking shortbread?"

Lizzie blinked twice in surprise. The woman had appeared meek at their first meeting, yet today she interrupted her man. No Athabascan woman would be so bold. Lizzie answered without thinking. "Sugar cookies."

The woman's face fell. "Oh. I'd hoped . . ."

Lizzie lowered her rifle. Slicing her arm through the air, she commanded, "Dogs, lie down!" Although they whined, they obeyed. Silence fell, lengthening as Lizzie stared across the small clearing at the pair of white people and they stared back. They'd received an answer to their question—why didn't they leave? Lizzie turned to go inside, but as she reached her door, the same loneliness that had plagued her earlier returned. Wouldn't it be pleasant to have someone to talk to? And they were harmless—a pair of *cheechakos*.

She whirled around. "Do you want one?"

They'd turned toward the woods, but at her abrupt question they halted in unison and peered over their shoulders at her. The man said, "One . . . what?"

"A cookie." Impatience sharpened Lizzie's tone. "You said you smelled them. Do you want one?"

The woman nodded eagerly. She took hold of the man's hand and pulled him forward. When they reached Lizzie, the woman's gaze bounced to the rifle cradled in Lizzie's arms. "We'd feel much more secure if you were to put away your weapon."

Lizzie felt more secure with the rifle in hand. What if they took advantage of her hospitality and tried to steal her furs? Unsmiling, she searched their faces, and a bit of her apprehension melted. They may have come to bring change in the Gwich'in village, but she sensed they didn't intend her harm. "Come in." She marched inside and placed the rifle on its pegs.

They entered, and their gazes roved the cabin, seeming to

examine every detail. Lizzie pointed to the rough-hewn table her father had constructed. "Sit." As compliant as her dogs, they crossed the hard-packed dirt floor. Clay Selby pulled out a chair for Vivian before seating himself. An odd spiral of longing rose in Lizzie's breast at his unexpected gesture. Did white men serve their women rather than waiting for their women to serve them? Pa was white, and she'd never witnessed him performing such a courtesy for Mama.

Confused by her reaction to Clay Selby's kind action, she whirled to face the stove. She scraped the cookies off the now-cool pan onto a battered tin plate and carried it to the table. Placing it between the pair, she commanded, "Eat." Then she returned to the stove to prepare another batch for baking. The dough had become sticky in her time away, but by flouring her hands she managed to form small amounts into balls and press them flat with the bottom of a tin can dipped in sugar. Soon the pleasant aroma of baking cookies filled the small cabin once again. Lizzie inhaled deeply, savoring the sweet scent that brought back equally sweet memories.

"Ahem." The sound of a clearing voice chased away her daydream. She turned toward the table, where her guests sat perched like a pair of otters watching guard from a flat rock. The man smiled, crinkles appearing in the corners of his eyes. "Are you going to join us?"

His kindly worded invitation, coupled with the gentle smile on his tanned face, affected Lizzie in an unfamiliar way. Nervous, but uncertain why, she shifted her gaze from his friendly expression to the plate on the table. It remained untouched. Confused, she looked at the man again, and then the woman. "I thought you wanted a cookie."

The woman smoothed her skirt over her knees and tipped her head slightly. Even though her hands looked chapped and a smear of dirt marred her chin, she carried herself regally. She spoke in a soft, pleasant voice. "It is customary for the hostess to be seated before guests partake of any treat."

Lizzie sensed no recrimination in the woman's tone or expression, yet defeat bowed her shoulders. No matter what Mama had said, Lizzie would never fit into her father's world. She didn't even know she should sit and eat with guests. She would bring shame to her father's household if she went to him. Yet she had no other choice.

Her gaze zipped from the man to the woman, her heart pounding so hard and fast her breath came in little spurts. They might deny the request that formed in her heart and strained for release, but for Mama's peace, she had to ask. Stumbling to the table, she held out her hands to the pair of visitors. "Will . . . will you teach me all that is customary? Will you teach me . . . to be white?"

Chapter Six

The native woman wouldn't have surprised Vivian more if she'd smacked her over the head with the cookie pan. For a moment, Vivian wondered if she had been whacked, because her world seemed to spin. She caught the edge of the table's rough top and tried to calm her galloping heart.

Did this woman truly want to learn to be white? Although Vivian had come to Alaska to be of service, she had few skills—she couldn't cook, and she couldn't construct buildings. It might be weeks before she had the opportunity to begin teaching the Gwich'in children the English language and then to read and write. But thanks to her attendance in Miss Roberts' finishing school, she knew etiquette.

The opportunity to be of use—to prove herself capable—stood before her dressed in a buckskin tunic, leggings, and beaded moccasins. It wouldn't be easy to transform this native woman into a proper lady, but she could do it. She squared her shoulders and opened her mouth to voice her agreement.

Clay cleared his throat. "Viv? Let's have a cookie, and then you and . . ." He sent a sheepish look toward the Athabascan woman. "Lizzie, is that right?" He waited until the woman gave a curt nod. "You and Lizzie can discuss exactly what she'd like to learn." Leaning sideways slightly on the stool, he added in a low tone, "Maybe you could swap lessons. Manners for cooking and trapping and so forth."

The woman stood staring at the pair of them with a stoic expression. Heat filled Vivian's face. She and Clay talking to each other as if Lizzie wasn't in the room was hardly proper protocol. What kind of a teacher modeled such a poor example? She indicated the open chair across the table with a graceful flick of her wrist. "Please, Lizzie. Sit and join us. While we partake of your gracious hospitality, we can discuss your specific needs."

Lizzie slid into the chair and stared across the table at Vivian. "My need is simple. I must be white." She lifted a cookie and took a bite.

Vivian examined Lizzie. Although she did everything abruptly, as if time was in danger of disappearing before her tasks were complete, she held an innate elegance of movement that Vivian couldn't help but admire. With her dusky skin, glistening hair, and vivid blue eyes, she was a striking woman.

"But you're a lovely native woman," Clay said, reaching for a cookie. "Why do you want to be white?"

Lizzie shot Clay a stern look. "You came to teach white man's ways to the children of Gwichyaa Saa. Will you withhold the same teachings from me?"

Vivian snatched up a cookie and nibbled it to hide her smile. Vivian often exhibited spunk, but hers was manufactured to mask her insecurities. This Gwich'in woman had genuine spunk. Perhaps she would learn a great deal from Lizzie.

Clay offered Lizzie one of his disarming grins. Mother

had laughingly said Clay could charm the stripes from a skunk, but Vivian sensed he'd met his match in this feisty Gwich'in woman. "Of course you're welcome to learn the same things we came to teach the children." Clay brushed crumbs from his shirt front and picked up a second cookie. "But I think you've misunderstood our purpose here. We don't intend to teach the children white man's ways—we've come to teach them God's ways."

Lizzie's fine eyebrows lowered. Her lips puckered, as if she found the flavor of her cookie unpleasant. "The ways of the white man's God are for white men. You've come to change the children. But the children are happy as Athabascans. They have no desire to change." She aimed her thumb at her chest. "I desire to change. Teach me instead. Leave the children alone."

Clay shook his head, his jaw jutting into a stubborn angle Vivian recognized all too well. "We've come to teach the children, and to preach God's Word to the entire village. We're happy to invite you to join us, but—"

The scent of scorched sugar filled the cabin. Lizzie jumped up and dashed to the stove. She whisked the tray from the heat chamber and smacked the pan onto the iron top. A tinny *clang* assaulted their ears. She shook her fingers, hissing through her teeth.

Vivian jumped up. "Did you burn your hand? Shall I fetch some cold water?" She spotted a water bucket on a low bench right inside the cabin's back door and moved in that direction.

"I'm fine." Lizzie's sharp retort brought Vivian to a halt in the middle of the floor. She stood, uncertain, while Lizzie glared at the burnt, broken cookies in the pan. Suddenly, Lizzie balled her hands on her hips and whirled, turning the seething look on Clay. "You will teach me here."

Clay chuckled softly. "But we're teaching in the mission, which is in the village."

"The village isn't open to me."

Clay rose and crossed the brief expanse of floor to reach Lizzie's side. "Why not?"

Vivian leaned forward slightly, eager to hear Lizzie's response. Over the past weeks of working in the village, she'd often pondered why Lizzie lived separate from the village. Now her curiosity would be satisfied.

Lizzie turned her back and began scraping bits of cookie from the tray. "That isn't your concern. But I can't go there. You'll have to come here." She looked past Clay, locking eyes with Vivian. "You'll come here . . . won't you?"

Vivian glimpsed a deep longing—almost a desperation—in the woman's unusual blue eyes. She knew she would be subjected to a reprimand from Clay later, but she couldn't refuse. "Of course I will." She sent a warning look at Clay, daring him to contradict her. He set his lips in a grim line and remained silent. Turning back to Lizzie, Vivian added, "And while I'm here, you can teach me, too."

Lizzie's eyebrows flew high. "What could I teach you?"

"Athabascan customs, so I don't offend the villagers." She chose not to mention cooking in front of Clay. She'd talk to Lizzie privately at another time.

Lizzie shook her head. "I am not the one to teach you how not to offend the villagers. I offend them with my presence."

Although her tone was harsh, Vivian believed pain underscored the fierce statement. How well she understood feeling unwanted. She'd been cast from her home, too. But what sin had this lovely, lonely Athabascan woman committed to earn the village's scorn?

Clay intervened. "I'm sure you'd be allowed to come to the mission. I'll speak to the village leaders and—"

"No!" Lizzie's face blazed red. She pointed to the open door. "You've eaten some cookies. Go."

Clay gulped. "But I didn't mean to—"

"Leave." Lizzie yanked up the crusty pan and pushed past Clay. She charged through the door and whirled around the corner, disappearing from view.

Clay and Vivian stood staring at each other in the quiet cabin. Vivian cocked her head and offered a sardonic look. "That went well."

Clay held out his arms. "I was only trying to help. Something's happened between Lizzie and the villagers. Perhaps God brought us here to reunite them. Look at where she lives, away from everyone . . ." His gaze roved the rustic yet neat cabin. "She must be lonely here." He curled his hand through Vivian's elbow. "We'll go because she asked us to, but I want you to come back, as often as possible. I think she needs companionship, and I believe you're the perfect one to reach her."

Vivian gaped at Clay. He saw her as capable of reaching Lizzie? Her heart gave a happy skip.

"You seem to be near the same age, and you're a woman, therefore not a threat." Clay led Vivian through the woods. Leaves crunched beneath their feet and slender, leaf-dotted branches waved in the light breeze, catching Vivian's hair. She crowded closer to Clay as he continued. "She asked for your help. If you abide by her request to come to her, then eventually you should be able to convince her to come to the mission school. That will be your goal."

Vivian dug in her heels, drawing Clay to a stumbling halt. He sent her a puzzled look, and she offered her sternest frown. "Clay Selby, I will not befriend that woman simply to persuade her to come to the village. It's dishonest."

"But—"

"I intend to help her, just as she asked. Hopefully she'll be willing to help me in return. But I'll not pressure her to enter the village." Vivian recalled the expression that crossed Lizzie's face when she'd said she offended the villagers with her presence. The woman carried a deep hurt, and Vivian would not rub salt in the wound by insisting she visit the place of her pain. Memories from her own personal place of pain tried to rise, but she pushed them aside. Hadn't she come to Alaska to forget?

"Then how will she hear the good news we've come to share?" Clay sounded more concerned than irritated, which removed Vivian's defensiveness. However, his question pricked.

"Can I not be trusted to speak of God to her without your assistance? I know Him, too, Clay." Vivian's heart panged. She didn't know God as intimately as her mother, stepfather, or stepbrother, but she'd been exposed to His teachings her entire life. She could share her faith even if a part of her questioned the reality of God's unconditional love and grace.

Clay hung his head. "Of course you can. I'm sorry if I sound as if I don't trust you. I need to remember . . . this ministry is ours rather than mine alone."

His comment was exactly the confirmation Vivian had been seeking since they'd set out on this journey together. Yet as he ushered her toward the village and the mission school, a weight seemed to press down upon her. Did she have the right to be an equal partner in a ministry when she held so many doubts herself?

∽

Clay left Vivian at her little hut with the promise he'd wake her from her nap an hour before suppertime. He headed for his own hut, but before he reached it, he turned around and walked through the center of the village instead. Perhaps one of the village leaders would be willing to talk to him about Lizzie.

She hadn't expressed a desire to join the village, but he sensed her loneliness. An image of her flicked through his mind—proudly angled shoulders and raised chin, blue eyes alight with passion. His heart rolled over his chest. Such a lovely woman. And so secluded. Bringing her into the village would give her an opportunity for companionship as well as protection. How did she survive out there all by herself? Couldn't whatever had transpired to separate her from the tribe be forgotten for compassion's sake?

He passed rows of sturdy log cabins with grass and wild flowers sprouting on the sod roofs. People nodded, offering lazy greetings that he returned in their native tongue. Although he hoped Vivian would eventually teach the villagers enough English for them to communicate in his language, for now he used his own mix of Kiowa and Athabascan as a means of developing relationships. Some people seemed amused by his attempts to master their tricky pronunciations. Others held their distance, as if uncertain of his trustworthiness. But none had openly ignored him. He viewed their hesitant reception as a positive step toward complete acceptance.

As he'd hoped, two of the band's elders sat outside their cabin. Shruh puffed on a hand-carved pipe and his wife, Co'Ozhii, busily stitched flowers formed of tiny beads onto the shank of a buckskin boot. They both looked up and nodded as Clay approached.

The man held his leathery palm to the spot of ground beside him. "Sit, Clay Selby. Smoke?" He held out the pipe in invitation.

Clay sat but didn't reach for the pipe. He'd tried smoking

his uncle's pipe once as a boy. Fifteen years later, he still remembered how his stomach had roiled afterward. He smiled and shook his head. "*Ęhę'ę, dogidinh*—thank you, but no."

They sat in silence for several minutes. One of the things Clay had learned long ago about the natives was they had no urge to fill time with unnecessary words. The few social events he'd attended away from the reservation—necessary events to gain financial support for his undertakings here in Alaska—had worn him out with the ceaseless chatter for chatter's sake. Even Vivian had a tendency to speak endlessly, as if she found silence distasteful. Although he had things he wanted to say to the man who contentedly puffed his pipe, he'd wait for his host to speak first rather than be considered discourteous.

Eventually, Shruh tapped out his pipe and fixed Clay with a steady look. "Your building nears completion. You have done well."

"I have had help," Clay replied in the man's native language. "Many of the village men have assisted."

Shruh nodded, as if approving Clay's humility. "They have assisted. But you led them. You have made buildings of logs before?"

Clay had helped his father construct their home on the Kiowa reservation. While the Kiowans lived in homes of mud bricks, Clay's father had used timbers as the foundation for the large building that served as both a home and church building. He nodded. "Once." He tapped his temple with one finger, smiling. "But I remember well."

Shruh chuckled, his eyes crinkling with humor. "You remember well." Then he faced forward, seeming to drift away in thought.

Clay cleared his throat, garnering the man's attention. "It is such a pretty day, Vivian and I went for a walk in the woods."

"A walk?" Co'Ozhii shot Clay an interested look.

"Yes. Walk." Clay searched for words to explain what he meant. "Not for the purpose of going anywhere. For enjoyment."

The older couple exchanged amused glances. Clay understood the reason for Co'Ozhii's interest in their activity. When a Gwich'in couple went walking, they were courting. He'd need to make it clear he and Vivian held no such affection for one another, but right now he had something more important to discuss. "We came upon a cabin and sat at the table of a woman named Lizzie. She is alone there, and I wondered if you might invite her to live in the village so she would have the protection of the band."

The warm amusement disappeared in an instant. The man stiffened, and the woman sucked in a sharp breath. Anger flashed in both pairs of dark eyes, and Clay felt as though they skewered him with their disapproving glares.

Co'Ozhii stabbed the bone needle through the pliant leather with force. She muttered, "*Ts'egid.*"

Heat filled Clay's face at the contemptuous tone. Co'Ozhii had called Lizzie trash. The younger woman must have done something horrible to deserve being discarded.

Shruh leaned toward Clay slightly, his demeanor challenging. "That woman is not welcome here."

Clay held out his hands in supplication. "The mission . . . it should be open to all who—"

Co'Ozhii rose, her movements stiff. She scooped up her handiwork and stormed into the cabin, leaving the two men alone. Shruh shook his head, his brow pinched into furrows of displeasure. "It will be open to all of Gwichyaa Saa. Our council agrees learning the English language will benefit us. Many white men would cheat us with confusing talk. What we learn from you will protect us. But Lu'qul Gitth'ihgi does not live here. Her mother—our daughter—made her choice, and Lu'qul Gitth'ihgi must honor that choice. She is no longer of our band."

Clay inwardly reeled. Lizzie was Shruh's granddaughter? How could he disown his own flesh? "But—"

"We will speak of this no more!" The man lurched to his feet and stood glaring down at Clay. "You have come to teach. This you must learn—traitors are banished. And if you choose to befriend a traitor, you become one yourself." He spun on his heel and entered his cabin, closing the door firmly behind him.

Clay recognized the action—he'd been dismissed. Trying to speak to Shruh or Co'Ozhii again today would only cause conflict—conflict he didn't dare stir if he hoped to win the tribe's trust.

His heart heavy, he scuffed his way to his own dwelling. Vivian had committed to teaching Lizzie. If she went back on her word, it would set a poor Christian example to the native woman, but if she honored her promise, the band might very well reject Vivian and him. He looked at the sky and held his arms outward, just as he had to Shruh. *Father, what should we do?*

Chapter Seven

Clay tossed and turned. The pine needles beneath his wool blanket shifted until there was a hollow in the middle. His backside connected with the dirt floor, and he grunted in frustration. Rolling to his knees, he tossed aside the heavy blanket and used his palms to sweep the needles into a pile again. Then he stretched the blanket over the mound and flopped down. He was more comfortable, but he still couldn't sleep.

How long would it take to adjust to the sun sending forth its light well into the nighttime hours? He and Vivian had been in the village for almost a month now, and his body still didn't seem to understand it must sleep, even though the sun remained awake. Vivian hadn't complained, but dark circles rimmed her eyes, and he assumed her sleep was also affected by the lingering sunlight. Maybe he should go whisper at her hut door—if she lay awake, too, they could talk about the blue-eyed woman named Lizzie and try to find a way to reach out to her without angering the village leaders.

He slipped from the makeshift bed, tugged on his boots, then stepped outside. Were it not for the silence in the village, he would have thought it was early evening rather than close to midnight. He headed toward Vivian's hut several yards east of his. A few dogs, tethered to stakes, lifted their heads as he passed by. Clay held his breath, but— apparently recognizing him as harmless—none barked or snarled. He heaved a sigh of relief. He didn't want to rouse the entire village. He reached Vivian's hut and tapped lightly on the doorframe.

"Who's there?" Her voice replied at once, confirming his suspicion that she couldn't sleep, either.

"It's me, Viv." He kept his voice low, glancing toward the village cabins to be sure he hadn't disturbed anyone. Rustling sounded from inside Vivian's hut, and then she tugged the blanket aside. Her hair hung in unruly waves across her shoulders, but she was fully dressed. She flipped her hand, inviting him inside. He ducked beneath the short door opening, and she dropped the blanket back in place.

Hugging herself, she blinked at him in alarm. "Is something wrong?"

"I couldn't sleep."

She grimaced. "Me either. It never really feels like night, does it?"

Clay shook his head. He gestured to the low bench he'd built out of half a log and two chunks of wood. They sat side by side, and Clay shifted slightly to face Vivian. Soft light filtered through cracks in the bark walls, offering enough illumination for Clay to recognize tiredness etched into her forehead and unsmiling lips. She needed rest—he should go. He started to rise, but she put her hand over his arm.

"I can't sleep because of the light. Why can't you sleep?"

He sank back down, releasing a sigh. "I've been thinking about Lizzie."

A funny little smirk appeared on Vivian's face.

He frowned. "Not like *that*." But his heart twinged in his chest, belying his statement.

"But isn't she lovely?" Vivian yawned behind her hand, her voice dreamy. "And so graceful—she reminds me of a fleet doe or a delicate swan. If it weren't for her dusky skin, dark hair, and buckskin clothing, she might pass for a woman of high society."

Images of Lizzie played through Clay's mind. He gulped, inwardly agreeing with his stepsister's assessment. "Yes. Yes, she is . . . lovely."

Another sly grin twitched the corners of Vivian's lips. He cleared his throat, eager to abandon the topic. He was here to preach, not to woo. And wooing a woman branded a traitor would not endear him to the tribe he wished to serve.

"Viv, listen." He repeated the troubling conversation he'd had with Shruh. Vivian's face changed from amused to indignant as he spoke. "So," he finished, "I'm not sure what to do."

She balled one fist and placed it against her hip. "I can tell you what we *aren't* going to do. We aren't going to abide by that silly edict. I told her I would help her, and I'm going to help her."

Clay bit the insides of his cheeks to keep from smiling. Despite his exhaustion and worry, it pleased him to see her so adamant about reaching out to Lizzie. Even so, they needed to consider the possible ramifications of going against the tribal leaders' order. "But what's the greater good, Viv? On one hand, we have an entire village of people who need to hear the gospel. On the other hand, we have an individual person who, for whatever reason, is all alone. If we can only reach one or the other, which direction should we go? Toward the village, or toward Lizzie?"

"Toward both." Vivian set her jaw at a stubborn angle.

Clay blew out an impatient breath, shaking his head. "You aren't listening to me. I just said—"

"I heard what you said. And I understand your concerns. But how can we not return to Lizzie after I've told her I'll help her? She's already been rejected by the tribe. We can't reject her, too." Her voice wavered with emotion.

Clay examined his stepsister with narrowed eyes. "You feel strongly about this."

She nodded, strands of red-gold hair flying around her face. But she didn't offer any further reason for her adamancy.

He gave her hand a pat and then leaned his elbows on his knees. "But we have to consider the consequences of going against the leaders' wishes—being branded traitors could result in our removal from the village. After all our work on the mission building, I don't want to start over somewhere else, do you?"

"Clay, you're making excuses." Vivian's tone, though gentle, cut him to the core. "You *know* the right thing to do."

Clay hung his head. Allowing Shruh's bitterness to override his conscience was wrong. "I do know what's right, Viv. You've given your word, and you have to honor it."

"So we'll visit Lizzie?"

"Yes. But you'll have to proceed carefully. If the village leaders suspect where you're going—"

Vivian caught his hand and gave it a tug. "You mean where *we're* going. You'll need to come, too."

His chest tightened in apprehension, but an element of eagerness to spend time with Lizzie also stirred within him. He assumed a defensive tone to hide the unexpected longing. "Why me?"

Vivian clasped both of Clay's hands, her fingers digging into his palms. "The man's position of leadership is valued by the natives. If you befriend her, it will help ease the pain of being cast aside by her grandfather." A shimmer of tears brightened Vivian's eyes. Her fingers convulsed on his. "You have to come, Clay. She needs you."

Even though Clay wanted to explore the strange emotions that tugged at him when he thought of Lizzie, he set aside his own reflections to focus on Vivian. Her emotional reaction seemed to go deeper than tiredness. "And what do *you* need, Vivian?"

She jerked away from him, her eyes wide. "We aren't talking about me. We're talking about Lizzie."

Clay lowered his voice to a gentle whisper. "But you seem to know her well, even though we've only spent a very short time with her. Are you sure—"

Vivian leapt up and strode to the hut opening. She lifted the blanket and pointed outside. "It's late, and we both need our rest. In the morning we can discuss ways to spend time with Lizzie without alarming the villagers."

Clay pushed to his feet and scuffed to the door. For now, he'd let it go. But he had to say one thing. "Viv? If you're reaching out to Lizzie to make yourself feel better, you've got ministry all backwards. You need to reach out to her for *her* good, not yours." Did he need to heed those words himself?

Her green eyes spit fire. "Good night, Clay."

He sighed "G'night." He returned to his hut, but sleep continued to elude him. He'd come to minister to the Athabascan people, but now he wondered if his most challenging task might be bringing an element of healing to Vivian's heart.

∽

Vivian folded her blue gingham dress over her arm and pushed aside the blanket that shrouded the hut's doorway. Stepping from the dim light of her hut into the sun's brightness made her squint, and she almost didn't see the two women bending over her small fire pit. She let out a little squeak of surprise.

The pair straightened and fixed her with sober looks. "You fire—it go out," one said in English as broken as Vivian's Athabascan.

Vivian smiled, trying to alleviate their concern. "I will light it again at suppertime." The days had warmed as June advanced—although when compared to the sweltering summer heat of Oklahoma, the temperature could still seem cool. Even so, Vivian's shawl provided adequate barrier against the morning chill. She had no need to hover beside a flame to warm herself. Besides, keeping the coals alive was an endless chore—one neither she nor Clay relished. He'd finally suggested they light a fresh cooking fire at mealtimes. Since he'd had the foresight to bring a good supply of matches, they could afford the luxury of beginning anew as needed.

The women murmured to each other, shaking their heads in dismay. Outside each of the Gwich'in cabins, a pit held coals that were carefully tended by the women. Thanks to Lizzie's tutelage, Vivian was beginning to feel more at ease in the village, but she wasn't and never would be Gwich'in. There were some things the natives would simply have to accept her doing differently.

The second woman pointed to the dress hanging from Vivian's arm. "You go to wash again, Viv-*ee*-an?" She extended Vivian's flowing name into three distinct sounds, emphasizing the middle syllable. When the natives spoke her name, it sounded guttural. They also seemed amused by her frequent trips to the river for wash water. Vivian wanted to ask Lizzie why bathing was so humorous to the Gwich'in, but she didn't want to offend her new friend.

She now contemplated how best to answer the women's question. So far, she'd managed to keep her visits to Lizzie's cabin a secret to avoid creating conflict with the villagers. More than half a dozen times over the past two weeks she'd slipped away without causing much concern—the natives assumed she was gathering berries, collecting fire-wood, or fetching water, since she always returned with something in hand.

Today, however, she wanted to take Lizzie the dress she'd modified to fit the native woman's more slender form. If Lizzie wanted to learn to live in the white man's world, the buckskin tunic and leggings would have to go. Vivian had brought three extra frocks from home, and she chose the one sewn from blue gingham for Lizzie because the color matched the woman's unusual eyes.

She bounced the dress slightly, unwilling to lie to the curious native women but fearful of telling the truth. She finally settled on a simple reply. "No, no washing today."

The pair shrugged and turned away, ambling toward the edge of the village where several other women worked in a communal vegetable garden. Blowing out a breath of relief, Vivian hastened in search of Clay. The sound of an axe connecting with wood alerted her, and she found Clay behind the mission school, turning fallen trees into firewood.

When she called his name, he set the axe aside, much to her relief. How she hated the sight and sound of an axe—it raised too many unpleasant memories. Despite the chill in the air, Clay's forehead glimmered with perspiration, and sweat created damp circles under his arms. Fixing her eyes on his flushed face, she informed him of her morning plans. "I left dried beef and a pan of corn bread in my hut for your lunch." Guilt panged when she considered how unsatisfying a cold lunch would be for a man who worked as hard as

Clay did. She added, "Or you could come to Lizzie's cabin at noontime. I'm sure she'll fix something better."

She hoped the promise of a good lunch would entice him to visit Lizzie. Despite her frequent prodding, he hadn't been to Lizzie's cabin since the day they'd sampled her sugar cookies. Each time she'd requested he accompany her, he frustrated her by making an excuse—he needed to work on the mission, or he needed to gather more firewood, or he needed to attend to some other pressing task. She didn't doubt the validity of his reasons, yet she grew impatient with them at the same time. When he'd finally completed every detail of the mission, would he find the time to visit Lizzie with her, or would he allow fear of retribution from the tribal leaders to dictate his actions? She wished she had the courage to confront him.

Clay reached underneath his shirt and removed the pistol he carried in the waistband of his trousers. "Take the gun."

Vivian disliked carrying the gun Clay's father had sent with them, but she understood the necessity. She held no hope she'd actually be able to hit anything at which she fired, but the noise should be enough to scare away any creature that might consider attacking her. The loud pop certainly frightened her. She took it gingerly and held it by the grip, aimed away from her body.

"That thing's loaded," Clay reminded her, his eyebrows high, "so be careful."

Vivian resisted rolling her eyes. Sometimes Clay fussed worse than a mother hen. "I will. 'Bye now." She shifted the folded dress to conceal the weapon and wove her way into the trees, skirting the village to avoid encountering any other villagers.

Humming, she followed the now-familiar path to Lizzie's house. Even though she'd traversed the woods safely several times, her heart still pounded in trepidation. Her gaze darted everywhere, her fingers twitching on the gun in case she needed to use it. Walking through the trees reminded her too much of a journey into the woods in the Dakota Territory many years ago. Clay had assured her no snakes lived in Alaska—it was too cold—yet she still feared a snake might slither through the leaves at her feet, as it had that day.

"Keep going," she urged herself, forcing her feet to move forward. "There are no snakes in Alaska—Clay said so, and Clay knows. I'm safe. I'm safe." But she knew a part of her would never be safe again.

To her relief, she reached the clearing beside Lizzie's cabin without incident. The dogs—accustomed to her presence by now—didn't even bark. They sat in their pen, looking at her with their tongues lolling from the sides of their mouths, almost as if they were smiling. For a moment, Vivian considered approaching the pen and trying to pet some of the beasts. How she desired the comfort of a warm, welcoming touch. But Lizzie had warned her to avoid the pen because the dogs' protectiveness might cause them to attack. Looking at their pointed teeth, Vivian decided not to test Lizzie's theory.

She glanced around, seeking the native woman, but she was nowhere in the yard. She peeked in the cabin's back door, which was propped open, as always. Empty. Had Lizzie forgotten that Vivian promised to visit this morning? Vivian cupped her hand beside her mouth and called, "Lizzie?"

Seconds later, Lizzie stepped from the trees at the back of the property. She moved with graceful ease, once again awing Vivian with her natural beauty. If attired in a velvet gown, with her hair in a sleek chignon, Lizzie would easily match society's most aristocratic members in appearance. Then Vivian noticed what the woman held, and she wrinkled her nose in distaste. No aristocrat would carry a fat rabbit by its ears in place of a beaded handbag.

Lizzie lifted the hare aloft as she approached, a sign of triumph. But she didn't smile. Lizzie rarely smiled. "I caught him in one of my snares." Although Lizzie had taught Vivian a few Athabascan words, she always addressed Vivian in English. "I'll show you how to skin and gut a rabbit and then cook it. You'll be able to please Clay with a fine meal."

Vivian's stomach roiled. She'd eaten rabbit before, but she'd only seen it after it had been cut into unrecognizable pieces. She had no desire to observe the process by which a rabbit was made ready for the frying pan, even if it would please Clay.

Lizzie, seemingly unaware of Vivian's discomfiture, pointed to the dress on Vivian's arm. "What did you bring?"

Vivian carefully placed the gun on the ground before straightening and shaking out the dress. "Remember when I took your measurements? I wanted to make sure I had a frock that would fit you. I had to tailor it."

Lizzie's forehead crunched. "Tailor?"

"Adjust its size," Vivian explained. "Your hips are narrower than mine." She didn't add that she'd needed to let out the seams at the bust. There were some topics best left unaddressed. She waited for some sort of response, but none came, creating a small niggle of discomfort within Vivian's chest. Although she'd spent several hours with Lizzie, she still hadn't found a place of complete ease with the native woman. Lizzie's stoicism held Vivian at a distance.

Lizzie dropped the rabbit, enticing a chorus of whines from the dogs. She clicked her tongue on her teeth, and they fell silent. Gliding forward on moccasin-covered feet, she reached for the dress, then held it at arm's length and looked it up and down. Her sober expression divulged nothing of her thoughts. Then, still holding the dress in front of her like a shield, she spun toward the cabin. "Bring the rabbit and come inside."

Too surprised to do otherwise, Vivian pinched the rabbit's nape between her index finger and thumb and snatched up the pistol with her other hand. With the pistol low against her thigh and the rabbit held well away from her body, she scurried after Lizzie.

Chapter Eight

Lizzie moved directly to the rope bed in the corner, dropped the dress Vivian had given her at the foot, and skimmed the tunic over her head. She tossed it in the middle of the bed and stepped out of her leggings. A scented breeze drifted through the open door, chilling her bare limbs, and she reached eagerly for the blue-and-white-checkered dress.

A startled gasp sounded behind her, and she stifled a sigh. What had frightened the white woman this time? Spiders, a dog's sudden yip, an owl flapping its wings—all of these things had brought a distressed reaction on past visits. Lizzie turned around. Vivian stood in the doorway, holding the rabbit the way Lizzie might hold a porcupine. Her cheeks glowed red, and she stared openmouthed.

Lizzie scanned the area but found nothing amiss. She angled her chin to the side. "What is it?"

Vivian deposited the rabbit and gun on the bench by the door and flapped her hands in Lizzie's direction. Her gaze bounced around the cabin, as frantic as a fly bumping against a windowpane. "Where are your . . . your . . . ?" She danced her fingers across her bodice. Her neck blotched as bright as her face.

Lizzie glanced down at her own length, puzzled. "My . . . ?"

"Undergarments," Vivian whispered.

Lizzie processed the English word. It was new, but she understood *under* and *garments*. She pointed at the discarded leggings on the floor next to her feet.

Vivian cleared her throat, seeming to examine the rafters. "I refer to drawers. And a chemise. I realize you couldn't wear a petticoat beneath your tunic, but . . ." She sucked in her lips as if she'd tasted an unripe rose hip and then spun around, presenting her stiff back. "Kindly cover yourself. The door is wide open, and—" She folded her arms across her ribs, reminding Lizzie of a turtle shrinking into its shell. "Quickly, if you please."

With a grunt of irritation, Lizzie turned the dress this way and that. How did a person find her way into such a voluminous costume? Donning her tunic was easy—pull it over her head and let it fall to her knees. But this dress, with its yards of fabric, defied entry. She marched across the room and thrust the wadded-up dress over Vivian's shoulder. "Help me."

Vivian let out a little yelp of surprise. She kept her arms pinned to her sides. "In polite circles, one requests assistance rather than demands it."

Lizzie pursed her lips tight.

Vivian said, "You should say, 'Would you help me, please?'" Her voice lilted sweetly.

Lizzie repeated flatly, "Would you help me, please?"

Vivian's head bobbed in agreement. Her gaze low, she plucked the dress from Lizzie's hands. With a few deft flicks of her wrists, she created an opening and popped the dress over Lizzie's head. Lizzie wrestled her arms into the long, tight-fitting sleeves, and then Vivian bustled behind her and began fastening the buttons that marched from the base of her spine to her neck. Such a lot of fuss, wearing this dress.

"You really shouldn't wear a dress without a chemise, drawers, and a petticoat," Vivian said in a scolding tone. "I had no idea you were . . . er . . . lacking such basic garments." She cleared her throat, and Lizzie imagined Vivian's face flooding with pink again. "I don't have extra to spare, but at my first opportunity I will prevail upon Clay to travel to Fort Yukon and purchase some batiste or lawn . . . or muslin if those fabrics aren't available. We must sew proper undergarments for you."

Lizzie stood silently while Vivian completed the buttons, contemplating wearing all of the unknown items the woman had mentioned. The dress felt strange enough—she had no desire to wear something else unusual. But if women in San Francisco wore chemises and petti-drawers, she would, too. She smoothed her hands over the full skirt and turned to face Vivian with a sigh. "I have much to learn."

"We both do." The white woman's tone lost its scolding edge. She clasped her hands under her chin and looked at Lizzie's hair. "May I unbraid your hair and try something?" She patted her skirt pocket. "I brought a comb and some pins. . . ."

Lizzie frowned. "Pins?"

Vivian pulled a handful of black squiggly things from her pocket. "Hairpins. To put your hair in a bun."

Lizzie circled Vivian, examining her red-gold hair. Swooped away from her face and twisted into a knot that resembled a bird's nest, it looked complicated. She pinched the puff of hair on the back of Vivian's head. "Like this?"

Vivian twisted her head slightly and stepped away from Lizzie's reach. "Yes. May I?"

Lizzie shrugged and dropped onto a chair. She fiddled with a loose thread on the dress's skirt, trying to sit still while Vivian pulled the comb through her hair and poked her head with the little pins.

Finally, Vivian moved in front of Lizzie and smiled. "There! All done, and I must say, it looks wonderful."

Lizzie carefully fingered the thick, coiled bulge at the back of her head. The light touch pulled the hair at her scalp, and she winced. "So I must wear a dress and build a nest of my hair. . . . What else will I learn today?"

Vivian touched her arm, and Lizzie met the other woman's gaze. Her cheeks bore a stain of pink, but her lips softened into a crooked half smile. "Lizzie, an important thing you should remember . . . a lady only disrobes in private or in the presence of a maidservant. Women who bare their bodies to others are considered"—she gulped, the color in her face brightening again—"indecent."

Another new word. Lizzie crunched her forehead. "Indecent—that's bad?"

Vivian nodded rapidly. "Indecent women aren't accepted in polite society. And this is what you want, isn't it? To be accepted?"

This time Lizzie nodded, but slowly, her thoughts tumbling. Mama had never hidden herself when undressing. For the first time, Lizzie experienced a rush of shame when considering nakedness. Maybe undressing freely was one of the reasons Pa had said Mama wouldn't fit in his world. Lizzie vowed to never remove her clothing in another's presence.

But Vivian had fastened the buttons up the back of the dress. How would Lizzie unbutton them on her own? She opened her mouth to ask, but the white woman began tugging at the shoulders of Lizzie's dress, her eyes roving across the bodice and down the skirt.

Finally, Vivian stepped back and put her hands on her hips. She nodded. "The hairstyle is becoming yet simple enough for you to fashion yourself, with some practice. And the dress fits you very well. The color . . ." She smiled. "I knew it would bring out the blue of your eyes. You look lovely, Lizzie."

Lizzie's chest tightened. When she reached San Francisco and located her father, would he recognize her by her sky-colored eyes that matched his own? "This dress . . . it is suitable for living in California? For San Francisco, California?"

Vivian's eyes sparked with interest. "Is that where you want to go?"

Lizzie nodded.

"You know someone there?"

Again, but with hesitance, Lizzie nodded.

Vivian looked the dress up and down, her brow pinching. "This dress is rather simple—more suitable for living on a farm or for small-town life." Her face brightened. "But I have several gowns in Oklahoma that would be appropriate for San Francisco. I'll write to Mother and ask her to send them. I have no need for them any longer, since I have no intention of ever leaving Alaska."

"You . . . will stay here forever?"

Pain seemed to flash across Vivian's face. "Yes."

"But why?"

Vivian tipped her head. "Why do you want to leave?"

Lizzie decided she'd rather not answer. Pinching her lower lip between her teeth, she rose and took a cautious stroll around the hard-packed dirt floor. The skirts brushed against her legs. The fabric felt strange yet not unpleasant against her skin. It swirled around her ankles and made a soft swishing sound. She frowned at the folds of fabric. She wouldn't be able to move silently in this dress. "It makes noise," she said.

"Noise?"

"Yes. A *whish-whish*. Animals might be frightened away when I hunt."

Light laughter trickled from Vivian's throat. She covered her lips with her fingers and stilled the sound. "In San Francisco, you won't need to hunt."

Lizzie supposed Vivian was right. She changed direction and started another loop.

"Don't hold your legs so stiffly when you walk." Vivian hurried to Lizzie's side and linked elbows with her. "Walk the same way you would if you were in your buckskin clothes. You have a very natural grace." She urged Lizzie across the floor.

Lizzie tried, but her legs refused to cooperate. The feel of the loose skirt was so different from her slim-fitting leggings. She tugged free of Vivian's light grasp. "*Dogidinh*— thank you—for fixing my hair and for bringing the dress. But I will put on my own clothes now." She turned toward the bed.

Vivian captured Lizzie's arm and drew her to a halt. "Oh no, you don't. If you truly intend to live in San Francisco, you must become accustomed to the clothing worn by white women."

Lizzie puckered her face into a scowl.

Vivian smiled. "I know it feels strange, but truly, you'll be comfortable in no time."

Lizzie raised one brow, uncertain.

"Please leave it on. You look lovely. I can't wait until Clay sees you—he'll be so surprised and pleased."

Heat rose in Lizzie's face at the notion of Clay finding her appearance pleasing. But she shouldn't want to please another woman's man. She pushed aside images of Clay's thick curling hair and easy grin and focused on the skirt. Catching hold of the folds of fabric, she held it away from her legs. "I won't remove the dress, but I will wear my leggings underneath."

Color streaked Vivian's cheeks. She tangled her hands in her skirt. "Very well—your leggings can serve as drawers until which time I can stitch a pair for you." She scurried toward the door. "I'll wait outside while you . . . you . . ." She bustled out.

Lizzie clicked her tongue on her teeth. As much as she wanted to learn white men's ways, this white woman puzzled her at times. Lizzie doubted she'd ever completely understand Vivian. She tugged her leggings into place and then looked longingly at the tunic. Her finger traced the line of red beads zigzagging around the tunic's neckline. Then she touched the simple scooped neck on the dress and slid her hands down the smooth, unadorned bodice. Not even the hem of this skirt bore any kind of beadwork or fringe. White women's clothing was plain compared to her embellished tunic. But she would be out of place in her father's world in her buckskin clothing, so as Vivian said, she'd learn to be comfortable in the dress.

She lifted the tunic and started to hang it on a wooden peg inserted in the wall, but the raucous barking of her dogs interrupted the task. She dropped the tunic and dashed for the door, forgetting about the swirling skirt of the unfamiliar dress. The fabric tangled around her legs, and before Lizzie could stop herself, she fell flat in the dirt. Pushing her hands against the ground, she raised her head and looked into the startled face of Clay Selby.

∽

Vivian, her eyes wide with alarm, dashed for Lizzie, but Clay got to her first. He grasped her elbow and lifted her to her feet. "Are you hurt?"

She swept her palms across the dress, removing dust and bits of grass and leaves. "I'm fine. But this skirt makes me clumsy."

Clay took a step back, his eyes traveling from the dusty, wrinkled skirt to Lizzie's face. She'd done something different with her hair—pulled it back the way Vivian wore hers. The change drew attention to her high cheekbones and delicate jawline. And her eyes seemed more vividly blue, perhaps enhanced by the blue checks on the dress. He stared, spellbound.

Something poked his shoulder, and he grunted at the intrusion.

"Clay?"

Vivian's voice held amusement. He glanced at her and caught her grinning. He cleared his throat. "What?"

"You're staring." She whispered, apparently trying to spare Lizzie's ears.

Clay looked again at the Gwich'in woman. She stood looking back, her face reflecting the same stoicism he often witnessed on the villagers' faces. If she'd heard Vivian's comment, he'd never know.

"Clay?"

He shifted his attention to Vivian.

"Why are you here?"

Why had he come? He tried to retrieve the purpose in coming to Lizzie's cabin, but the reason eluded him. The sight of the Gwich'in woman with her hair up and attired in the blue gingham dress had stolen his ability to think. "I . . . um . . ."

Vivian snickered. She held her hand toward Lizzie. "She looks wonderful, doesn't she? Like a real lady."

Clay swallowed, offering a slow nod. "Yes. She's . . . lovely." He allowed himself a lingering head-to-toe look. Lizzie was lovely, as he'd said, yet an element of disappointment also wriggled through his mind. Somehow the voluminous dress and American hairstyle stole something from Lizzie. But Vivian looked so pleased with herself, he didn't dare voice the thought.

Lizzie gave the skirt of the dress another vicious swipe with her hand. "It will take time for me to learn to walk in this dress." She caught the hem and raised it several inches, revealing her buckskin leggings and moccasins. "It's much easier to move in my leggings."

Vivian gasped.

Clay coughed to cover a laugh.

Vivian dashed forward. She pulled the fabric from Lizzie's hand and smoothed the skirt back into place. "Lizzie, Lizzie, remember what I told you?"

Lizzie's dark brows crunched together. "I didn't remove the dress."

"But you mustn't show people what you're wearing *underneath* it, either!"

Clay nearly swallowed his tongue, holding his laughter inside. Vivian had managed to transform Lizzie's exterior, but it might take a few more visits to bring change to the native woman's long-held habits. But maybe Vivian shouldn't try to change Lizzie—she was enchanting just as she was.

He rubbed his finger under his nose, finally recalling why he'd come seeking Vivian. "Viv, a trader came to the village today and delivered your stove from Fort Yukon."

Vivian's face lit. "Already?"

He'd sent a message with a passing trapper to order the stove only two weeks ago. He hadn't expected to receive it so quickly, but he knew Vivian would want to use it right away rather than continuing to ruin their food over an open fire. "I'll put it together for you this afternoon, but I wondered where you wanted it placed in the school."

She clapped her hands. "Oh, I think you should put it in the very center of the large room. Then it can be used as a heat source in the winter. Don't you agree?"

"That's what I would have chosen, but I wanted to be sure it wouldn't be inconvenient for you when you use it for cooking." Clay's gaze drifted to Lizzie, who stood with her hands on the back of her head, her face set in a displeased scowl. "Is something wrong?"

She grimaced. "This nest . . . it pulls."

"Nest?"

Vivian caught Lizzie's hands and drew them away from her hair. "Not a nest, a *bun*." She moved behind Lizzie and seemed to inspect the hairstyle. "It pulls because your hair is so long and thick, which makes it heavy. We might have to cut—"

"No!" Lizzie and Clay burst out with the word at the same time. Both women shot Clay a startled look.

Heat built in his face. "I, um, meant to say . . . a woman's hair is her crowning glory. If at all possible, you should refrain from . . ." He used his fingers to mimic a scissors.

Vivian put her hand on her hip. "That's easy for you to say. You don't have to suffer headaches from the pull of a weighty coil of hair." She plucked the pins from Lizzie's hair and let it tumble free. The thick, straight tresses fell nearly to Lizzie's waist. Immediately, the native woman divided the locks into two portions. She deftly twisted one braid, then a second. Even without ribbon at the ends, the shining ebony plaits held their shape.

Clay realized he was staring again. He waved one hand in the direction of Gwichyaa Saa and inched backward. "Well, if you trust me to place the stove, I'll return to the village and . . ."

"Can you stay a little longer?" A playful grin twitched

the corners of Vivian's mouth. "Lizzie is going to teach me to"—for a moment, her face puckered—"prepare a rabbit for frying." She swallowed, and the teasing glint reappeared in her eyes. "You can sample my efforts."

Lizzie nodded hard enough for the ends of her braids to unravel. "You stay, Clay Selby, and watch Vivian learn the Athabascan way of cooking a spring hare. You'll see if she is as good a learner as she is a teacher."

Chapter Nine

C lay grinned at Vivian's red-streaked cheeks. Lizzie's praise pleased her—and him, too. He'd worried whether Vivian would be more hindrance than help in Alaska, but she was obviously impacting this Gwich'in woman. With a relationship established, it would be an easy transition for Vivian to tell Lizzie about God's love.

Jealousy struck so hard his knees almost buckled—he'd wanted to be the one to tell Lizzie about Christ. Reeling, he turned to Lizzie. "I . . . I can't stay." Real disappointment swept over him, but he gave himself a mental kick—for what purpose had he come to Alaska? Vivian was making progress in reaching Lizzie. He had an entire village waiting for his preaching. "I have work to do. You teach Vivian, and she'll be able to serve rabbit for me another time."

He drew Vivian to the edge of the clearing and lowered his voice. "As soon as you've finished preparing the rabbit, come straight back. I may need your help getting the stovepipe up. And we'll need—"

She pinched his arm, bringing his rush of words to a halt. "What is your hurry? You could take a little time, stay for a bit, and get to know Lizzie better. She invited you—doesn't that mean we're building her trust? But if you run off . . ." Her brows rose, allowing her expression to complete her thought.

Clay glanced toward Lizzie. She'd crossed the yard to the dog pen. He watched her scratch the ears of one dog, then the ruff of another, seeming to give a portion of attention to each. His heart caught at the sight. Were the dogs her only friends? The desire to remain—to truly reach out to Lizzie and to get better acquainted—welled up in him again. But God's work called.

Reluctantly, he turned back to Vivian. "After I get everything finished at the mission school, I'll be able to take time for visits. But I have to complete the school first."

A feeling akin to panic filled his chest. He'd already spent a month on the building, and he still needed to chink the walls, build a door, order windows, portion off sleeping areas for each of them, and more. So much to do before he could open the doors of the mission for classes and services. Each day of delay could mean a lost opportunity to win a soul. He took another step toward the woods.

"Viv, enjoy your time with Lizzie." He tipped forward and delivered a brotherly kiss on her cheek. "Save me a piece of fried rabbit. I'll see you later." Before she could voice another excuse to hold him, he whirled on his heel and strode into the woods.

His mind raced ahead to the waiting tasks. Had it taken his father so long to get the mission school on the reservation running? When Clay was twelve, not quite a year after Pa remarried, Pa had moved him and Vivian's mother to the Kiowa reservation in Oklahoma Territory to minister to the people displaced by government mandates. Try as he might, he couldn't recall lengthy delays. It seemed Pa had begun his ministry immediately. And effectively.

Clay kicked at the decaying leaves under his feet, wishing he could scatter the unpleasant feelings of incompetence that arose when he compared himself to his father. For as long as he could remember, he'd wanted to be like Pa—strong, confident, capable. Judson Selby had been mother and father all through Clay's growing up, and somehow he'd filled both roles so well Clay never missed a mother's presence.

As an itinerant preacher, Pa had carted Clay all over Minnesota and the Dakotas, and Clay had grown up listening to his father's booming voice deliver messages of faith and inspiration. Pa had enough faith—and muscle strength—to move mountains. As a boy, Clay had believed there was nothing his pa couldn't do. As an adult, he still believed it. And Clay wanted to be just like him.

But first he had to get his mission built. Envisioning the day he'd finally be able to stand behind a podium and preach from the Bible, he sped his pace. By the end of the day, he'd have Vivian's stove in place. Then he'd turn his hands to chinking, and then building a door, and then—

A bird swooped over his head, chirping a shrill warning. Clay grinned. Then he would preach. Boldly, and vehemently. Just like Pa.

When he reached the village, he headed straight for the mission school. Two dozen or more Gwich'in gathered at the corner of the building with their backs to Clay, their jabbering voices raised in curious excitement. Clay had discovered anything new fascinated the villagers, and he had to watch to be certain the youngsters didn't run off with his tools. If they'd discovered the crate holding the stove pieces, he might already be missing some parts.

He broke into a jog, covering the ground quickly. "Excuse me," he said, working his way to the center of the group. To his relief, the stove crate remained untouched. Instead, two barrels—barrels he hadn't seen before—lay on their sides, minus their lids. Various clothing items lay scattered on the ground or in the hands of grinning natives.

For a moment, confusion smote him, but then he remembered the letter Vivian had sent prior to their leaving Oklahoma to the members of the church she'd attended in Hampshire County, Massachusetts, with her aunt and uncle. She'd requested clothing items for the children who would attend Clay's mission. Apparently, they'd honored her request. The mercantile owner in Fort Yukon must have sent the barrels with a trapper or trader who'd delivered them while he'd been at Lizzie's cabin.

A little girl named Naibi tugged on Clay's pant leg and held up a pink calico dress. Her brown eyes sparkled, her round face wreathed in a hopeful smile. "You give to me? I wear—look like Missus Viv-ee-an."

Clay delighted in how many English words the child had already adopted. He took the dress and held it against Naibi's front. He didn't know much about children's clothing, but it appeared the dress would swallow the child. He shook his head. "This is *t'si chux*—too big." The child's face clouded. He tweaked her nose and offered a soothing promise in Athabascan. "But we will find one that will fit." Sweeping the group with a bright smile, he added, "We'll find something for all of you."

Like vultures on a fresh kill, the villagers pressed in, hands reaching, voices jabbering. In a few minutes, all of the clothing articles had been claimed by eager natives, and Clay was left with two empty barrels. He carried them inside the mission. With their lids intact, they could serve as stools until he could build something better. They would also provide much-needed storage. He hoped the church would send more barrels of clothing later.

Whistling, he set to work putting the stove together for Vivian. The pieces fit together like a big puzzle, although working with the heavy iron challenged him more than the wooden puzzles of his childhood. He spent more than an hour securely attaching the iron feet and scrolled door to the heating chamber and assembling the flue pipe.

Hot, dusty, and sweaty, he stepped back to admire his handiwork. The McClary Brandon black iron stove hunkered in the center of the large square room. The top angled downward on one side—the result of placing the stove on an uneven dirt floor. But if he waited until he had a wood floor in the mission, it might be next year—or even later—before Vivian would be able to make use of the stove. Crooked wasn't perfect, but it would have to do. Hopefully its ability to cook food and heat the room wouldn't be affected by its slight list to the right.

He scratched his head, grimacing. He hoped Vivian would be satisfied. He'd not been able to afford a top-of-the-line model with warming hobs, a water reservoir, or even multiple heating chambers. This stove possessed an oven and three removable stove lids—a simple model, to be sure. But it should be a huge improvement from cooking over an open fire, and he hoped it would improve the taste of the food she prepared.

As if in response to his musings, his stomach growled, reminding him it was past time for lunch. He headed outside, placing a cut tree branch across the door opening of the mission to serve as a barrier. Oddly, the natives viewed the tiny obstruction like a closed door and wouldn't enter without permission when the branch was in place. However, if it wasn't there, they'd wander inside at will, younger ones climbing the unchinked walls and older ones examining every inch of the unadorned interior.

He entered Vivian's hut and located the dried beef and corn bread in a small crate. Unwilling to eat inside the dismal hut, he carried the crate outside and sat on the log he and Vivian used as outdoor seating. He offered thanks for the meal and then ate his dreary lunch. While he chewed, his thoughts drifted through the woods to Lizzie's lonely cabin. Were Vivian and Lizzie enjoying the fried rabbit? If it turned out half as good as the cookies Lizzie had given them, it would have been worth waiting for. The company would have been nice, too.

"I'll bet Pa never had such selfish thoughts," he muttered. He finished eating quickly, then returned the empty crate to Vivian's hut. His stomach full, he wandered back to the mission school, eager to get Vivian's stove ready for use so he could move on to other tasks.

He slid his hand across the shiny top, his eyes traveling the distance from the stove to the roof's peak twelve feet above his head. He could use some help in putting up the flue pipe, but who should he ask? Vivian hadn't yet returned. Half of the villagers had gone to their summer fishing camps to catch and dry salmon, taking the older children with them, and those remaining stayed busy with gardens and constructing articles of clothing from the caches of fur caught during the cold winter months. He didn't want to take others from their duties.

Sucking in a fortifying breath, he made a decision. This was *his* mission, and *he* would be responsible for it. He gathered the remaining lengths of pipe and connected them, piece by piece, ascertaining the bands were tight enough to hold without crimping the tin. Then, his muscles quivering, he held the joined length straight up and down and tried to force the end between the branches that held the sod roof in place.

He grunted with the effort, holding back exclamations of frustration. After several tries, he finally managed to find a crack wide enough to accept the pipe. He said through gritted teeth, "C'mon, go through . . ." Chunks of dirt and bits of bark fell, peppering his hair, face, and shoulders. He blinked rapidly, crunching his face against the onslaught, and pushed harder. But it wouldn't penetrate the thick sod.

Panting with exertion, he propped the bottom end of the pipe into the opening on the stove. He lifted his shirt tail to clean the grime from his sweat-dampened face and then looked again at the ceiling. He'd have to break a hole from the outside in rather than the inside out. Hopefully, a small portion of the pipe would show through on the roof.

For a moment, he paused. Should he pull the pipe down and move the stove closer to the wall? It would be easier to keep the pipe secure if it weren't in the center of the room, and it would require less climbing on the roof. But Vivian's observation had been right—the stove would do a better job of projecting heat to the entire space in its present location. He'd leave it in the middle. Somehow he'd get that pipe through the roof.

He picked up the tin cap for the pipe. It was too large for his pocket, so he tucked it inside his shirt. It rubbed against his ribs, an unwieldy distraction as he wedged his fingers and toes between cracks on the log wall and climbed upward. He reached the roof and paused to examine the expanse of sod. There, just a few inches from the peak, he located a small bulge of dirt—displaced by the pipe.

Nodding, he gritted his teeth and heaved himself onto the roof. On hands and knees, he inched his way to the bulge. The scent of the grass-covered sod filled his nostrils, a fresh scent that made him want to smile. When he reached the bulge, he pulled several tufts of grass loose and scooped out the sod. A circular tin pipe peeped out, and Clay nearly shouted in exultation. He shifted fully to his knees and grasped the pipe with both hands. Slowly, firmly, he pulled until he'd freed a suitable length of pipe.

With one hand stabilizing the pipe, he used his other hand to reach beneath his shirt for the cap. His weight shifted to his right knee with the movement, and the sod beneath his knee dipped. Alarmed, Clay angled his body the opposite direction. To his horror, the sod beneath both knees crumbled. He dropped the cap and reached to support himself, but his knees broke through the sod and caught in the branches that held the sod in place. He wriggled to free himself, but the movement only resulted in more sod breaking loose.

He forced himself to hold perfectly still, but his heart pounded as he peered through the opening in the branches to the floor of the mission school below. Would the branches give way and send him plummeting? His mouth dry and chest heaving, he searched the village grounds, seeking anyone who might be able to assist him. The only people within shouting distance were a few women working in the garden and a group of giggling children playing a chasing game.

He'd have to depend on himself. He drew in several calming breaths, bringing his erratic pulse under control. Then, gingerly, he began working his left leg free of the tangle of branches. Hope soared when he managed to release his leg, but the elation was short-lived when the shift in weight pushed his right leg deeper into the roof. His leg twisted in the branches, and pain shot from his knee to his hip. Grunting with frustration, Clay planted both palms on the sod and tried to arch his back to release his right leg.

Sharp points of branches tore his pant leg, digging into his flesh, but he gritted his teeth and pulled again. Several smaller branches broke, their cracks sounding above the pound of his heartbeat in his ears. One more pull and—

The branches gave way. Clay plunged through the narrow gap.

Chapter Ten

Vivian licked her fingers, then giggled to herself. Had she ever displayed such poor manners? But who would have believed rabbit fried in bear fat could be so delicious? She didn't want to waste a single morsel.

Lizzie bobbed her head at the picked-clean bones on Vivian's plate. "The rabbit . . . you enjoyed it?"

"Oh yes. It's the best meal I've had since Clay and I arrived in Alaska—even better than anything we ate on the way." Although initially queasy, Vivian prided herself on observing the entire preparation process and then cutting the skinned, gutted rabbit into pieces herself. With Lizzie's supervision, she'd then cooked the meat to perfection. Lizzie was an excellent teacher.

She heaved a deep sigh. "I feel badly, though, for having such a wonderful lunch when poor Clay is eating dried beef and yesterday's corn bread."

Lizzie used her finger to pry loose a tiny bit of meat from the last bone on her plate. "It was his choice to return to the village."

Vivian nodded thoughtfully. Yes, it had been Clay's choice to leave. He'd almost given the impression of one escaping

100

when he'd darted back toward the village. Clay's drive to complete the mission school—to begin his ministry—was admirable. He pushed himself so hard. Regret mingled with guilt twined through Vivian's middle. She'd spent too much time away today. She needed to return and assist him, as he'd requested.

Giving her thumb one last swipe with her tongue, she pushed away from the table. "Let me help you clean up, and then I should go back."

Lizzie dumped the bones from Vivian's plate on top of her own. "I don't need your help. Go."

The dismissing words would have hurt Vivian if she hadn't already spent quite a bit of time with Lizzie. She'd learned the native woman was often abrupt, but Vivian didn't believe Lizzie intended to be unkind. "Are you sure?"

"Take the snare we made and set it up in the brush near your hut. Check it in the morning." Lizzie, plate of bones in hand, headed out the door. Vivian scurried after her as she continued. "Maybe you'll be able to serve your man rabbit for breakfast tomorrow."

Heat filled Vivian's face. She caught Lizzie's arm. "Lizzie, Clay isn't my man. He's my brother."

Lizzie gawked at her, her face more expressive than Vivian had ever seen it. "Brother? But I . . . I thought . . ." Lizzie jerked loose of Vivian's hold and darted toward the dog pen.

Vivian followed, hoping Lizzie might complete her thought. But the dogs provided too much of a distraction. They lined up along the fence, wagging their tails and yipping in excitement. Lizzie tossed the bones over the enclosure. Snarls and sharp barks erupted as the animals scrambled to retrieve a treat. Only half of them secured a bone, and the lucky ones hunkered low, snarling over their prizes. One brown-faced dog tried to snatch the bone from another male, and he got his paw nipped for his efforts. Whimpering, the unsuccessful dog slinked to the corner of the pen to lick his wound.

Vivian pointed to the injured dog. "The poor thing . . . Why didn't you wait until you'd killed a second rabbit? Then there would be enough bones to go around."

Lizzie sent Vivian an odd look. "I throw in fewer pieces so the dogs establish leadership amongst themselves."

Vivian stared at Lizzie in shock. "But that's so . . . heartless!"

"Not at all." Lizzie spoke matter-of-factly. "Some of them have to follow. Otherwise they'd never be able to pull my sled as a team."

Vivian gazed at the sad dog in the corner of the pen. "But it doesn't seem fair."

Lizzie shrugged and whirled for the cabin. "Many things aren't fair. Learning is often hard. But hard-won lessons usually serve us the best."

Vivian turned away from the pen and hastened again after Lizzie. "I'll go now, but I'll try to come back tomorrow."

Lizzie dropped the empty plate into the wash bucket by the back door with a tinny clang, then headed for the table. "I won't be here. The salmon are running. I'll miss securing my catch if I don't go soon."

"But I thought you planned to leave by winter." Vivian reached for the skillet in the middle of the table, but Lizzie snatched it up first. She followed the native woman back to the wash bucket.

"I do." For a moment, Lizzie paused in her endless rush of busyness and stared out the open door, as if seeking something. "But if Denali doesn't show me favor, I might have to . . ." Her voice drifted away, her eyes clouding.

Vivian touched Lizzie's sleeve. "Lizzie, why do you want to leave this place? It's your home."

Lizzie shot Vivian a sharp look. "You left your home to come here—to Gwichyaa Saa. If Clay is . . ." The strange blush crept across Lizzie's face again. "Your brother, he has no authority over you. So why did you come?"

Vivian blinked twice in surprise. "I came to teach."

"And your reasons are important to you?"

Vivian contemplated Lizzie's question. If she were successful at teaching, if she could help Clay in the saving of souls, perhaps God would finally forgive her. She nodded. "Yes. They're important."

A knowing smile curved Lizzie's lips. "Yet you don't share the reasons with me."

Vivian bit down on her lower lip. She couldn't share the deepest reason. Not without divulging the horrible thing she'd done. Lizzie would certainly run away in revulsion if she knew Vivian had killed her own father.

Lizzie pointed to her chest. "I have reasons, too. But I think it's not as important for you to know them as it is for me to know them. So I will keep mine inside, as well." She picked up a bucket. "You need to go, and I need to fetch water. I'll return from my fish camp in four days. Come back then if you'd like to learn to dry the salmon."

"Four days? But what of your dogs?"

Lizzie shook her head, clicking her teeth on her tongue. "The dogs go with me, of course." She marched around Vivian and out the door, calling over her shoulder, "Come back in four days' time. You still have much to learn."

⚭

Clay sat on the floor, rubbing his aching hip and staring up at the ragged hole in the roof. He silently berated himself—how could he have been so foolish? He should have known poking that hole would weaken the roof. Why hadn't he taken the time to place several branches crosswise and used them as a support before climbing across the sod? He'd been too impatient to complete the task, unwilling to admit he needed help.

Proverbs 29:23 flitted through his mind like an admonition: *"A man's pride shall bring him low . . ."* He slapped the hard-packed floor. His pride had plummeted him from the roof to the hard ground below. Even so, the Lord had watched over him. Other than several scratches and bruises, he didn't believe he'd done any real damage to himself. He'd heal. It would take more effort to correct the damage done to the roof and the stovepipe.

He glared at the bent pipe pointing at the patch of blue sky. "Another delay." Groaning, he pushed to his feet. Chunks of sod, shattered bits of tree branches, and tufts of grass littered the floor beneath him. He hung his head, discouragement weighing him down. His father wouldn't have made such a mess.

Sighing, he limped into the sunshine in time to see Vivian step out of the trees. A smile graced her face, and she hummed a cheerful tune. Her lightheartedness in the face of his despondence stirred his anger.

Balling his hand on his hip, he scowled at her. "It's about time you showed up. Didn't I tell you to hurry?"

The tune died on her lips. "I would've been here sooner, but I stopped to put out a snare Lizzie and I made so—" Her eyes widened, and she dashed forward, reaching for his face. "Clay! What happened to you? You're all beat up! Did the villagers attack you?"

Her fingers traced his cheek, the touch bringing a fierce sting. He pushed her hand down. "You and your ridiculous imagination. No one attacked me. I fell through the roof."

"You—you what?"

"Fell through the roof." He ignored her aghast expression and pointed, disgusted. "Trying to get the stovepipe up. The roof collapsed on me, and I bent the flue pipe. So now I've got another mess to fix before I can move on to chinking."

"Oh, Clay . . ." Her dismayed tone matched his feelings. "I'm so sorry."

Clay set his jaw. "Sorry doesn't fix it." The hole seemed to mock him, proclaiming his incompetence. "It means more time before I can open the mission for classes." He shook his head. "I'll need to weave some branches in where I broke through to strengthen the roof support before I lay on more sod." Clay retrieved his hatchet from his hut and then turned toward the woods. His right hip ached worse than a bad tooth, and it stabbed when he put pressure on the leg, but he kept moving. "I hope I can find some dead branches so I don't have to cut down a sapling or two—not sure I'm up to it."

Vivian caught up to him and grabbed his arm. "Clay, please, come to my hut and let me tend your wounds."

Her fingers dug into his flesh, and he grimaced. "I don't have time! I need to—"

Her hold tightened. "I know, I know, you have all of these other tasks waiting. But you're bleeding! Mother well equipped me with bandages and salve. Let me help you. Please?" She tugged at him, trying to draw him back toward the huts.

Clay glowered down at her. If a few scratches upset her this badly, she'd be useless to him in a real emergency. Impatience sharpened his tone. "I don't need tending. I need to collect branches."

Her fingers fell away from his arm. Tears glittered in her eyes. "But you're hurt, Clay. And I . . . I need—I want t-to help."

Looking into her fright-filled face, Clay suddenly understood. He grasped her by the shoulders and gentled his voice, hoping she'd accept his tender tone as apology for his earlier impatience. "I'm not hurt that badly, Vivian. I won't bleed to death over a few scratches. Your father—"

She jerked loose, backing away from him with her eyes as wide and terrified as a cornered rabbit's. "H-how do you know about my father?"

Clay shrugged slowly, his muscles complaining. "Pa told me years ago when I asked how he'd died—said he'd bled to death after cutting his leg with an axe." He held out his arm. A tear in his sleeve revealed a scratch, the blood already dried into a jagged scab. "But look. Just scratches. So you don't need to be troubled over me."

She worried her lower lip between her teeth, her brow furrowed into lines of distress.

Clay sighed. "If I let you put some bandages on these *scratches*"—unconsciously, he emphasized the word, revealing his inner frustration—"will you then allow me to gather the branches I need?"

She nodded rapidly, twisting her fingers together at her waist. "But I want to come with you. May I come with you? I'll carry the branches for you."

"All right. But hurry. I have work to do." He followed Vivian to her hut, but his thoughts railed against the delay. *Lord, when will I be able to begin the ministry of my heart?*

Chapter Eleven

Lizzie pulled her handmade dip net from the water and flung the wildly flapping salmon onto the bank. Her dogs, tethered well away from the edge of the river, barked in excitement. She decided not to quiet them—hearing them celebrate the catch encouraged her to keep working. Over her two days at the fish camp, she'd brought in almost seven dozen fat salmon. She wanted to catch ten dozen—half of what she'd caught last year—and then she would return to her cabin.

Ignoring the ache in her shoulders, she swung the net into the water again and waited for the tug that signaled a catch. From upriver, chattering let her know groups of villagers from Gwichyaa Saa were also at work, catching salmon. They would remain at their summer camps for weeks, drying the salmon and enjoying one another's company. Mama's childhood stories of going to fish camp with her parents had always stirred Lizzie's envy. As a girl, she'd wished she could be part of the village merriment. She still carried a desire to belong, but not with the villagers. Never again with the villagers.

As soon as she'd caught what she wanted, she would load the fish onto travoises and give her dogs the chore of carting the fish to her cabin. There, she would dry the salmon in her drying hut and then turn her attention to the chores that had gone neglected over her time away. If she had a family, the duties would be distributed, but—her heart panged—only she bore the responsibility for gathering food, tending the garden, and caring for the dogs. And she still had a coat to complete.

A salmon caught in her net. Two-handed, she tossed it up with the others, and then dipped the net again, the actions as natural as breathing. Her thoughts drifted to Vitse's coat. By now she'd hoped to have the pieces sewn together, ready to receive the elaborate embellishments that would take weeks to complete. But her time with the white woman—learning table manners, proper conversation topics, and appropriate means of dress, as well as teaching Vivian ways to cook, clean, and trap, had stolen her precious free time. Yet she couldn't begrudge her time with Vivian. For the first time since Mama's death, she felt as though she had a friend. And she'd gained so much knowledge.

Embarrassment flooded her frame as she recalled how she envied the woman. She'd believed Vivian had a tender husband, one who performed little kindnesses and looked after her. Lizzie had often wondered how Vivian resisted running her fingers through the thick curls framing Clay's ears and neck. Now she understood—a sister wouldn't behave affectionately toward her brother. Lizzie sighed. If Clay were *her* man, she would explore those soft-looking curls at every opportunity.

She gave herself a little shake. She must stop thinking of Clay in such familiar ways. When she'd finished the coat and honored her mother's dying request, she would leave this place. Clay and Vivian intended to stay. Allowing herself to ponder what it would be like if Clay were her man did her no good. Her chest panged painfully. Before she'd met these two white people, she had no reason to stay. But she would miss Clay and Vivian more than she cared to admit.

She glanced down at her customary buckskin clothes. Vivian wouldn't be happy to see her wearing something other than the blue-checked dress, but she couldn't stand ankle-deep in water with a skirt dragging in the current. She'd considered wearing it with the skirt pulled between her legs and tied at her waist to keep it out of her way and allow her to move freely. But Vivian had indicated a lady didn't show what she wore beneath a dress. Pulling up the skirt would expose her leggings, and the remembrance of Clay's startled reaction the day she'd revealed her leggings made her face heat. So she'd donned her buckskin tunic instead and hoped neither Clay nor Vivian would wander by and catch her.

Behind her, the dogs set up a series of growls and low-pitched barks. She spun to see them leaping against their tethers, teeth bared, their pointed faces all aimed at the bank where she'd tossed the caught salmon. Frowning, she turned in that direction, and to her shock, the pile of rose-colored fish appeared smaller. Lizzie dropped the net and dashed to the area, seeking animal tracks. Had a bear been brazen enough to wander close enough to steal her catch? Usually the smell of the dogs was enough to keep the big marauding creatures at bay.

Lizzie sucked in a sharp breath. No paw prints were imbedded in the moist ground, but she found evidence that a pair of two-legged predators had prowled around her salmon . . . and apparently sneaked away with some. The prints led directly into the brush. Her dogs continued to growl in warning, but her sharp hiss hushed them. In the silence that fell, she tapped her lips with her fingertips, trying to decide what to do.

Whoever had sneaked up behind her had taken perhaps four salmon. She could recover that number in a half hour's time, so it wasn't a devastating loss, but it angered her that someone would be lazy enough to simply take what she'd worked hard to gain. Based upon the size of the footprints, the thieves were young—perhaps no more than eight or nine years. But even a child of that age knew stealing was wrong. They should be reprimanded, perhaps punished, so they wouldn't choose to take something that didn't belong to them again.

Leaving her dip net on the bank, Lizzie took the time to strap the morning's remaining salmon onto a travois and cover them with pine boughs to mask the scent of the fish, as she'd done with the previously caught fish. She moved Martha, her most trustworthy dog, closer to the line of birch travoises. "Down, Martha. Stay." The dog whined low in her throat, but she hunkered down and rested her chin on her paws. "Good girl."

Lizzie then untethered Andy—the fiercest looking of all her dogs with his bent ear, two-toned eyes, and a scar on his forehead from a tussle with George when he was still a pup—and set her lips in a grim line. "We'll catch those little thieves, Andy, and you can give them a good scare when we do."

Coiling the end of Andy's tether firmly around her hand, she allowed him to lead her into the brush. It wasn't difficult to follow the trail—broken branch tips on bushes and trampled leaves showed the course the thieves had taken. Their carelessness proved their youth and inexperience. When she and Andy were no more than two dozen yards into the woods, Andy's ear perked up. Lizzie heard it, too—giggles. The dog curled his lips to show his teeth, but she gave a gentle tug on the tether, silencing any growls.

Lizzie tiptoed forward, holding Andy close at her side, and peeked between leafy branches into a small clearing. Two children, a girl and a boy, had gathered the makings for a fire. The boy sat on his haunches, striking a flint against a stone to light the pile of dry leaves. The girl sat off to the side, busily skewering a salmon with a sharpened stick. Her tongue stuck out of the corner of her mouth and her little brow puckered in concentration. Clearly, they'd cooked fish over an open fire before.

Lizzie looked past their expertise to their clothing. Could these children be from Gwichyaa Saa? Neither child wore the typical buckskin tunics of the Gwich'in tribe. Instead, the boy had on a shirt similar to the one worn by Clay Selby. The shirt, man-sized, hung below the boy's knees, with the sleeves rolled into bulky wads at the child's elbows. The girl's dirty bare legs stuck out below the hem of a brown dress printed all over in little yellow and orange flowers.

Curiosity overcame Lizzie, and she stepped from the brush with Andy bristling beside her. Both children lurched to their feet, their frightened gazes fixed on Andy. The girl dropped the fish on top of the tiny flame. A sizzle sounded, accompanied by a thin coil of smoke as the fire died.

Lizzie pointed at the boy—the taller of the pair—and asked in Athabascan, "Where did you get those clothes?"

The boy licked his lips, his gaze darting back and forth between Andy and Lizzie. "From Clay Selby—a white man who lives in our village."

Lizzie's silly heart gave a jump at the sound of Clay's name. She squelched the happy reaction. She should be angry with Clay for putting the children into white man's clothing. Were their buckskin tunics not good enough? Yet, despite her best effort, she couldn't conjure up indignation.

The little girl added in a shrill voice, "He gave them to us. We did not steal them."

Lizzie frowned, partly because of their answers and partly because evidence of their thievery lay at their feet in the leaves. "But you stole my salmon."

"Only three." The fearful look fled the boy's eyes, replaced by defiance. "You have many fish, but you are only one person. You have no need of them all."

Lizzie dismissed his excuse with a wave of her hand. "You are here with one of the fish camps?"

Both children nodded.

"Then eat your own fish. Leave mine alone."

The boy's lip curled in derision, and he tugged the girl tight against his side. "Our vitse is old—she cannot catch as well as you."

"It is only three fish," the little girl challenged, her chin sticking out stubbornly.

Lizzie stifled a frustrated sigh. They'd wronged her. Why couldn't they understand? She should talk to their grandmother, who apparently was raising them without teaching them principles. She took a step closer to the pair. "Where is your vitse?"

The little girl's eyes flooded with tears. She sent a frantic look to the boy. His face hardened. "Why?"

"I want to tell her she has thieves for grandchildren."

The girl clutched her brother's hands. He squared his skinny shoulders. "Take your fish—we do not want them anymore."

Lizzie glanced at the dead salmon, their bright scales coated with dry leaves and dirt. Then she looked again at the children. Despite the boy's brave posture, she sensed a real fear underneath his bluster. Her heart softened. What were three fish, anyway? "Come, Andy." She turned to go back to her camp.

"Are you going to take your fish?" The boy's voice called after her.

Andy released a little growl in reply, but Lizzie gave his tether a pull and continued walking without responding to the child. She ruffled Andy's ears. "Hush now. They're just children. And they're hungry." The boy was even younger than she'd been when Pa left her alone with Mama. She remembered hunger. She wouldn't wish it on these children. "As they said, it's just three fish."

⁂

Clay wiped his mouth with his sleeve and sat back on his barrel chair, shooting a grin at Vivian across the table he'd built inside the school. "That was good, Viv. Really good."

Vivian nibbled the last of the rabbit from the bone and offered a smile in reply. "It was good, wasn't it? Although, I have to say, the rabbit I had at Lizzie's cooked in bear fat was even better. But lard will have to do. Now that I've learned to use a snare, we'll be able to enjoy fresh meat now and then."

Clay wouldn't have imagined his squeamish stepsister finding the courage to kill and prepare small game for their table. Yet she'd surprised him twice in the past three days, first with a fat grouse and today with a rabbit. Her time with Lizzie was bringing changes that would serve them well as they established a home in Gwichyaa Saa. Vivian might make a fine missionary after all.

She lifted her chin, sniffing the air. The enticing aroma of smoked fish lingered over the entire village and drifted through the door and window openings. "I'd hoped some of them might choose to share a bit of their catches with us, but I suppose we're on our own."

Clay toyed with the edge of his plate. He'd cleared a sizable piece of ground behind the mission school and instructed

Vivian to plant a garden with the seeds they'd brought from home, but he needed to contribute to their food stores, as well. They'd managed thus far on the canned milk, dried beef, and dry goods they'd brought from home, but eventually those items would be used up. Vivian's snare wouldn't feed them all through the winter months.

"We need to provide for ourselves, Viv. Everyone is expected to carry his or her weight in the tribe. Besides . . ." He pointed at her with a well-gnawed bone. "We're here to serve, not to be served, remember?"

Vivian sent him an impatient look. "You needn't preach at me, Clay. I know our purpose. But when we open the school and have children here each day, are you going to ask them to bring their own lunches? Or do you intend to provide a meal for them?"

Clay grimaced. "I imagine we'll need to feed them." Which meant he would need a larger supply of food than he'd first imagined. The natives stored their dried salmon and other foods in log caches set on stilts, safe from dogs or other animals. Perhaps when he'd finally completed the mission school, he would build a cache for their use and then turn his attention to hunting. If he felled a moose or an elk, their needs would be met for several months.

Of course, hunting would take him away from the village and its people. He nearly groaned. His heart ached with the desire to preach. But other tasks ate up every bit of his time.

"I worry about not having enough food this winter." Vivian's anxious voice cut into Clay's thoughts. "I wonder when the supplies the Mission Committee said they'd send are going to arrive. I expected them before now."

Clay wondered the same thing. The Mission Committee that arranged his placement in Alaska had assured him he'd receive support in the way of food—sacks of flour, sugar, cornmeal, potatoes, onions, and turnips—and school supplies such as paper tablets, books, and slates. But so far, the only items they'd received were the stove he'd ordered and the barrels of clothing sent by Vivian's church friends.

He voiced an idle worry. "Maybe they arrived in Fort Yukon, and the folks on the docks peeked in all the crates and decided to keep the things they liked rather than send them on for the *Indians* to use."

Vivian wrinkled her nose. "You sound like that awful man who gave us the canoe ride." Then her face clouded. "But do you think it's possible someone absconded with our supplies?"

Clay patted her hand. "Brother Mercer assured me he had a reliable contact in Fort Yukon who would be responsible for transporting any goods to us here in the village. You know how long it took the things we shipped from Oklahoma to arrive. I'm sure the goods are just delayed."

Vivian sniffed and began clearing the makeshift table. "Well, if they don't hurry, the potatoes might very well be rotten before they reach us. And I may have eaten a rabbit I skinned and gutted myself, but I refuse to eat a rotten potato!"

Clay laughed and rose. Over the past few days, the soreness from his fall had eased, but he still felt a catch in his right hip if he moved too quickly. He tried not to favor the leg too much, though, because his limp always brought a frown of concern to Vivian's face. "I'm taking the bushel basket to the river for clay. I hope to have a good portion of the north wall chinked by bedtime."

"Let me clear these dishes, and then I'll go with you."

Ever since his fall, Vivian had hovered near, as if afraid to let him out of her sight. While he appreciated her concern, her attentiveness was starting to feel cloying. He shook his head. "No, you stay here."

"But—"

"I'd rather you weeded the garden." He ignored her crestfallen expression and started out the door, but then he turned back. "When do you intend to see Lizzie again?" Oddly, mentioning the woman's name raised a desire to see her himself.

Vivian brushed a few stray strands of hair from her face. "The day after tomorrow, probably. She said she would be at the river, fishing, for four days. Why?"

"Do you think she'd be willing to hunt for us? Something bigger than a rabbit—something that would feed us for a long time. Maybe we could offer her a bushel of potatoes or . . . or some cornmeal or sugar in trade . . . when the supplies finally arrive."

Vivian stacked the dishes, her expression thoughtful. "I can ask. I don't know that she'll have need of a food trade, though. She's planning to leave Alaska."

Something akin to panic caught in Clay's breastbone. "She's leaving?"

"Yes. That's why she wishes to learn to be white. She said she's moving to San Francisco and won't return." Vivian's lips puckered into a pout. "I'll miss her. She's so different than any of my friends from Hampshire County, but I've grown fond of her. I wish I could convince her to stay."

"Do you know why she wants to leave?"

Vivian laughed softly, shaking her head. "I've asked her twice, and both times she's changed the subject. She is quite secretive about her reasons."

"When does she intend to go?"

Vivian banged dishes together. "She wants to be gone soon—before winter, certainly."

Soon . . . The prick of panic grew. Clay needed to hurry even more. After visiting with Shruh and Co'Ozhii, he'd decided his first sermons to the Gwich'ins of the village must focus on the concept of forgiveness. If he preached it well, they might pardon whatever transgression Lizzie's mother had committed and welcome Lizzie into their tribe. Surely the lonely woman would be grateful to receive their pardon and acceptance. Maybe it would be enough to make her stay.

He gave himself a little jerk that spurred his feet into motion. "I'm heading to the river now. Remember those weeds—they're choking out our plants."

Vivian released a long-suffering sigh. "Yes, Clay, I'll remember."

He hustled out the door, rubbing his aching hip as a prayer filled his mind. *Please let her change her mind and stay. Vivian relies on her friendship.* His steps slowed, his thoughts rumbling to a halt. Did he want Lizzie to stay for Vivian's sake . . . or his own?

Chapter Twelve

Lizzie hung the last of the salmon filets over the smoke-darkened beams of her smoking hut and closed the door. She had hoped Vivian might come and assist in preparing the salmon for smoking. Several times during the day, Lizzie had paused to search the break in the trees, eager for the white woman's arrival, but the entire day had slipped by. Vivian must be with Clay. Desire for companionship stirred in Lizzie's heart—to never be alone must be a glorious thing. *And I will know that glory very soon.*

Rubbing the base of her spine with both hands, she angled her gaze to the distance, where the proud mountain Denali disappeared into the clouds. Mama had always said they were never alone because they lived in Denali's shadow. Mama found comfort in Denali's presence, but Lizzie wanted more than a mountain as a companion.

Tiredness washed over her, and she longed to enter her cabin and crawl into bed until her aching arms and shoulders found relief. But she had one more chore that must be tended—burying the fish bones and skins between the rows in her vegetable garden. With a sigh, she retrieved her shovel. The stench of the rotting pile drew insects and

soured the air around her cabin. No matter how tired she
was from her days of fishing and then preparing the meat,
she would put that detestable mess underground where it
would serve as fertilizer.

With the shovel propped on her shoulder, she trudged to
the garden plot between the cabin and the dog pens. Her
father had carved away all the wild growth years ago, leaving
a clear expanse where the sun could spread its warmth on
the corn, squash, pumpkins, cabbages, and carrots. Wearily,
she pressed the shovel's blade into the dirt and turned the
soil, creating a shallow ravine all along the garden's edge.
Then, her feet dragging, she plopped shovelful after shovelful of salmon remains into the ravine before scooping the
dirt back into place.

Her dogs slept, tired from dragging the huge cache of fish to
Lizzie's cabin. They'd dozed the day away and would probably
sleep until tomorrow morning. Lizzie envied their ability to
drop to the ground, curl into a ball, and drift away.

She had just begun digging the fourth and final ravine
when a rustle in the brush caught her attention. Two of the
dogs lifted their heads in curiosity, but after sniffing the
air, they lay back down. Lizzie kept her gaze aimed at the
place she'd heard the sound, waiting. Moments later, Vivian
stepped into the clearing with a basket swinging on her arm.

Lizzie's spirits lifted at the sight of her friend. Then she
looked past Vivian, searching for a glimpse of Clay. She
pushed aside the brief pang of disappointment that Vivian
was alone and moved to greet the white woman. "You've
come in the evening? You always come in the morning."

Vivian smiled. "I know, but it doesn't grow dark, so I can
find my way."

"But it isn't as safe," Lizzie chided. Clutching the shovel
with both hands, she said, "Animals hunt in the evening

hours. You shouldn't come alone." If she frightened Vivian enough, perhaps next time she'd bring Clay with her.

Worry briefly flashed in Vivian's eyes. "I'll remember for next time." Then her expression cleared, a smile chasing away the concern. "I missed you while you were gone." She wrinkled her nose, waving her hand in front of her face. "But, *phew*, you smell of fish." Then she put her hands on her hips. "And you aren't wearing your dress."

Lizzie ducked her head. "It gets in the way of fishing."

Vivian laughed. "I suppose you're right." She reached into the basket and lifted out a bundle wrapped in a piece of burlap. "I brought you something. Clay got my stove working, so I was able to bake this afternoon. I made cookies. Shortbread—like the ones my mother baked for me before I left Oklahoma." Her eyes misted with tears, and she blinked rapidly. "I hope you'll enjoy them."

Lizzie dropped the shovel and reached for the package. No one had given her a gift since she was a little girl. She wasn't sure how to react. So she stood silently with the little bundle balanced on her palms, staring into Vivian's face. After several seconds, she blurted, "You love your mother."

The tears reappeared, deepening the green of Vivian's eyes. "Yes, I do."

"She's alive—you've told me so. If she is alive, why aren't you with her?" If Lizzie's mother were alive, nothing would compel her to go somewhere else.

Vivian sighed. "It's hard to explain, Lizzie. I love my mother, and I know she loves me, but I lived away from her for many years. Ever since my father . . . my father . . ." She gulped, and one tear trickled down her cheek. "Since he died." She sucked in a great breath, as if saying the words robbed her of air. "Now my mother and I are . . . strangers. It's somehow easier to be apart."

Lizzie frowned. Being apart from her mother and Pa had never gotten easier.

Vivian went on. "So I came here to help Clay. This is my home now." As she spoke, her voice gained strength. "From now on, I'll be an Alaskan."

Lizzie curled her hands around the package of cookies. "This is what you truly want? To stay here, away from the mother you love?"

For a moment, Vivian looked off to the side, as if traveling somewhere in her mind. Then she gave a brusque nod. "Yes. This is where I must remain." Her chin jerked, and she faced Lizzie again. "Are you leaving because your mother is gone? Or is it because of your grandparents?"

Lizzie took a step backward. "Why do you ask this?"

Vivian stretched one hand toward Lizzie, her expression remorseful. "Please don't be offended by my question. I only ask because I care. I know your grandparents rejected your mother, but I don't know why. Clay and I would like to help you bring an end to your differences."

Anxiety coursed through Lizzie's chest. The joy of receiving a gift, of seeing her friend come to visit, fled with the rush of emotion. "You have spoken to my grandmother? About me?"

"No, but Clay has. He's very concerned about—"

"Tell him to leave my grandmother alone. Tell him it isn't his concern. Tell him—" Lizzie spun and charged to her cabin. She plunked the cookies on the bench inside the door and pressed her fists to her temples. Her mother's dying wish had been for Lizzie to reconcile with her grandparents. If the white people intruded, then she wouldn't be able to claim the deed as her own. Her mother's request would go unfulfilled, and then how would Mama rest in peace?

"Lizzie?" Vivian's voice came from behind Lizzie, both hurt and puzzled.

Lizzie whirled to face her friend, who stood uncertainly in the cabin's doorway. She angled her chin high. "You are my friend, Vivian. You've given me much—have taught me much—and I am grateful. But in this thing you must not interfere. Teach me, yes. Learn from me, yes. But leave my grandmother alone. If you can't honor my request, then we can no longer be friends."

She pushed past Vivian, marched across the yard, and snatched up the shovel. Even though Vivian lingered, wringing her hands and pacing along the edge of the garden plot, Lizzie ignored her. When she finished her task, she cleaned the shovel, put it in its spot in the lean-to, and entered her cabin. She closed the door without acknowledging Vivian's presence.

Her heart aching, she dropped onto her bed. How it pained her to treat Vivian so callously, but how else would she make the woman understand? She must make peace with Vitse her own way. Shifting her gaze to the window, she sought the great mountain that had given her mother tranquility and security. Her shoulders wilted. Clouds, mottled gray and white, stood guard. Hiding . . . the mountain was hiding.

When she fulfilled Mama's final wish, would Denali make itself known to her? Then would she, too, know contentment?

⁂

"She was so cold, Clay—angry. Lizzie has never been one to be openly demonstrative, but she was friendly to me. I feel I've ruined our friendship by prying."

For the past half hour, Vivian's tears had flowed despite Clay's best efforts to reassure her. Although sympathy for his stepsister's heartache made his chest feel tight, he recognized part of his discomfort was unease. How did a man cope with a woman's tears?

Clay reached across the table and gave her hand several gentle pats. "She's probably tired, Viv. Think of how hard it must have been during the days of fishing, all on her own. When people are tired, they react differently. Just wait—you'll go see her tomorrow, and she'll be more like the Lizzie you know."

"Do you think so?" Vivian sniffled, her chin quivering. "I didn't realize until she closed the door in my face how much I've come to depend on her friendship. I . . . I get lonely here."

Clay could understand Vivian's hurt feelings, but how could she be lonely in the village? They were constantly surrounded by others. He couldn't even wash his face and shave in the morning without gathering a small crowd. The natives watched him lather his cheeks and chin, clicking their tongues on their teeth or chortling. They observed his work on the school and followed him into the trees or to the river when he went to gather firewood or water. He always had company.

Vivian released a heavy sigh, her face shiny from dried tears. "I almost regret teaching her to be white because she'll feel confident to leave now."

Clay didn't want Lizzie to leave, either. "I wish we knew for sure why she was going." He slipped from the barrel chair and walked to the window. He peered out at the quietly busy village. Family groups gathered in small circles in the cleared areas in front of their cabins. Men smoked their pipes and women busied themselves with handwork while youngsters giggled and darted around in childish games. Without turning from the village scene, he mused, "Do you suppose she'd stay if her grandparents would welcome her? Living all alone—relying completely on herself—must be difficult for her."

"You'd never guess it by watching her." Vivian joined Clay at the window. She rested her elbow on the unfinished sill and propped her chin in her hand. "I've never met a more self-sufficient person than Lizzie. She doesn't seem to have need of anyone."

Clay raised one eyebrow. "Needs and wants are two different things, Viv. She might possess the skills necessary to survive alone, but I suspect she wants others around. Otherwise, she wouldn't have welcomed you." The now-familiar prick of envy accompanied his words. Considering how little time he'd spent with the woman, she had weaseled her way into the center of his thoughts. A part of him wanted her near—he couldn't deny it.

"I don't know that she'll welcome me again, after I angered her so . . ."

Clay, confused by his own thoughts and uncertain how to respond to Vivian's melancholy reflection, chose not to respond. She'd spoken so softly she might have been speaking to herself anyway. He pushed away from the window. "It's late—we should get some sleep." Slipping his arm around Vivian's shoulders, he aimed her for their huts. "Da'ago offered me the use of his canoe and said I could take his largest travois to tote our supplies from the river to the village. I told him I'd like to go to Fort Yukon tomorrow. While I'm there, I'll check on our supplies."

He couldn't afford a day away from the mission—he still had two full walls to chink—but he feared their precious food stores might be rotting on a dock somewhere, waiting for someone to find the time to deliver them. He also needed to purchase glass for the mission's windows and hinges for the door, which required a trip to Fort Yukon.

Vivian looked up at him, hopefulness sprouting on her face. "Could you purchase some fabric for me while you're there? I prefer something lightweight, such as batiste. But I'll take muslin if that's all they have—six yards, please."

Clay paused outside Vivian's hut door, mentally counting the amount remaining in his money pouch. "Is the fabric a want or a need, Viv? We only have funds for needs."

Her face flushed with pink. "I assure you, it's a need."

"All right, then. I'll see what I can find."

"Thank you, Clay."

"You're welcome." He turned for his hut.

"Clay?"

He paused.

"Tomorrow . . . on your way to Fort Yukon . . . might you find the time to stop by Lizzie's and tell her I still want to be her friend?"

Clay hesitated, torn by the pain in Vivian's voice and expression.

"I neglected to ask her about hunting for meat for us. You could discuss a trade . . ."

The mission needed a good supply of meat for the winter. And Vivian needed an element of assurance. Besides, the idea of seeing Lizzie was appealing. "All right, Viv. I'll stop by her cabin tomorrow."

Vivian's face broke into a relieved smile. "Thank you."

"Sleep well now," he said.

"You too."

Clay closed himself inside his hut, kicked off his boots, and flopped onto his bed. Propping his hands beneath his head, he stared into the shadows, inwardly planning tomorrow's activities. One day to visit Lizzie, reach Fort Yukon, purchase glass and fabric and possibly a few food stores if those promised by the Mission Committee were unavailable, and return. At least he knew he'd have enough sunlight to find his way, regardless of how late he returned.

Should he visit Lizzie on his way out or his way back? Lizzie probably rose early, like most of the natives, since she would have chores waiting. The hour might be too late if he waited until the return trip. He nodded, his decision made—he'd see her on his way to Fort Yukon. His heart gave a little leap of delighted excitement, but he told himself he was only eager to restore harmony between the women for Vivian's sake.

He closed his eyes and ignored the little voice inside his head that scoffed, *You aren't fooling anyone, least of all yourself.*

Chapter Thirteen

I n the morning, birdsong accompanied Clay on his walk
to the river. The sun sent fingers of light between tree
branches, gilding the foot-carved pathway. He pulled
an empty travois, which he intended to leave at the river's
edge for his use when he returned. The sturdy willow sup-
ports stirred decaying leaves and raised the fresh scent of soil.
Despite the worries of having too much to do in too short a
time, he couldn't deny a sense of pleasure from the scents,
sounds, and sights of nature on this crisp morning.

Vivian's many trips through the woods to Lizzie's cabin
had created a clear path that Clay had no difficulty following. When he heard the dogs bark, he knew the cabin
waited nearby, so he called out a greeting. "Lizzie! It's Clay
Selby." He announced himself twice before stepping into
the clearing beside her cabin. She stood in the center of the
yard with her rifle at her side.

He lifted his hand in a wave and paused at the edge of
the yard. "May I . . . draw near?" He glanced at the dogs,
who continued to bark and paw the fence.

Lizzie sliced her hand through the air and whistled. With
a series of whimpers, the dogs calmed.

Clay took her actions as an invitation to enter the yard. He strode within a few feet of her and offered a quick wave. "Good morning, Lizzie."

"Good morning."

She wore Vivian's blue-checked dress, and the sun glistened on her dark hair, which she had fashioned into a misshapen lump on the back of her head. He discovered he missed her braids—the simple style suited her so well. Yet he drew in a breath of relief at the sight. Despite the lack of warmth in her tone and the absence of a welcoming smile, she hadn't cast aside Vivian's teachings. Vivian would be comforted when he told her.

"I'm on my way to Fort Yukon, but Vivian asked me to stop by and see you." The native woman's sober expression gave Clay an uneasy feeling in the pit of his stomach. He wished she wouldn't stare at him so intensely, as if she could examine his thoughts. If she read the deepest ones, he'd scare her to death.

"Is Vivian coming today?"

Since he'd left his stepsister thoroughly scrubbing the interior of the mission school in preparation for fitting the windows, he doubted Vivian would leave the village today. He shook his head. "Not today."

Lizzie's face gave away nothing of her thoughts, but he believed he glimpsed a brief flash of regret in her blue eyes. He added, "But she can come tomorrow, if . . . if you'd like a visit."

"She may visit." Lizzie's chin raised. "But I must ask that she—and you—respect my wishes and do not speak to my grandparents about me."

The stubborn jut of Lizzie's jaw reminded Clay of Co'Ozhii. He didn't figure either woman would appreciate the comparison. "Neither of us want to cause you distress, Lizzie.

We're concerned about you, living here alone and fending for yourself. It must be lonely, and even dangerous. We wish the comfort and protection of the village for you." His voice rose with fervor as he spoke, his desire to provide this woman with comfort and protection overriding all else.

Lizzie lifted the rifle. "I have protection." She pointed to the pen, where the dogs sat looking in her direction, their faces attentive. "And my dogs provide comfort. I don't need the village." She spoke with conviction, but her voice quavered slightly, making Clay wonder if she intended to convince him or herself of her statement's truth. "I want to learn from Vivian. I'm willing to teach her. But I am the leader of my . . . family . . . and as leader I insist you honor my request. Do not speak of me to my grandparents."

Could he honestly vow to honor Lizzie's request? And if he refused, would she then refuse their company? The remembrance of Vivian's deep hurt and worry from the night before pierced him.

He drew in a slow breath and released it, offering a reluctant nod. "Very well. I will not mention your name to your grandparents again." But he would still present the idea of forgiveness and reconciliation, and pray the rifts between family members would be mended.

"Good."

"May I ask you a favor?"

She tipped her head, her brow pinching.

"Vivian and I have need of meat for the winter. Would you kill an elk or moose for us? I'm willing to make a trade—dry goods, clothing . . . whatever you might need in exchange for the meat."

The slightest hint of a smile twitched at the woman's lips. "You're asking me to hunt for you?"

Heat built in Clay's face. No able-bodied native man would

ask a woman to provide for him. Her amusement bruised his pride, but he had to be honest. "My days are full, building the mission. I don't have time to hunt." Then he considered all of Lizzie's responsibilities, living on her own. It was selfish to ask one more thing of her. He opened his mouth to tell her not to bother, but she spoke first.

"I'll try to make a large kill for you. I wouldn't want my friend Vivian to starve during her very first winter in Alaska."

Had she teased him? She looked so sober, he couldn't be sure, yet he detected a hint of humor in her statement. "Thank you. Please let me know what you'd like in trade."

"I'll keep the hide," she said. "I can sell it in White Horse. That will be trade enough."

That didn't sound like a fair exchange to Clay. "Are you sure? I'd be glad to—"

"Vivian is my friend. I choose to help her." Pink bloomed on her dusky cheeks. "And you." She pointed toward the woods with her rifle barrel, inching around him. "I must check my traps. Tell Vivian to come tomorrow. When winter arrives, she'll need warm mittens and a hat. You will, too. If the Great One, Denali, has blessed my traps with rabbits, I'll show her how to prepare a hide for tanning and help her sew mittens that will keep your hands from freezing."

"That's kind of you." He lowered his voice, injecting fervor in his tone. "And I will pray that God has blessed your traps so you're able to make what you need."

Lizzie's brow furrowed. "Then you will utter a worthless prayer. Your God has no use for me."

Her blunt statement startled Clay. "Why would you say that?"

"I'm not white."

Clay shook his head adamantly. "My God—the Father of us all—loves you very much, Lizzie."

The woman snorted.

Clay ignored the derisive sound. "Didn't you ask Vivian to teach you?"

"Yes."

"You're wearing a white woman's dress. You style your hair in a white woman's fashion. Does that mean you accept the things she's taught you?"

Lizzie's sky-colored eyes glinted with apprehension, but she nodded.

"Vivian and I both came to teach. So why do you doubt what I tell you? God loves you." Clay's heart caught, remembering the day he'd accepted God's love for himself. Only a child—six years old—but carried to truth by his father's earnest teaching. In his mind's eye, he viewed his father's fervent face proclaiming the truth of God's great love to the Kiowa people. Holding his hand to Lizzie, he said, "In the Bible it says God loved the world so much, He sent His only Son to die for the sins of the world so we could all be clean and unblemished before Him. *The world*, Lizzie. Everyone ever born. That means you, too."

Lizzie twisted her lips, as if tasting his statement and trying to decide whether she found the flavor pleasing. Then she stuck out her arm, showing him the back of her hand. "Your words are fine and good for white people. You can be clean. But see my skin? Brown . . . Always brown. I'll never be clean enough for your God. I can only hope I am clean enough for my father and his family."

Clay opened his mouth to protest, but she swung away from him.

"I must check my traps. Good-bye, Clay."

Clay watched her stalk away, his heart heavy. He considered following her, prevailing upon her to listen to him, but too many other responsibilities awaited him. He headed for the river, resolve lengthening his stride. Up until now, he'd denied Vivian's requests that he visit Lizzie, but no more. Lizzie needed lessons beyond what Vivian had presented. It would mean time away from the mission, but he would make known the truth of God's love to this native woman who, somehow, inexplicably, had wormed her way into the center of his heart.

––––––

Clay's trip to Fort Yukon proved more frustrating than fulfilling. His elation that the Mission Committee had sent supplies was dashed when he discovered the crates and bags had been left, unattended, in the back of a well-frequented livery stable. Consequently, nearly all of them had been opened and scavenged. He located the livery owner asleep in the loft. The man wasn't happy to have his nap disturbed, but Clay ignored his disgruntled mutters and lodged a complaint about his lost goods.

The man shrugged. "Things come in, things go out." He coughed, not even bothering to cover his mouth. "I store 'em an' don't get so much as a penny for my trouble. Can't be expected to keep guard, too." He rubbed his temples and squinted at Clay with watery eyes. "You got issues, mister, take it up with the law." The man doubled over in another coughing fit, and Clay quickly departed.

Clay suspected Fort Yukon's lawman wouldn't care much about the loss of items intended for a native village, so he didn't bother following the liveryman's advice. He loaded the remaining supplies in the canoe and then paid a scruffy-looking boy fifty cents to keep watch and holler like his pants had caught fire if anyone approached his belongings. Then he went shopping.

His lungs nearly exploded with his gasp at the asking price for twelve-inch square panes of glass. The merchant expressed no more sympathy than the livery owner had. "Any idea what I pay for freight for fragile items like glass? Mister, these here'd be a bargain at ten dollars apiece, an' that's a fact."

Clay had hoped to put glass in all five window openings, but after seeing the prices he decided they'd make do with oiled paper. At least for their first year. Maybe the Mission Committee could find the funds for windows later. He purchased iron hinges and a door latch, cringing at the amount of money he had to hand over even for such basic items that couldn't possibly be considered fragile.

The ramshackle mercantile next to the hardware store offered a surprisingly wide selection of fabrics, including a snow-white batiste Clay knew would please Vivian. But bleached muslin was less than half the price, so he asked for it instead. After the owner cut the fabric, he said, "Hey, ain't you one o' them missionaries what took up residence at a siwash village north o' here?"

Clay gritted his teeth to hold back words of admonition and nodded.

"Some mail come for you." The man lifted a crate from under the counter and pawed through it. "Had a whole passel o' mail this month—pret' near a dozen letters! Two of 'em's for you an' your woman." He withdrew the crumpled envelopes and thrust them across the counter at Clay with a big grin. "There ya go, mister. *Two* of 'em."

"Thank you." Clay glanced at the envelopes—a letter for Vivian from her mother, and one for him from Pa. His fingers itched to tear into his immediately, but he needed to get back. The reading would have to wait. He slipped them into his shirt pocket, tucked his paper-wrapped parcels under his arm, and returned to the borrowed canoe.

His jaw dropped and feet stumbled when he spotted three

ragtag urchins sitting on the crates, munching raw potatoes. Where was the boy he'd paid? Righteous indignation filled Clay's chest and exploded from his mouth as he broke into a run. "You there! What do you think you're doing? Get away from my things!" He'd never spoken so harshly to children, but he'd never had his patience tried to such extremes.

The boys hopped from the canoe, the smallest one losing his hat in his scramble to escape. He spun to retrieve it, but Clay glared at him, and he took off after the others, bareheaded.

Disgusted, Clay gave the tattered hat a toss after the fleeing child and then wedged his packages between crates.

Taking up the paddle, he rowed with all his might, expending some of the frustrations of the day. By the time he rounded the bend that hid the town from sight, his aching shoulders begged for respite. Drawing a deep breath, he slowed the pace of his paddling and allowed his racing pulse to calm. He passed a small group of rafting otters. Their bright eyes followed him. On another day Clay would have chuckled at the animals' lazy curiosity, but today he couldn't manage so much as a tired smile.

"Everything that could go wrong went wrong," he said, snorting with disgust. "Supplies stolen. Items priced beyond any reasonable means." He gave the paddle a vicious swipe, his ire mounting again. He left the otters behind, but he continued to speak to the passing landscape. "Fifty cents squandered on a boy who proved untrustworthy. An entire day spent away from the mission school. And—" He clamped his mouth shut, unwilling to voice the most distressing of all—his failure to convince Lizzie that God loved her.

Clay pushed the paddle through the water, propelling the canoe along, while his thoughts drifted backward in time. For Clay's first eight years of life, his pa hadn't stood behind a pulpit in a church building—they'd traveled all over the Dakotas on horseback. Town to town, homestead to homestead, Pa preached wherever God called. Sometimes he opened his Bible in the middle of a busy street, sometimes in schoolhouses or barns. He preached to crowds so large he had to holler to be heard, and he shared just as exuberantly one-on-one in the dirt yard of a sod house while the housewife snapped peas and chickens pecked in the dirt around his feet. Wherever Pa went, he reached folks.

Passionate. Sincere. Zealous. Clay applied all of those words and more to Judson Selby. The man drew people like a magnet drew steel, and not once in all of his years of observing his father had Clay seen anyone turn his back on Pa's teachings. Maybe Pa's size—six foot four in his stocking feet—discouraged folks from ignoring him. But Clay suspected it was more than Pa's intimidating size that kept ears attentively tuned—it was his presentation. When Pa spoke, folks listened and accepted, and that was that.

Clay's chest tightened, a familiar worry rising to choke him. He didn't have his pa's size—he wasn't a small man, but he lacked his father's unusual height and muscular build. He didn't have his pa's booming voice, either. He believed he had his father's zeal and desire to point lost souls to their Savior, but he lacked the element of magnetism his father possessed. An ache built in the center of his chest. What good was it to have a desire to preach if folks wouldn't listen?

He gave the paddle a firm sweep that sent the canoe onto the bank. He tugged it well away from the water's edge so the current couldn't carry it away. The travois waited, right where he'd put it that morning, along with a coil of rope to secure the supplies to its willow-and-deer-hide frame. He'd need to make more than one trip to get everything to the village, so he loaded the things he thought they needed most—the half-emptied gunnysacks of potatoes, onions, and carrots, the oiled paper and metal door workings, and Vivian's muslin—on the travois and left the other items in the canoe.

As he tucked a square tarp over the crates in the canoe's belly, he prayed it wouldn't be bothered by curious animals or thieving humans. "I can't afford anything else getting lost." *Lost* . . . The word taunted him. Raising his eyes to the cloud-dusted sky, he held his arms out in a gesture of supplication. "I came here so the native people would find their way to You—so they won't be lost eternally. I came to do *right*, God. So why are so many things going wrong?"

Chapter Fourteen

Vivian paced outside the mission school, watching for Clay's return. Even during the hours she'd stayed busy—hoeing and watering the garden, picking the first plump pea pods, and sweeping the mission school's floor with a handmade willow broom until it practically gleamed—she'd caught herself looking toward the break in the brush where he'd disappeared that morning, pulling an empty travois behind him.

She leaned against the corner of the building and gnawed on a hangnail. Although no stars showed in the sky, nighttime had arrived—the little pendant watch Aunt Vesta and Uncle Matthew had given her their last Christmas with her proved it. And still no Clay. What if something had happened to him? The fretful thought wouldn't leave her head.

She tried so hard to resist living with a cloud of fear haunting her, but no amount of effort successfully held the worries at bay. So many unpleasant things could befall a person. He could have been attacked by a bear or a moose. Perhaps his canoe overturned and the river carried him away. In town, might he have met with some unsavory fellows who accosted him to steal his supplies? Vivian's imagination conjured one tragedy after another until her heart pounded so hard it hurt to draw a breath.

Simply waiting was too difficult—she needed to stay busy. She'd already completed the chores Clay had left for her, as well as a few of her own choosing. A fresh pan of corn bread waited for Clay in his hut, she'd stacked a good supply of wood inside the school for the stove, and she'd even ventured into the deeper brush to set her snare. What else could she do? She clapped her palms together. Washing! Clay wore the same trousers and shirt every day for work, but he'd donned clean clothes before leaving for town. She could retrieve his dirty clothing and wash it.

She carried bucket after bucket from the river until she'd filled the rusty tin washtub that sat outside her hut. As she'd come to expect, a small number of native women gathered to watch her. Each time she or Clay used the wash bucket to clean their hands and faces or Vivian prepared to launder their clothing, the natives stood nearby, jabbering and chortling to themselves. Vivian had grown accustomed to having an audience, even if the lack of privacy occasionally frustrated her.

Tonight, however, she appreciated their presence. They unwittingly offered a welcome distraction.

Vivian shaved a bit of lye soap from a bar into the water and stirred it with her hands, managing to create a few dismal suds. She plunged Clay's shirt into the water again and again, glancing up to acknowledge her grinning audience every few seconds. When she felt she'd removed the majority of the grime, she shook it out, spraying the watching crowd with water droplets, then draped the shirt over a bush to dry.

She reached for Clay's trousers, but a little girl with round, rosy cheeks and two missing front teeth thrust a little calico dress at her. "Missus Viv-*ee*-an, *ngideloy ton-gilax*?"

Vivian mimed placing the dress in the washtub and repeated the child's request in English. "Wash your clothes?"

"Wass," the child said, and the women broke out in a fresh round of guttural murmurs.

Crooking her finger, Vivian gestured for the child to step between her and the washtub. Hunching her shoulders and giggling wildly, she complied. Vivian gave her the dress and then, holding the child's hands, she pushed the dress and the little girl's arms into the water. The child squealed, and Vivian laughed. Together, they gave the dress a thorough scrubbing while the watching women *ooh*ed and made clucking sounds with their teeth. The little girl hung the soggy dress next to Clay's shirt to dry. Then she dashed away, her bare feet slapping the hardened ground and her delighted giggle filling the air.

With the child's departure, the others apparently decided it was time to turn in. They ambled toward their cabins, leaving Vivian to finish the final pieces of laundry. Alone again, her thoughts once more turned troublesome. How she wished she had someone to talk to—someone who would understand rather than judge her fearful thoughts. Mother, Aunt Vesta, even Clay's father repeatedly lectured her that being afraid meant she didn't trust God to take care of her and those she loved. But how could she completely trust God when He'd let her down before?

Vivian dipped a bucketful of the murky wash water and carried it to the garden so it wouldn't be wasted. Midstride, she paused and stared at the open spot in the brush, willing Clay to emerge from the thick growth. The hour neared ten o'clock—what could be keeping him?

The rustle in the brush alerted Lizzie to an animal's presence. A large animal, based on the amount of noise. She slowly separated the boughs of a thick rose-hip bush with the tip of her Winchester rifle and stared down the barrel, waiting for the creature to cross her path.

Late at night or early in the morning—either were ideal times for hunting. It didn't seem to matter to the creatures that light still shone rather than giving them the cover of dark. The thick trees offered the security of shadows. They were hungry, and so they ventured out to forage, giving Lizzie an opportunity to fill her cache with meat. Or to fill Clay's—*Vivian's*, she corrected herself—cache with meat.

The thrashing grew louder. The animal was near. Lizzie hunkered low, her back stiff, one eye squinted shut, her senses alert. She cocked the hammer slowly, cringing at the muffled click. But when the animal—a bear?—showed itself, she'd be ready. Lizzie held her breath, her finger poised on the trigger. A lumbering shape, cloaked in gray shadows, emerged from the brush. She squeezed the trigger.

A scream rent the air. The animal—but not an animal, Lizzie now realized—flailed, bringing up his head where a weak band of sunlight briefly illuminated his features. Lizzie bolted out of the bushes and raced for him, watching in revulsion as he crumpled and landed facedown in the fern-strewn forest floor.

Panting, heart racing, she rolled him onto his back. She gasped and sank back on her haunches. A scream of horror built in her throat, and she covered her mouth with both hands to hold it inside. *Clay!* She'd killed Clay Selby.

∞

"Vivian? Vivian, wake up!"
The frantic whisper cut through Vivian's sleep-fogged

brain. Tiredness had finally won out, and in spite of her worries concerning Clay's continued absence, she'd crawled into her bed and fallen into a restless sleep. Now she sat up and groggily rubbed her eyes. Had she only imagined the voice?

"Vivian!"

She staggered to her feet, finally recognizing the caller. Pulling aside the blanket that covered her doorway, she looked at Lizzie. "What are you doing here?" She flung a frantic look across the quiet village.

"Come." Lizzie grabbed Vivian's arm and dragged her behind the hut.

Vivian stumbled on an exposed root, but Lizzie's firm hold kept her upright. "Lizzie, what—?"

Instead of replying, Lizzie pointed to a travois that lay in a gray triangle of shade. A still, bulky shape lay strapped to the conveyance. Vivian squinted through the dim light— what on earth? Then her knees buckled. She let out a cry of alarm. "Clay!"

She dropped to her knees and placed her hand on Clay's hair. Something felt sticky. Blood. Her stomach whirled. She looked into Lizzie's grim face. "What happened to him?"

"I shot him."

Vivian's jaw fell open. She tried to speak—to ask why Lizzie would shoot Clay—but words wouldn't form.

"I was hunting for meat, as he asked me to do."

Buzzing filled the inside of Vivian's head. Did Lizzie mean to blame Clay? She forced herself to listen to Lizzie's words.

"He sounded like a bear, dragging supplies through the brush. So I shot him." Lizzie held her shoulders stiff. Her low voice held no emotion.

Vivian jerked her attention to Clay. Although he hadn't moved, his flesh felt warm to the touch. His chest rose and fell in slow but steady breaths. He wasn't dead. A flicker of hope ignited in her breast. "Help me get him into his hut."

They each grabbed one support on the travois and dragged it across the brief expanse to Clay's hut. Vivian panted with exertion. How had Lizzie managed to tote Clay all the way to the village by herself? They weren't able to maneuver the travois through the doorway, so they lifted Clay by his arms and legs and carried him to his bed.

He lay on the blanket with his arms outstretched and his head lolling to the side like a discarded ragdoll, completely unaware. Vivian knelt beside him. "I need a lantern. There's one in the corner there. Would you light it, please? You'll find a tin of matches on that little shelf." She didn't shift her gaze from Clay.

Squeaks, a soft *skritch*, and then a flare of light let Vivian know Lizzie followed her directions. A soft yellow glow lit the cabin. Lizzie set the lantern on the floor next to Clay's head and crouched beside Vivian.

"I thought I'd killed him." Lizzie's voice still held no emotion, yet Vivian sensed a deep agony beneath the woman's surface. "But he breathes. . . ." She pointed at his softly rising chest.

"Yes, I see." Vivian didn't add she hoped he would continue to breathe. The comment would only add to Lizzie's guilt, and what good would it do? She pulled the lantern closer, examining Clay's head. An ugly wound, four inches long and almost a half inch wide, glared up at her, but to her relief it appeared the bullet had skimmed alongside his skull rather than penetrating the bone.

She had never treated a bullet wound, but she'd tended Clay's scratches when he fell through the mission roof. Those scratches were healing well. Surely this wound would, too, with the same ministrations. She swung her gaze to meet

Lizzie's stoic expression. "Will you fetch some water and heat it on the stove in the mission school? I want to clean his wound, but the water should be boiled first."

Lizzie's face pinched with uncertainty. "I need to leave, Vivian. It will not serve you well if others awake and find me here."

Vivian grabbed Lizzie's hands. "Please, Lizzie. He's unconscious, but if he wakens he might try to get up. He could start the wound bleeding again. He's already lost much blood—I can see it in his hair and along his face." The sight repulsed her, and she had to swallow before continuing. "He shouldn't be left alone."

Lizzie chewed her lip for a moment. Then she pulled Vivian to her feet. "You get the water and heat the stove. I'll stay here with him. If the others see you out moving around, they won't be alarmed. But . . ."

Although Vivian preferred to remain at Clay's side, she understood Lizzie's apprehension. Arguing would only prolong seeing to Clay's wound. "All right. Stay very close." Her voice caught. "And call me if . . ." Lifting her skirt, she raced out of the hut.

Vivian ran to the river, grateful for the murky sunlight. She scooped up a pan of water and spun toward the village, sloshing water over the rim. Hissing through her teeth, she slowed her pace—she didn't want to make a second trip.

In the mission building, she added wood to the coals in the stove and placed the pan on top, then dashed to the hut to check on Clay. As she'd directed, Lizzie sat near, her hand on Clay's shoulder.

"Any change?"

Lizzie shook her head, her braids swinging with the movement. She turned her tortured face to Vivian. "I am so sorry, Vivian." Her voice broke.

In her weeks of visiting the native woman, Vivian had never seen her express such sorrow. She couldn't allow Lizzie to carry a burden of guilt—she understood far too well that agonizing weight. Vivian curled her hand over Lizzie's shoulder. "It wasn't deliberate. I don't blame you. Don't blame yourself."

Lizzie nodded, shifting her head to look back down at Clay. "Is the water heated?"

Vivian hustled to the school to check the pan. The water wasn't boiling yet, but steam rose in a wispy cloud. It would do. Using her skirt to protect her hands, she carried the pan to Clay's hut and then shifted Lizzie out of the way. She retrieved Clay's shirt—the cleanest piece of fabric she could locate quickly—from the bush outside and dipped it in the water. The heat stung her fingers, but she ignored her pain and gently brushed the wadded cloth across the wound. Clay groaned, rolling his head away from her touch.

"Hold him still," Vivian said. Lizzie pinned Clay by the shoulders. He fought against her restraining hands, but the native woman held firmly. Vivian was able to continue cleansing the area until she'd removed all of the dried blood and bits of dirt and leaves that clung in his tousled hair. "I need to get bandages from my hut. Stay here—I'll be right back."

Once again she dashed through the night and retrieved the box of rudimentary medical supplies her mother had sent with them. She returned to Clay's hut and knelt beside his bed. She dipped salve with her finger and smeared it on the raw, ugly gash. After Clay's fall, she'd used one roll of bandages and a good portion of the salve doctoring his many scratches. The little glass jar contained less than half its original contents. "I hope I'll have enough salve and bandages to care for his injury."

Lizzie unraveled the roll of white cotton bandage. "I'll make a paste for you to use. Slippery elm bark and calendula flowers have healing powers."

Vivian tried to memorize the names of the plants. No doubt the knowledge would prove useful in other times. She took the length of bandage from Lizzie and wrapped it gently around Clay's head. He didn't stir, which simplified her task but also frightened her. Was it good for him to be so still, or did it indicate the bullet had done damage inside his head as well?

Tears stung behind her nose, and she sniffed hard. "What Clay will think we need most is someone to chink the mission walls. He doesn't care about himself—only the mission. He's worked so hard to finish the building so we can begin teaching. But now—"

"What is this woman doing in Gwichyaa Saa?"

The thundering question stated in Athabascan startled Vivian so badly, she jerked. Her knuckles banged into Clay's temple, and she immediately cupped his cheeks and examined the bandage covering the wound. Would it start bleeding again?

Lizzie leapt to her feet and backed into the corner, staring stoically at the man who filled the doorway with his ominous presence.

Convinced she hadn't hurt Clay, Vivian rose. She used her stumbling Athabascan mixed with Kiowa—a combination Shruh would understand better than English—to address the tribal leader. "She helps me." She flipped her hand toward Clay, who hunched white and silent. "Clay was hurt. She brought him to me so I could tend his wound."

Shruh stepped into the hut. The narrow space seemed to shrink with his commanding presence. He leaned forward and examined Clay with a fierce frown. "He hit his head?"

Vivian wouldn't lie, but neither could she tell the truth. She didn't reply.

Lizzie raised her chin. "I did it."

Shruh swung to face Lizzie. The room fairly sizzled with the animosity emanating between grandfather and granddaughter. He barked, "How?"

"I shot him."

Vivian waited for Lizzie to offer an excuse, an apology, or even an explanation. But none came. As much as she admired Lizzie's courage in the face of Shruh's derision, she couldn't allow Shruh to believe Lizzie had hurt Clay on purpose. She started to speak, but Lizzie stepped past Shruh and touched Vivian's arm.

"If you need me, you know where to find me." Lizzie spoke in English, sending a furtive glance in Shruh's direction. "Anything you need . . ." Then she slipped out of the hut.

Chapter Fifteen

Lizzie ran through the woods, fleet-footed as a deer. Images of Clay—collapsed in the ferns, white and still on the travois, face contorted in pain while Vivian cleansed his wound—flashed in her mind, torturing her with the realization of what she'd done.

She'd shot a man. And not just any man—Clay. The missionary who'd come to serve her mother's tribe. The brother of the woman who'd befriended her. The man who crept through her dreams and made her wish she was white. Guilt entangled her, as tenacious as the wild grape vines that took command of the rose-hip bushes in the woods. A sob escaped her throat, and her race came to a stumbling halt.

She staggered to the nearest aspen and sagged against the pale bark. She closed her eyes, wishing she were asleep in her bed—that the recent events had been only a dream. But wishing changed nothing—this nightmare was real. Sinking downward, Lizzie sat on the mossy ground beneath the tree and buried her face in her hands. Why would her grandparents desire peace with her after what she'd done? How would she face Vivian again?

A groan left her throat, and she pounded the ground

with her fists. It was useless now to finish the coat. Useless to expect Vivian to teach her any longer. Useless to stay even another day in this place. Lifting her face toward her mother's source of comfort, she whispered, "I must say good-bye . . . sooner than I'd planned. As soon as I know if Clay Selby will live, I'll go to find my father." Pain stabbed as she realized what leaving early meant. She hugged herself. "My mother will never be at peace now. I've failed her. I've failed her . . ."

Collapsing over her lap, Lizzie allowed her grief to spill forth in a song of mourning that split her heart in two.

◦∕◦

Shruh paced back and forth in the small hut, his anger palpable, although he didn't speak a word. Vivian gritted her teeth and sat close to Clay's inert form, allowing the tribal leader as much space as possible. His foot brushed her skirts on each pass, but she didn't reach out and pull them out of his way. She feared even breathing too loudly, uncertain of how he would respond.

After long minutes of silent, seething fury, he suddenly stopped and clamped his arms across his broad chest. "Vivian Selby, stand."

Vivian understood the curt command spoken in the man's native language, but she wished she could pretend ignorance and dive under a blanket to hide. Her limbs quivering, she pushed herself upright and faced him.

"You know Lu'qul Gitth'ighi well?"

Swallowing, Vivian offered a hesitant nod. She struggled to find the right words to communicate clearly. "I have visited her cabin. She teaches me to cook and use a snare." Tears burned the back of Vivian's nose. "She is my friend."

Shruh's eyes narrowed. "You have defied the village edict

of excommunication." His heavy brows beetled into a thick line of condemnation. "I am willing to grant you allowance because you are not of our tribe and therefore unfamiliar with our ways."

Vivian's head ached with the effort of translating his words into English. When understanding dawned, her heart beat with hope. Might he be willing to grant permission for her to continue her relationship with Lizzie? *Please, please . . .*

"Considering your ignorance, I will not demand immediate removal. I will offer you another chance to be allowed to remain in Gwichyaa Saa." He jabbed his finger at her. "To stay, you must vow to me that from this moment on, you will have no contact with Lu'qul Gitth'ihgi."

Vivian's hope plummeted. "But—"

Shruh held up his hand, stilling her words. "Make your vow."

Vivian wove her fingers together, pressing her joined hands tight against her ribs. Her entire body trembled in nervousness. "I . . . I cannot."

The man's dark face contorted, his eyes nearly disappearing into slits. "Then you choose to suffer the same fate as your friend. By this time tomorrow, you must be gone from Gwichyaa Saa."

Vivian gasped. She held her hands toward Clay. "But my brother! He is hurt. He needs care. I cannot move him. It might kill him!"

Shruh glanced at Clay's still form, his face impassive. He met Vivian's gaze again and spoke in the same emotionless tone Vivian had often heard Lizzie use. "Then vow to end all contact with Lu'qul Gitth'ihgi. You will be forgiven and allowed continued sanctuary in Gwichyaa Saa."

A war took place in Vivian's heart, the battle so intense she feared her chest might turn inside out. How could she reject Lizzie . . . and how could she not, given Clay's dire situation? Tears flooded her eyes. She opened her mouth, but no words spilled forth. From his blanket bed, Clay released a low moan. Vivian dropped to her knees beside him and placed her hand on his tangled hair. She sent a pleading look to Shruh. "M-may I have until tomorrow to give you my decision?"

Shruh looked again at Clay, and for a moment his stern expression softened. But his voice was harsh when he replied, "Tomorrow. You make your choice." He tossed the door covering aside and stormed out. Before the blanket had settled back over the opening, Vivian received a glimpse of the night. Dark had finally fallen.

A deep moan awakened Vivian. She scowled, uncoiling reluctantly, and her elbow bumped something soft and warm. The moan came again, brief but louder. She blinked into the dim light, trying to make sense of her location. Why was she curled on the floor of Clay's hut? Then memories of the previous night returned in a torrent, and she jerked to her knees.

"Clay? Clay, are you awake?" She ran her fingers along his prickly jaw, searching his face for signs that he understood her question. His eyelids fluttered, and she sucked in a sharp breath, holding it until his lids slid upward to reveal his bleary, red-rimmed eyes. Happy tears distorted her vision. "You're awake! Oh, Clay, talk to me."

He licked his dry lips, blinking so slowly it seemed as though his eyelashes carried weights. "My head hurts."

Vivian laughed, a joyous explosion that brought a fresh rush of tears.

Clay grimaced, shaking his head slightly. "Not funny."

She cupped his cheeks, smiling through her tears. "I'm

not laughing because I think it's funny—I'm happy you can speak to me and it makes sense." She sniffed and swiped at the tears that ran in warm rivulets down her cheeks. "I was so afraid you might—" But sharing her fear wasn't necessary. Stroking his cheek again, she said, "Are you hungry? Would you like some corn bread?" She started to rise and retrieve the pan she'd baked yesterday evening while waiting for his return.

His hand snaked out and caught her wrist. The grip was weak, but she sank back down. "No food. Not hungry." He swallowed, making a horrible face. He released her wrist and groped the bandage that surrounded his head. "What happened to me?"

Vivian pulled his hand away from the bandages and held it between her palms. "Don't you remember?" She hoped he would recall the events himself. She didn't want to be the one to tell him Lizzie had shot him.

His brow furrowed, his lips pinching into a tight line of pain. "I was in the woods, bringing our supplies . . . what was left of our supplies . . . and I . . . I can't remember anything after that."

Vivian took a deep breath and made her explanation brief. "There was an accident and you were shot. You have a nasty gash, and you'll have a headache for quite a while, I'm afraid, but you're alive. That's all that matters."

Confusion marred his brow. "How did I get here?"

Vivian tried to smile, but her lips refused to cooperate. "Lizzie put you on a travois and brought you to the village."

For long seconds Clay lay, looking into Vivian's face without speaking. She read nothing in his blank expression, but she sensed he was silently putting together the pieces and drawing an accurate conclusion. Suddenly he planted his elbows on the blanket and struggled to lift himself.

Vivian released a surprised squawk and pressed him back down. "Lie still! You were unconscious for hours. You need to rest."

He struggled weakly against her restraining hands. "Our supplies—I left the bags of food in the woods. Some of it was already stolen. We can't lose the rest of it."

"I'll send one of the villagers to search for the food." They liked Clay—they'd be willing to help him. Unless Shruh, in his anger with her, had ordered the tribe to stay away from both of the missionaries. Clay stopped fighting and relaxed against the blanket. She gave his shoulder a gentle pat. "I want to change your bandage, and then you should try to eat a little something."

He made a face. "Stomach's upset. I don't want food."

"Then some tea?" Clay had developed a fondness for tea steeped from rose hips. Vivian braced to run into the nearby woods and pluck a few plump pods.

"Later."

Although she wanted to argue, she decided rest might be his best medicine right now. "All right. Lie still while I heat some water. Then I'll return and—"

"Vivian Selby?" Shruh's deep voice interrupted from outside the hut.

Vivian scrambled to her feet and pulled the blanket aside. The man's appearance was as foreboding as it had been in last night's deep shadows. His wife, Co'Ozhii, stood beside him, her lined face impassive. Several of the village men clustered near, their expressions severe and their arms folded over their chests. Vivian gulped. "Y-yes?"

"*Sidox xinehayh*—come talk to me."

Co'Ozhii tipped sideways and peeked past Vivian. "Clay Selby . . . he is . . . ?"

A strand of hair slipped alongside Vivian's cheek, tickling

her jaw. She tucked it behind her ear, imagining how disheveled she must appear after her restless night on the floor. She replied as best she could in her Indian mix. "Alive. I believe he will be fine." Then she squared her shoulders and gave Shruh a challenging look. "But he needs quiet and rest. Can we speak later?"

Clay's worried voice called, "Viv?"

Vivian adopted a soothing tone and spoke to Clay in English. "It's all right, Clay. Sleep now." She stepped out of the hut, pulling the blanket across the doorway. She clutched handfuls of the thick woven cloth behind her back and drew again on her limited Athabascan. "I must see to Clay. He is weak. If you have medicine to strengthen him, I would welcome it." She sent the request in Co'Ozhii's direction, believing the woman would be most likely to respond.

Shruh cleared his throat. "We need to—"

Co'Ozhii put her hand on her husband's arm. "Meat will build his strength. And chamomile tea will soothe him so he can sleep."

Shruh grunted.

His wife offered a disapproving look. "We will not send a weak man's helper away from the village. If he cannot fend for himself, his death will be on our hands."

Vivian wondered how the native woman could extend such consideration to Clay—a stranger—while ignoring the fact that her own granddaughter had been left to fend for herself. She bit down on the tip of her tongue. Offending the tribal leaders would gain nothing. She needed time—time to let Clay heal and time to conceive a way to convince the village to allow her friendship with Lizzie to continue.

Vivian lowered her head slightly, a gesture of submission she hoped would pacify Shruh. "I know we must talk, but

I ask that you allow me to care for Clay first. When he is able to work, then he can be a part of our talk, too." She flicked a glance at the man's face, searching for a small sign of agreement. "Clay is the head of our mission. He should be included—yes?" She held her breath.

✀

Lizzie paused outside the village and peered through a gap in the pin cherry bushes. The sight made her mouth go dry. A group of villagers, led by her grandparents, crowded near Clay's hut. Vivian faced the angry mob. Although her view was obstructed by the many people in the way, she glimpsed Vivian's pale face and wide eyes. Her heart twisted in sympathy. After last night's unpleasant encounter in Clay's tent, Lizzie had no doubt her grandfather had gathered the others to act in hostility toward Vivian and Clay.

But what should she do? Even though she held deep resentment concerning the edict that banned her from entering the village, her respect for the tribal laws went deeper than resentment. She wouldn't have violated the ban last night had the situation not been urgent—she couldn't leave Clay on that trail unattended. Even now, she wondered how she'd found the courage to set foot on village ground.

She glanced over her shoulder at the tumble of supplies she'd carted from the woods. She'd been forced to leave them behind when she put Clay on the travois, but early this morning she'd retrieved them. Clay and Vivian needed the supplies for survival. She'd hoped to place them inside Vivian's hut while the village slept, but it had taken longer than she'd expected. Now that the village was greeting a new day, she couldn't give the items to Vivian without being seen.

The deep rumble of her grandfather's voice reached Lizzie's ears. She recognized sternness in the tone, but the birds chattering in the branches overhead masked the words. She pushed a branch aside, gaining a better view. If she could see Vitsiy's face, perhaps she could construe what he spoke to Vivian. But too many others surrounded him. The statement was lost.

Lizzie sat back, allowing the branches to close and shield her. Chewing her lip in consternation, she placed her hand on the nearest bag, which contained fat potatoes. If she left them here along the pathway that led to her cabin, Vivian would surely come upon them eventually. But if she didn't find them soon, squirrels and other small creatures would raid the bags. Whatever the animals left behind would be ruined by invading insects.

Then again, Vivian visited her nearly every day. The bags wouldn't lie here, undiscovered, for long—maybe a day, at most. For a moment, her heart lifted. But grim realization chased away the glimmer of hope. She'd shot Clay. Vivian, caught up in seeing to Clay's needs, hadn't blamed her last night, but she'd certainly have changed her mind this morning. Lizzie had done Vivian a terrible wrong by shooting her brother. No one could forgive such a misdeed.

She sighed. She couldn't enter the camp, and she couldn't leave the bags here. Unless . . . She clicked her tongue on her teeth. She would come back tonight, after everyone had gone to their cabins for sleep. If the bags were still here, she'd tote them to Vivian's hut and leave them outside the woman's door. If the bags were gone, she'd know Vivian had found them and been able to tote them herself.

Although still apprehensive about leaving the bags in the brush, she assured herself she'd chosen the best solution. A glance through the bushes showed the circle of visitors outside Clay's hut had grown larger, but Vivian no longer stood in their midst. They jabbered softly amongst themselves. Their voices would cover the sound of her creeping away. She braced her hands on her knees, prepared to rise and return to her cabin.

"Why are you hiding in the bushes?"

Chapter Sixteen

Lizzie clutched her chest, nearly toppling in surprise at the sound of a childish voice right behind her. She whirled and found herself face-to-face with the two children who'd stolen from her pile of salmon at the river. The little girl opened her mouth to speak again, but Lizzie hissed, "Shh!" She glanced at the villagers. None turned in her direction. She blew out a breath of relief. Then she grabbed each child by the fronts of their white-man's clothing and pulled them down next to her. "What are you doing here?" she demanded in Athabascan.

The boy pulled loose and straightened his shirt. "What are *you* doing?"

Lizzie ignored his challenging tone. "I brought food."

The girl's eyes brightened. She jabbed her brother with her elbow. "See? She *is* nice. Just like she let us keep the fish—she brought us food."

Lizzie shook her head. "Not for you. For Clay and Vivian Selby."

The child's face fell. "*Iy,* not for us . . ."

Despite her aggravation at being accosted by these two scamps a second time, Lizzie's sympathy stirred. "Y-you are without food?"

"We have some," the little girl said, "but—"

The boy grasped her arm and gave her a silencing look. He lifted his chin and faced Lizzie. "We are fine."

Lizzie nibbled her lip, uncertain. She needed to return to her cabin before her grandfather or one of the tribal leaders caught sight of her lurking outside the village, but how could she leave these children if what she suspected was true? Their vitse was old—they'd said so. Pride would keep the old woman from asking for help, and the children would continue to go hungry.

She had an idea, but she couldn't talk to the children so close to the village where they might be overheard. Gesturing for them to follow, Lizzie inched backward, staying low. Without hesitation, the girl followed, and the boy—his face wreathed with uneasiness—skittered after his sister. Lizzie led them well into the trees. When she felt they were safe from listening ears, she crouched to their level. "What are your names?"

The girl grinned, showing a gap where her front teeth should be. "I am Naibi. My brother is Etu."

"Naibi and Etu, I cannot give you the food you saw in the bushes—it does not belong to me. It belongs to the missionaries, Clay and Vivian Selby." Their dark eyes stared at her, reflecting hopelessness, and Lizzie's heart constricted. Would her next words encourage them? "The food is for the mission, but the mission is for the village. I am sure they will share with you and your grandmother."

Naibi released a happy squeal and brought her pudgy hands together. She beamed at her brother, but the boy didn't look assured.

Lizzie turned to Etu. "Will your vitse accept food from the mission?"

The boy, his face too old for his young years, offered a slow shrug. "She is afraid to let others know she is having trouble gathering food for us."

Naibi added, "She does not want to be seen as useless." Her bright voice contrasted the sadness of the statement.

Lizzie didn't know the children's grandmother, but she understood the woman's concern. There was no worse designation than useless among the Gwich'in people. "Your parents . . . they do not help her?"

Naibi hung her head, and Etu answered. "They are dead. As is Vitsiy. It is just Vitse and us now."

"Etu is getting bigger. He is nine years already." Naibi's chin bounced up, her expression cheerful again. "He can plant squash, and fish, and even hunt if someone will teach him."

Lizzie nodded thoughtfully, looking Etu up and down. Although young, he appeared to be an intelligent, sturdy boy, capable of helping his family. But boys learned from their fathers, and Etu had no father. Who would teach him the skills he needed?

Naibi touched Lizzie's hand. "We watched you at the river. You are good at fish catching. You caught many more fish than Vitse." She tipped her head, her tangled hair spilling across her round cheek. "Will you teach Etu to fish?"

Lizzie warmed at the innocent question. These children didn't know her, yet they trusted her. She wished she had time to teach Etu to fish, to hunt, and to trap. But she was preparing to leave this place—she had no time to spare. "No." Her voice carried the heavy tone of regret, and her remorse doubled when the little girl's face fell. "But I have much food at my cabin."

If she left for California before winter set in, she wouldn't need all of the meat and fish she'd stored. She'd intended to sell the surplus, along with her furs, but perhaps it could be put to better use right here in Gwichyaa Saa. Why she cared about these children—children who'd stolen from her!—she couldn't explain, yet the thought of them going hungry created an ache in the center of her heart. "The missionaries know how to find me. If you have need of more food than what is in those bags, you tell them. They will come to me, and I will give them food for you."

Naibi flashed a happy smile at Etu, but the boy remained solemn.

"I need to go now. Will you tell the missionaries where to find the bags of food?" She gave the pair a stern look. "Remember, it is *their* food, not yours. Stealing is *wrong*." She softened her tone. "But the missionaries have come to help. They will share their food with those who need it."

Naibi nodded. "We will tell them. Come, Etu!" She grabbed her brother's hand and tugged him toward the village. Etu trotted behind his sister, but he kept his face angled toward Lizzie, his eyes seeming to beg her for . . . something. But Lizzie had nothing to offer these children. She'd done all she could. She hardened her heart and turned away from Etu's seeking eyes.

✑

After three days of lying on his pine-needle-and-blanket bed, Clay told Vivian, "I'm getting up, and nothing you say will stop me." She begged and threatened and almost cried, but he pulled on his boots, buttoned his shirt, and headed for the mission with Vivian scampering along at his heels.

The sunlight hurt his eyes—he'd grown accustomed to

the hut, where only dim streaks of light penetrated the bark walls and ceiling. The headache that had plagued him unceasingly for the past few days intensified. He shielded his eyes with his hand and ducked his head, wincing.

Vivian caught his arm and drew him to a stop. "I told you it was too soon. You're hurting—I can tell. " She glowered at him, but then her expression turned pleading. "Please, Clay. Go back to your hut. Just one more day. If you are up too soon, you might open the wound. I worry it might start bleeding again." She flicked a glance toward the village, her brow puckering.

He stifled a frustrated sigh. "Viv, I've been lying around for too many days already. Is the clay going to march from the riverbank and fill the gaps between these logs?" She flinched, and he regretted that his sarcasm hurt her, but she had to let him work. The mission building had to be completed. He needed a place to teach and preach—his ministry depended on this structure. "Who else will do the chinking if I don't do it?"

He pulled loose of her light grasp and entered the mission. Stepping over the threshold brought a rush of emotion he didn't quite understand. He turned a slow circle, examining the room by increments while a mighty lump welled in his throat. He mentally calculated the time he'd need to finish chinking the walls, build the sleeping rooms, and construct benches. Another two weeks? A month? Fingering the bandage on his head, he silently lamented the injury that had prevented progress on the building.

He strode to the northwest corner, where the gunnysacks, crates, and barrels containing their food supplies lay in a disorganized heap. "I need to build a small storage loft for our supplies." He sent a weary look in Vivian's direction. "I'm grateful to Lizzie for retrieving these and bringing them to the village for us." A reparation for bouncing a bullet off his head, perhaps.

"She took a terrible chance, coming into the village."

Vivian had sung Lizzie's praises repeatedly over the past days, reminding Clay again and again he might not be alive if Lizzie hadn't broken the excommunication edict and brought him to the village. What she neglected to remember was he wouldn't have been hurt at all if Lizzie hadn't mistaken him for a prowling animal. He didn't want to feel angry at Lizzie, but the emotion welled up against his will. *Lord, help me forgive her—she didn't deliberately harm me and slow my progress.*

Vivian sent a glance out the door, her eyes flashing in apprehension. Her expression raised questions that had plagued him for the past several days. Clay moved to her side and touched her arm. She jumped, casting the frightened look on him. Something unpleasant had transpired while he lay, half-asleep and unaware. Now that he was on his feet again, it was time for answers.

"Viv, while I was recovering, Shruh visited frequently. You and he argued."

Vivian scuttled backward a few inches. "You heard us?"

"I heard your voices, but never the words. What was the disagreement about?" Clay waited, but Vivian drew in a breath and stared at him in silence, her eyes reflecting worry. "Viv?"

Her breath whooshed out, and she seemed to wilt. "I'd hoped he might change his mind, but . . ." Lifting her head, she fixed him with a resigned look. "Clay, Shruh is angry because—" Murmured voices carried from outside, and Vivian whirled to face the door opening. She clasped her hands at her throat. "Here he comes." Her voice sounded strained. "I suppose he'll tell you."

Clay hurried to Vivian's side. "He'll tell me what?"

But Vivian, focused on the approaching cluster of men, didn't answer. Clay stepped into the yard to greet Shruh, Da'ago, and several other tribal leaders. Although an unnamed worry seized him, he formed a welcoming smile and greeted them in Athabascan. "*Ade'*—hello. It is good to be up and working again." He let his gaze bounce from one unsmiling face to another, his unease mounting, and forced a light laugh. "If any of you would like to assist me with chinking, I would accept your help."

"We must talk." Shruh spoke abruptly, as if Clay hadn't offered any words of greeting.

Clay cupped his hand above his eyes. "Very well. Would you like to step out of the sun?" Even with his shielding hand in place, he had to squint. His head throbbed.

Shruh looked as if he would refuse, but then he glanced at Clay's bandage and gave a brusque nod. He flipped his hand at the gathered men, and they surged across the threshold.

The villagers had explored the mission building on many occasions, but once more their faces angled this way and that as they examined Clay's handiwork. The building wasn't a work of art, but it was well built—strong enough to withstand rain and wind. It would serve the villagers well. Pride swelled. They wouldn't find fault with his craftsmanship.

Shruh crossed his arms over his chest and set his feet wide. "Clay Selby, we must speak of the woman Lu'qul Gitth'ihgi."

Clay glanced at Vivian, who had scuttled into the far corner and huddled there, wringing her hands. He gestured for her to join him, but she shook her head. Puzzled, he turned to Shruh. "I know she hurt me, but it was not intentional. We should not hold her accountable." He spoke to himself as much as to Shruh. "I owe her my appreciation for bringing me to safety, where Vivian could see to my wound."

163

Shruh sliced his hand through the air. "I do not wish to speak of what *she* has done, but of what *Vivian Selby* has done."

Clay crunched his brow. "I—"

"I told you contact with this woman was forbidden. Yet Vivian admits making visits to her cabin—many visits. I warned you of the consequences, but she disregarded my warnings." The elder's lined face hardened. "Do you have words of defense?"

Clay licked his dry lips. His head pounded, and he wished Vivian would at least stand beside him. He felt terribly alone facing Shruh's anger. "Our only defense, Shruh, is that God sent us to Alaska to share His love with the Athabascan people. Although Lu'qul Gitth'ighi does not reside within Gwchyaa Saa, she is an Athabascan, so our ministry extends to her, as well."

Shruh's eyes narrowed. "Have you, like the woman, sought her out?"

Although Clay hadn't visited as frequently as Vivian, he couldn't lie. "Yes, sir. I have."

The men muttered to one another, sending disapproving glances in Clay's direction. Shruh's lips twitched. "As I told your woman, you are newcomers—unacquainted with tribal law. As such, I wish to grant you leniency and the privilege of residing within our village. But I cannot do so unless I am guaranteed you now understand the excommunication and will honor it."

Shruh flung a sour look toward Vivian. "This woman has repeatedly refused to discontinue her relationship with Lu'qul Gitth'ighi. But you are the head of the mission, and she must abide by your decision. So I ask you—will you intentionally seek to spend time with the banished woman again?"

Chapter Seventeen

Clay's head pounded with an intensity that made him queasy. Simple . . . it would be so simple to acquiesce to Shruh's demand. After all, Lizzie was only one person . . . although she'd become an important person, intriguing him in ways he little understood. But what good would come of admitting his interest in her? She'd been banished from the tribe he'd come to serve. She planned to leave Alaska to reside in California. He'd have to say good-bye to her soon anyway, so what harm would there be in agreeing to stay away from her? By doing so, he'd secure a place in the village, where he and Vivian could minister to the entire tribe of Gwich'ins.

It's for the best, isn't it, Lord? He drew in a fortifying breath, ready to assure Shruh that he and Vivian would abide by the excommunication, but a wave of weakness attacked him. The ground beneath him seemed to tip, and he lost his balance. Vivian dashed to his side and slipped beneath his arm, preventing him from toppling onto the mission's dirt floor.

Vivian snapped, "Someone help me!" Da'ago stepped forward and grabbed Clay's other arm. Vivian glared at Shruh, surprising Clay with her defiance. "Talk later. My brother needs to rest now."

She aimed Clay for the doorway, and she and Da'ago assisted him back to his hut. Although less than half an hour ago he'd insisted on leaving his bed, he sank back down willingly, his eyes falling closed of their own accord. To his relief, now that he wasn't on his feet, the dizzy feeling eased.

"Thank you, Da'ago." Vivian's voice lost its sharp edge as she addressed the tribal elder. "I appreciate your help."

"You are welcome, Missus Vivian." Footsteps retreated, signaling the man's departure.

A cool hand touched Clay's brow, and he opened his eyes to find Vivian looking at him with both exasperation and concern. Despite the throbbing pain in his temple, he released a light laugh. "I guess I should have listened to you when you said it was too soon."

She grimaced. "I knew the moment you appeared, Shruh would swoop down like a vulture. He's been waiting to talk to us ever since he found Lizzie in your hut the night you were hurt."

"You mean the night she hurt me." Clay hadn't intended to voice the thought, but maybe it was best if he made his feelings known. Holding resentment inside was much like letting a closed sore fester. Breaking it open led to healing.

"Surely you don't blame her." Vivian gaped at him in dismay.

He rubbed his aching head. "I know she didn't mean to shoot me, but the fact remains she fired her rifle and hit me. She might have killed me, Viv. It's hard to forget that."

Vivian hung her head. "I know." She fiddled with the edge of the blanket, chewing her lower lip. "Does this mean . . . you aren't willing for us to spend time with her anymore?"

Sleep beckoned—his brief venture out had tired him more than he thought possible. Or maybe facing Shruh's ire had exhausted him. Clay sighed. *Most likely, it's the thought of never seeing Lizzie again that creates such a heaviness in my heart.*

"I want to see her," he admitted. A part of him pined for time with the beautiful woman with raven hair and sky-blue eyes. "But our seeing her angers the villagers. Especially Shruh. The Mission Committee sent us here to minister to the tribe. I don't want to be branded a failure." The pain in his head stabbed, but a greater pain pierced his heart. He didn't want to cast Lizzie aside, the way the villagers had done. But he couldn't lose the opportunity to minister to the Gwich'in. Pa would be so disappointed if Clay failed in his attempts to establish a mission in Gwichyaa Saa.

Tears pooled in Vivian's eyes. "But, Clay, think of all the Bible stories about Jesus dining with those rejected by the Pharisees. Shouldn't we set an example of forgiveness and acceptance to everyone, the same way Jesus did?"

If it weren't for the pounding in his head, Clay would have laughed. He'd questioned whether Vivian would make a good missionary, but there she sat, preaching a sermon. One he couldn't ignore. "You've given this much thought."

"I've thought of little else since the night Shruh found Lizzie in your hut." She caught his hand between hers, the fierce grip expressing the depth of her emotion. "If you succumb to Shruh's rules about excommunication, how can you ever teach about acceptance and love? Your words would be a farce."

Clay's head hurt too much to think. "I need to sleep, Vivian."

She sighed. After a moment, she released his hand and pulled the blanket across him, her face sad. "All right. But as soon as you're awake and set foot outside, Shruh will be here demanding an answer."

Clay ground his teeth together, eager to block out Vivian's ominous prediction. "Viv, I promise . . . before I go to sleep, I'll ask God to tell me what He would have me do. All right?"

A relieved, albeit sad, smile tipped up the corners of Vivian's lips. She offered a nod. "That's wise, Clay. After all, He's the one who brought you here to minister." She rose and left the hut.

Allowing his eyes to slip closed, Clay rasped a heartfelt prayer: "You brought me here, God. Please tell me how far this ministry is intended to reach." He fell asleep before he received an answer.

∽

Lizzie sat in a slice of shade behind her cabin and stitched a blue bead into place, completing another delicate forget-me-not. She held the coat at arm's length and admired the row of blossoms dancing from shoulder to shoulder. Perfect. She showed the coat to Martha, who lay on the grass nearby. "What do you think?"

Martha raised one ear, tipping her head as if forming an opinion. She gave a yip, and Lizzie smiled. Then her smile faded, her gaze drifting in the direction of Gwichyaa Saa. Had Clay recovered? Did Vivian need salve? She wished someone would come and let her know how they were doing.

As much as she appreciated Martha's faithful presence, talking to the dog wasn't the same as talking to Vivian. The past days had been lonelier than those prior to Vivian and Clay Selby's arrival. Having experienced human companionship, she felt a keener absence now that it was gone.

"I don't know why I'm completing the coat," Lizzie told Martha as she reached into the little hide pouch at her hip for a green bead. She held the little bead to the light, envisioning an entire leafy vine trailing down the coat's front. "My grandmother will surely never accept it now that I've done Clay such harm." Her chest ached with the remembrance. If only one could turn back time. If given a second chance, she wouldn't squeeze the trigger. The picture of him crumpling, then lying white and still on the fern-strewn pathway would haunt her forever. "But I need something to do—to keep myself busy until my garden is ready to harvest."

By the time Lizzie had returned to her cabin after leaving the food bags near the village, she'd decided she would leave for California at the end of the growing season. Clay and Vivian could make use of the extra food stores, and allowing her plants to wither and die, unattended, went against her conscience. Two more months. She could stay here, alone, two more months if it meant the opportunity to make restitution to the missionary pair. But then she would have to leave and never look back. The feelings for Clay rising to life deep inside her couldn't be allowed to blossom. Leaving was her only option.

Lizzie rubbed Martha's stomach with her bare foot as she continued stitching. "I'll do as much on the coat as I can with the time I have. It won't be as nice as the one I'd planned to give to Vitse, but it will still fetch a good price in White Horse." One of the traders in the town especially liked native clothing—he sold the pieces to a man who ran a Wild West show in America. Lizzie didn't know what he meant by a Wild West show, but she would gladly allow him to fill her pocket with coins. She'd need all the travel money she could get.

Her hands fell idle as she tried to envision California. Pa had been gone for so long, she'd nearly forgotten his stories of living in the city. She knew he'd had a big house, because he often complained about the small size of their cabin, and she knew his family was wealthy because he frequently bragged to Mama about his fortune in furs being equal to his father's success in the '49 gold rush. Lizzie recalled asking him why he didn't search for gold in Alaska like so many others were doing, and he'd laughed and said, "Why should I get my hands dirty? Furs are cleaner." Lizzie hadn't understood his meaning—preparing furs was stinky work. But when Papa laughed, she laughed too, and the meaning hadn't mattered nearly so much as his joyfulness.

Martha whined, reminding Lizzie she wanted more scratching. Lizzie bobbed her foot and carefully applied another bead to the coat. Green beads, like Vivian's eyes. And blue beads, like Pa's eyes. Her eyes, too. She let her eyelids slip closed as an image of her father appeared in her memory. Voss Dawson—tall, slender, with thick hair that stood on end and a beard so full and soft she could lose her fingers in it. A learned man who taught her to read, write, and cipher before her seventh year. A rugged man who trained her to be self-sufficient. A man who claimed to love her, and then left her behind.

In her memory, she heard her father's voice—"Never forget, Lizzie, you have a father in San Francisco who loves you." She'd never forgotten. And soon she'd see him face-to-face. Would he be proud of the woman she'd become?

Tears stung behind Lizzie's eyelids. Before she could go, she had work to complete. She sniffed, opened her eyes, and determinedly returned to stitching. Martha fell asleep, stretched out in the grass. The breeze teased Lizzie's hair as she stitched, weaving the vine that would eventually reach from the coat's neckline to the hem. The vine was the length of her hand from longest fingertip to wrist when Martha suddenly growled and jumped to her feet. Fur bristling, she stared into the brush.

Lizzie set the coat aside and grabbed for her ready rifle. Whoever neared, it was a stranger—Martha wouldn't respond so suspiciously to someone with a familiar scent. The dogs in the pen came to attention, their pointed snouts aimed in the same direction Martha looked. Martha growled again, crouching into a position of attack. Her lips curled back to reveal white, pointed teeth.

Lizzie soothed, "Easy, girl, easy. Stay . . ." She would reverse her words if the visitor proved to be a threat.

Suddenly, two little heads popped up above the pin cherry bushes. Two pairs of dark eyes met Lizzie's. Lizzie relaxed her tense shoulders. "Down, Martha."

Martha sank down, releasing a low-toned growl of complaint. The other dogs added their whines and growls to Martha's. Lizzie leaned her rifle against the cabin wall and strode across the yard to greet the two little visitors. Naibi ran straight to Lizzie, but Etu headed toward the dog pen.

"Etu, no! They bite!" Lizzie called in Athabascan.

The boy slowed his pace momentarily, but then he dashed to the pen and curled his fingers in the wire. The dogs went wild. Lizzie, fear making her clumsy, ran over. To her surprise, rather than snarling with fur on end, the dogs wagged their tails and lolled their tongues in a happy welcome while leaping against the fence.

Etu grinned up at her. "They like me."

Naibi skipped over to join Etu. She poked her hand into the pen, and Martin, Dolly, and Thomas all competed to lick it. Martha loped across the yard and sniffed the back of Naibi's head. Naibi giggled wildly, hunching her shoulders. Then she turned around and wrapped her arms around Martha's broad neck. Martha swiped the child's cheek with her tongue.

Lizzie watched in amazement as the dogs made friends

with the two children. A wishful idea formed: If only Etu and Naibi had a father who might be interested in purchasing her team. Then she could leave, assured the dogs would at least be loved by the children. Or maybe she could gift the children with the dogs. Their grandmother would surely benefit from having the animals to pull the travois or sled. She discounted the thought. The grandmother didn't have enough food for the children—the dogs would starve if left with Etu, Naibi, and their vitse. Leaving them with strangers would be hard for her, but she had to consider their welfare.

Lizzie allowed the children and the dogs several minutes of play, and then she tugged the children away from the pen. Although a part of her thrilled to have the unexpected company, she knew she couldn't encourage the children to seek her out. She put her hands on her hips. "Does your grandmother know you're this far away from the village?"

The pair exchanged guilty looks.

"You didn't ask her permission?"

They shook their heads in unison, hands linked behind their backs. They looked so innocent, Lizzie had a difficult time not smiling. But she couldn't encourage them to run all over the woods, unattended. Her pulse raced when she thought about the various dangers that could befall two small children.

"It isn't safe to venture so far through the woods by yourself." She turned a stern gaze on Etu, the older and—supposedly—more responsible of the pair. "What would you do if you came upon a bear?"

Etu puffed his chest. "I have a knife." He patted a tiny, scarred sheath hanging on a length of rawhide around his waist. "I would protect Naibi."

Lizzie snorted. She hated to dash the boy's pride, but

his knife wouldn't intimidate a gopher. "A knife like that would only tickle a bear and make him mad." She shook her head. "Etu, you need to use good judgment. Naibi depends on you."

Naibi pulled on her lower lip with one finger and rocked from side to side. The little flowered dress, its hem now torn and muddied, swayed above her dirty bare feet. "Etu takes good care of me. That is why he brought me here."

Etu nudged her, his brows forming a V.

Naibi shifted away from him, her expression guileless. "He remembered you said you had lots of food. And we are hungry."

Compassion filled Lizzie, followed by a rush of concern. "Did you tell Vivian about the food I left in the bushes?"

Etu nodded his head hard. "We showed her where you put it. And we helped her carry it into the log house Mister Clay builds." Then he shrugged. "But she gave us none of it."

Lizzie wondered why Vivian would be so thoughtless. Didn't she realize the children were hungry? Or was she too busy taking care of Clay to think about anyone else? "I do have food, and I will feed you today. But"—she forced a firm tone—"you may not come here whenever you choose for something to eat. It is unsafe for you to be in the woods on your own, and members of the tribe are not supposed to visit me. So do not come again, do you hear me?"

Both children nodded. Etu said, "We will not come here on our own again."

Naibi skipped forward and clasped Lizzie's hand, beaming up with her gap-toothed grin. She swung Lizzie's hand. "Can we go eat now?"

Lizzie curled her fingers tightly around the little girl's hand. The contact felt good. Her lips lifted into a smile. "Do you like baked acorn squash? And smoked salmon?"

She didn't mention the sugar cookies that filled a crock on her shelf. She'd surprise them with the treat.

Naibi licked her lips, and Etu's eyebrows rose in anticipation.

"Then come." As Lizzie led the skipping children across the yard to her cabin, she told herself she mustn't grow attached to them. She wasn't staying, and they were members of a village in which she wasn't welcome. But even as she composed the inner warnings, she feared it was too late. Naibi and Etu had already captured a portion of her heart.

Chapter Eighteen

Vivian deliberately stayed away from Clay's hut and allowed him the day to rest. And to think. She wanted to advise him on how to respond to Shruh's demand for them to reject Lizzie the way the rest of the village had done, but harping at him would only lead to resentment. Clay was stubborn—maybe even more stubborn than she. So she busied herself using the flour the Mission Committee had sent to bake several loaves of bread, cleaning and roasting the grouse that had been foolish enough to get its foot caught in her snare, and carting all of her nonpersonal items from her hut to the mission building to give herself a little more space in her tiny dwelling.

By midafternoon, she'd given away most of the bread. Although she hated to lose so much of the food she'd prepared, she could hardly blame the natives for requesting a portion—the aroma was enticing and so different from the usual scents surrounding the village. But she wrapped the last two loaves in burlap and hid them in the bottom of a crate so she and Clay would at least get to enjoy some of her bounty.

She'd just sent two natives away empty-handed when a rough-looking trapper leading a gray-muzzled pack mule ambled through the middle of the village and approached the mission. Vivian stifled a groan. Had the scent of baking bread brought him from the woods?

"Good afternoon," Vivian said when the man stopped outside the mission doors. "Is there something I can do for you?"

The man swept his battered hat from his head, revealing salt-and-pepper hair badly in need of a cut. "I be huntin' a white woman name o' Vivian Selby. I got a package for her—mercantile owner in Fort Yukon sent it out with me yesterday." He turned his head and coughed.

Vivian waited for the coughing spell to pass, and then she moved a few inches closer to the man. "I'm Vivian Selby."

His grin broadened, exposing shreds of chewing tobacco caught in crooked, yellowed teeth. "Well, then, right nice to make your acquaintance, Miz Selby. Here now . . ." He unbuckled one of the straps securing an odd assortment of items onto the poor mule's bowed back. "Feller in town told me the writin' on the box says it came all the way from Massy-chusetts, Yoo-nited States of America."

He paused to touch his hand to his chest and look sky-ward, his expression reverent. Then he jerked a good-sized wooden crate free and plunked it on the ground at Vivian's feet. It took great self-control to resist diving on the crate immediately. If it came from Massachusetts, it held gifts from Aunt Vesta and Uncle Matthew. Anticipation made her giddy.

But she coiled her fingers together and waited while the man adjusted the remaining straps, gave the mule's rump a whack, and aimed another smile at Vivian. "Yes, ma'am, I told that mercantile feller I didn't mind a bit makin' a delivery—wouldn't even charge him, seein' as how the box was comin' to a white woman."

He laughed, but the laugh turned into another coughing spell. He stomped the ground, bringing the cough under control, then offered a sly grin. "An' you don't need to be payin' me nothin', neither. It's enough of a treat just to take a gander at you, purdy lady." He waggled his wiry brows. Tipping sideways, he let loose a stream of tobacco-colored spittle that landed very near the crate.

Vivian scuttled forward and pulled the box away from the man. She wished Clay were with her. The way the trapper looked her up and down made her uncomfortable. "Thank you for delivering my crate. If you'll excuse me, I'd like to examine the contents."

The man cackled as if she'd made a joke. "'Course you do, 'course you do." He jerked on the mule's reins, and the big animal stumbled forward a step. The man plopped his hat in place. "I'll be moseyin' on now. You have a good day, ma'am."

Vivian waited until he rounded the bend at the far side of the village before retrieving Clay's claw hammer and prying the top off the crate. She pawed past a layer of straw, then gasped in delight. A beautiful teapot and a pair of matching cups and saucers painted with pink rosebuds nestled within the folds of a mint green gown lovely enough to grace the high society luncheons in Boston.

Vivian lifted out the teapot and ran her fingers over the delicate blooms, her eyes misting as she remembered sweet tea parties with Aunt Vesta in her fine parlor. She scanned the beautiful but rugged landscape surrounding the mission. The tea set certainly didn't fit the surroundings, but holding it gave her such a feeling of home. She hugged the little pot to her chest and sighed. "Thank you, Aunt Vesta."

She set the pot aside and reached into the box again. A second gown, daffodil yellow with yards of snow-white lace, unfolded in her hands. "Oh my . . ." She'd thought the green gown lovely, but this one must be the loveliest ever sewn. Holding it brought another rush of remembrances, ending with a strong desire to return to the years she'd spent with her aunt and uncle. Away from the untamed prairie lands, she'd felt secure and safe.

Guilt fell over her so abruptly she drew in a strangled gasp. She didn't deserve to hide away, secure and safe—she had restitution to make. And she would make it here, on a frontier even more rugged than the one of her childhood homestead. She started to shove the dress back into the box, but desire stilled her movement. Instead, she held the gown against her front and looked down its length. Her gaze drifted past lovely yellow flounces to a double row of creamy lace . . . to the toes of her scuffed brown shoes. A laugh trickled from her throat—such an incongruous pairing!

Sighing, Vivian crushed the dress to her aching heart. She would never wear this gown, or the mint one—they were far too fine for a missionary teacher on the Alaskan frontier. She gave a little jolt. But what about . . . ? She examined the gown again, her heart pounding in happy speculation. This was exactly the kind of gown that would fit well in the upper social classes of San Francisco.

She'd had Clay post a letter to her mother, requesting dresses, but nothing Vivian left behind in Oklahoma compared to the daffodil gown. Lizzie would have no need to hide in shame if she entered the city attired in the delightful, regal gown, with her hair pinned up. This evening, Vivian would pen an exuberantly worded letter of thanks to her dear aunt, try each dress on one time for the sheer enjoyment of it, and then find a way to present them to Lizzie.

"I shall keep the teapot and teacups, however," she vowed aloud. Perhaps they'd improve the flavor of the herb teas she and Clay drank in lieu of imported black pekoe.

She folded the pair of dresses and began to place them back in the crate, but she spotted an envelope lying in the bottom of the wood-slatted box. Black, scrolled script formed a single line on its front: *For my dear Vivian.* The sight of Aunt Vesta's familiar handwriting sent a coil of homesickness through Vivian's breast. Even though she'd been sent to her aunt and uncle in disgrace, they'd never treated her unkindly. Returning to Mother when she'd finished school had been difficult, and when she thought of home, Aunt Vesta and Uncle Matt's charming, gingerbread-bedecked bungalow on the edge of Huntington's town square always came to mind.

Squatting beside the box, she ripped open the envelope and eagerly unfolded the pages. As she read, her hands began to shake. By the time she'd finished, the pages rustled as if caught in a stiff breeze, and tears coursed down her face. She crushed the pages to her heart, her head low. "What should I do? Oh, what should I do?"

∽

What should she do? Lizzie stood at the pathway's foot with Naibi clinging to her hand as if she never wanted to let go. She'd told the children they shouldn't venture into the woods alone, yet she had to send them back. Given the hour of the afternoon, the villagers would be in their yards—the women preparing an evening meal, the youngest children playing, and men gathering in groups to visit. The likelihood of being seen was increased with the activity at this hour. Being seen would create problems.

Naibi pulled on her hand. "Walk with us, Lizzie."

Even Etu, brave boy that he was, looked at Lizzie expectantly.

Lizzie chuckled to herself. Had there ever been any choice? "Let's go."

The path was too narrow for three abreast, and even two made a tight fit when one of the two was a full-grown woman wearing a wide-skirted dress. But Naibi refused to release Lizzie's hand and walk on her own, unlike Etu, who prowled the path ahead, his hand on the little knife sheath and his fierce gaze searching the bushes for any animal brazen enough to attack. Branches tickled Lizzie's arm and tried to tear the skirt of her blue-checked dress. She caught a handful of fabric and tucked the skirt closer to her body rather than sending Naibi ahead.

The little girl hummed, occasionally flashing a bright smile upward, which Lizzie couldn't resist returning. She hadn't smiled as much in the past two years as she had during the two hours Naibi and Etu visited. She'd laughed aloud, watching them frolic on the grass with Martha and two other dogs. Naibi had admired the beadwork on the coat, and Etu's eyes widened in amazement when she showed him her cache of furs ready for market. Having them there—talking with them, listening to their childish babble, seeing wonder in their eyes—had given her such a lift.

Her heart ached as she considered the children's bleak future. If their vitse was as old and feeble as the children had indicated, they might be completely alone soon. But Clay and Vivian were building their mission school. Even though Lizzie still believed they should be cautious in placing too much knowledge of the white world in the children's heads, surely this pair would benefit from the missionaries being in the village. Someone would be available to provide for Etu and Naibi.

Jealousy twined through Lizzie's heart—a foolish emotion, but an honest one. Her hours with them had proved Etu and Naibi were fine, good-hearted children, and a part of her wished she could claim them as her own. But she was leaving—and she couldn't take them with her. She must arrive in San Francisco completely unencumbered to begin her new life. Her father had intimated Athabascan ways had no place in California. She must leave every vestige of her past behind.

Naibi's toe connected with a root. Lizzie curved her arms around the little girl to prevent her from falling, and Naibi giggled her thanks. Etu glanced back, rolled his eyes in a long-suffering manner, then resumed his protective stance. Naibi swung Lizzie's hand, a happy melody pouring from her throat.

Lizzie swallowed. Some parts of her past would be harder to forget than others.

Several yards from the village, Lizzie drew Naibi to a stop. "Etu?" The boy whirled, planting his feet wide. "Take your sister on from here."

Naibi sent a wide-eyed gaze upward. "But what of the bears and wolves? Are you not afraid they will eat us up?"

Lizzie nearly choked, trying to hold back her laughter. Such a conniving little urchin. She smoothed the child's tangled hair from her cheeks. "You are close enough now to be safe. But go straight to the village." She aimed the warning at Etu. "No wandering in the woods now, do you hear?"

The boy nodded in agreement. He held out his hand. "Come, Naibi."

Naibi cupped both hands around Lizzie's. "You come, too. A bear might get you if we leave you here alone." Her dark eyes begged.

Lizzie gently disengaged the child's hands. "Go with your

brother now. And remember what I told you—do not come through the woods alone again." She gave the little girl a slight push toward Etu. He darted forward and put his arm around his sister's shoulders. Together, the pair moved toward the village. Lizzie remained on the pathway until they rounded a bend and disappeared from sight. Even then she waited, her senses attuned in case Naibi chose to break free of Etu's arm and run back to her. But the children didn't return.

Sighing, both relieved and disappointed, she turned to retrace her steps to her cabin. She took one step, and the bushes on her right rustled. Lizzie froze, her breath held in her lungs. Her hand automatically reached for her knife sheath. But it wasn't there—she'd removed it while working on the coat and hadn't put it back on. Neither had she brought her rifle. Fear created a sour taste in her mouth, and she poised, ready to run as fast as the blue-checked dress would allow.

Another rustle, and someone emerged from the bushes—a tall Gwich'in woman wearing feathers in her gray-streaked hair. She stepped directly into Lizzie's path and fixed her with a solemn frown. "*Adé*, Lu'qul Gitth'ighi . . ." The woman's chin raised, her gaze narrowing. "How are you, my grand-daughter?"

Chapter Nineteen

Lizzie stared at Co'Ozhii—her mother's mother, to whom she hadn't spoken since she was a girl so small Pa had carried her from place to place on his hip. She held no specific memories of her own of this woman, yet she knew her well. From her mother's many woeful tales. She bobbed her head in a jerky greeting. "*Adé*—hello, Vitse."

Co'Ozhii lifted one brow. "You stand before me in a dress not of our people, yet you speak in my tongue. Your white father did not rob you of your mother's language."

"My father robbed me of nothing." Her grandmother's lips tightened into a grim line, and Lizzie instantly regretted her defensive reply. She lowered her head and added in a respectful tone, "He insisted I know the tongue of *Dine'e*, the People. He said it is my heritage."

Co'Ozhii's eyes flashed. "Your father speaks foolishness. And that foolishness resides in you, as well."

Lizzie bristled. After years apart, her grandmother approached her only to hurl insults? "Why do you call me foolish?"

The older woman's face twisted with scorn. "You cannot help it. It is the white man's blood coursing in your veins.

Only so little of it in your mother's, yet there was enough to make her choose unwisely."

Lizzie frowned, confused.

"And these two white people who enter my village, who build their school and talk of teaching our children." She snorted, followed by a cough. "They can do no good, planting foolishness in the minds of innocent children. But I see my people become enamored with the man who coaxes music from a box. Intrigued, they listen. They believe learning his language will be of benefit to us." For a moment, it seemed fear glimmered in the woman's eyes. "Soon they will accept his ways, and they will change. As my daughter changed. Much harm will come."

Lizzie shook her head, thoroughly perplexed. "I do not understand what you are telling me."

Co'Ozhii seared Lizzie with a stern glare. "Then open your ears and listen. Listen with the part of you that still remembers the heritage of your mother." She paused to cough again, the harsh sound grating. "These white people bring trouble into our village. They defy our laws by consorting with those excommunicated—"

Lizzie's face heated.

"—and force their teaching on our young. Already conflict arises between husband and wife, parent and child. They need to leave."

Holding out her hands, Lizzie gave her grandmother a helpless look. "But why do you tell me? I do not live in the village. I have no say in what happens there."

"But you have made friends with Vivian Selby. She respects you, yes?"

Slowly, Lizzie nodded. "As I respect her."

"Then tell her to go. Her white skin, her hair of autumn leaves and eyes like grass in springtime . . . our young men look upon her with longing. She brings much trouble by staying in the village. Tell her . . . she must go." Co'Ozhii's voice rose in fervor, and another coughing bout gripped her.

"If I tell her . . ." Lizzie licked her lips, her mouth suddenly dry. "Will you then look with favor upon me?"

For long moments the older woman stared, unblinking, her mouth set in a stern line of uncertainty. Finally she shifted her gaze to stare somewhere into the trees, as if seeing something in her memory. "Favor I cannot offer. It would mean giving you honor. There is no honor for you. You have been tainted by the sins of my grandfather, as was your mother. But . . ." She met Lizzie's gaze again, cold resolve showing in the unyielding set of her square jaw. "You can spare the same pain befalling another child. Perhaps the High One will choose to look upon you with favor."

Without offering a good-bye, Co'Ozhii brushed past Lizzie and strode down the path. Lizzie stared after her grandmother, one phrase from their short conversation—*"You have been tainted by the sins of my grandfather"*—repeating itself in her memory. Troubling ideas began to roll in the back of her mind. She needed answers.

∽

Clay grabbed the bucket that rested on the floor inside the door of his hut. Bending over brought a stab of pain behind his left eye, and he winced. But he couldn't allow the pain to hinder any further activities. Somehow he'd have to work whether his head hurt or not.

He stepped into the yard and paused, allowing his eyes to adjust to the evening light. Although the sun still shone, the intensity had lessened as the nighttime hours approached, and he didn't find it as difficult to bear as he had that morning. He bounced the bucket against his leg, gathering the energy to walk to the river. Hopefully a good wash would awaken him enough to get some work done. He'd slept the entire day away. He rounded his hut and nearly collided nose to nose with Shruh's wife, Co'Ozhii.

She halted, the feathers in her hair continuing to sway, and met his startled gaze with an unsmiling look. "You are recovered?"

The blunt question, delivered on a note of irritation, tickled Clay. She seemed disappointed to see him on his feet. He gave a cautious nod, aware that too much movement might cause his head to pound again. "I am better, yes. *Dogidihn*—thank you."

She snorted. "I will tell Shruh. He wishes words with you."

Clay watched her storm away, his stomach churning. Going for water now could be misconstrued as an attempt to escape. He turned the bucket upside down and sat on it. Propping his elbows on his knees, he heaved a mighty sigh. What would he tell Shruh? The tribal elder would follow through on his threat to banish him and Vivian if they didn't agree to stay away from Lizzie. He'd prayed again and again about what he should do, but no answer had fallen from the sky.

"You're up. . . ." Vivian approached from the mission building. "I have your supper ready."

The way his stomach felt, he wasn't sure he'd be able to eat anything this evening. "Shruh is coming to talk to me."

Vivian crouched beside him. Her eyes were red rimmed, mute evidence of her heartache over their situation. "What are you going to tell him?"

He sighed, rubbing his hand down his face. "What else can I tell him, Viv? If we refuse, we're done here. The Mission Committee will have wasted time and money on us. I don't know that we have any choice except to—"

A tear trickled down Vivian's cheek.

He took her hand. "I know how hard this is for you. I'm sorry."

Vivian slipped her hand into her apron pocket. "Clay, I received a letter, and—"

Lizzie burst from the bushes. Both Vivian and Clay jumped. She stumbled toward them, the hem of the blue-checked dress dragging in the dirt. Vivian's face paled. She leapt up and met her. "Lizzie! You shouldn't be here, especially not now. Shruh—"

Lizzie pulled loose of Vivian's grasp. "I'm not leaving. I wish to speak to Co'Ozhii."

Vivian shot a frantic look over her shoulder at Clay as he rose and stumbled toward the women. He curled his hand over Lizzie's shoulder. "Shruh is already angry." Protectiveness welled up, surprising him with its intensity. "This isn't a good time for you to try to speak to your grandparents."

Voices carried from the village. Vivian clutched at Clay's arm. "They're coming."

Clay lowered his voice. "Lizzie, please go now. You being here will cause further conflict. Please . . ."

But instead of responding to Clay's request, Lizzie charged forward to meet the approaching cluster of villagers. Clay grabbed Vivian's arm and started after her. Vivian resisted, but he gave a stronger tug, and she stumbled alongside him, clumsier than he'd ever seen her.

Shruh stopped, forcing everyone behind him to do the same. He pointed at Lizzie. "You . . ." His angry gaze swung to include Clay. "You brought her here?"

"I came on my own." Lizzie stepped in front of Clay. If he hadn't known better, he might have thought she was trying to shield him. "I need to talk to Co'Ozhii."

Co'Ozhii's face pinched with rage. "I have nothing more to say to you."

Shruh sent his wife a sharp look. "You have spoken to—"

Lizzie interrupted, her gaze boring into Co'Ozhii's. "You know you do." She stood with shoulders square, her head at a proud angle. Her hair, unfettered, hung down her back in a thick waterfall of glistening black. In her gingham dress, she faced the accusatory crowd with courage and grace. Clay likened her to David facing the Philistine giant with only a stone and a sling. Just as David emerged the victor against great odds, he suspected Lizzie would win this contest of wills.

Co'Ozhii tipped toward Lizzie, her eyes snapping. She dropped her voice to a raspy whisper. "Will you shame me in front of my own people?"

Shruh stared into his wife's sullen face while she glared at Lizzie. Then he spun to the tribe members. "To your cabins. We must speak to the white people and to Lu'qul Gitth'ighi alone."

The group muttered, and Da'ago stepped forward. "A ban or its removal"—he glanced at Lizzie—"must be approved by all elders. We should stay."

Shruh shook his head, his graying braids slapping against his shoulders. "*Ęhę'ę*—no. This is a private matter, not a tribal one. Go."

Although the men still murmured among themselves, they turned and ambled back toward the center of the village. Shruh stepped past Lizzie to address Clay. "We will go to your mission. Come." He set off with a long, determined stride, and Co'Ozhii hurried after him.

Lizzie turned to Clay and Vivian. "You need not come. As my grandfather said, it is a private matter."

Vivian clutched his arm, her expression pleading. "Let them go on their own. Then we can . . . talk."

Shruh spun to face them. "Clay Selby and Vivian, you come, too. We have much to discuss."

Clay looked at Lizzie. He kept his voice low and spoke in English, knowing Shruh wouldn't be able to understand everything he said. "It's your decision. We'll come with you, if you like, and try to help bring peace between you and your grandparents. Or we'll stay away. Whatever you want." He fully expected her to turn them away. She'd proven her independent spirit and had warned them away in the past. But he prayed she'd accept his help. Even if she didn't need it, he hoped she would want his support.

Lizzie looked at her grandparents by turn, then at Vivian, and finally at Clay. Her gaze lingered, and his scalp tingled at the intensity. Finally, she gave a nod, as if agreeing with some silent voice, and held her hand toward the mission. "We'll go." Her expression turned hard. "It will do my grandmother good to share her secrets before all of those she holds in contempt."

Chapter Twenty

L izzie, arms swinging with determination, stalked after her grandparents, with Clay and Vivian following behind her. After living alone for so long and facing every conflict without support or assistance, her heart pattered in appreciation for their presence. Their friendship. Their unconditional acceptance. It helped ease the sting of her grandparents' rejection.

Inside the mission, Clay dragged several barrels across the floor and formed a rough circle, then gestured for the others to sit. Lizzie sat first, a gesture intended to indicate she had seized control of the meeting. Her glowering grandfather and grandmother quickly chose barrels directly across from her, their fierce gazes pinned on Lizzie's face.

Vivian sank onto the barrel next to Lizzie and offered a feeble smile. She leaned toward Lizzie and whispered, "How can you be so composed and strong? I am terrified!"

Lizzie squared her shoulders and admitted in a low tone, "I, too, am fearful. But fear will not earn regard from my grandparents. I must be strong."

Vivian nodded. Then she sat up straight and lifted her chin, although it quivered.

The moment the seat of Clay's pants met the lid of the remaining barrel, Shruh spoke. "What do you wish of us?"

Lizzie narrowed her eyes, an expression she knew could be construed as defiant, yet she used it to mask her deep pain. "I wish answers." Lizzie gazed steadily into her grandmother's stoic face. "You claimed white blood coursed through my mother's veins. How can this be?"

Shruh cast an angry glance at his wife. The room seemed to shrink beneath the weight of his fury. But Co'Ozhii did not waver under his glare, her dark eyes boring into Lizzie's without so much as a blink in response. Neither of her grandparents spoke for several moments.

Clay cleared his throat. "Co'Ozhii, of all the people in the village, you have been the most apprehensive about my presence here. I understand not all white men have treated the Gwich'in fairly, yet your feelings seem to be more . . . personal." Clay paused, his Adam's apple bobbing in his neck.

Vivian grasped his hand. Lizzie wished she could do the same. She wove her fingers together in her lap as Clay continued softly.

"Was there . . . someone . . . long ago who gave you reason to hate?"

Co'Ozhii's expression hardened, her eyes snapping, and then she took on the appearance of someone drifting far, far away. She rocked gently on the barrel, her arms over her chest. When she spoke, her tone became singsong, as if sharing a bedtime story with a child. "In the days of forests and warring tribes—before the white men came and built their towns amongst us—my grandmother ventured to the river at her mother's request to fetch water for the cooking pot. She was a maiden of tender years, beautiful, and promised to a man of a neighboring band. Their union was meant to bring peace between her village and his."

Although Lizzie had never heard the story, she believed she knew the ending. She wanted to plug her ears, but instead she clamped her fingers more tightly together. They felt icy cold.

"While at the river, a man approached—a man with hair the color of autumn leaves and eyes blue like the berries that grow wild in the briars." Co'Ozhii paused to cough into her hand. The cough lasted several seconds, and then she drew in a shuddering breath that brought it under control. She continued to rock, the barrel staves squeaking in discordant accompaniment to her tale. "My grandmother—young and foolish—was transfixed by the sight. He spoke kindly to her in a tongue she'd never heard before. He wooed her with gifts of glass beads and woven cloth. He asked her to meet him the next day, and then the next. She forgot her promise to wed the neighboring tribesman and instead submitted to this autumn-haired man with a smooth tongue and smiling eyes."

She abruptly ceased rocking, jerking her face to stare accusingly at Clay. "By the time my mother was born, the man had gone. He left my grandmother to bear his shame alone. The village leaders forgave my grandmother's indiscretion and accepted my mother into the tribe. But my grandmother never wed—no Gwich'in man would have her. She spent her remaining years in bitterness, abandoned by the father of her only child."

Clay hung his head, as if the unknown white man's deceitful actions had been transferred to him.

Co'Ozhii doubled over in another coughing fit, and when she rose, fury shone in her dark eyes. "The disgrace of my mother's lineage was never mentioned in the village. She wed one of our men, and I was born to their union." Co'Ozhii held out her arm. "I bear the dark skin of my people, but underneath . . . underneath is the blood of the one who wronged my grandmother." She hugged herself, wrapping both arms tight across her middle and burying her hands beneath her armpits. "I prayed to Denali that the white blood would be washed from future generations, but my daughter—my foolish daughter—chose a man with white skin and eyes of blue. I warned her. I told her we would not accept this union, would excommunicate her. But she chose him anyway. And then she gave birth to you." Co'Ozhii's cold gaze fell on Lizzie.

Lizzie stared back, determined to hide the emotions that tumbled wildly through her frame.

"You hold more white blood than even your great-grandmother. More white than Gwich'in. Your mother named you aptly, *White* Feather. You do not belong with us." She rose stiffly, her shoulders slumping as if she bore a great weight. "Do you have your answers now, Lu'qul Gitth'ighi?"

Very slowly, her eyes never wavering from her grandmother's impassive face, Lizzie bobbed her head in a nod.

"Then go." Co'Ozhii, still hugging herself, broke into a new round of coughing. Bent low, she scuttled out of the mission building.

Shruh rose and spoke to Clay and Vivian. "You will not speak of what you heard today to anyone in the village. My wife has spent years burying her shame. I will not have it unearthed by you"—his gaze jerked to include Lizzie—"or you." He drew in a deep breath, turning once more to Clay. "I will summon the other elders, and we will return to extract your promise to honor our tribal law of excommunication." He spun and strode out the door.

Now that her grandparents were gone, Lizzie gave in to the strain of the past minutes. She slumped forward and shook her head, watching the play of her hair swinging across the bodice of the blue gingham dress. "My mother prayed daily to the High One for peace between herself and her parents, but her prayers will be denied. I'll never have peace with them—my grandmother's anger runs too deep within her."

Clay shook loose of Vivian's grasp. He reached past her to cup his hand over Lizzie's. "You can't give up. There's always hope."

Vivian stared at Clay, her green eyes wide. "Didn't you hear the story Co'Ozhii shared? Lizzie is right—the woman holds generations of anger. It will take a miracle for her to set aside her resentment."

"You forget," Clay said softly, "that God can perform miracles."

Lizzie snorted. "You speak of God the way my mother did. But He ignored my mother's pleas. I have no reason to hope He'll listen to mine." With a deep sigh, she pushed from the barrel and stood unsmiling before them. "My being here causes trouble for you. I'll go now, and I won't bother you again." She started toward the door.

Clay leapt up and stepped into her pathway. "Lizzie, I agree that you should go now. Your grandmother asked you to leave, and you'll show respect if you abide by her request. But I don't want you to abandon your friendship with Vivian . . . or me."

Lizzie's heart doubled its tempo. Clay's open admittance that he saw her as a friend moved her more deeply than anything before. He held his hand toward Vivian, and she hurried to his side.

As much as Lizzie appreciated their support, they needed to face truth. "You know what my grandfather requires. If you want to stay here and teach the children, you can't spend time with me anymore." Pain seared her heart, making her wince. "You should be pleased to tell me good-bye. After I hurt you . . . why would you wish time with me?"

Clay shook his head, and something seemed to break across his face—a realization that made Lizzie catch her breath. His lips slowly tipped into a tender smile. "Lizzie, that bullet finding my head was an accident."

"Then you . . . you forgive me?" Lizzie searched Clay's face.

"There's nothing to forgive," Clay said, his smile warm. "Now . . . let's join hands. I want to pray." Clay already held Vivian's hand, but he stretched the other toward Lizzie. Vivian reached, as well. With hesitance, Lizzie grasped hands with them. Clay and Vivian bowed their heads, but Lizzie kept her head erect and her eyes open. She angled her gaze to the doorway, watching for Shruh so she could warn Clay of the man's approach.

Clay began to pray. "Lord, You made it possible for Vivian and me to come to Gwichyaa Saa and share the truth of Your love with the people here. I believe You intend Lizzie to be one of those who experience Your touch."

Something warm and welcoming coiled through Lizzie's middle. She swallowed a lump of desire that seemed to fill her throat and blinked away the sting of tears.

"So I ask that You soften Shruh's and Co'Ozhii's hearts toward Lizzie," Clay continued, his voice sincere yet expectant. "Bring reconciliation between grandparents and grandchild. You are a God of peace, and I ask that peace bloom in this village so that You will be glorified. In Your Son's name I pray. Amen."

As Clay lifted his head, Lizzie pointed to the approaching cluster of men, led by Shruh. "They're coming." She hurried to the door. "I'll go." She paused and glanced back over her shoulder, her gaze bouncing between Clay and Vivian and then lingering on Clay. "I don't expect your God to answer, but I thank you for asking for peace. I will always remember your kindness to me." She slipped out the door and dashed for the sheltering woods.

∽

Clay stepped into the mission's doorway and propped his hand on the doorjamb. Vivian crept up behind him, peering past him to the elders, who moved with slow, purposeful strides toward the mission building. She curled her trembling hand over Clay's shoulder. "Do you really think they'll let us be friends with Lizzie and stay here?"

Clay glanced at her. His brow furrowed. "Don't you believe God answers prayer?"

Vivian recalled her fervent prayers the day of her father's funeral. She'd begged God to bring her precious papa back to life, to remove the horrible burden of his death from her soul. Yet her father lay cold in his grave and the guilt still plagued her.

"What He wills, Vivian, will happen here." Clay sounded more certain than she'd ever heard him. "He sent us to this place. He has a purpose. We'll answer to Him first and men second, and trust that He'll make the way for us to minister to *all* of the Gwich'in people."

Vivian slipped her hand over her skirt pocket, where Aunt Vesta's letter rested—the letter that informed her of Uncle Matthew's illness and held her aunt's heartbreaking appeal for Vivian's return to Hampshire County. How she wanted to honor Aunt Vesta's request. Vesta and Matthew had cared for Vivian in her time of need—could she do any less for her dear aunt and uncle? But she'd committed to helping Clay in his ministry. She must stay for as long as he stayed. And he would stay forever—unless Shruh insisted they leave.

Vivian held her breath as Clay stepped back and allowed the men to enter the mission building. Her heart felt torn in two. If God honored Clay's prayer, they would stay and Aunt Vesta would struggle on without Vivian's help. If God denied Clay's request, she would be able to go to her aunt, but at the cost of many lost souls. *God, I don't know what to ask!*

There weren't enough barrels for everyone to sit, so the men stood in a group with Shruh at the front. He folded his arms over his chest and looked at Clay with lowered brows. "We wait to hear your assurance, Clay Selby. Speak."

Vivian bit down on her lower lip, clinging to Clay's arm. The muscle in his jaw twitched as he drew in a breath that expanded his chest. He opened his mouth to speak, but a childish screech intruded. Vivian jumped back as Clay dashed to the door. The men clustered behind him, murmuring in confusion.

A little girl raced through the center of the village toward the mission, her bare feet raising a small cloud of dust. Tears streamed down her face. Clay stepped out to meet her, and she fell into his arms. She peered up at him with wide, fear-filled eyes and gasped, "Mister Clay, you come. My vitse—she is asleep and Etu cannot wake her. You must wake her for us. Come! Come!"

∽

Lizzie tugged the gate aside and stepped into the dog pen. She crouched down and allowed the furry beasts to swarm her. She relished the warmth of their licking tongues while shifting to avoid their gleefully wagging tails. Her hands stroked napes and scratched ears while she murmured words of endearment. But even while she accepted the dogs' affection, her thoughts drifted elsewhere. Back to the village, to the log enclosure constructed by Clay Selby. His words rang in her memory.

"There's nothing to forgive," he'd said. She'd shot him. She might have killed him. But he held no grudge. Lizzie wrapped her arms around Martha's thick neck while the other dogs continued to bump her shoulders, her back, her hands, begging for her attention. But she barely felt them, reveling in the wonderful feeling of release Clay's words had offered.

And then he'd prayed. His petition for reconciliation between her grandparents and herself echoed again and again in her soul. Deep within her breast, hope flickered. Would God hear? Would God answer? Might her mother, at long last, be able to rest in peace? She released Martha and pushed to her feet. The dogs pressed against her legs, making it difficult for her to move, but she wound her way between them and left the pen.

She'd never found comfort in sitting beside the patch of ground that cradled her mother's body, but for some reason her feet carried her to the back corner of her plot of ground—to the mound of rocks that marked Mama's resting place. She knelt, placing her palms over two rough, sun-warmed stones.

"Mama, I didn't understand until today what you meant about me being more white than Athabascan. Vitse shared the tale of her grandmother—your great-grandmother. Seeing you repeat her grandmother's choice has embittered her against us. But another white man, a man named Clay," —her heart began to thud wildly in her chest as the little flicker of hope tried to ignite a fire of belief—"prayed for peace to bloom between Vitse and Vitsiy and me. If his prayers are answered, then you, too, will have peace. I wish peace for you, Mama."

Lizzie crunched her eyes closed, seeing behind her closed lids her mother kneeling in prayer with her face aimed toward the mighty mountain Denali. Lizzie wanted to seek Denali, too, but fear that the peak would be shrouded in clouds kept her lids firmly closed. She couldn't bear to have her hopes dashed. Not now.

She swallowed the tears that formed in the back of her throat and whispered, "I'll wait to see if peace comes, and then I'll do as you asked and leave here. I will seek my father and live in his world, where you said I belong. But, Mama?" She dared open her eyes, her gaze slowly lifting above the trees in search of the mountain's snowy peak. "My heart longs to stay here, with Clay Selby, just as you must have longed to be with Pa and my great-great-grandmother must have longed for a lifetime with my white great-great-grandfather. And I—"

Her words fell silent, her hopes plummeting. No snowy peak glistened in the sunshine. Only gray, wispy clouds. Disenchantment assailed her. She hung her head, tears burning behind her nose. Her grandmother had called her foolish, and she now accepted the accusation. Only a fool would place her hope in a God she couldn't see.

Chapter Twenty-One

C lay forked another serving of smoked salmon onto a flat piece of bark and handed it to Etu. The boy sank to his haunches and began eating at once. Clay, watching Etu, heaved a sorrowful sigh. With their grandmother's passing, Etu and his younger sister were on their own, but at least for this day they would be well fed. As was customary, every family in the village had contributed food for the funeral dinner. The children, rather than refusing to eat, took full advantage of the potlatch by sampling everything from caribou to steamed squash.

Clay helped himself to something that resembled mashed sweet potatoes and sat on the ground next to Etu. Across the small clearing, Vivian shared a log seat with Naibi. The child sat so close, she was nearly in Vivian's lap. Vivian kept her arm snugly around Naibi's shoulders, occasionally leaning down to whisper something in the little girl's ear. Watching the pair, Clay experienced a rush of appreciation for Vivian's tender care of the child. Naibi needed a woman's affection.

The little girl hadn't left Vivian's side since several village men had carried the lifeless body of her grandmother from their ramshackle log home three days ago. The elders would meet at the end of the day to decide with whom to place the children in the village. Clay intended to ask permission to bring Etu and Naibi into the mission. Their grandmother's death had turned everyone's focus from Lizzie to the children, but as soon as the day of mourning ended, Shruh would no doubt resume his demand for Clay and Vivian to denounce their friendship with Lizzie. Maybe their willingness to provide a home to the children would soften the elderly tribe leader toward them, and he would allow them to stay even if they chose to continue seeing Lizzie.

Etu plopped the empty piece of bark aside and poked Clay on the shoulder. "Mister Clay? Naibi and I have no gifts."

The boy's worried face pierced Clay. Traditionally, the family of the deceased provided gifts to every person attending the burial ceremony. Etu proved his desire to be responsible by wishing to bestow thank-you gifts to those attending his grandmother's funeral, but Clay assumed the village would extend understanding if the two youngsters didn't observe the practice.

He slung his arm around Etu's skinny shoulders. "It's all right, Etu. I think the people know it's hard for you and Naibi to find enough gifts for everyone."

Etu's face didn't clear. "But my grandmother—she will have no honor without gifts." Tears glittered in the boy's dark eyes. "I have a basket of rocks we collected from the riverbank. They are pretty. Could we give one to everyone? As a gift?"

Clay's throat tightened. The more elaborate the gifts, the more honor was given to the deceased. Many might look upon rocks as a very inadequate gift, but Etu was offering the best he had. He tousled the boy's thick hair. "You get the basket, and I will ask your sister to help you distribute them."

A relieved smile lit Etu's face. He shot off.

Clay rose and wove his way through the gathered villagers to Vivian and Naibi. He placed his hand on Vivian's shoulder. "Are you all right?" Dark circles under Vivian's eyes evidenced her lack of sleep.

She offered a weary smile. "Naibi is missing someone."

Clay frowned. Of course the child was missing someone—her grandmother.

Naibi leaned against Vivian's shoulder and peered up at Clay with wide brown eyes. "I want Missus Lizzie. I wish she was here."

Clay's heart caught. Lizzie had kept her promise to stay away. Knowing she was holding herself aloof from him and Vivian made him long for her presence.

Naibi tugged his pant leg. "Missus Lizzie is my friend. I thought all your friends came to the potlatch."

Vivian sent Clay a helpless look. Clay hunkered down and used a strand of Naibi's hair to tickle her nose. He responded in the child's language. "Lizzie does not live in the village, so she probably does not know about your grandmother."

Naibi sighed. "Can we go tell her? I want her to know Vitse is gone."

Etu panted to a halt beside Clay. Rocks rattled in the bottom of the woven basket he cradled against his stomach. "Come, Naibi. We will give everyone a rock for coming to Vitse's funeral."

Naibi hunched her shoulders. Tears pooled in her eyes. "I want to keep my pretty rocks."

Etu stomped his foot. "You will come *now*. The guests will not honor Vitse without gifts."

Clay curled his hand around the back of Etu's neck and gave a gentle squeeze. "Since you are the head of your family now, you present gifts to everyone, Etu."

Etu frowned. "But Vitse is *her* grandmother, too. She should help."

Clay propped his hands on his knees and looked directly into Etu's eyes. "But Naibi is just a little girl, and her heart is hurting. Let Naibi stay here with Missus Vivian."

Naibi stood and smoothed the skirt of her calico dress. "It is all right, Mister Clay. I will help Etu." Resignedly, the child scuffed away after her brother.

Vivian watched them go, her face sad. She patted the spot on the log Naibi had vacated, and Clay sat. Vivian said, "What's going to happen to them, Clay?"

The concern in her tone warmed him. Surely she'd agree with his plan to take the children in. "I intend to ask Shruh to let them stay with us."

Vivian's head swiveled so quickly she nearly unseated herself. "With us?"

He frowned, surprised by her stunned reaction. "Well, yes. You've had Naibi with you the past two nights, just as Etu has stayed with me. They seem secure with us. I'm sure Shruh would allow us to provide for them."

"I didn't know we were opening a boarding school."

Clay nibbled his dry lower lip, pondering Vivian's strange response. He replied cautiously. "Providing sanctuary to Etu and Naibi doesn't mean we're starting a boarding school. The other children will attend during the day, and the families will come for services on Sunday, just as we've planned." *If I ever finish the building*. "Etu and Naibi don't have any other relatives. What are they supposed to do?"

"Have you mentioned this to the children? Have you made promises to them?"

"I asked Etu last night if he would like to stay in the mission house with us. He seemed very relieved to know someone wanted him."

Vivian looked away, her lips twitching as if she'd placed something sour on her tongue. Clay grabbed her hand. "Vivian, what's the matter?"

She jerked her hand free. "You're making promises we might not be able to keep. I don't even know if—" She clamped her lips together.

An uneasy tingle crept across Clay's scalp. "Viv, what are you saying?"

She whirled on him. "Clay, I've needed to talk to you about something for several days, but we haven't had time alone. I received a letter from my aunt in Hampshire County. She asked me—"

"Clay Selby?"

Vivian folded her arms over her chest and stared off to the side. Clay looked up into Da'ago's solemn face.

"It is time to say good-bye to Nara. The children want you to say some words, too."

Clay's heart turned over in his chest. He wasn't Gwich'in, yet he was wanted and needed by two small children. God had to allow him to remain here in Gwichyaa Saa. "I'm coming." Da'ago strode away, and Clay turned to Vivian. "Are you coming?"

She rose, her face resigned. "Of course I'm coming. Naibi and Etu need us. But I must speak with you this evening. It's very important."

✑

Vivian lay on her side, facing Naibi, who slept soundly beside her. Dried tears left shiny trails on the child's cheeks. She'd finally cried herself to sleep half an hour ago. As much as it had pained Vivian to listen to the child's mournful sobs, she couldn't deny impatience at being forced to put off her conversation with Clay again.

204

After the burial, the villagers had danced well into the evening hours. She and Clay had stayed for the dancing, and Clay even joined in—although he'd looked ridiculously out of place in his black wool suit alongside the embellished buckskin tunics of the other dancers. His participation seemed to comfort the children, however, so even if the custom was very different from the solemn funeral affairs of home, Vivian hadn't complained.

When everyone returned to their cabins, she'd asked Clay to join her in the mission building. But Etu clung to Clay's arm, and Naibi clung to Vivian's waist, and Clay had suggested they put off their talk until tomorrow. Would she ever have the chance to tell Clay she needed to leave?

Or maybe I'm not meant to leave.

The thought had teased her mind since Aunt Vesta's letter had arrived. She shifted on the bed, cringing when the pine needles beneath her crackled. But Naibi didn't stir. Vivian carefully rolled to her back and stared at the dark bark ceiling. What should she do?

When she'd stated her intentions to accompany Clay to Alaska and assist him in establishing the mission, her mother and stepfather had done their best to discourage her. They told her the work would be too hard, the frontier too rigorous for her. But finally, they'd given their blessing, and Vivian had inwardly celebrated. She'd have the opportunity to prove herself capable and useful. She'd fully intended to stay in Alaska forever.

Until the letter came, informing her of Uncle Matthew's stroke. Aunt Vesta needed her. When she'd needed somewhere to go—when Mother didn't want her—her aunt and uncle had taken her in. They'd offered the love and security Mother, in her grief and anger over Papa's passing, was unable to give. How could she deny her aunt's request?

She had to go to Massachusetts. Clay would understand. He was strong and able—he'd be able to run the mission by himself. What did he need her for, anyway? *Cooking, cleaning, teaching the children to read . . .* Would he be able to do all of that and preach, too? Vivian pushed aside the arguments that filled her mind. He could hire a native woman to cook and clean. As for the teaching, he knew how to read and write. Anyone who knew how to perform the tasks could show someone else how to do them.

Even if she had only a few snatches of time with Clay tomorrow, a few minutes would be enough to say what needed saying. She practiced the statement, whispering into the quiet night, "Clay, Aunt Vesta needs me and I'm going to Huntington." She waited for a feeling of satisfaction to wash over her, but instead a cloak of dread seemed to fall from the ceiling and smother her.

Naibi wriggled, moaning in her sleep. Vivian automatically reached out to rub the child's back. The child quieted, curling her body until it nestled against Vivian's side.

When Vivian finally fell asleep much later, tears were still drying on her cheeks.

Chapter Twenty-Two

I f you really must go, I understand." Clay forced the assurance past stiff lips. Underneath, he raged against Vivian's proclamation that she was needed elsewhere. As much as he'd originally balked about bringing her, he'd come to depend on her. And now she wanted to leave. He supposed he should have expected as much—they all knew Vivian was too fragile for this harsh lifestyle.

He set his fork aside and patted his stepsister's arm. "I'll contact the Mission Board as soon as possible and make arrangements for your transport to the States."

Vivian sighed, her head low. She dabbed at the gravy in her plate with a folded piece of bread. "Thank you, Clay." For someone who'd just been given approval to do what she wished, she didn't seem happy. "How . . . how long do you think it will be . . . before you hear from the board?"

Clay pushed his empty plate aside and rested his elbows on the table's edge. "Given the slow nature of communication, I would assume two weeks at least." Two weeks—he'd need to use the time to complete the sleeping rooms inside the mission building. Etu and Naibi could share one, and he'd take the other one.

"I'm glad you'll have the children with you." Vivian lifted her chin and offered a sad smile. "At least you won't be alone."

Clay nodded. He'd been greatly relieved when Shruh had agreed to allow him to assume responsibility for the children. Now, knowing Vivian wouldn't share in the caretaking, he hoped he hadn't taken on more than he could comfortably handle. But Vivian was right—the children would be company. And, he reassured himself, they could help in the mission.

Etu had already proven his usefulness by helping chink the walls. Naibi was small, but she could push a broom and wield a dust rag. Even if they couldn't teach or cook, as he'd planned for Vivian to do, they were willing to assist through whatever means they could. The moment they'd finished supper this evening, they'd dashed off in search of berries so Vivian could bake a pie. He should ask her to teach him so he'd be able to bake pies after she'd left.

"Do you suppose Shruh's consent for you to care for Etu and Naibi means he won't cast you away from the village?"

Clay considered Vivian's question. He still hadn't openly declared his intention to abandon his relationship with Lizzie, but Shruh and the others had stopped pressing him. An odd sickness had entered the village—a deep, wracking cough accompanied by fever—and the villagers' focus had shifted to fighting the illness. Co'Ozhii was among those stricken, and Shruh spent his days with her.

"I pray so," he finally answered.

Vivian began clearing their dishes.

He followed her outside to the wash bucket. "I'll send word to the Mission Board as quickly as I can." He watched her make a stack of the dishes on the half-log that served as a work surface. "But until we receive a reply, it would be helpful if you'd continue here as usual. I'd rather the children didn't know you were leaving until we have a date set. They've already lost so much."

Vivian cringed. Her hands stilled in their task, and she sucked in a long breath. She held it for several seconds, and then released it. Raising her head, she sent Clay a repentant look. "I don't want to leave, Clay. Honestly. I wish . . ." She lowered her gaze again, biting down on her lower lip. Tears glittered briefly in her eyes, and she blinked several times. "I wish things could be different, but Aunt Vesta needs me. How can I refuse her?"

"You can't." Clay hadn't meant to speak so abruptly, but his inner frustrations came through against his will.

Vivian pinched her lips into a scowl that seemed half rebellious, half regretful. "Aunt Vesta and Uncle Matthew took me in when Mother didn't want me. They didn't have to love me, but they—"

Clay frowned. "What do you mean, your mother didn't want you?"

Vivian released a little huff, fixing Clay with a chastising look. "Come now, Clay, if you know how my father died, you surely know that my mother could no longer bear to look at me. I served as a reminder of his death. So she sent me away."

Shaking his head, Clay plopped down on the far end of the worktable. "She sent you to your aunt and uncle to protect you. She knew establishing the mission in Oklahoma would be even more rugged than living on the Dakota plains. She wanted what was best for you."

Another disbelieving huff left Vivian's lips.

Clay grabbed her hand. "Viv, believe me—you weren't sent away as punishment, but as protection."

She refused to meet his gaze.

With a sigh, he released her hand. "But don't worry about me. I'll be fine. You go do . . . what you need to do."

Without a word, she went back to clinking dishes together.

Clay considered pursuing her flawed beliefs about why she'd been sent to Massachusetts, but the stubborn jut of her jaw dissuaded him. Instead, he made a silent note to write to his stepmother and encourage her to send assurances to Vivian. Maybe Myrtle would be more convincing. The decision made, he changed topics.

"I assume you'll want as much time as possible with Lizzie before you go." He leaned against the mission wall and crossed his ankles, hoping his relaxed pose would decrease the tension between them. "She hasn't learned all she needs to know to live in San Francisco, has she?"

"No. And I still need to finish sewing her—" Vivian's face flamed. She snatched up the bucket. "I'm going after water." She bustled off, leaving Clay wondering what she'd meant to say. As Vivian headed for the river, Etu and Naibi burst from the brush at the opposite side of the village.

Etu held out the basket. "We found many berries, Mister Clay!" The boy, his face flushed and sweaty, beamed. He looked around. "Where is Missus Vivian? I want to see if this is enough."

"We want two pies—one for each of us." Naibi held up two pudgy, purple-stained fingers, her smile bright. "She will bake them, yes?"

"I'm sure she will," Clay assured the pair, "but not until tomorrow. It's too close to bedtime. Put the berries inside the mission, and then take the buckets to the river for water. You two need to wash before you turn in."

The children groaned. Etu groused, "Mister Clay, you are always making us too clean."

"Cleanliness is next to godliness," Clay quipped. The

children's brows furrowed in confusion. Clay laughed. "Being clean is a good thing. It will keep you from getting sick. Now do as I said."

They grumbled under their breath, but they moved to obey. Once they were heading down the pathway toward the river, each swinging a bucket, Clay stepped inside the mission and turned a slow circle, examining the structure with a critical eye. He'd made a great deal of progress, but there was still much to accomplish. The sense of urgency that plagued him whenever he thought of his purpose here returned, but even stronger than before. Vivian's departure would change so many things.

He closed his eyes and bowed his head. "When she leaves, Lord, I'll have to do my own cooking, cleaning, and clothes washing. I'll have to teach as well as preach. I've come to rely on her assistance, and now I wonder . . . can I truly run this mission on my own? I need a helper, Lord—one who has the strength and desire to live in this untamed land."

Behind his closed eyelids, a picture formed of Lizzie standing tall and proud in the face of Shruh's fury. His eyes popped open and he shook his head hard, dispelling the image. He couldn't rely on Lizzie—she wasn't welcome in the village, and she intended to leave. Clay's shoulders sagged in defeat. Unless the Mission Board sent someone from the States to be his assistant, he would be on his own.

I don't think I can do it, Lord. Please help me.

∽

Lizzie filled the dogs' water trough and made her way out of the pen, holding her skirts well above her ankles to keep from catching them on the wire enclosure. Outside the pen, she let the folds of fabric fall, and she moved easily across the ground toward her cabin.

Over the weeks of wearing the blue-checked dress, she'd finally begun feeling comfortable in the full, sweeping skirts and snug-fitting bodice. The hem of the dress appeared frayed, however, and she'd rubbed one spot on the back of the skirt nearly all the way through on her cleaning stone trying to remove a sticky smear of pine sap. The weary-looking gown was fine for working, but she would certainly shame her father if she appeared at his doorstep in the dress.

She entered her cabin and crossed to the stove to check the pan of corn bread she'd prepared earlier. It looked browned, so she used her skirts to protect her hands and removed it. She set it on the windowsill to cool, then stood staring out at the quiet side yard. Ever since her encounter with Vitse and Vitsiy, she'd caught herself on several occasions staring unseeingly across the grounds.

The realization that she truly was more white than Athabascan had come as a shock, and she wondered if the recognition should change how she viewed the world. Yet her eyes took in the same familiar fern- and moss-covered ground, the same thick pin cherry bushes and tall aspens, the same garden plot awaiting her attention. Nothing on the outside had changed. So why did she feel so different on the inside?

Giving herself a little shake, she moved to the bureau Pa had used to store his clothing and picked up the comb Vivian had left for her. She combed her thick hair back from her face and twisted it into a rope that she then formed into a heavy coil. She jabbed pins into the coil until she could tug on it and it didn't shift. Satisfied her hair was secure, she moved back to the windowsill and checked the corn bread. Steam no longer rose from the mealy bread—she could eat.

But the moment she sat, her hunger fled. She linked her hands in her lap and stared at the empty spaces around the table. Loneliness assailed her with such intensity, tears stung. She closed her eyes, striving to imagine Pa and Mama seated at the table with her. But instead of images of her parents appearing in her mind's eye, Clay and Vivian Selby emerged. She slapped the tabletop, and the images scooted into the shadows.

"I need to eat," she told herself, using her firmest voice. She had work to do and must be well nourished. She broke a chunk of bread free of the pan and plopped it on her plate. After slathering the bread with honey, she stabbed her fork into the crumbly chunk and lifted a bite. But she didn't put it in her mouth. Dropping the fork, she snatched up the plate and headed for the slop bucket to dispose of the corn bread. Just as she tipped the plate, her dogs began to whimper, and then she heard someone call her name.

Jerking upright, Lizzie sought the source of the sound. Etu and Naibi burst into her yard and darted straight for the dog pen. Lizzie set the plate aside and jogged across the ground to meet them. Joy at seeing them battled with worry about them journeying through the woods, unprotected.

She caught their arms, drawing them away from the pen. "Did I not tell you to never come here again?" she scolded in Athabascan.

"You said not to come alone." Etu pulled his arm free and pointed toward the woods. "Missus Vivian brought us."

Vivian stepped out of the brush and hurried to join them. Her cheeks were flushed, and her breath came in little puffs. She shook her finger at the children. "Shame on you for running ahead that way," she scolded the children in English. "You need to stay with me." She removed a pack from her shoulders and dropped it on the ground beside her feet, then fanned herself with both hands. She sent a weary smile in Lizzie's direction. "These two are as nimble-footed as a pair of squirrels. I couldn't keep up with them."

Lizzie gave the children's arms a little shake and used English in deference to Vivian. "You listen to Missus Vivian and stay with her from now on." Sighing, she addressed Vivian. "Their grandmother needs to keep a better watch over them—they're good children, but she lets them run too wild."

Naibi's lower lip poked out. "Vitse . . . her spirit goes. We bury her body."

Lizzie's jaw fell. "W-what?"

"You did not come to potlatch." Etu's voice held a hint of accusation.

"When?" Lizzie pressed her palms to her aching chest.

Vivian answered quietly. "A week ago."

"Oh, Etu and Naibi . . ." Memories of her first painful days after her mother's death returned. Sympathy welled, bringing a rush of tears. Lizzie dropped to her knees and embraced both children. Naibi nestled against Lizzie's shoulder, but Etu stood stiffly within her encircling arm. "I'm so sorry your vitse is gone." She looked at Vivian over Naibi's shoulder. "What happened to her?"

Vivian shrugged, her face sad. "Perhaps she just drifted away, as older people sometimes do. Perhaps the sickness claimed her. We aren't sure."

"Sickness?"

Etu pulled loose. He abandoned English for his more familiar Athabascan. "Some people in the village are sick. They cough and get very hot. Mister Clay is worried their spirits will leave, the way Vitse's did."

Lizzie's heart clutched in fear. When she'd seen her grandmother, the woman had been coughing. Might her

214

grandmother die, too? Two conflicting thoughts collided in the center of Lizzie's mind: If Vitse were gone, the village might finally accept her into their fold. But if Vitse died, her opportunity for restored peace would die with her. For which should she hope?

Chapter Twenty-Three

Lizzie pushed to her feet and forced her lips into a smile her heart didn't feel. "Children, there is a pan of corn bread and a jug of honey on my table. Would you like some?"

Without hesitation, the pair dashed toward the house.

Vivian watched after them, shaking her head. "They just finished breakfast—flapjacks and fried fish—before we walked over here. They shouldn't be hungry." Then her face pursed into a grimace of sympathy. "But I suppose their last weeks with their grandmother, when food was far from plentiful, affected their appetites. They would eat constantly if I let them."

Lizzie brushed the bits of grass from her knees. A few green smears remained, marring the blue-checked cloth. "The children are staying with you?"

"For now." Pain flashed briefly in Vivian's eyes.

"This sickness . . ." Lizzie chose her words carefully. "Have any other villagers succumbed to it?"

"Not yet." Vivian sighed. "But both Clay and I are concerned. If things don't improve soon, Clay intends to canoe to Fort Yukon and request assistance from the doctor."

Lizzie released a soft snort. "No doctor will come to the village."

"But perhaps he'll tell Clay how to treat the illness and provide him with some medicine," Vivian replied.

Lizzie doubted a white doctor would even offer that much help to the villagers, but she didn't say so.

Vivian drew a deep breath. "Lizzie, while the children are occupied, I need to talk to you about something important."

A prickle of trepidation wound its way down Lizzie's spine. She pointed to the garden. "Can you talk while I weed? My plants need attention."

"You weed and I'll stitch," Vivian said. She picked up the bundle she'd dropped and followed Lizzie to the garden plot. Lizzie reached for her hoe, and Vivian seated herself on the grass with her feet tucked to the side. She withdrew several cut pieces of creamy-looking cloth, thread, and a slim silver needle.

Lizzie chop-chopped the ground, one eye on the plants, one eye on Vivian. "What are you making?"

Vivian shot a quick glance toward the cabin before replying. "Your . . . pantaloons. Drawers to wear beneath your dress." She cleared her throat, zipping the needle in and out of the cloth. "I finished the chemise and petticoats last week. I brought them along for you."

Lizzie moved forward a few feet and gently hacked at the ground around the squash. "So many items . . . and I must wear them all, every day?"

Vivian set her lips in a stern line and nodded.

"It will take some getting used to. . . ."

"You'll manage." Vivian flashed a smile. "When you're

finished here and we go into the cabin, I'll show you what else I brought you."

Lizzie raised her eyebrows in silent query, her hands slowing.

"Two beautiful gowns. Even though I'm . . ." For a moment, Vivian seemed to drift away, her eyes clouding. Then she gave herself a little shake. "They will be perfect for you when you go to San Francisco."

Lizzie paused, two-fisting the hoe and resting her cheek against her knuckles. "You said you had something important to tell me."

The pain Lizzie had glimpsed earlier returned and then quickly disappeared when Vivian raised her chin and squared her shoulders. She dropped the cloth to her lap and pinned Lizzie with a serious look. "I wanted you to know I will be leaving soon, so our lessons together will come to an end."

Lizzie blinked in surprise. Her heart seemed to trip within her chest. "You and C-Clay are leaving?"

"Not Clay. Only me."

Lizzie's confusion grew. "But I thought you intended to remain in Alaska and help C-Clay." Embarrassment heated her cheeks. Why couldn't she speak the man's name without stammering? She put the hoe to work to cover her blunder.

Vivian lifted the pieces of cloth and returned to stitching, her brow puckered. "My uncle has fallen ill, and my aunt needs my assistance in caring for him. So as soon as the Mission Board that sent Clay and me to Alaska gives approval, I shall depart for Massachusetts."

Lizzie narrowed her eyes and peered hard at Vivian. "Massachusetts . . . to an aunt and uncle." She tapped the hoe a couple of times and then said, "You must love them very much to go to them."

Without pausing in her stitching, Vivian nodded. "I owe

them a great deal. They took care of me when my mother sent me away."

Lizzie froze. Vivian's words reminded her of Co'Ozhii rejecting Lizzie's mother and, subsequently, Lizzie. Curiosity overcame her usual reserve. Leaning on the hoe, she asked, "What sin did you commit for your mother to send you away?"

Vivian's chin quivered. "I . . . I killed my father."

The hoe fell from Lizzie's hands.

Cheerful cries intruded, and Etu and Naibi ran from the cabin toward the women. "Missus Lizzie, can we play with the dogs?" Etu asked.

Lizzie picked up the hoe with shaking hands and leaned it on the wire mesh that surrounded her garden. "Not all of them. You wouldn't be able to control them. But I'll release Martha for you—she will enjoy a time of play." The children scampered along beside her as she moved to the dog pen. She smiled in reply to their thanks and patted Martha's head as if all was well, but underneath, her thoughts churned. Vivian—so sweet and well-mannered and *weak*—had killed her own father? Her feet stumbled on the way back to the garden plot, her limbs stiff in response to the startling revelation.

Vivian met Lizzie's gaze. "You're shocked."

Shocked couldn't begin to define how Lizzie felt. She picked up the hoe, but she didn't put it to use. "I would not have taken you for a . . . a murderer."

Vivian winced. "When Clay stated his intentions to come to Alaska and develop a mission where he would win souls for the Lord, I saw an opportunity to redeem my own soul. I hoped, by working hard, I might absolve myself of the great burden of guilt. Perhaps, had I been given enough time, I might have discovered freedom, but now . . ." Tears flooded the woman's green eyes. "I can only hope that caring for my uncle will accomplish the same objective and God will accept my efforts as sufficient atonement."

Lizzie crossed to the edge of the garden. "How did it happen?"

Vivian blinked rapidly and took up the needle again. Her fingers worked busily while she spun a tale of a little girl, a lunch basket, a working man's errant swing of an axe, a serpent slithering at a child's feet, and the child running in terror rather than delivering the basket. Vivian finished on a strangled moan. "Had I gone to him, as my mother directed, I could have saved him. The doctor said if help had reached him in time, he would not have bled to death. But help didn't come because, in cowardice, I ran and hid."

Lizzie carefully processed the story. Then she left the garden and knelt beside Vivian. She took the woman's hand between her palms. "You didn't swing the axe. You didn't kill him."

Vivian jerked her hand free, glaring at Lizzie. "I let him die!"

"But you didn't know he was hurt." Lizzie frowned, puzzled over Vivian's stubborn refusal to see the truth. "How could you have known? It's foolish to blame yourself."

Vivian stared at Lizzie, her mouth set in a grim line and her eyes wide and angry. "Who else can I blame?"

The children's laughter drifted across the yard, filling Lizzie's ears. Despite their recent loss, Etu and Naibi still found reasons for joy. A romp in the sunshine with a tongue-lolling dog, and all was well. If only happiness could be restored so easily to her friend.

She turned her attention back to Vivian. "When I shot Clay, you did not blame me. Why?"

Vivian blinked several times, her brow furrowing. "You didn't deliberately shoot him. It was an accident."

"But if he'd died—if I had killed him, even by accident—would you have blamed me?"

For several seconds, Vivian sat in silence. When she spoke, her voice sounded raspy, as if her throat was very dry. "I would have mourned, and I might have struggled to find the ability to forgive you, but knowing it was an accident, I would have forgiven you."

Lizzie took Vivian's hand again, squeezing hard. "If you could forgive me, then why can you not forgive yourself?"

∽

Clay pounded an upright half log into place, finishing the frame for the doorway leading to the second sleeping room. He wiped the sweat from his brow and stepped back to admire the fruits of his labor. Portioning off the front third of the mission school to create sleeping rooms resulted in a much smaller sanctuary than he'd originally planned, but careful arrangements of benches would provide enough seating space for both school work and church services.

He headed to the water bucket for a drink. After guzzling two full dippers of water, he splashed a third over his face, shuddering as the cool water dribbled down his hot skin. He glanced toward the village, frowning at how few people gathered in their yards as the evening hours approached. Many of the villagers remained in their cabins rather than mingling together as was their normal custom. The fever had everyone nervous.

Clay whispered a heartfelt prayer for the illness to run its course quickly without claiming any other lives, then he headed back inside to determine what else he could accomplish before bedtime. He ran his hand along the newly constructed wall, noting the large cracks between logs that would require chinking. He might have been able to get a large portion of the chinking completed today if he'd kept Etu with him instead of letting him go to Lizzie's with Vivian. But knowing the children would soon have to say good-bye to her, he'd chosen to allow them the day together. Besides, Vivian had put off telling Lizzie of her plans for too long. His heart panged. He wasn't ready to say good-bye to his stepsister or the blue-eyed native woman. He'd be very alone when they were both gone.

His stomach rumbled, and he checked his timepiece. Nearly seven o'clock. He frowned. Why hadn't Vivian and the children returned? They'd left right after breakfast. He hadn't expected them to stay away all day. He scrounged in the barrels and crates lurking in the corner of the mission building and found a half loaf of bread, some dried meat, and a tin can of peaches. A dismal supper, but far better than nothing. He sat at the makeshift table and ate his simple meal while watching out the window for Vivian's return.

Not until a little after eight did she and the children emerge from the brush. Etu held a fat grouse by its feet, and Naibi carried a small burlap bag. They both dashed to Clay when they spotted him sitting outside the building.

"Mister Clay, Mister Clay!" Etu waved the grouse in Clay's face. "Missus Lizzie helped me make a snare, and already I caught a bird! Missus Vivian says she will cook it for our breakfast!"

Clay duly admired the bird before turning to Naibi. He asked in their language, "And what did you catch?"

Naibi giggled. "Mushrooms. But I only had to pick them."

Clay smacked his lips, and both children laughed. He gestured to the mission door and spoke in simple English. They'd never learn it if he didn't use it regularly. "Put your prizes inside. Then wash. When you are clean, I will show you your new sleeping room."

The children raced for the door. Clay caught Vivian's elbow and drew her to the far corner of the building, away from the children's listening ears. "You were gone much longer than I expected. Did you have a good day with Lizzie?" A little prickle of jealousy teased the back of his heart.

"We spent most of the afternoon sewing, and she showed Etu how to make that snare." A soft smile lit Vivian's tired face. "He was so proud when he found the grouse caught in it. His chest puffed so much I thought he might pop the buttons off his shirt."

Clay chuckled, imagining the boy's delight. "Did you tell her you plan to leave soon?"

Vivian's smile faded. "Yes. And we had a talk that . . ." She paused, sucking in her lips and pinching her brow. "Clay, I'm doing the right thing, aren't I?"

"You mean by leaving?"

She nodded.

Clay shrugged. "Viv, I can't tell you what's right for you. You have to make the choice. Your aunt needs you—I understand why you want to go."

Vivian hung her head, heaving a mighty sigh. "I want to go . . . but I also want to stay. I'm very confused."

"Have you prayed about it?" His father's standard question to every dilemma slid easily from Clay's lips.

"Yes, but—"

"Mister Clay!" Etu and Naibi thundered to Clay's side. Naibi tugged at his shirt while Etu held out his hands. The boy said, "We wash our hands and faces. Show us our room now!"

Clay allowed the children to drag him toward the mission door, but he looked at Vivian over his shoulder. Her forlorn expression pulled at his heart. As soon as he got the children settled in their room, he planned to sit down and try to draw out Vivian's reasons for melancholy.

But by the time he'd helped them arrange their beds and few belongings in their new space, Vivian had already retreated into her hut. He decided she'd had a long day and he should let her rest. He headed to his room in the mission school with the silent promise to carve out time to speak with her tomorrow.

Chapter Twenty-Four

Clay handed Vivian her valise. Apprehension churned in his middle as he looked beyond her to the paddleboat that would transport her to Fairbanks. From there, she would catch a train for the second leg of her lengthy journey through Canada, into the United States, and eventually to Massachusetts. "I don't feel right, sending you by yourself." Anything could happen to a woman traveling alone.

Vivian lips twitched into a funny half smile. "I'll be all right, Clay. Don't worry." She released a light laugh. "These next weeks of travel will be good for me. I'll have to depend on myself rather than on someone else."

"Remember God is only a prayer away," Clay said. He committed to praying daily for her safety and strength. "He'll always be there for you."

"I know." The words carried surety, but her tone lacked confidence. Before he could say anything else, she tipped forward and planted a kiss on his cheek. "Take good care of Etu and Naibi. As soon as they've learned to write, have them send me letters." Tears flooded her eyes. "I . . . I shall miss them." She tugged a handkerchief from her reticule and dabbed her cheeks.

The paddleboat captain blasted the air horn, and Vivian jumped. Their gazes connected, and he said, "It's time." She gave a slight nod, and he escorted her onto the boat. At the end of the gangplank, he gave her a hug and whispered, "Take care, Viv. Send me word when you get there, and I pray you will—" He stopped himself before he uttered, "heal." He wished he'd had the time to help her overcome whatever fear or pain held her captive. He felt as though he'd failed her somehow.

"You write, too, so I know how the people of Gwichyaa Saa are faring." She backed up slowly, the valise bouncing against her knees. Her eyes glittered, but she blinked several times and gave him a wobbly smile. "And take the children to see Lizzie—she'll be lonely without their company."

"I will—as often as I can." His heart skipped a beat as he made the promise. He wanted the children to have time with Lizzie, but he wanted time with her, too. All too soon, she would leave, and he would lose the opportunity to share God's unfailing love with her. As if in response to his inner thoughts, his feet shuffled backward, carrying him to the shore.

Workers dashed out to release the restraining ropes, setting the paddleboat free of the moorings. Clay waved his hand over his head. "Good-bye, Viv! God bless you!"

She waved back, wind tossing little strands of hair around her face. Then she turned from the spindled railing and left the deck. With Vivian gone, Clay had no reason to remain on the bank staring across the water, but his feet remained rooted for several minutes. Behind him, men loaded boxes, barrels, and sacks into waiting wagons. Voices—some angry, others pleading—filled the air. Life in Fort Yukon went on as usual, but for Clay, everything had changed. He was now on his own.

But didn't you just tell Vivian God is only a prayer away?

The admonition might have come from the heavens, it resounded so loudly in his head. He was the worst kind of hypocrite, standing there feeling alone after lecturing Vivian on the same topic. Slapping his hat onto his head, he turned and forced himself to wend his way through the milling activity of the docks to the center of Fort Yukon in search of the doctor. After several inquiries, someone directed him to one of the local saloons.

Unpleasant aromas—stale tobacco smoke, yeasty beer, and men's body odors—assaulted his nose as he stepped into the rough wood structure. He breathed as shallowly as possible as he made his way to the bar, where the doctor hunched over a tall mug of amber liquid. He cleared his throat to gain the man's attention. The doctor turned his bleary gaze in Clay's direction and grunted.

"Sir, I wondered if I could purchase some medicine from you." Clay explained the malady spreading from one villager to another. "I fear there will be deaths if we're not able to bring the fever under control."

The doctor took a swig of his drink and backhanded his lips. "Have it here in Fort Yukon, too. Somebody brought it in and it's been bouncing all around town. Spreads like a bad habit."

"So you have a medicine that works?"

"Nope." The man pushed off the stool and stood before Clay, wavering slightly. "Just been telling everybody to keep to themselves—less likely to catch it that way."

Clay restrained a snort—the doctor might be telling people to keep to themselves, but based on the number of folks he'd just seen working at the docks and frequenting the stores, they weren't listening. "So there's no treatment?"

"Treatment's simple—ply 'em with whiskey for the cough, keep the patient cool, and hold off on feeding them 'til the fever's run its course."

Considering how long some of the villagers had suffered from the fever, they might very well starve the victims to death if he followed the doctor's advice. Clay scowled at the man. "Are you sure this is what you're telling everyone, or is the treatment only for the natives?"

The doctor scowled back. He pointed a stubby finger at Clay. "Don't be hurling insults at me, young man. I took a pledge to treat all folks the same. I'm telling you what I'd advise anybody, and that's a fact." The man whirled toward the barkeeper. "Sell this fellow the biggest bottle of whiskey you got." He squinted at Clay. "Tablespoon as needed to stop the cough. That's the best I can do for you."

Even though Clay knew he should hurry back to the village—he'd left Etu and Naibi in the care of an older Athabascan girl named Nayeli—he decided to make a stop at Lizzie's cabin and check on her well-being. Vivian hadn't mentioned Lizzie coughing or seeming ill, but he'd seen how quickly the sickness could strike. He'd rest easier if he knew she was all right.

As he approached her clearing, he heard her dogs bark in warning. Having had a bullet bounce off his skull once, he didn't care to repeat the experience. He paused and cupped his hands beside his mouth. "Lizzie! Lizzie Dawson! It's me—Clay. Can I come onto your yard?"

A shrill whistle pierced the air, and the dogs fell silent. Then he heard her call, "Come ahead."

His pulse immediately sped. He pressed his palm to his chest, willing his heart to settle down. The threat of being fired upon was gone—so why the racing heartbeat? He pushed through the brush to enter her yard. And when he caught sight of her, his heart fired into his throat and lodged, making it difficult for him to draw a breath.

Lizzie stood just outside her cabin, attired in a buttery, swoop-skirted gown bedecked with layers of frothy lace. The pale yellow accented her glimmering hair of darkest night and made her eyes appear even more vividly blue. He came to a stumbling halt, staring in shock at the change. Vivian had worked a miracle in transforming the earthy native woman into a lady of culture.

"Y-you're beautiful." Clay spoke without thinking.

Lizzie toyed with a stray strand of hair that lay along her long, graceful neck. "Th-thank you." She drew her hands down the length of the gown, her expression bashful. "I was missing Vivian, so I tried on one of the dresses she gave me. I . . . I did not realize I would have anyone visit."

Clay gulped, happy he'd taken the time to stop by. He wouldn't have wanted to miss seeing Lizzie in such finery. He whistled through his teeth, shaking his head in wonder. "You will certainly set the city of San Francisco on its ear when you arrive."

She took a step closer, revealing a bare foot beneath the gown's hem. Her dusky toes poking out from the flurry of lace amused him. "I don't care about the city. I only care about one man."

Clay nearly staggered. "Do . . . do you have a beau in San Francisco?"

"A beau?" Her brow puckered for a moment, then cleared. "No. My father is there."

Clay's jaw dropped. "You *know* your father?" He regretted his impulsive outburst when she folded her arms over her chest and gave him a stony glare.

"Of course I do. He built this cabin. He lived here with my mother and me until my twelfth year."

Clay gentled his voice. "And you've been in touch with him over the years? He wants you to come to California?"

Lizzie's face didn't change expression, but something akin to desperation flickered in her eyes. "Why would he not? He is my father. Would not any father want his child to be with him?"

Clay wondered why her father hadn't taken her with him in the first place, but before he could ask, she continued.

"My mother wished me to go to him. I intend to honor her request." She turned her gaze to the side, releasing a sad sigh. "I have nothing holding me here anymore."

Clay wished he could gather her in his arms and ask if he might be a reason to stay. But he jammed his fists into his pockets and pushed the desire aside. It would be selfish to ask her to change her plans. Yet worry nibbled at the back of his mind. "Lizzie, have you been in contact with your father? Does he know you're coming?"

Lizzie set her lips in a firm line. She smoothed a few dark tendrils of hair from her cheek and raised her chin. "Did you come today for a reason?"

Clay blinked twice, scrambling for the initial purpose of his call. He rubbed his finger beneath his nose to rein in his galloping thoughts. "I wanted to make sure you were well. We have a sickness in the village." He patted the bag that hung from his shoulder, made bulky by the rectangular whiskey bottle. "If you need medicine, I'll leave some for you."

Lizzie's eyebrows flew high. "The doctor—he gave you medicine for the Gwich'in people?"

Clay made a face. "Well, not medicine exactly. He said there wasn't medicine for this sickness. But . . ." He slipped the bottle free and held it up. "This should help with the cough."

The gown's gentle movements made Lizzie appear to float as she glided across the grass to reach him. She leaned forward and read the bottle's label, then pulled back with a sour look on her face. "Spirits. That isn't medicine. It steals a man's intelligence."

Did she think he would be foolhardy enough to encourage drunkenness? Under ordinary circumstances, he wouldn't offer whiskey to anyone, but the sick people needed relief. "I'll only give a small amount to anyone who has the cough."

Lizzie didn't look reassured.

Her lack of confidence pierced him. He slipped the bottle back into his bag. "Now that I know you're all right, I suppose—"

She held her hand to him. "My grandmother . . . she is one of the sick ones?"

Clay nodded. "Yes, Co'Ohzii was one of the first to fall ill." He wouldn't tell Lizzie how worried he was about the older woman. Even though she refused to allow him to visit, he'd gotten a glimpse of her thin, pale face when he'd knocked on the door and Shruh opened it wide enough for him to peek in. He didn't approve of drinking alcohol, but if the liquid in the bottle would stifle her cough and allow her to rest and recover, he'd make sure Shruh gave it to her.

Lizzie looked to the side. Clay watched a myriad of emotions—fear, anger, worry, and finally grim resignation—play across her features before she jerked her gaze to meet his again.

Her expression turned pleading. "Send Etu and Naibi to me. Here, away from the village, they will be less likely to fall ill, too."

Clay worried his lip between his teeth. Her suggestion

made sense, but he didn't relish losing the children's companionship. Besides, Shruh had entrusted them to him. If he sent them away, to a woman banished from the tribe, the man would have further reason to condemn Clay. "I . . . I'm not sure that's wise. . . ."

Lizzie's brow pinched. "You do not trust me to care for the children?"

"I trust you," Clay assured her. He explained his hesitation.

Lizzie's expression gentled. She offered a nod that made her hair bob up and down. "But would they not be safer away from the sickness? Surely Shruh couldn't fault you for trying to protect the children he placed in your care."

Clay contemplated Lizzie's reasoning. The children would be safer here, where the cough couldn't reach them. He'd be lonely without them, but he'd also be free to work long and hard and finally finish the mission building. Of course he'd visit them daily to be certain they fared well . . . which meant he'd see Lizzie each day.

He drew in a steadying breath. "It's a fine idea, Lizzie." *Very fine.* "I'll bring them tomorrow morning."

Chapter Twenty-Five

"Missus Lizzie?"

Lizzie glanced over her shoulder, and a fond smile pulled at her lips. Naibi, faithful as a puppy dog, followed Lizzie between the rows of corn. The child asked endless questions, but Lizzie didn't mind. Over her week of caring for the children, they'd weaseled their way firmly into her heart.

"Yes? What do you want now?" She fingered a plump ear, checking for signs of readiness.

"Why do you live here all alone instead of in the village with Dine'e?"

Lizzie jerked, the innocent question stabbing like a knife in her breast. How could she explain that the People had no use for her? It would be far too confusing for a girl of such tender years. "I . . . I like it here. It's my home." She moved to the next tall, rustling stalk.

"But don't you get lonely?" Naibi imitated Lizzie's actions, gently pinching an ear while her face crunched in concentration.

Lizzie drew in a deep breath. She wouldn't lie to the child. "Sometimes." *But my loneliness will soon end. Soon I will be with my father.* She forced a grin, tweaking Naibi's nose. "But I have you and Etu."

The little girl pinned Lizzie with a serious stare. "But Etu and I will leave soon. When the sickness is gone, we will go back to the village and live in the mission building. So you will be alone again." Her expression turned hopeful. "But you have George and Martha and Thomas and all the other dogs. So you will not be lonely, yes?"

The child's concern warmed Lizzie to the center of her being. "I'll be fine."

"Good." Naibi threw her arms around Lizzie's middle and hugged her hard. She tilted her head back, her tangled bangs catching in her thick eyelashes. "And we will come visit you—me and Etu and Mister Clay."

Mister Clay . . . Her heart gave a happy skip at the sound of his name. He'd stopped by her cabin every day to check on the children. The exuberant pair always raced across the yard to greet him. With effort, she'd managed to suppress her desire to follow their example and run into his arms. It would be foolhardy to express her growing feelings for the kindhearted man who bestowed hugs and smiles on the children—he was here to serve the village, and she was preparing for a life far away from the village. Admitting the affection that blossomed ever greater with each visit would only lead to heartache.

"That would be wonderful." Lizzie returned Naibi's hug. "But for now, Etu caught a rabbit in his snare—we need to fry it up. So let's go wash our hands and prepare our lunch."

Naibi crinkled her nose. "You are like Mister Clay. Always wash, wash, wash." She giggled and raced out of the garden, her bare feet pounding the grass.

Lizzie followed more slowly. *You are like Mister Clay.* The child's comment rang in her mind. Perhaps in that one way, she and Clay were alike. And in their shared fondness for the children. But in every other way? She envisioned his hair, the rich brown of a cattail's skin threaded with strands of autumn gold—thick, curling hair that lifted at his collar and around his ears, so different from the black, straight hair of the Gwich'in. His skin had tanned brown under the sun, closely matching her own tawny color, but she'd glimpsed his throat when his top shirt button opened. Underneath, he was white.

And he persisted in placing his trust in an invisible God who resided somewhere above the clouds. A God he called Father. At each visit, he shared from a black book supposedly written by this unseen God, his face fervent as he did his utmost to convince her she was loved, wanted, by his Father God who could be hers, too, if only she asked Him to be.

Lizzie shook her head, blowing out a little breath of scornful disbelief. On the outside, she and Clay were different. And deep underneath, in their hearts, they were very, very different.

She paused in her trek across the yard and examined the back of her hand. One would never guess she carried the white blood of her father or her great-great-grandfather. Her mother's blood ran deeper, stronger, and colored her all the way to the surface. She rubbed her skin, but the color remained. Brown. Always brown.

Scuffing forward again, she allowed her thoughts to look into the future. If she joined with a white man—a likely happening when she entered her father's world—would her children carry the dark skin of her mother's people, or would they be gifted with their father's paler hue? How she hoped the pure white of their father's heritage might wash out the muddied blood of her mixed heritage, resulting in white-skinned children. If they showed white on the outside, no one would look at them with derision. White meant acceptance.

Inside the cabin, she found Naibi and Etu busily setting plates, cups, and spoons on the table in readiness for their noonday meal. They laughed together, their round faces beaming and dark eyes sparkling. Their obvious cheerfulness raised a coil of envy. She reminded herself she, too, would experience unfettered bliss when her father welcomed her into his house.

Her time in the garden had proven the vegetables neared their time of harvest. Which meant Lizzie's moment of joy waited just around the bend. Her heart pattered with hope. But then a grim reminder chased the patter away. How could she feel truly joyful unless she fulfilled her mother's wish for reconciliation with her grandparents? Her shoulders sagged in defeat. It would be wiser to simply accept that joy did not exist for her—not here, and not with her father.

∽

Vivian sank into the delightful softness of the hotel's featherbed and released a sigh of pleasure. Her week of train travel and sleeping in a hard berth had created a permanent ache in her lower spine. From Fairbanks, through Canada, the American Northwest, and then to Carson City, Nevada, she'd traveled steadily south. And tomorrow she would begin her eastward trek across the vast United States to Massachusetts and Aunt Vesta. But tonight—for one glorious night—she would savor a hotel room, a bath, and the luxury of a bed.

She fingered the paper money wired to the hotel by her dear aunt, grateful for the security it provided. The telegram accompanying the packet of cash had included an outline of her carefully laid itinerary and tickets for every remaining leg of the journey. Vivian returned the money to the same little pocket in her reticule that held the tickets, whispering a silent prayer of gratitude for her aunt's diligent planning. She had merely to follow the directions at each depot, and in a little over two weeks, she'd be under the roof of Aunt Vesta and Uncle Matthew's stately townhouse.

As much as she anticipated reuniting with her aunt and uncle, she couldn't cast off the cloak of regret that had fallen over her from the moment she'd made the decision to leave Alaska. Were the villagers recovered from the bout of sickness? Had any of them succumbed to the fever? And Clay—was he keeping a careful watch over Etu and Naibi? Had he completed the mission so he could begin the ministry of his heart? Was he visiting Lizzie, as she'd requested, so the native woman wouldn't feel so alone? So many questions—and no way to find answers.

She pushed off the bed and crossed to the window. She looked out at a busy city scene. Just gazing at the dusty, crowded streets filled with various conveyances and people bustling here and there made her feel hemmed in. She missed the openness of the Alaskan wilderness, the slower pace of the natives who resided in the quiet village. Her brow puckered in confusion. How had only a few short weeks created such a change within her? She would never have imagined the city stifling her. She'd need to adjust her thinking before she reached Hampshire County.

"The amenities of Huntington are preferable to the rugged conditions in Gwichyaa Saa," she reminded herself, her fingertips on the glass as she peered outward. "I shall have opportunities to visit the opera hall, engage in delightful teas with Aunt Vesta and her friends, and partake of carriage rides with the other young people. . . ." She shifted slightly, gaining a better view of a passing horse-drawn, well-fringed surrey. A whiff of her own musty body odor reached her nose, and she grimaced. "And I shall enjoy the convenience of indoor plumbing."

She whirled from the window and charged to her valise. After withdrawing a clean gown and the other items necessary for bathing, she stepped into the hallway. A bathing room specifically for female guests waited at the far end. When she'd checked it earlier, someone else was making use of it. But surely by now the woman would have left and Vivian could enjoy a leisurely soak. Her skin prickled in anticipation. Vivian attempted to turn the knob.

"Occupied!" A frantic voice screeched from behind the closed door.

Vivian tipped her face close to the raised-panel door. "Will you be much longer?"

"Five minutes." The reply carried over the sounds of splashing.

Vivian leaned against the wall with her belongings draped over her arm, determined to remain beside the door so she could enter the moment the other woman vacated the room. Guests milled up and down the hallway on their way to their rooms or to the dining room on the main floor. She nodded and smiled when they greeted her, all the while battling embarrassment at her disheveled, travel-weary appearance. But not responding would be impolite. If only the woman inside the bathing room would hurry!

A middle-aged gentleman came up the stairs and ambled toward her. He stopped and tipped his fashionable black bowler, offering a broad grin. "Hello, miss."

Vivian hugged her clean clothing to her ribs. The man, attired in a fancy pinstriped suit and sporting a neatly trimmed mustache, oozed charm and sophistication. How slovenly she must appear in comparison. "H-hello."

"I believe I saw you at the train station earlier this afternoon." He glanced up and down the hallway, his thick brows briefly dipping. "You're traveling alone?"

Was it wise to acknowledge her lack of chaperonage? Vivian bit down on her lip, uncertainty holding her silent.

He must have guessed the reason for her hesitation, because he chuckled lightly. "Now, now, I'm giving the wrong impression. Believe me, my query is entirely chivalrous." His smile broadened. "I have a daughter, Mathilda Rose, who is the apple of my eye. She's near your age. In fact, you remind me of her with your green eyes and heart-shaped face." He sighed, shaking his head in a rueful manner. "I'm afraid my fatherly inclinations aren't easily squelched."

Vivian couldn't resist displaying a grin. How sweet for him to be concerned about her. "Where is she?"

"Home in Ely with her mother. I'll be joining them tomorrow now that my business dealings are complete." He sighed again. "I've spent the past two weeks in San Francisco, overseeing the sale of a client's business. Such a tiresome activity! I'm very ready to be home again." Planting his feet wide, he slipped his hands into his jacket pockets. "And you, young lady? Are you heading home, too?"

Vivian opened her mouth to heartily agree, but for some reason the statement didn't leave her lips. She'd always considered her aunt and uncle's home her own. Why, then, did an image of Gwichyaa Saa fill her mind's eye? She replied, "I'm going to visit relatives."

"So you've left your home behind," he mused.

Vivian swallowed a knot of sadness. "Yes, sir."

"Well, then, I wish you safe travels, an enjoyable time with your relatives, and a speedy return to your home."

Even though his final wish would not be fulfilled, Vivian smiled. "Th-thank you, sir."

"I believe I'll retire now. The train leaves early tomorrow morning." He reached beneath his jacket and withdrew a folded newspaper. "Might you enjoy reading this before you turn in? It's already a week old, but—"

"Oh yes, please!" Vivian reached eagerly for the paper. Living in the village, she'd fallen woefully out of touch with happenings in the country. Perhaps reabsorbing herself in newsworthy events might help her feel at ease in the city again. "Thank you very much."

"You're quite welcome. Good night now, young lady." He touched the brim of his hat again, offered a dapper bow, and strode down the hallway.

The doorknob squeaked, and a plump woman with frizzy hair sticking out from beneath a ruffled mob cap stepped from the steamy bathing room. "There you are. I gave the tub a quick rinse. There's plenty of hot water—enjoy." The woman bustled around the corner and slammed herself into a room.

Vivian darted into the bathroom. She turned the brass spigots as high as they would go, smiling at the musical spatter of water against the tub's cast-iron bottom. She dropped her dirty clothes in a heap and stepped into the tub. When the water reached a mere six inches from the tub's rolled rim, she twisted the spigots to the off position and eased against the sloped back. Hot water lapped all the way to her chin. She closed her eyes, releasing a long sigh. *Luxury, pure luxury.*

She'd placed the newspaper on a nearby table next to her folded nightclothes. Wouldn't it be pleasant to read while soaking? Her heels squeaked against the tub's surface as she raised herself up to grab the paper. Holding the pages well above the water, she reclined and read every article on the front page.

The paper grew damp from the steam, and Vivian considered laying it aside rather than ruining it. One more page, she decided. Exercising great care, she turned to the second page and, immediately, an article caught her attention: WELL-RESPECTED BUSINESSMAN VOSS EDWARD DAWSON KILLED IN ROBBERY ATTEMPT. *How sad*, came the automatic thought. Angling the paper to better catch the light, she began to read.

Suddenly she gasped, sitting upright. Water splashed the pages and cascaded over the edge of the tub. She tossed the paper aside and clambered out, grabbing up a towel to mop the floor before water dripped to the room below. Assured she'd dried the floor as best she could, she draped the towel over the tub's rolled rim and stared at the crumpled paper lying open on the floor at her feet.

Her pulse pounded as she located the line that had nearly stilled her heartbeat: *"Mr. Dawson began Dawson Industries with wealth gained from fur trapping on the Alaskan frontier. . . ."*

Chapter Twenty-Six

Vivian's motions turned clumsy as she scrambled into her clean clothing, brushed her damp hair away from her face, and carried her soiled clothing to her room. In one of her conversations with Lizzie, the native woman had shared her full name—Lu'qul Gitth'ighi Elizabeth Dawson—White Feather at her mother's choosing, and Elizabeth Dawson after her paternal grandmother.

Dawson . . . Lizzie had never admitted her reason for wanting to go to San Francisco, but was it possible Lizzie intended to seek her father's family? Might the Voss Dawson listed in the newspaper be one of Lizzie's relatives? Perhaps even her father? If Clay were here, he'd no doubt advise her she was allowing her imagination to run wild. But she needed answers, for Lizzie's sake.

Perhaps the man who'd given her the paper could provide more information. Throwing on a dress, she pressed her memory—behind which doorway had the man disappeared? She tapped on two incorrect doors before she located the right one. He'd changed from his suit and hat into a satin dressing robe and slippers. His graying hair looked mussed, as if he'd been lying down before she disturbed him.

"Why . . . hello again." The surprised look on the man's mustached face nearly sent her scuttling back to her own room, but she had to ask what he knew about the death of the man who might be Lizzie's father.

"I . . . I'm so sorry to bother you, but this article . . ." Vivian held up the paper, folded to the story in question. "You said you were in San Francisco recently. Can you tell me anything more about . . . about . . . ?"

The man plucked the newspaper from Vivian's hand and frowned at it for a few seconds. Then he nodded. "Oh yes . . . tragic event. The entire town murmured about it. Apparently this gentleman was quite well known and well liked."

"What happened?" Vivian clasped her hands to her throat, her mouth dry.

"Isn't that clear from the article?" He tapped the page with the backs of his fingers. "Robbers accosted Mr. Dawson as he left his place of business, demanded money, and when he refused, they shot him. Right there on the street."

The man's emotionless recital chilled Vivian.

"I didn't attend his funeral, but my business dealings had to be delayed because all of my associates went. According to their reports, half the city of San Francisco turned out to pay their respects."

Vivian took the paper from the man's hand, staring at the headline. "It says he spent time in Alaska. . . ."

"Yes. In the eighteen sixties and seventies, my associates indicated."

Vivian's heart skipped a beat. The timing would be perfect. She gulped.

"Are you a friend to Mr. Dawson?"

Vivian jerked her gaze away from the paper. "What? Oh. No, I didn't know him at all. But . . ." She swallowed the tears that gathered in her throat. If her assumptions were correct, Lizzie knew him. Poor, poor Lizzie.

"I believe on the society pages there is an expansive obituary." The man yawned behind his hand. He began inching his door closed. "Good evening, miss."

An obituary would list survivors. Vivian thanked the man and hurried back to her room. She spread the paper on the bed and turned the pages until she located the obituary page. The gentleman was right—most obituaries were a mere one to two inches of column space. Mr. Dawson's stretched for more than six inches, disclosing all of his community involvements, business successes, awards he'd received, and family connections. The final paragraph listed his survivors, and Vivian underlined the names with her finger as she read.

"The death of Voss E. Dawson is mourned by his Parents, Edward and Elizabeth (Tanner) Dawson; Brothers Virgil and Victor; his Beloved Wife of eight years, Margaret (Hopemeister) Dawson; his only Son, Timothy, age seven; and precious Daughters, Elizabeth (nicknamed Lizzie) . . ."

Vivian gasped. They'd listed Lizzie! So Voss Dawson was her father—and he'd told his new wife about her. But then she read on, and her elation crumbled.

". . . age six, and Lydia, age four, all of San Francisco."

Vivian wadded the paper and pressed it to her aching chest. If this man was Lizzie's father, not only had he abandoned his first child many years ago, he had replaced her by naming a second daughter Elizabeth and had nicknamed her Lizzie. Certainly his "Beloved Wife Margaret" had no idea her husband had once married a Gwich'in maiden and fathered a half-breed child.

Tossing the paper aside, Vivian began to pace the room. Anger mingled with intense sorrow. Lizzie needed to know about this.

Vivian dropped sideways on the bed, hugging a plump pillow the way she wished she could embrace Lizzie to lighten the pain the woman was sure to bear if Voss Dawson was, in fact, her father. Then Vivian sat upright, shaking her head. "I could be wrong. Lizzie might be going to San Francisco for some other reason." She sagged onto the bed again. "But just in case, I must tell her about this man's death." Vivian moaned, closing her eyes against the sting of tears. "But how?"

✀

Clay tucked his Bible into his knapsack and hung the strap around his neck. Then, on a whim, he reached for his accordion box. How long had it been since he'd played the cheerful musical instrument? Not since his first weeks in Gwichyaa Saa. Recalling how much the villagers, particularly the children, had enjoyed listening to him play, he decided a few tunes would bring some cheer. Especially to those in mourning—to his great heartbreak three villagers had lost their battles with the illness in the past two days—or to those who lay sick and miserable on their sleeping mats.

But first he needed to visit Lizzie's cabin and check on Etu and Naibi. He prayed daily that the fever jumping from one cabin to another hadn't made its way through the woods to Lizzie's home. He'd spend a couple of hours playing games with the children, reading from the Bible to Lizzie whether she wanted to listen or not, and getting reacquainted with the keyboard on his piano-accordion. No doubt his fingers were rusty from their long break, but Etu and Naibi wouldn't complain. And hopefully Lizzie wouldn't be offended if he hit some sour notes. *She'd probably rather hear sour notes on the accordion than sweet verses from the Bible.*

He slipped between some trees at the edge of the village

and followed the familiar pathway. His thoughts raced ahead to the welcome he knew he'd receive. It gave him such a lift to see Etu and Naibi's faces light up when he stepped into Lizzie's yard. And their hugs—tight, their sweaty heads pressed to his ribs—gave him a sense of belonging. He smiled, picking up his pace. He knew what it must feel like to be a father, having been the recipient of their heartfelt greetings.

But he needed to exercise caution. The daily visits were planting ideas in his head. Ideas that had no place there. When the children came running, he caught himself looking beyond them to Lizzie, wishing she would hold out her arms in welcome, too. Just thinking about it now, far from her cabin on a trampled pathway lined by thick brush, brought a rush of heat from his chest to his face. Or maybe it was just the effort of carrying the heavy accordion. He'd let himself believe the latter.

The sound of giggles carried over the gentle melody of the wind, reaching his ears. Obviously the children weren't ill. *Thank You, Lord, for protecting them. Please continue to keep them healthy.* As he completed the prayer, he stepped into Lizzie's clearing. The children, in the middle of a game involving some sort of odd-looking balloon, looked up and spotted him. Etu dropped the plaything, and they both came running.

Clay dropped to one knee and braced himself, laughing as they plunged against him. "It looks as though you were having fun."

"We play catch," Etu announced. Over their time with Lizzie, both children's English had improved mightily. Etu dashed to retrieve the toy and offered it to Clay. "Missus Lizzie made a ball by blowing air into a moose's bladder."

"A bladder?" Clay made a face. "You keep it."

Etu laughed, his eyes crinkling in merriment. "Mister

Clay is scare of bladder!" Still laughing, he spun and ran toward the cabin, hollering, "Missus Lizzie! Missus Lizzie! Mister Clay comes, and he is scare of the ball you make!"

Naibi gave Clay's upraised knee a pat. "It is all right, Mister Clay. Everyone is scare of somefing."

Clay snorted in amusement. He slipped his arms free of the accordion case and propped it against a tree trunk at the edge of the yard. Then he took Naibi's hand and walked with her toward the cabin. When they were halfway across the yard, Lizzie emerged from her cabin. As he'd come to expect, she wore the blue-checked dress Vivian had given her, but today she'd braided her hair in one long plait that fell down her spine and ended a scant inch above the dress's waist. Even such a simple style enhanced her high cheek bones and delicate jawline. *What a beautiful woman* . . .

"You're late today," Lizzie said by way of greeting, but her voice held no recrimination. "You usually come closer to noon."

He needed to let her know what was happening in the village, but he didn't want the children to overhear. There was no sense in frightening them. He put his hand on Naibi's head. "You two go finish your game. I'm going to talk to Missus Lizzie for a bit, and then I'll play with you."

Naibi snatched the ball from Etu's hands and darted off. Etu thundered in pursuit. When they were fully engaged in their game, Clay turned to Lizzie. "Can we talk?"

Lizzie gestured to a low bench tucked along her cabin wall, and they seated themselves at opposite ends. Clay wished he could scoot close and hold her hand. Partly because he feared his news would be upsetting, and partly because he longed to touch her, just once.

Clay drew in a breath and assumed his most gentle tone. "We've lost three people from the village to the fever.

Yesterday evening, an elderly man named Taima died, then a few hours later I received word that a young woman—newly married—had also died." The woman was close to Lizzie's age. He tipped his head. "Did you know Magema?"

Lizzie's forehead crinkled. "I know only my grandparents. But my mother probably knew both of them." Her gaze drifted toward a stand of trees, where a rock pile signified a grave. "I wonder if she knows their spirits have departed. . . ." She returned her attention to Clay. "My grandmother . . . she still lives?"

"Yes." Clay hung his head. The third death, only that morning, affected him the most. He'd spent several hours with the parents, offering comfort, but he doubted his efforts had eased their deep pain. "The last one to fall prey to the fever was a little boy, not even a year old yet." How sad that the child wouldn't have the opportunity to experience the joy of boyhood, to grow into manhood and become a husband and father. Yet Clay knew without a doubt God had embraced this little one into His holy presence, where the child would live forever in joy and peace. God wouldn't turn away such an innocent soul.

His heart panged for the other two who were lost. He hadn't had a chance to share the truth of Jesus's sacrifice with them. Did that mean, in God's eyes, they were also innocent and would enjoy eternity with the one true God?

"Clay?"

He hadn't realized he'd drifted away in thought until Lizzie's puzzled voice reached his ears. He shifted to look into her concerned face.

"You care deeply for the villagers." She spoke in her usual matter-of-fact tone, but he saw a glimmer of approval shining in the depths of her blue eyes.

He nodded. "Yes. I do."

"Why? They are not your people."

Again, he sensed no accusation, only a desire to under-stand. Unconsciously, his hand stretched across the brief gap separating them and curled over hers. The simple contact—so impersonal—had a very personal effect on his senses. He forced himself to focus on her question and the best way to answer.

"But you see, Lizzie, they *are* my people. They were cre-ated by the same God who knit me together within my mother's womb. Each of them possesses a heart that yearns for a relationship with their Maker." He tightened his grip on her fingers, desire for her to accept the truth he shared as her own rising inside of him and tangling his emotions. "The Bible tells us everyone comes to the Father through the Son, Jesus Christ. Once they accept Jesus as their Savior, God becomes their Father, and we are all bound by love. We become brothers and sisters in Christ."

Lizzie sat for long seconds, peering into his face with a stoic expression. He wished he could read her thoughts. Her lips parted, and he held his breath, praying silently that she might finally ask the question his heart pined to hear: *May I ask your God to become my God?*

"Is it safe, with people dying in the village, for you to come back and forth? What if you carry the sickness with you and give it to Etu or Naibi?"

Clay's breath whooshed out. His shoulders slumped. He released Lizzie's hand and cupped his palm over his knee, battling a mighty wave of disappointment. Why did this woman so stringently resist mention of God? "I hadn't con-sidered that. I thought with them away from the village, they'd be safe. But . . ." He sighed. "Are you saying you don't want me to come here anymore?"

Something flashed in her eyes. Regret. Perhaps a longing.

But she lowered her gaze, and when she raised her head again she held the unemotional expression that was far too familiar. "I don't want to say you aren't welcome, but it might be best . . . for the children's sake."

Clay suspected her real reason for asking him to stay away was to avoid hearing any more of his talk about God. Clamping his teeth together in frustration, he looked across the yard, where Etu and Naibi had collapsed and lay on their sides, chins propped on elbows, examining something in the grass. His heart flooded with affection for the pair. As difficult as it would be to stay away, perhaps Lizzie's suggestion was wise.

"All right." He rose, his legs resisting the movement. "I'll spend some time with them, then explain why I won't be back for a while. Do you . . ." He didn't attempt to hide his sadness as he gazed at her. "Have need of anything before I go? Wood chopped . . . snares checked . . . anything?" He supposed he should be ashamed of his blatant attempt to prolong his leave-taking. But he wasn't.

"We'll be fine." Lizzie stood, smoothing out her skirt. Her gaze skittered everywhere but directly at him. "I've survived just fine on my own for these many years."

And that was the problem, Clay finally realized. She'd survived so well, she didn't believe she had need of anyone or anything, including a Savior. *Lord, help her realize her need of You, however that may be. And act swiftly.*

Chapter Twenty-Seven

C lay did his best to fill his days with frenetic activity. Taking time off only to attend the funeral ceremonies for those who died, he utilized nearly every moment of light to work, work, work. With the arrival of July, the sun lit the sky almost the entire day, with a few hours of dark between midnight and four in the morning. The long days led to exhaustion, but overwhelming tiredness was better than the pressing ache of loneliness.

He split logs to make benches for the main room and used saplings and rope to build makeshift bed frames for the sleeping rooms, topping the beds with simple mattresses of thick wool blankets folded around piles of pine needles and dried leaves. Using packing crates and strips of bark removed from the huts he and Vivian had used as shelters, he built shelves for the children and him to store their belongings in the sleeping rooms.

After completing the loft, he neatly stored all their food supplies, marveling at how much larger the main room felt without the clutter of boxes, barrels, and burlap sacks. Then, to give himself extra work space for studying or meal preparation, he added a long narrow counter along the wall where he'd attached the table. For good measure, he built shelves underneath it to hold dishes, pots, pans, and other kitchen utensils. The shelves put all items within easy reach of even little Naibi.

Six days after telling Lizzie he would stay away until the sickness left the village for good, he hammered the final window casing into place on the mission school and stepped back to admire the completed building. Grayish chinking filled the gaps between the rough log walls, well-oiled paper served as windows, and a sturdy planked door stood open, inviting people to cross the smooth rock stoop and enter the mission. He walked a slow circle around the structure, examining every inch from the rock foundation supporting the logs to the grass- and daisy-strewn roof protecting the insides from rain.

He berated himself for failing to add a second door on the back side of the building for the sake of ventilation and to be used as an escape should the need ever arise. "I can always chop another one out later," he muttered to a ground squirrel that popped from its hole and seemed to give the log building a perusal. He smacked the solid wall with his open palm, scaring the little striped creature into scrambling for cover, and assured himself that for now the single door facing the village would serve him fine.

With long strides he rounded the building and stepped through the doorway, pausing just over the threshold. He crossed to the front and stood between the two doors leading to the sleeping rooms. Satisfaction filled him as his gaze roved across the rows of rough-hewn benches. He imagined a host of Gwich'in villagers seated, attentive, absorbing the message he shared from God's holy word. A lump filled his throat.

Clay dropped to his knees on the hard-packed dirt floor and folded his hands. His heart sang in praise. *Thank You,*

Lord, that the building is complete. Now my ministry can finally begin. His prayer continued, branching from gratitude to pleas for an end to the sickness and for protection for Vivian as she traveled, and ended with a heartfelt request. *Give me the words, dear Father, to reach the Gwich'in people with Your love and grace. And please, please, soften Lizzie's heart that she might embrace You.*

He rose and rubbed his aching knees. His stomach rumbled, reminding him he'd gone the entire day without eating. Again. Vivian would be appalled. Recalling her frequent reprimand—*"Clay, you cannot work on an empty stomach. You'll make yourself sick. So sit down and eat!"*—he smiled. She'd turned out to be a decent cook between the iron cookstove and Lizzie's lessons.

As always, thoughts of Lizzie made his chest ache. While he sat at the table by himself and ate a simple meal of dried salmon, a thank-you gift from Taima's family for his visits after the man's death, he allowed himself to visit Lizzie in his mind. When would this sickness finally depart so he could go to her, check on the children, talk with her again? Each sunrise drew them closer to the day she would pack her belongings and leave. He didn't have time to waste.

He'd finished the salmon and rose, intending to fetch water to wash his plate, when a shadow fell across the floor. Clay jumped, nearly dropping the plate. He looked into Shruh's drawn face. The long days of caring for Co'Ozhii had aged the older man. Shruh cleared his throat. "Clay Selby? I would speak with you."

Clay set the plate aside and crossed quickly to Shruh. "What is it?"

The man sent a glance around the room, his brow furrowed. Without a word, he plodded to the first sleeping room and opened the door. After a look inside, he moved to the second door and repeated the inspection. Clay, puzzled, waited for him to share his concern. Shruh returned to Clay and folded his arms over his chest.

"Two tribesmen, Da'ago and Kiona, visited my cabin earlier today with a strange tale."

Shruh's condemning tone held Clay captive. His chest tightened in trepidation. "A-about me?"

"About you, the boy child Etu, and the girl child Naibi. They say you took the children into the woods several days ago, but when you returned they were not with you. They have watched each day for the children's return. But no children have come from the woods." Shruh's scowl deepened. "I put the children in your care, trusting you to provide well for them, but now I wonder if my trust was misplaced." He looked around again, holding his hands wide. "Where are the children?"

Clay's mouth went dry. He'd enjoyed his reprieve from Shruh's fierce insistence that he abandon his relationship with Lizzie. Admitting he'd allowed the children to stay with her would no doubt raise another round of disapproval and could very well result in his expulsion from the village just when he'd finally completed the mission and could begin teaching and preaching. He struggled to find a way to tell the truth without inciting Shruh's ire. *Father, help me.*

"Where are the children?" Shruh's voice thundered, a command Clay could not ignore.

"With Lu'qul Gitth'ighi."

"What?" After his deep-throated, demanding query, the simple one-word question emerged as soft as a bird feather drifting from overhead.

But Clay wasn't deceived by the calm tone. Shruh's eyes sparked with fury, and his quivering muscles communicated his tenuous hold on his temper. He faced Shruh squarely and responded in a strong, unrepentant-yet-respectful voice. "With the illness spreading through the village, I worried for their safety. I placed them with Lizzie—with Lu'qul Gitth'ighi—so the sickness wouldn't be able to reach them."

"With a banished woman."

With your granddaughter, you stubborn old coot. "Yes."

Shruh paced away, his gait stiff. He stopped on the opposite side of the room and stood with his back to Clay, yet his voice carried clearly across the expanse of benches. "Again and again you choose to ignore the edicts of our tribe. You seem to be a good man—an honorable man, seeking to care for orphaned children and offering comfort to those whose hearts are broken by loss." A note of confusion crept into the man's tone. "Yet you cannot abide by rules."

He spun to face Clay, his lined face wreathed with a mixture of anger and remorse. "If I allow you to stay, my people will not respect me. They will say Shruh does not honor his own tribe's council."

Clay scurried between two rows of benches to stand before Shruh. "I know I acted against tribal dictates by seeing a woman who'd been excommunicated." A picture of Lizzie formed in his mind, making his heart swell with the desire to go to her again. "But I did it out of concern for Etu and Naibi." *Lord, pave the way to reconciliation.* "If I address the council members and assure them of my reasons for going against your law, might they choose to let me stay? Then the fault will not fall on you. It will be their decision."

Shruh stared into Clay's face, his mouth pinched into a tight line of uncertainty. "You speak to them. But first, you bring the children back to the village. They belong here, not in the home of a woman who is not of our tribe. Bring them here, and then come see me. I will arrange the meeting between you and the council. We will decide what to do with you."

∽

Lizzie snapped the final ear of corn from the stalk and dropped it into the woven basket at her feet. The children worked together in the next row, picking the corn and filling their own basket. So many ears—an abundant harvest. Lizzie's heart filled with gratitude for nature's favor, even while she ached at the realization that with harvest nearly complete, she would say good-bye to Etu, Naibi, and—she pressed her palm to her traitorous heart—Clay.

Etu peeked between the long, crackling leaves of the shoulder-high stalks. "Missus Lizzie, you roast corn for lunch today?"

Lizzie had intended to send the children to the cabin for leftover corn muffins and dried caribou for lunch so she could continue working, but how could she deny Etu's hopeful request? Especially since her time with the children neared its end. "Of course. It always tastes best when fresh-picked."

Naibi's happy squeal rang, earning a few barks of surprise from the penned dogs.

With her basket full, it seemed a good time to take a break and prepare several ears for roasting. She dragged the basket to the waiting travois and slid it onto the willow cross branches. Then she grasped the poles and toted the basket to the side of the house, where a hollow clay mound served as her roasting pit.

Naibi skipped from the vegetable patch to observe Lizzie. With her hands behind her back, her chin tucked low, and her little mouth puckered, she resembled a wise old owl. A wise old owl in a beflowered dress. Lizzie stifled an amused chuckle as she removed several ears from the basket and lined them up side by side inside the pit.

The child pointed. "Do you soak them? Vitse soaked ears in water first."

"These are fresh ears," Lizzie explained, "still holding moisture from their time on the stalk. We don't need to soak them unless they dry out."

"Ohhh."

The single-word response ran up a scale and down, reminding Lizzie of the notes Clay played on his music box. She pushed aside thoughts of Clay and returned to her task. The pit held up to a dozen ears, but she chose to roast eight. Surely two or three ears apiece would satisfy the children's healthy appetites.

Just as she layered in the kindling to start the fire, the dogs began to whine, alerting her to someone's presence. She jerked to her feet, ready to dash for the rifle that waited at the edge of the vegetable patch, but her heart leapt in joy when she spotted Clay stepping from the trees.

He'd come! She hadn't realized the depth of her longing for him until the moment she saw him again. She took two stumbling steps in his direction, a laugh of pure delight forming in her throat. But then she met his solemn gaze, and trepidation stilled the sound.

Naibi turned and looked across the yard. She let out a little squeal of delight and started to run to Clay. Lizzie captured her arm and drew her to a halt. "Go back and help your brother."

Naibi flung her hand toward Clay. "But—"

"Later," Lizzie said, and the child huffed. With one more pleading look toward Clay, she turned and scuffed back to the garden. Lizzie hurried across the ground to meet Clay. "What is wrong? More deaths?" Her heart panged at his sadness.

Although she didn't understand his deep caring for the people of Gwichyaa Saa, she admired it. It hurt her to see his sorrow.

He hung his head. "No, praise God, no others have died, but . . ." He sighed, meeting her gaze. With stilted, apologetic words, he shared the villagers' concerns and his need to take the children back to the village with him. As he spoke, Lizzie's ire stirred.

"They would put the children in harm's way rather than allow them to be with me?"

"I'm sorry, Lizzie. I tried to convince him to leave them here, but—"

"Him." Lizzie nearly spat the word. She crossed her arms over her chest. "My grandfather, yes? Is it the village's concern or merely Vitsiy's concern?"

"He came to me with the concern, but villagers had gone to him."

Lizzie searched Clay's face. Would he lie to protect her feelings?

"They saw me take the children into the woods and return without them." Clay chuckled softly, rubbing his finger beneath his nose in a gesture that spoke of his embarrassment. "I guess they thought I left them alone somewhere . . . or disposed of them."

"My grandfather would have found that preferable to leaving them with me." Lizzie made no attempt to hide her bitterness.

Clay's expression softened, compassion glowing in his brown-flecked eyes of grayish green. "Your grandfather was more upset with me—for ignoring the village edict of excommunication. I knew when I brought the children here I was going against tribal law. But I hoped . . ."

He didn't complete the sentence, but Lizzie filled it in for him. "They would change their minds?"

Clay nodded.

Lizzie spun and charged toward the roasting pit, aware of Clay following on her heels. "They will never change their minds about me. I am tainted by my great-great-grandfather's and my mother's sins." She waved her hand in the direction of Denali, drawing on scorn to hold the deep pain of rejection at bay. "Every day of my mother's life, she prayed for reconciliation between herself, her parents, and Dine'e. But the High One never listened. She is gone now, and her requests lie dead, as well."

She whirled to face him again, blinking away the hot tears that gathered in her eyes. Without conscious thought, she slipped into Athabascan. "It is pointless to hope, Clay Selby. They will never change. They will make me carry the disgrace of my white blood to my own grave." Raising her chin, she gulped back the painful sting of the village-imposed disdain. "But I will have the victory." Resolve stiffened her spine. "I will find the strength to live happily far from here. In my father's house, I will find a place of acceptance. And those who have rejected me from the days of my birth will no longer be remembered in my heart."

Chapter Twenty-Eight

Clay propped open the mission building's door with a round rock and stood on the stoop. The service wasn't scheduled for another hour, but nervousness combined with anticipation had awakened him early. He'd enjoy the crisp scent of morning and count down the minutes until the villagers began ambling toward the mission.

He slipped his trembling hands in the pockets of his black wool suit jacket and gazed toward the center of the village. How many would come? He'd gone from cabin to cabin yesterday evening, informing each family of his intention to hold the first church service this morning. Although he didn't expect everyone to attend—many were still in bed with the fever that passed from one person to another and seemed to make circles around the village—he hoped for a good attendance.

Of course, some might stay away for reasons other than sickness. Not everyone in the village approved of the council's decision to allow Clay to remain in Gwichyaa Saa. The leaders had cast their votes for and against his removal. The narrow margin—four to three—still made his stomach

260

queasy. His past kindnesses had swayed some in his favor, but they'd taken Etu and Naibi from him, placing the children with an elderly cousin of their grandmother. The old man didn't seem capable of caring for himself, let alone two active children, but Clay didn't dare argue. One more breach of their trust, and they'd disregard whatever good he'd done and toss him out.

When he'd visited the man's cabin last night, saving it for last so he could spend a little time visiting with the children, he'd reminded them they could come to the school each morning for lessons. It wasn't the same as caring for them every day, all day, but at least he would be able to make sure they were fed and that they bathed regularly.

A bird perched in a nearby tree, pouring forth a bright morning song. Clay smiled in reply, the last stanza of "Awake, My Soul, and With the Sun" filling his heart. He sang out loud and strong, "Praise God from Whom all blessings flow. Praise Him all creatures here below . . ." Several other birds joined the first one's chorus, finishing the verse with Clay, and he laughed, unable to squelch a rush of happiness.

This first service had been so long in coming, so earnestly prayed over, his stomach trembled in eagerness. He'd prepared his first sermon from the second book of Acts, relying heavily on Peter's words on the day of Pentecost. Many had accepted the truth of salvation on that day, and he hoped for the same awakening in the village of Gwichyaa Saa.

"Let them come, Lord," he whispered to the clear sky. "Let them come, and open their hearts to believe."

An hour slipped by while Clay remained in the doorway, watching. He observed cabin doors opening and faces peeking out, as if ascertaining the mission and Clay were still there on the edge of the village. His heart leapt in anticipation with each squeak of a door hinge. But after a few seconds, the doors would snap closed, sealing the residents inside. No one came.

He grew warm in his jacket, so he slipped it off and held it over his arm. His timepiece showed twenty minutes past the hour, but he didn't let the time discourage him. Only twenty minutes late. They might still come. He'd learned over his months in the village that the natives moved at their own pace. The ten o'clock hour meant little to them. They might start ambling in his direction at any moment. He'd stay right here until they chose to come.

At forty minutes past the hour, he sat on the stoop, leaned against the doorjamb, and stretched his legs into the patch of sunshine. A beetle scurried between his feet, and he said, "Did you want to come inside? I'm ready for you." The beetle disappeared in a crack in the hard ground, reminding Clay of the people hiding behind their planked doors. He stifled a groan.

He considered going inside and retrieving his Bible to review his notes one more time. Not because he didn't know the sermon well—he'd practice it a dozen times already—but the sitting and doing nothing wore on his nerves. Putting his hands against the rock slab, he started to push himself to his feet. But a sudden thought stopped him midrise. Would leaving his post signal an unwillingness to hold the service? He wouldn't risk it. He settled back onto the slab and went over the sermon in his mind, rehashing phrases best delivered with quiet fervency and others that warranted a more emphatic tone. Absorbed in inner thought, he lost track of time.

When he glanced at his timepiece again, he gave a start of surprise. Eleven-thirty! A full hour and a half past the time he'd intended to begin. Disappointment, frustration, and—yes, he admitted it—anger swirled through him, all battling for first place in his soul. He rested his head against the rough doorjamb. Closing his eyes to block out the sight of the quiet village, he allowed disappointment to rise to the top.

All of his work to build the mission, all of his prayerful preparation on the sermon, and here he sat, alone. *At least Vivian isn't here to witness my failure.* The thought did little to comfort him. Being a failure without an audience didn't change his standing. He'd promised Pa a lengthy letter, disclosing every detail of his first service with the Gwich'in people. The letter would be simple to write. He only required one sentence: *No one came.*

∽

Vivian stared at the passing countryside. Flat, treeless plains greeted her eyes, reminding her of the sparse land that surrounded her parents' reservation in Oklahoma. Days of travel mushed together in her mind, making it difficult to discern either the date or her location. According to the train's conductor, however, this was Sunday and they were crossing Kansas. Kansas . . . which bordered the Oklahoma Territory.

I wish I could stop by the reservation and see Mother.

The thought took her by surprise. She'd felt distanced from her mother for so long. Their estrangement held them apart even when they sat side by side in the same room. Most often she wanted to escape the woman's presence. Perhaps that was part of the reason Alaska had held such appeal. Now, closer in miles but separated by circumstances, she longed to turn back time to her little-girl days. Back to when she felt comfortable with Mother. And a Sunday might be the perfect time to recapture their lost closeness.

Sundays were always relaxed days, especially on the

reservation. Her stepfather led the Kiowa in hymns, his rich baritone voice booming over all the others. Then he preached God's word, his Bible draped across his broad palm as if it were an extension of his arm. Somehow Vivian had felt closer to God in the little adobe chapel on the reservation than anywhere else. Her stepfather's strong yet tender voice reminded her of what God must sound like—wise, patient, loving.

If she could visit today—on a relaxed Sunday—she and Mother might be able to explore the hurts that had driven them apart. Perhaps they would finally bridge the great chasm between them. For a moment, her heart soared with hope. But then she discounted the ridiculous notion.

The Union Pacific Railroad didn't extend into Oklahoma. Even if it did, no rails reached the Kiowa reservation where her mother and stepfather served. Besides, a visit would delay her arrival in Massachusetts. She must set aside her desire and continue this trek as planned. Yet the need to communicate with Mother—to connect with her on at least a very small level—persisted.

A letter, perhaps? She'd taken the time to send a short note along with the article about Voss Dawson to Clay in care of the mercantile in Fort Yukon before leaving Carson City. She hoped Clay had retrieved it by now and had found a gentle way to approach Lizzie. She hoped she was wrong—that Voss Dawson was no relation to Lizzie at all—but she'd rather err on the side of caution and notify Lizzie than allow her friend to discover the news in a less kind manner.

She dropped the curtain over the window and settled into her seat, tapping her lips in silent contemplation. Had the death of Voss Dawson stirred this desire for reconciliation with her mother to life? If Voss was Lizzie's father, she'd never be able to reunite with him. Might a similar fate await her if she delayed reaching out to her mother? Panic gripped Vivian, shredding the edges of her heart. She'd worked so hard to put aside her fears and live confidently, exhibiting strength and courage rather than constant worry. She was good at pretending. Even Clay believed she had changed. But she knew the truth—her courage was a farce. What would it take to finally overcome the crippling apprehensions?

She closed her eyes, her mind drifting to the day Clay had seen her off at the dock in Fort Yukon. He'd reminded her she wasn't traveling alone—*"God is only a prayer away,"* he'd assured her. A passage from the Bible, one of Aunt Vesta's favorite psalms, whispered to her heart: *"Yea, though I walk through the valley of the shadow of death, I will fear no evil: for thou art with me . . ."*

Vivian covered her face with her hands and slumped forward over her lap, desire to believe God was with her warring against her long-held resentment. *"Thou art with me . . ."* Where had God been the day her father died? *"I will fear no evil . . ."* Why hadn't He given her the strength to ignore the fearsome snake and go to Papa?

"Why didn't You prevent me from letting him die?" The agonized question, explored so many times over the years, wrenched from her lips, but just as in times past, she received no answer.

⁕

Lizzie sat in the sheltering band of shade stretching out beside her cabin and painstakingly attached another fluffy red-and-white foxtail to the bottom edge of the moose-hide coat. With careful trimming, she'd managed to make each tail appear identical in length, even though the foxes she'd trapped had been various sizes. Spaced so each bushy tail brushed against the ones on either side, she'd used two dozen tails to completely embellish the edge. The extravagant fringe work would add much value to the coat, as well as increase its beauty.

Today she'd brought white-faced Abigail from the pen to keep her company as she worked. The dog wasn't as attentive as Martha, but she lay nearby and licked her paws, her presence a welcome diversion from Lizzie's loneliness. With the children's departure, she'd leaned more heavily on the dogs for companionship, but she'd tried to distance herself a bit from her favorite ones. It pierced her to witness Martha's drooping ears and low-slung head—the dog didn't understand Lizzie's detachment—but pulling away now might make parting a little easier when the time came. And the time was coming quickly.

"I've nearly finished clearing the vegetable garden," Lizzie informed Abigail, who went on washing her paws as if her mistress hadn't spoken. "The turnips won't be ready for a while yet, but I won't worry about digging them this year. If someone wants to come later and harvest them, that's fine. But I have corn, and squash, and beans. A good harvest—food that will carry Etu and Naibi"—*and Clay*— "through the winter."

Leaving the food behind, knowing it would provide for the ones she held dear, comforted her. She cradled the knowledge, assuring herself it, too, would make her leave-taking easier. She'd be remembered.

She spread the coat across her knees. Too heavy for the warmth of midsummer, the weight was uncomfortable, but she left it there and examined every bit of the intricate beadwork. Her mother had possessed a gift for creating beauty, and she'd taught Lizzie well. The sweet forget-me-nots and curving vines created a pleasing design across the shoulders and down the front. A simple zigzag of alternating blue, yellow, red, and green beads added color to the cuffs and the coat's bottom edge above the red foxtails.

Smoothing her hand over the lush beaver collar, she gave a satisfied nod. "It's the loveliest coat I've ever made, Abigail. And next week, before we leave for Fort Yukon, I will take it to Vitse and Vitsiy's cabin and give them one more chance to make peace with me. If they refuse, I will take my coat and leave. But my conscience will be clear, knowing I did my best."

She pushed away the inner reminder that unless she honored Mama's dying request for peace, her conscience would prick her for the rest of her life. Had Vitse recovered from the fever yet? Clay hadn't visited in several days. She surmised the village leaders had forbidden him from contacting her. She drew a slow breath, a feeble attempt to ease the pain of missing him. If her grandmother's spirit slipped away, surely he'd be given permission to share the news with her. Or her grandfather would come instead. If she had to hear sad news, she preferred it came from Clay. At least he cared about her and would seek to comfort her.

Her hands stilled on the coat, her heart *trip-tripping* as she replayed her final thought. *He cares about me.* What a glorious feeling, to know a man cared for her. Although he'd never voiced the words, she'd read it in his eyes. Felt it in the touch of his hand on hers. Witnessed it in his willingness to spend time with her and perform tasks for her. But the glory of knowing he cared was buried beneath the deep ache of separation from him.

He'd come to serve in the village. His heart lay with Etu and Naibi and the Gwich'ins. Hadn't he told her so many times? He wouldn't choose her over the villagers any more than Pa would choose Mama over his life in San Francisco.

For the first time, a worrisome thought found its way to

the forefront of Lizzie's consciousness. Would Pa welcome her, or would he tell her she belonged in Alaska, the way he'd told Mama? "He *has* to welcome me," she stated aloud. "There is no one else to accept me."

Lizzie set the coat aside and gathered Abigail near. The dog rested her broad head on Lizzie's chest and whined softly in complaint when Lizzie surrounded her neck with both arms, but Lizzie didn't release her hold. She needed the comfort of the dog's warm, sturdy body. "I will visit the village one more time before I go. I will offer my beautiful coat to Vitse. And afterward I will ask Clay to escort me to Fort Yukon. A proper good-bye, Abigail, will help me let him go."

She kissed the top of the dog's head and set her aside. Taking the coat with her, she headed for her cabin. She wanted to pray for the strength to release her love for Clay and her ties to this land. Her eyes drifted to the place where Denali stood proudly, its tip masked by an embracing puff of white.

She shook her head at the obscuring clouds. "The High One hides from me again. When will I accept the truth? There is no help for me."

Chapter Twenty-Nine

On Monday morning, Clay stepped into the sunny yard of the mission building and ran his fingers up and down the keys of the accordion. Saturday, when he'd visited the cabins to tell the villagers about the first worship service, he'd also told them the school would open to anyone who desired to learn to read and write in the English language. He'd concluded, "I'll play the piano-box. When you hear it, you come."

So he stood in the yard and played a tune—a rousing rendition of "Onward Christian Soldiers." He sang all four verses at the top of his lungs. Twice. Many Gwich'in paused to listen, and Clay met their gazes, smiling no matter if they appeared amused, irritated, or stony. When he finished he waved his arm and called in Athabascan, "Come! Lessons beginning now!"

He'd hoped for a crowd. Only two children came running. Regardless of the low number, his heart lifted. He held out his arms in welcome. "Etu and Naibi!"

They barreled against him, bumping their heads on the accordion and then retreating. But they laughed, unhurt.

Clay tousled their tangled hair. "Let me put this away, and—"

"No!" Etu voiced the protest. "Play more, Mister Clay."

Clay glanced toward the village. Parents stood with their hands on their children's shoulders, holding them back. He read longing on several little faces. A grin twitched at his cheeks. He knew how persuasive Etu and Naibi could be. Perhaps the other children would be able to sway their parents if he gave them cause to beg.

"I'll play, and you two dance." Clay wriggled his shoulders, adjusting the accordion into a more secure position, and began a cheerful tune. Giggling, Naibi caught Etu's hands and tugged him into a jig in the mission yard. Clay whisked surreptitious looks toward the other children. Little heads tipped toward their parents and begging hands stirred the air.

That's right—ask.

Clay transitioned into a second song, giving the others an opportunity to join him, Etu, and Naibi. But by the end of the second song, parents had herded their children toward the garden or back into their cabins. Clay allowed the accordion to wheeze into silence, releasing his own sigh at the same time.

Only two students for his school. For one brief second, discouragement tried to take hold, but he cast it aside. Two was better than none. Etu and Naibi desired an education, so he would provide it. Gesturing to the open doorway, he said, "Go in, children. Choose a seat—whichever one you want—and we will start learning some letters."

They spent a pleasant hour focusing on the letters A, B, and C. They drew pictures of items beginning with each letter, chanted the sounds they made, and traced the letters again and again, first in the air with their fingers, then on the ground with a stick, and finally on a piece of bark with a bit of charcoal. While they worked, Clay glanced out the door repeatedly, hoping another student or two might wander in. But the others remained stubbornly absent.

Why had the council allowed him to remain in the village if they intended to pretend he didn't exist? Clay's empathy for Lizzie, living within reach of the village yet divided by silence and indifference, increased by a hundredfold over the course of the morning. How had she borne the isolation for so many years? After only a few days, he was ready to climb out of his own skin.

Lunchtime neared, and Clay let the children help him cut up carrots, potatoes, and turnips—three each—and measure them into a soup pot. The activity gave them a chance to prepare a tasty soup but also provided an opportunity to learn to count. On a whim, he incorporated a simple lesson on addition as well, adding together the number of vegetables that went into the pot.

Watching the children's serious yet attentive faces, he couldn't help but experience a rush of pride that he was managing so well. He'd worried that his lack of experience as a teacher would hinder him from any real success, yet so far things had developed naturally. The children were eager to learn—he only had to guide them. Clay didn't miss Vivian until they sat on a log under the sun to enjoy their soup and they didn't have any bread to dip in the watery broth.

Etu straddled the log with the bowl balanced between his knees. "Mister Clay, when we are done eating, can we go in the room you built for us?"

Clay lowered his spoon and considered the boy's question. What would be best? He'd seen the cabin where the children now lived—a dark, dirty one-room structure that smelled of rank furs and spoiled food. The children slept on a pile of mouse-eaten caribou hides laid out on the dirt floor in the corner. By contrast, the room in the mission would look like a palace. Was it kind to allow them to see the beds and shelves he'd made, knowing they wouldn't be able to stay?

Naibi fluttered her thick lashes. "We will not touch and make things dirty. We promise."

Clay's heart melted. How could he deny children who possessed nearly nothing a peek into a room that should have been theirs? "When we're done, we'll go to the room together."

The children ate quickly, each devouring several bowls of the vegetable soup. Clay had hoped there might be some left over for his supper so he wouldn't need to cook again, but he'd suffer hunger himself rather than let the children go without. Each time they asked, as Vivian had taught them, "May I have more?" he allowed them to return to the pot until only a tiny bit of broth remained in the bottom.

When the food was gone, he insisted they fetch water and wash their dishes. He supposed in real schools, pupils weren't required to do dish washing, but given their circumstances, they needed housekeeping skills as well as book learning. They grumbled, but he helped, and they ended up giggling throughout the clean-up tasks.

The moment they placed the stack of clean bowls on the shelves, Naibi grabbed Clay's hand. "Our room, Mister Clay! Let us go into our room!"

Clay shouldn't permit the children to think of the extra sleeping room as theirs any longer. He replied, "All right. We'll go see *the* room now."

He knew they'd missed the subtle emphasis in his wording when they burst into the room and immediately began exploring from corner to corner. They touched everything with eager fingers while their joyful cries echoed from the beamed underside of the loft.

"Shelves!"

"Our own window!"

"Look, Etu—such nice beds! One for me and one for you!"

Clay's spirits bounced between joy at their obvious delight and regret because they wouldn't be able to enjoy the room. He felt as though he rode a teeter-totter.

Etu flopped onto the bed near the window and stretched out, folding his arms under his head. He grinned from ear to ear. Naibi clambered into the second one. She giggled, bounced on her bottom a couple of times, and then smoothed her hands over the now-rumpled blanket.

"Oh, it is so soft and nice, Mister Clay." The little girl sent Clay a dimpled smile, her dark eyes bright. "I love this bed." She curled on her side, using her stacked hands as a pillow. "I could sleep here for forever." She yawned.

Clay looked at Etu. The boy's eyes drooped. Clay said, "Are you tired?"

"*Ayi*—yes." Etu gave a lazy shrug. "It is hard to sleep in our new home. The hides, they are scratchy, and little animals crawl on us at night."

Clay tried not to shudder. He needed to talk to Tabu about ridding his house of mice. Maybe he didn't mind sharing with the little pests, but the children deserved better. "Would you . . . like to sleep here?"

Both children's eyebrows shot upward in happy speculation.

He added quickly, "Just a nap."

Their expressions fell. Naibi said, "Not night?"

Clay thought his heart might break, but he had to be honest. "No, not at night. The village leaders said you're to stay with your uncle Tabu."

"He is not our uncle," Etu groused, his brows pinching into a scowl. "He does not even want us. He said so."

Etu's comment didn't surprise Clay. Why would an elderly man want to care for two young, active children? He crossed to the bed and curled his hand over Etu's shoulder. "I'm sorry you and Naibi aren't happy, but we have to do what the tribal leaders say. So you have to stay with Tabu. But you can come here for school every day, and if you like, you can use these beds to take a nap." He gave Etu's chin a little flick and winked at Naibi. "But I won't let you sleep all day. We still have schoolwork to do."

Both children pretended to groan, and Clay laughed. Then, in unison, they closed their eyes. They looked so peaceful, a lump formed in Clay's throat. How he wished they could stay with him.

Clay closed the door, then pressed his forehead to the smooth sanded wood. His heart ached. For the children, who needed a better home. For Lizzie, who needed the love of God and the comfort of family. For the villagers, whose stubbornness held them back from hearing the message of God's grace. And for himself. Even for himself.

Turning from the door, he moved to the front bench and sat, staring at the log wall in front of him. So many lofty plans had brought him to this place. And nothing had turned out the way he'd intended. Why had things gone so awry?

He pushed to his feet, planning to lay out the items needed for bread baking, but when he looked toward the work counter, another idea took precedence. More than he needed bread, he needed advice. And he knew who could provide it. After retrieving his writing paper, ink, and pen, he seated himself on a barrel and dipped the pen in the ink. *Dear Pa . . .*

∽

Vivian paused, chewing the end of the pencil the telegrapher had provided for her to record her message on a small square of paper. He'd cautioned her to keep the message short—ten words or less. How could she condense the message and still express her heart's desire? Years of pent-up confusion, hurt, and anger longed for release. She'd already written one word: *Mother*.

She stared at it, a picture of her mother forming in her mind. Tall, slender, a serious face graced with kind eyes. Eyes that had lost a bit of their sparkle with Papa's death. Eyes that had watched Vivian from across the room the day of Papa's funeral, so much pain reflected that Vivian couldn't look at her for more than a few seconds at a time. Yet the remembrance was burned forever into her memory.

"Miss?" The man across the counter toyed with his little cap. "Train's due to pull out in five minutes. You best get to writing. 'Less you changed your mind about sending a telegram?"

Vivian jerked, startled from her reverie. "No, I . . . I haven't changed my mind. It's just—" The train's warning whistle blared. She needed to hurry. Pressing the rounded point to the paper, she scrawled a quick message: *Need to talk. Will write long letter from Vesta's.* Her hand shaking, she finished: *Love, Vivian*.

The man took it from her and scowled at it for a moment. "Gotta cut a word for it to go at forty cents." He pressed the paper against the scarred counter and drew a line through the word *love*. Vivian covered her quivering lips with her fingers. The man's action served as a reminder of the change in her relationship with Mother after Papa died.

"Forty cents." He held out his hand in expectation.

She withdrew four Liberty Head dimes from her little coin

purse and dropped them in the telegrapher's hand just as the train blared its whistle again—a long, piercing shriek.

"That's the last 'un," the man hollered over the shrill sound. "You best skedaddle!"

Vivian snatched up her reticule, dashed out of the office, and clattered across the wooden boarding deck. The train's conductor stood outside the passenger train, obviously seeking someone. When he spotted her, he waved frantically. He hopped onto the little landing and held out his hand. She grabbed hold, and he hefted her up at the same time steam *chug-chugged* and the train's big wheels squeaked into motion.

He opened the door to the passenger car and ushered Vivian through. She scuttled to her seat and sat, smoothing her skirts into place. She offered the conductor a relieved smile. "Thank you for your assistance, sir."

He tipped his hat, his mustache twitching with a grin. "Glad we got you onboard. I was afraid you were going to miss your last chance." He shuffled between the aisles, requesting tickets.

Vivian sank into the seat, the man's final words echoing through her mind. *"Your last chance . . ."* Might the letter she intended to write to Mother be her last chance to set things right? A second thought followed, one that made her mouth go dry. *What if my last chance fails? Will I be forced to carry the weight of Papa's death to my own grave?*

Chapter Thirty

Lizzie gave a mighty, final tug to the ropes securing the cured hides to the travois. Nothing shifted. Nodding in satisfaction, she moved to the next travois. She could have filled four travoises with furs, but she only owned three. So she'd piled them high and tied them securely. At least two thousand dollars worth of furs awaited transport to the trading post in Fort Yukon. But she'd be lucky to get half that amount.

Pursing her lips with regret, she double-checked a knot on the final travois. She'd get more if she could take the furs to White Horse instead, but the dogs wouldn't be able to drag the travoises that distance. If she wanted to sell in White Horse, she'd need to wait until the snows fell and she could mush the dogs with the loaded sled. Sailing over snow was much easier than dragging poles across the ground. But the snows were still months away. She had no desire to stay here by herself that much longer. Besides, a thousand dollars was plenty of money. More than enough to take her to California, with much left over to give to Pa. She admired the well-filled travoises, satisfaction puffing her chest. Wouldn't Pa be proud to see how successful she'd become?

Raucous barking intruded in her thoughts. The dogs leapt against their enclosure, releasing excited yips. Lizzie laughed, shaking her head. The animals knew what the loaded travoises meant, and they were eager to work. She crossed to the pen and reached over the wire, scratching their ears by turn. "Yes, yes, I know you want to help me." Her voice caught. Such good dogs. Such faithful companions. She swallowed tears. She would miss them. "We'll go soon. Not yet, but soon. Down. Down." Whining low in their throats, they obeyed.

Spinning on the soft heel of her moccasin, she headed for her cabin. She charged through the door, intending to grab the last two items she wanted to take with her—the moose-hide coat and her pa's rifle—and leave. But when she stepped over the threshold something made her pause. Weeks of anticipation and days of frantic preparation had led her to this moment of departure. Now that the time had arrived, she wasn't ready to go.

She stood, looking into the single room that had been her home her entire life. Memories tumbled on top of one another in a dizzying explosion of thought and feeling. Everything in the room, from the ragged curtains of bleached muslin billowing gently in the breeze to the braided rag rugs on the floor held meaning and value. Her eyes skittered from one item to another, her mind flipping through memories. Mama had made this; Pa had used that. The back of her nose stung, and she sniffed hard.

It hurt to leave so many belongings behind, but of what use would her battered pots and pans, her traps, and her well-used books be in California, the land of extravagance? She'd decided to take only those things that could serve her well in the city—the dresses and underclothes Vivian had given her and small items of personal use, such as the silver teapot Pa had given to Mama their first year together and the beautiful beaded necklace Mama had made for her shortly before she died.

The furniture, her few tunics and leggings—except those she now wore for travel, and her cooking items must all stay behind. Lizzie moved to the bed and sat. The old ropes creaked with her weight, the sound as familiar as a lullaby. She smoothed her hand over the straw mattress, bare now since she'd used the blankets to protect her furs from the bite of the ropes. She'd been birthed on this bed. Probably even conceived on this bed. And now, with the cabin standing empty, passing trappers and traders would come in and sleep on it. Perhaps Athabascan hunters from other villages might choose to stay in her cabin rather than in the hunting shacks that peppered the woods—the cabin would be much warmer than the simple bark or hide huts, the bed more comfortable than a pile of pine needles covered with a blanket.

Curling her fingers around the edge of the mattress, she shifted her attention from the bed to the old rusty cookstove. In her mind's eyes, she imagined strangers in *her* home, lighting a fire in *her* cookstove, making use of *her* things. Her chest tightened until she could barely draw a breath. She jumped to her feet. Where were the iron padlocks Pa had used to secure his fur caches? They must still be here somewhere. She should find the padlocks and put them on her doors to keep everyone away.

She gave herself a little shake. Drawing in a long, slow breath, she brought her racing pulse under control. She unclenched her hands and made a sweeping gesture, as if wiping the notion from her head. "You don't want these things anymore. You'll be living in a fine house with your father. Why shouldn't someone else use this old cabin and these old things?" But she looked again at the bed fashioned by her father's hands more than twenty years ago, and the jealousy pinching her heart didn't release.

"Enough. Time to go." Setting her jaw at a determined angle, she marched to the corner and grabbed up the coat she'd made for Vitse. She whispered her plans aloud, slipping easily into the Athabascan tongue. "One last visit to the village of my mother's birth. I will see my grandparents and try, for the sake of my mother, to restore peace. Then I will offer the food stores in my cache to Clay Selby for his use."

What pleasure she would find in offering Clay the supply of smoked moose and salmon, the bushel baskets of corn and squash and pumpkins. Knowing he wouldn't go hungry thanks to her made her want to dance and sing. She hugged the coat to her chest, savoring the unique sensation of lightness and joy.

Then she released a little gasp. Still cradling the coat, she jerked her gaze around the room, examining her belongings again. The table and chairs, bureau, and kitchen breakfront cupboard, although well used, were all still serviceable. She much preferred thinking of Clay using her belongings—and perhaps remembering her with each use—than strangers putting their dirty hands on them.

An idea quickly formed in her mind. "Yes, yes . . ." She nodded, happy with the plan. It would mean at least an extra hour of work before she could visit the village, but what was an hour? She'd spend a hundred hours if it meant gifting the man who'd stolen a piece of her heart. She draped the coat over one of the rough-hewn chairs her father had built and then lifted the coat and chair together. She bustled toward the door, smiling, her moccasin-covered feet padding softly against the floor. One last task and then she could begin her new life.

⁓

"G," Naibi announced slowly, sliding the square of bark bearing the letter into place between the squares marked with F and I, "and O." She placed the final square with a broad, round O filling it, at the very end of the row of letters. Using her finger as a pointer, she bounced it along the squiggly line of squares stretched across the mission building floor. "A, B, C, D, E, F, G, H, I, J, K, L, M, N, and O!" She clapped her hands in delight.

"Well done, Naibi—you remembered them all." Clay captured her in a hug, wincing at the musty smell of the little girl's hair. Over the past week, both Naibi and Etu had grown grimier in appearance. Apparently Tabu never required them to bathe. But despite their uncleanliness, their minds worked well. Their English vocabulary expanded daily. They'd learned the first half of the alphabet, the sounds the letters made, and were already able to write short words such as "man" and "dog." Clay surmised by the end of the next week, with all the letters tucked into their knowledge banks, they'd be ready to begin real reading lessons.

Naibi wriggled loose and beamed at him. "I remembered!" Her bright smile faded to a look of uncertainty. "I am smart, right, Mister Clay?"

Clay hugged her again and repeated the assurance he'd already given twice since noon. He wished he could pinch Tabu's lips shut. Daily, the old man berated the children for going to school. Just that morning, he had hobbled into the mission yard, pointed at them by turn, and stated, *"Yigginh git'itadhit."* Clay had bitten down on the end of his tongue to keep from bellowing, "They are not stupid!" He'd held his temper partly because Tabu was old and probably needed their help during the day, but mostly because he was supposed to set a good example. If he yelled in anger at their caretaker, he'd set the poorest example.

But now he had a new responsibility—undoing the harm the old man inflicted with his careless tongue. "You are the smartest girl in school."

Naibi stared at him for a moment, her lips slightly parted, and then she burst out laughing. She rose from her crouched position next to the letters and grinned at Etu, who straddled a bench and put together a simple wooden puzzle Clay had made by carving apart an old crate slat. "Etu, you smartest boy in school."

Etu straightened his shoulders, his skinny chest puffing. Then he scowled. "You make joke at me. I am only boy in school."

Naibi flipped her hands outward. "So you be smartest, yes?"

"Naibi, *yigginh git'itadhit.*" Etu spat the words.

Clay strode across the classroom and sat, facing Etu. Even though he knew Etu only repeated what he'd heard, he couldn't allow him to wound his sister. He took the boy's chin in his hand. "Etu, you should never call someone a name that will hurt them. And that goes especially for your sister. She looks up to you—admires you. You should protect her, not insult her."

Etu tugged loose, twisting his face into a sneer. "She says stupid things. She makes me look dumb."

"No one can make you look dumb without your permission." Clay lowered his voice. "Etu, I know Tabu sometimes says things he shouldn't. He's wrong. But that doesn't mean you can be wrong, too. Hurting someone is always wrong. What verse did we work on yesterday during our Bible time?"

Etu crunched his face, concentrating. He recited slowly, " 'Be ye kind one to another . . .' "

"That's right." Clay wanted the children to memorize all of Ephesians 4:32, but he'd broken it into sections to make it easier for them. He needed to focus on the second half soon—he had a feeling that if the children remained with Tabu, they would have need of the reminder to forgive. "Is calling someone stupid kind?"

The boy hung his head. "No."

"Then what should you do?"

After several seconds of sullen silence, Etu finally sighed. "I should say sorry."

"Good boy."

Etu scuffed across the floor to his sister, his head low. The children whispered together, and finally they hugged. Etu remained with Naibi, playing with the bark alphabet letters.

Clay stayed on the opposite side of the room, allowing them to make their peace, his heart heavy. After only a short time with Tabu, the children had changed so much. He sensed a growing resentment in Etu, and Naibi had developed a penchant for whining. He berated himself for his stupidity in losing them to Tabu. If he'd exercised better judgment, they might still be with him.

"I can't turn back time," Clay murmured, half admonition, half prayer. "All I can do is try to abide by the village dictates from now on so I don't give them further cause to mistrust me. Maybe Shruh and the other leaders will see how ill-kempt the children are and ask me to take them again." His heart swelled with hope. A second hope quickly followed. "And maybe they'll take pity on Lizzie, too, and welcome her into the tribe."

And maybe I'll grow wings and fly to the moon.

Why did he persist in trying to bring Lizzie into the village? She didn't want to come—she was leaving. Would he never get that into his head? He sagged on the bench, his chin low. Could it be the problem wasn't getting the realization into his head, but convincing his heart?

"Mister Clay?"

Etu's concerned voice captured Clay's attention. He stood and moved quickly to the children. "Yes? What is it?"

The children shifted to their knees and looked toward the open doorway, their faces pinched in concern. Etu said, "Something is wrong."

Clay hurried to the door. Villagers milled in confusion, their mutterings carrying to Clay's ears. They seemed to be looking toward the southwest, but from inside the building, Clay couldn't determine what held their attention.

"School is over for today. You two go to Tabu now," he directed the children as he stepped outside. He moved toward the center of the village, his gaze seeking. He spotted what appeared to be a spiral of smoke lifting above the trees. He stopped near a group of women and asked in Athabascan, "Is someone smoking meat?"

Most of them ignored him, but the one standing nearest looked at him the way Tabu often looked at the children. He half expected her to call him stupid. "Too large for a fire from a smokehouse. And too black."

"No firebolts have come from the sky," another one said, confusion underscoring her tone. "So it must not be trees." The others mumbled their agreements.

The one who had first addressed Clay bobbed her head, sending a knowing look across the group. "See the size? And the black smoke? Dead wood. Much dead wood burns. It is a cabin fire."

The women wandered off, chattering amongst themselves.

Clay stared at the black spiral that rose and then drifted with the breeze, marring the clear blue sky with dingy smudges. It appeared more ominous by the moment. A cabin fire, the woman had said—*Lizzie!* His heart leapt into his throat and, without a thought for the possible consequences, he took off running through the woods.

Chapter Thirty-One

Lizzie stood next to the dog pen, her hand buried in Martha's ruff, and watched her cabin burn. Smoke swirled above the treetops. Flames danced behind the windows and licked their way beneath the eaves. The roar and crackle became a melody of cleansing. Although a part of her ached to see her home destroyed, a greater part of her rejoiced that she would never have need to imagine strangers within its walls.

Martha whined, bumping her master's hand with her dry nose. Lizzie automatically stroked the dog's head. "Shh, girl, we are safe. All is well."

The heat touched her face and raised perspiration on her forehead. She swiped it away with the back of her hand and then wiped her hand on her tunic. *The Gwich'in villagers will have no record of my presence here. I will carry my memories of Mama and Pa away with me and leave only ashes behind.* The thought brought equal measures of satisfaction and regret.

She turned and faced the dog pen. The dogs crowded against the wire fence, their curious eyes fixed on her face. She smiled and cupped Martha's square jaw in her palms while allowing her gaze to sweep over all of them. "You needn't worry. The fire will burn itself out. I'll put you in your rigging soon and we'll—"

"Lizzie! Lizzie!"

The frantic cry carrying from the woods brought Lizzie's words to a halt. She turned from the pen to see Clay burst from the trees, his face etched with fear. He dashed halfway across the yard and then stopped so abruptly it appeared he'd collided with an immovable force. His head bobbed here and there, seeming to take in the scattered furniture and the blazing cabin. Then he spun around and spotted her beside the pen. Relief broke across his face.

"Lizzie!" He raced to her and, without warning, swept her off her feet. His face pressed against her hair. "Lizzie . . . oh, Lizzie . . . thank the Lord you're safe . . ." He rocked her, continuing to murmur.

His encircling arms bound her own to her sides so she couldn't reach up and return the embrace. But she wanted to. Oh, how she wanted to. Her heart nearly burst with the all-consuming wonder of being held in this man's arms. She pressed her cheek to his shoulder, glorying in being held. In feeling valued. In feeling loved. Tears sprang into Lizzie's eyes, an overflow of the myriad emotions welling in her chest.

Finally, Clay set her down and cupped her cheeks. He peered directly into her face, his dear gray-green eyes alight with concern. "You're all right?" He shifted back a few inches. His hands smoothed her hair, her shoulders, her upper arms, and then returned to gently cradle her face in his palms while he looked her up and down. "You aren't burned?"

She curled her hands around his wrists and smiled at him through the tears that distorted her vision. "I am fine. Unhurt. Don't worry." *But hold me again. Please hold me again.* . . .

As if reading her secret thoughts, he wrapped her once more in his embrace. She nestled against him, the warmth of his body and the musky scent of his skin more welcome than anything she'd known before.

His voice rasped, "Thank God. When I saw the smoke, I thought—" He pulled back again and turned his face toward the yard. His brow furrowed. "How did you get so many items out of the cabin?" He clamped his hands over her shoulders and gave her a little shake. "You might have been killed trying to save your belongings!"

Looking into his fear-filled eyes, compassion swelled in Lizzie's breast. She touched his whisker-shadowed cheek, offering a reassuring smile. "I took everything out before I started the fire. I was never in danger."

The furrows in his brow deepened. Then he released her and stumbled back. "You . . . you started the fire . . . deliberately?"

She couldn't determine from his tone whether he was angry or merely confused. "Yes. I am leaving, so . . ." The explanation died in her throat. She was leaving. Leaving this land. Leaving this *man*. The ecstatic bliss of moments ago faded into a blur of mingled regret and sorrow.

❦

Clay clenched his fists and pressed them to his thighs, a futile attempt to bring his tangled emotions under control. When he'd seen the smoke—and had envisioned Lizzie in danger—he'd reacted on instinct. His frenzied race through the woods left him breathless and terrified. Then, when he'd seen her safe and untouched by the flames, gratefulness had nearly buckled his knees. Capturing her in his arms as an expression of his great relief, however, resulted in the mightiest reaction of all.

Even now his arms tingled from their contact with her, eager to once again enfold her—to hold her tight to his heart. She'd fit so perfectly, her head nestling into the curve of his neck, her slender form aligning to his contours. Like two pieces of a puzzle they were, designed for one another. But what foolishness, to allow himself to embrace Lizzie. Now that he'd held her, how could he let her go?

"But why burn the cabin?" he asked. Unbidden, anger swelled. He'd spent weeks building the mission, yet Lizzie had set fire to a perfectly good home.

"I . . . I couldn't bear to think of others using it." She toyed with the buckskin tie on one braid. "An empty cabin is an invitation. I didn't want strangers in my home."

What difference did it make if she no longer had use for it? Clay snorted. "It was a *selfish* act, Lizzie."

Her face contorted—in anger or hurt?—but before she could respond, a roar filled the air. Instinctively, Clay dove for her, shielding her with his body. Arms wound around one another, they watched the cabin's roof and walls collapse inward, sending up a great shower of sparks. Yellow and orange flames shot up to swallow the sparks. Soon the cabin would be reduced to chunks of charred wood and a pile of black ash. Clay feared his heart would bear a similar fate if he didn't release this woman. He forced his traitorous arms to relinquish their hold.

Stepping several feet away, he spoke sternly, more for himself than for Lizzie. "Why not burn everything, then?" He swept his arm to indicate the items standing under the sun in the yard. "Were you also going to burn your furnishings one by one?"

"No." Her dark eyes flickered with uncertainty. "I meant to offer them . . . to you. For use in your mission. But . . ." She ducked her head.

He stared at the part in her raven-dark hair, guilt chasing away his anger. *"Be ye kind one to another, tenderhearted, forgiving one another . . ."* The words he'd asked Etu to recall earlier that afternoon winged through Clay's heart, flaying him in admonition. He'd told the boy it was always wrong to hurt someone, and he'd chosen harshness for the purpose of distancing himself from Lizzie.

He stretched his hand toward her. "Lizzie, I'm sorry. The cabin . . . it was yours, and you should be able to do whatever you wish with it. Even if that means burning it."

She tipped her head slightly, peering at him through her fringe of lashes.

"I was scared. For you." Clay gulped. If she didn't stop looking at him in that crestfallen way he might do more than put his arms around her. He might wash away the expression with a torrent of kisses. He pushed his hands into his pockets and spoke again, using the tone he might use to comfort Naibi. "I let fear make me speak in anger. Will you forgive me?"

Slowly, so slowly he thought he might have imagined it, she bobbed her head in agreement.

He smiled, and when she offered a shy smile in return he nearly melted. Such a beautiful woman with a tender heart. *But she can't be yours.*

She lowered her head and smoothed the grass with her moccasin-covered toe. "I . . . I also have a full cache. Moose and salmon, vegetables . . ." She flicked a glance at him and then looked down again. "I have no need for it, since I am . . . I am leaving."

Did her voice break, or did he only imagine it? Between

the dogs' persistent whining, the continued noise of the fire, and the wind's whisper through the trees, he found it difficult to hear her.

Lizzie's head bounced up, her gaze colliding with his. "You will take these things from me? The food? The furniture and . . . and the pans and other things? You will use them?" Her dark eyes seemed to beg.

Clay nodded emphatically. "Yes. And each time I use them, I'll" —he swallowed—"think of you."

Her face lit, transforming her. The apprehension, the hint of anger—all disappeared beneath a beaming smile of gratitude. But Clay should be the grateful one. She'd just given him a tremendous gift. He wanted to gift her in return, but how? Her beautiful face, aimed at him with such admiration and appreciation, put inappropriate ideas in his head. Turning away, he spotted the travoises waiting beneath the shelter of aspen trees. He pointed. "You're taking those with you?"

She stepped to his side. Her nearness, although she didn't touch him, sent a tingle of awareness from his scalp down his spine. "Only to Fort Yukon. I must sell the furs for money for my journey."

"May I . . . accompany you?" Surely she'd appreciate having someone with her. Someone to see her off, to give her a proper good-bye.

"You would do that for me?"

Her astonishment touched him. He brushed her cheek with his fingertips. "It's not so much."

But her eyes told him it was much. Very much. For long seconds, she held him captive with her adoring gaze, and then she sucked in a sharp breath. "If you would go with me to Fort Yukon, might you . . ." She let out several little huffs of air, as if gathering courage. She bustled to one of the travoises and lifted a coat from the top of the pile. Holding it toward him, she said, "I made this."

Clay walked slowly toward her, admiring the coat. He'd seen many beautifully embellished coats worn by the natives at the funeral potlatches, but this one far exceeded all others. He smoothed his hands across the thick beaver ruff. "This is lovely, Lizzie." A sudden thought struck, and he jerked his hand back. "You aren't giving this to *me*."

She hugged the coat to her chest, her eyes wide. "To Vitse. For a peace offering." Once again, she dipped her head, shrinking inside herself. "So my mother might be honored."

Clay had witnessed the last ugly exchange between Lizzie and her grandmother. He couldn't imagine the older woman softening enough to accept this coat. But he wouldn't speak of that to Lizzie. He offered, "Would you like me to be with you when you speak to your grandmother?" How he wanted to help her—to give her strength. He held his breath, waiting for her reply.

"I would like that, Clay. Thank you."

Clay released the breath, relief making his legs weak. He leaned against the nearest tree. "You want to do this before going to Fort Yukon, yes?"

She nodded.

"Well, then, let's go see her now." He pushed away from the tree and reached for her hand. "But first, Lizzie, let's pray and ask God to prepare the way to healing between yourself and your grandparents." If she could experience one miracle—one seemingly impossible happening—then perhaps she could leave with the knowledge of God in her heart. And if he knew she carried God with her when she left, surely he would have an easier time letting her go.

He knelt, looking up at her expectantly, his hand still

stretched toward her. She stared at the cabin, where red coals glowed in a blackened pile of timbers. He waited, praying silently for God to win the battle taking place inside her soul. Finally, she sighed. She draped the coat back over the furs, knelt, and placed her hand in his.

"Pray to your God, Clay Selby. And may He have ears to hear."

Chapter Thirty-Two

Lizzie lifted the moose-hide coat from the first travois. Sending a stern look toward the wriggling, eager dogs, she said, "Down." She waited until they obeyed. "Stay." She ignored their complaining whines and followed Clay to the door of her grandparents' cabin.

She allowed Clay the privilege of knocking on the weathered door. Her hands, trembling and clumsy, refused to obey her wishes. Clay's prayer—a prayer requesting peace and a restored relationship between Lizzie, Vitse, and Vitsiy—echoed in her mind. His impassioned yet personal tone as he addressed the God he called Father reminded her of Mama's voice when she spoke to the High One. How she wanted to believe all those prayers would finally be answered.

Clay stepped back from the door and lifted his shoulders in a shrug. "They don't answer. Do you want to—"

The door swung open, revealing Co'Ozhii. Lizzie stifled a gasp when she got a view of her grandmother in the sunlight. In the weeks since they'd argued at the mission, it seemed Vitse had aged a dozen years. Her skin hung in sallow folds on her face, and deep purple smudges underlined her sunken eyes. Her tunic hung loose on a frame far too thin. Her gray hair, lank and lusterless, flared out from unraveling braids.

Vitse turned her unsmiling gaze from Clay to Lizzie. "What do you want?"

Not even a hint of her former defiance colored her tone. She just sounded tired. So very, very tired. Even after all the pain this woman had inflicted, Lizzie's heart stirred with concern. The illness had taken much from her grandmother.

"I wanted to see you." She took care to speak in the Athabascan tongue. "I am leaving soon, traveling to California. Then I will trouble you no longer." She searched her grandmother's face, seeking a sign of either relief or—better—regret. But the woman's face remained impassive. Lizzie held out the coat, which draped across both of her arms. "I brought a gift. I made it. For you."

Vitse's eyes flicked to the coat, but they didn't linger to admire the foxtails, delicate beading, or flawless hide. She lifted her tired gaze to Lizzie once more. "Why?"

Lizzie stepped forward, forcing Clay to move aside. But he stayed close, providing comfort and support with his presence. "To bring peace to my mother's soul." She needed to provide no further explanation. Her grandmother would understand the value and purpose of a peace gift. She bounced the coat slightly, battling the urge to force it into Vitse's hands. "Will you accept it?" *Will you let peace blossom between us before I leave you forever?*

A deep, wracking cough sounded from inside the cabin. Co'Ozhii whirled toward the sound. The sudden movement must have made her dizzy, because she clutched for the door frame and missed. Clay jumped forward and caught her before she fell. He guided her into the cabin, and Lizzie followed, concern making her stomach twist.

Clay pressed Co'Ozhii into a chair and then crouched beside her. "You are still sick?"

Clay spoke with such kindness. He truly cared about her grandparents.

"I am recovered." Vitse's weakness disproved her words. "But now Shruh lies ill. I gave the fever to him." She gestured to the deeply shadowed corner where a blanket-covered lump signified Shruh's body. "I must see to him." She tried to rise, but her legs gave way and she collapsed into the chair.

Clay rose and crossed to the pine-needle bed. He spoke to Shruh in a soft voice, but Lizzie couldn't hear the words. She considered going to her grandfather, too, but she feared her grandmother might fall from the chair if someone didn't remain near. She placed the coat on the table and pulled out another chair to sit close to Vitse.

Lizzie stared at her grandmother's hands—wrinkled hands with crooked joints and yellowed nails. Old hands. The sight made her sad. "How long has the cough held him?"

"A week." Vitse sighed, her gaze never wavering from the bed in the corner. "He tired himself, caring for me, and then he fell ill. Now I care for him." Her flat tone took on a slightly bitter edge. "If our only child did not betray us and did not now lie cold in a grave, I would have—" She bit down on her lip. Her head swiveled quickly, her hard gaze boring into Lizzie's. "It is too late. One cannot make peace with the dead."

Lizzie leaned forward slightly. "But you could make peace with me. Then Mother can lie at rest, knowing peace exists between her daughter and her mother."

"And if we make peace, you will stay here as a daughter would, and care for your aged vitsiy and vitse?" Vitse released a derisive snort. "You go, daughter of a white man, and live in his world. There is no peace for us."

The lump in the bed shifted, bringing Vitsiy's face into a weak beam of sunlight drifting through the open window. "My wife, come near with our granddaughter."

Lizzie cringed at his weak, trembly tone. The wizened man calling from the bed bore no resemblance to her powerful grandfather. She rose and held her arm to Co'Ozhii. Her grandmother made a face, but she took Lizzie's arm and allowed her to assist her to the bed. Clay moved aside, and Co'Ozhii sat on the mattress near Shruh's hip. Lizzie stood beside her grandmother, looking over her shoulder at her grandfather's thin, pain-riddled features.

Shruh took Co'Ozhii's hand and then drew in a rattling breath. "You vowed to banish our daughter if she married a white man. You brought honor to yourself by keeping your vow." His words escaped on a near-whisper, his voice so raspy it reminded Lizzie of sandpaper on rough wood. "Now our daughter lies dead. You can bring an end to the banishment . . . if you wish. No honor will be lost."

Co'Ozhii's spine stiffened. She yanked her hand free. "You ask me to make peace with the one who bears the blood of traitorous white men?"

Shruh's face contorted, and his body rose involuntarily as he coughed—a horrible, deep, painful cough that made Lizzie clutch her own chest in agony. When he finished, he collapsed, his lank gray hair fanning out across the mattress. He spoke, his voice whisper-soft. "I only tell you what you can do without losing honor. The choice, my wife, is yours." His eyes slipped closed, and a wheezing breath eased from his slack lips.

Clay rushed forward and leaned over Shruh, his ear close to Shruh's chest. Then he straightened and put his hand beneath Shruh's nose. Lizzie sat frozen, staring at Vitsiy's still face. She knew the truth, but her heart didn't want to accept it. Clay braced his hands on the bed and stood for long seconds, his head low and eyes closed. Finally he looked into Lizzie's face.

"I'm so sorry. He's gone."

Lizzie nodded, clamping her teeth together to hold back a cry of distress. Something deep inside of her broke, and she feared it would never be mended. Her grandfather was dead, and she'd never truly known him.

Clay had spoken in English, but apparently Vitse had understood. With an animal cry of grief, she pushed Clay aside. She wrapped her arms around Shruh and held him to her chest while wails of mourning poured from her throat.

Lizzie wanted to look away from her grandmother's anguished pose, but her eyes refused to cooperate. The image—Vitse's tenacious hold on Vitsiy's lifeless body, her straggly gray hair falling across Vitsiy's face—burned into her memory. Suddenly, Co'Ozhii swung one arm outward. The movement pushed Shruh's lifeless arm off the mattress's edge, where it dangled, a narrow shaft of light highlighting its fragility. With her face still buried against Shruh's limp neck, Co'Ozhii sobbed, "Go away. I wish to mourn alone."

Lizzie had mourned alone when her mother died, and she didn't wish such sadness—such lonely emptiness—on her grandmother. She remained rooted in place.

Another wail tore from Co'Ozhii's chest. "Go!" Her mournful cries echoed off the log walls.

Clay caught Lizzie's arm and drew her away from the bed. "Come. We'll tell the others of Shruh's passing. She'll allow her tribesmen to comfort her. It's best for us to go."

Lizzie agreed with Clay, but it stung that Co'Ozhii preferred comfort from anyone other than her granddaughter. She swallowed the fierce knot of sorrow that filled her throat.

"Yes. We'll go." She slipped out the door with Clay, but she left the coat behind.

⁓

Vivian sat at the desk in the room that had been hers during her growing-up years. The room was exactly as Vivian had left it when she'd gone to Oklahoma a little over a year ago, but the familiar surroundings—comforting and secure when she'd lived here—now felt strange. Vivian couldn't cast aside the feeling that she didn't belong here.

Someone tapped at the door, and Vivian called, "Come in."

The door cracked open, and Aunt Vesta's smiling face appeared. "So this is where you escaped. You disappeared so quickly after supper—I turned my back for a moment, and you were gone."

Vivian grimaced. She had slipped upstairs after finishing her meal, but she hadn't meant for her actions to be construed as escape. "Did you or Uncle Matthew need me? He seemed fine." In fact, he'd made remarkable progress between the date of Aunt Vesta's letter and Vivian's arrival in Hampshire County. Vivian wondered if she was needed here after all. "And you were busy with the kitchen maid, so I came on up."

"No need to apologize, Vivian. You are correct that you weren't needed. I merely wanted to check on you." Aunt Vesta entered the room and sat at the foot of the quilt-covered bed, smiling at Vivian. Her red-gold hair, threaded with silver, shone in the soft yellow glow of the desk lamp. "Will you turn in early tonight? I'm sure you're still exhausted from your lengthy journey and last night's late arrival."

Vivian shifted sideways in the gracefully scrolled chair and absently smoothed her hands over the soft fabric of the ruffled dressing gown she'd found hanging in her wardrobe. "Yes, I'll turn in soon, after I finish—" She glanced at the letter she'd begun. Only a few paragraphs thus far—a few stilted, ill-worded paragraphs. She should throw it away and start over. If only she could gather her thoughts into a sensible bundle.

Aunt Vesta raised her chin and peered down her nose at the page on the desk. "What are you working on there?"

Vivian flicked the paper's corner with her thumbnail. "A letter. To Mother."

"Ahh." Her aunt nodded wisely. "Assuring her of your safe arrival. That's very kind of you, Vivian."

"It isn't what you think." Vivian's words came out more tartly than she'd intended. She sighed. "Aunt Vesta, I need to . . . well, clear the air, so to speak . . . with Mother. But I'm not sure how to begin. Could you help me?"

"Why, certainly, dear." Aunt Vesta tipped her head, her expression attentive, as Vivian had come to expect. "When clearing the air, the best place to go is to the root of the disagreement. What do you perceive as the root?"

Vivian's mind skipped backward a dozen years and stumbled to a halt on the day Papa died. Her chin quivered, and she set her teeth together to stop the childish tears. "She has never forgiven me for killing Papa."

Her aunt's eyebrows shot skyward, disappearing beneath the soft fluff of her bangs. "Why, Vivian, what on earth makes you think such a thing?"

Vivian braced her hands on her knees and leaned slightly forward. "What else can I believe? After Papa died—after I neglected to go to him as she'd instructed and find him in time to summon help—she never hugged me or kissed me." Her hands balled into fists, her nails biting into her soft flesh. But she welcomed the discomfort. It took her focus away, albeit briefly, from the deep, abiding pain in her heart. "I would catch her staring across the room at me with this look of . . . of *betrayal* on her face.

"Then as soon as she remarried and we moved to the reservation, she packed me up and sent me to you, as if she feared I would bring death upon a second father." Vivian's throat tightened, the hurt and resentment of the past years rising up to strangle her. "I want so much to return to the days when Mother loved me. But I don't know how to go there."

She flipped her hands outward in a helpless gesture. "I can't bring Papa back to life for her, Aunt Vesta. What else can I do to earn Mother's love again?"

Aunt Vesta covered her mouth with her fingers, her eyes wide and distressed. Tears flooded her eyes, making her green irises shimmer. "My dear child, all this time . . ." She opened her arms. "Come here, Vivian."

Vivian slipped from the chair to the bed and allowed her aunt to draw her head to her shoulder. She'd sat close to Aunt Vesta many times as a young girl. Then, as now, she'd longed for her mother to hold her in that same way. How she hoped Aunt Vesta would discover a means of bridging the gap between herself and Mother.

Aunt Vesta stroked Vivian's hair. "Vivian, your mother didn't blame you for your father's death. She couldn't have. She was too busy blaming herself."

Vivian tried to sit up so she could look into her aunt's eyes, but Aunt Vesta held her tight, her fingers coiling into Vivian's unbound hair. Vivian snuggled her cheek more fully against her aunt's shoulder and stayed within her embrace.

"Your mother blamed herself for asking you, just a little slip of a girl, to enter those woods where you might have been bitten by the snake that so frightened you. She blamed herself that you had to grow up without a father."

Aunt Vesta's words, so gently spoken, penetrated the center of the hurt Vivian carried. "She was consumed by guilt—so much so she couldn't bear to look at you. She saw the burden of pain and fear you carried, and she hated herself for causing it. That's why I suggested she send you to live with your uncle and me."

Vivian jolted loose of her aunt's hold and sat upright. "Y-you suggested?"

"Yes, it was all my idea for you to leave the reservation where your mother and new stepfather had chosen to serve." Aunt Vesta took a lacy handkerchief from her pocket and began mopping at Vivian's cheeks.

Vivian drew back in surprise. Was she crying? She touched her face and found it moist with tears.

Aunt Vesta pressed the handkerchief into Vivian's lap and continued. "When she remarried and moved to an even more rugged landscape than the one she'd left behind, she worried something terrible might befall you, too. She nearly ate herself up with worry. So Uncle Matthew and I offered to keep you with us, where you'd be safe."

"So Clay was right . . ." He'd told her she'd been sent away for her safety. But she surmised it was because of *her* fears, not her mother's fears.

Aunt Vesta took Vivian's hands and squeezed. "Dear girl, your mother loves you dearly, and she wants nothing more than a close, loving relationship with you." She paused, her fine brows pinching together thoughtfully. "Do you want to know how to regain the untarnished love you once shared?"

Vivian nodded eagerly. "Yes. Please tell me what I can do."

With a sweet smile, Aunt Vesta leaned forward and brushed a kiss on Vivian's cheek. "Tell her you forgive her—and mean it. It's all she needs to hear, and it will set both of you free."

Chapter Thirty-Three

Lizzie knelt beside the closest team of dogs and draped her arm across Martin's back. He whined softly, bobbing his head against her ribs, but remained obediently on his belly as she'd directed. Lizzie's chest ached so badly she could scarcely draw a breath. Clay had prayed for peace between her grandparents and herself. But Vitsiy was dead and Vitse had demanded she leave. Where was the peace she so desperately needed?

Clay crossed to her, his long shadow falling across her and the dogs. Then he crouched, causing his shadow to cover only her. Somehow, huddling within the protection of his shadow offered a small measure of comfort.

"It's too late for you to leave for Fort Yukon now." Clay's hand started to reach for her, but then he jerked it back. He curled his hands over his knees. "You should wait until tomorrow morning. You can say good-bye to Etu and Naibi, and I'll accompany you—help you with the dogs, in selling your furs, and making arrangements for travel."

Her fuzzy brain, weary from the tiring day and emotional battles, found no argument but one. "I burned my cabin. I have no place to go except to Fort Yukon."

Clay scowled. "It's too late. And you're tired . . ." He rubbed his finger beneath his nose for a moment. Then he snapped his fingers. "I know. Come to the mission. We'll find a way to tether the dogs behind the building, and you can stay in the room I prepared for Etu and Naibi."

He wished her to sleep under his roof? Only a man wanting to take a woman to be his own would make such a request. Hope coiled through her middle, but she pushed the fleeting emotion back down. He didn't want her in that way, or he wouldn't sit there with his hands gripping his knees—he'd draw her to his body instead.

She shook her head. "The tribal leaders would not approve. I can return to my land and sleep under the cache." The food cache sat several feet above the ground, keeping the food safe from marauding creatures. The spot provided shelter enough for a summer sleep.

Clay's scowl deepened. "You'll not sleep in a shack or on the ground when I have a perfectly good bed at the mission." He rose, holding out his hand. "Come. I'll get you and the dogs settled, and then I need to inform the villagers of Shruh's passing. Co'Ozhii will need their support and strength."

For years she'd made her own decisions. Allowing Clay to direct her should make her feel weak, yet she felt oddly relieved to have someone else take control for a little while. Lizzie took his hand and allowed him to pull her upright. She sighed. "Thank you, Clay. For taking care of me, and for seeing to Vitse's needs."

She whistled to the dogs, and they leapt up, dancing in excitement. As she and Clay led the teams through the village, his shadow continued to enfold hers. A fleeting wish winged through her heart: *If only this caring man could enfold me forever.*

❧

Clay emerged from the bark hut he'd occupied before completing the mission. He'd peeled away portions of it, using the wood to build shelves inside the mission, and the sunlight pouring through the large gaps had kept him awake most of the night. *God, grant me all I need to meet the challenges of this day.* He knew he would face physical challenges, taking Lizzie all the way to Fort Yukon, but mostly he was concerned about the emotional challenges.

How would he find the strength to bid Lizzie farewell today? The woman had woven herself into the deepest part of his being. Lifting his eyes to the clear sky, he whispered, "Help me, Lord."

The village already buzzed with activity. Preparations for Shruh's potlatch were well under way. He hoped the villagers would forgive him for seeing to Lizzie's needs today rather than staying and helping. As he headed for the river to draw water for a morning wash, the sound of pounding footsteps intruded. Etu and Naibi bounded to his side, offering good-morning greetings.

He gave them each a hug and pointed to the extra buckets sitting outside the mission door. "There won't be any lessons today. But grab those and come with me. We'll have enough water for all of us—you, me, and Missus Lizzie—to wash."

The children's faces had sagged in disappointment until he'd mentioned Lizzie. Then they broke into broad smiles. Naibi clapped her chubby hands. "Missus Lizzie, she moves to the village?"

Clay quickly corrected the child, his own heart stinging at the change in the little girl's demeanor when she learned

Lizzie would be leaving. How well he understood her sadness. He added, "But you'll get to see her one more time before she leaves, and I know she'll be glad to see you. But come—let's get the water before we wake her."

When they returned from the river, low whines and high-pitched yips greeted them—Lizzie's dogs, awake and ready to face the day. Etu shot a startled look in Clay's direction. "Mister Clay, you did not say Missus Lizzie brought her dogs!" Both children abandoned their buckets on the pathway and dashed behind the building to greet the animals.

As Clay stood watching, Lizzie stepped from the cabin. Her hands deftly twisted her hair into matching braids as she rounded the building. Clay stifled his chuckle when she put her hands on her hips and gave the children a mock scowl. "Who is bothering my dogs?"

The children looked up. Broad smiles creased their faces, and they ran to Lizzie, arms outstretched. "Missus Lizzie! Missus Lizzie!" She laughed, bestowing hugs and kisses.

Clay's heart turned over in his chest. The love so clearly exhibited between the woman and the children rivaled the beauty of the summer morning. Sunlight shimmered on three dark heads, laughter joining the birdsong. Clay wished he could spend every morning in just this way, observing a joyous celebration of togetherness.

He strode to the happy trio. "Children, would you like to take care of Lizzie's dogs this morning? Give them some water and dried salmon from the loft? Then you can have breakfast with Missus Lizzie and me. It will give you time with her before she leaves."

Naibi clung to Lizzie's hand, her expression doleful. "You are really leaving?"

Lizzie smoothed the child's tangled hair from her eyes. "I must go to my father now. It is my new home."

306

Etu sighed. "We will miss you."

"And I you."

The shine of the morning dimmed with their shared sadness. Clay intervened once more. "See to the dogs, then bring the extra buckets into the mission." He lifted a bucket, took hold of Lizzie's elbow with his other hand, and guided her to the mission doors. A glance over his shoulder confirmed the children followed his directions. Lizzie also peered backward, her expression pensive. He offered her a smile. "They've become very responsible."

He and Lizzie chatted together as they prepared breakfast at the cookstove—Lizzie frying johnny cakes and Clay stirring a pot of cornmeal mush. The children, so happy to have Lizzie with them, didn't even argue when he instructed them to wash well before eating. They came to the table with clean hands and shining faces. The meal passed happily, with laughter and more chatter, but all too soon the food was gone, the dishes washed and put away, and Lizzie announced that it was time to go.

Etu's lower lip poked out. "I don't want you to go."

"Or me." Tears shimmered in Naibi's eyes.

Lizzie gathered both children close. Clay thought his heart might break when her eyes slipped closed and her face contorted with unshed tears. He touched her back and whispered, "It's a long journey to Fort Yukon."

With a nod, she set the children aside. She bestowed one more kiss on each of their round cheeks and then rose. "I'll ready the dogs." She dashed out.

They spoke little as they drove the travois-bearing dogs through the woods. Lizzie had taken this route before—a path that ended at a ferry that would carry them across the river and into Fort Yukon.

By noon, Clay was ready to sit and rest, but a hearty lunch

of dried salmon, cornmeal cakes, and berries picked along the river refreshed his body. And his spirits were lifted by sharing conversation with Lizzie beneath whispering aspens while the river sang a sweet song nearby. He only wished they could tarry longer.

They reached the ferry by four in the afternoon. Clay paid the fare, choosing not to argue when the owner charged double for each team of dogs. All too soon they entered the busy city. Lizzie marched straight through town, hardly glancing at the tumbledown buildings, the wagon- and mule-filled streets, and the hodgepodge of people bustling here and there. Would she maintain her disinterested stoicism when she reached San Francisco?

She led the way to the trading post at the far edge of Fort Yukon. Watching her dicker with the grimy, rough-looking owner of the post, Clay's admiration for the woman doubled. She knew what her furs were worth, and despite her tiredness from their long walk, she was determined to get a fair price. Forty minutes later, she tucked a thick roll of paper money in a little pouch beneath her tunic and sent Clay a tired look.

"I am finished here."

The words held a meaning Clay wished he could ignore, but he offered a nod. "Let's go."

Clay fell behind the travoises so Lizzie could control her dogs. Now that the travoises were all but empty—one still held Lizzie's trunk of personal belongings—the animals seemed to think their work was done. She clicked her teeth, whistled, and jerked their traces to hold them to a slow walk as they retraced their footsteps.

Clay called, "Where are we going now?"

Lizzie didn't turn around. "The mercantile. I can buy my paddleboat ticket there, and I want to find a ready-made dress. My buckskin tunic can't go with me to California, and the ones Vivian gave me are too fine to wear while traveling."

Clay wondered if the men in California would find Lizzie as appealing in her buckskin tunic and leggings as he did. Jealousy attacked, and he was grinding his teeth when he stepped through the mercantile's swinging doors.

The owner turned from straightening tin cans on a shelf and shot Clay a smile. The smile faltered when his gaze bounced to Lizzie, but he offered a halfhearted welcome.

Clay returned the man's greeting with more warmth than the owner had exhibited. "Lizzie needs—"

"Do you have any ready-made dresses?" Lizzie interrupted, and Clay stepped back to allow her to take charge.

The owner poked his thumb toward the east wall. "Seamstress in town keeps me supplied with a few."

Lizzie turned toward the rack without a word. While she perused the limited selection, Clay filled the time by peeking in the barrels at the front of the store. Crackers, shriveled apples, pickles swimming in a briny liquid . . . He'd worked up an appetite with all the walking. Surely Lizzie was hungry, too. Maybe they could have a picnic before she departed.

Lizzie moved to a tiny room at the back of the store to try on the dresses she'd selected, and Clay asked the owner for two handfuls of crackers and a half pound of fat sausages. "I'll take a wedge from that yellow cheese behind the counter, too."

The man filled the order, his eyes repeatedly flicking to the corner where Lizzie had disappeared. Scuffling noises carried from beneath the ill-fitting door, filling Clay's head with images he had no business exploring. He forced himself to focus on the owner's packaging of his purchases.

Just as Clay paid for the items he'd chosen, the door creaked and Lizzie strode to the counter. The buckskin tunic was gone, and in its place she wore a simple, unadorned muslin gown of deep green—the color of the moss that grew along the riverbank. The brown wooden buttons marching from the rounded neckline to the waist called attention to her lithe frame, and the full skirt skimmed her slim hips and swished above the toes of her moccasins.

She stopped in front of Clay and held out her hands. "It seems to fit. Is this a suitable traveling dress?"

Clay held back the words of praise that trembled on his tongue. How could she be so unaware of her natural beauty? He forced his head to bob in agreement.

"Good." Lizzie faced the owner. "I'll take it. I also need a ticket for the paddleboat."

Clay inched toward the front door, unwilling to watch Lizzie purchase the ticket that would carry her away from him, but the mercantile owner called him back.

"Nearly forgot. It's been sittin' here near a week now." He shuffled something around beneath the counter and finally emerged with an envelope in his hand. "You got a letter." He shoved it across the counter at Clay.

Clay tucked the bundle of food under his arm and reached eagerly for the letter. He'd been waiting for word from his father—he hoped his pa would offer advice on reaching the villagers—but a glance at the neat hand-writing let him know this came from Vivian instead. Although a niggle of disappointment gripped him, he knew Lizzie would be happy to read a message from Vivian. He thanked the storekeeper and hurried outside. A few moments later, Lizzie emerged, a paddleboat ticket in her hand.

Clay lifted his gaze from the ticket and gave Lizzie a

wobbly smile. "I bought some food. Let's go sit by the dock and eat. We can look at Vivian's letter together."

Lizzie delayed them briefly to enter the bakery and purchase a half dozen loaves of dried-out bread to feed the dogs. Then they found a spot along the riverbank, well away from the boarding dock. Lizzie tossed chunks of bread to the dogs, her expression sad. "The trader who bought my furs said he knew a man—new in town—who was looking for a good team. But I wondered if you . . ." She gave him a hopeful look.

"What, Lizzie?" When she turned that sweet expression on him, he'd do anything for her.

"If you'd like to have them."

"Me?"

"You might have need of a team come winter, and they're all good dogs. They work well together." She spoke so rapidly, Clay had a hard time catching all the words. "I don't want to leave them with strangers, and Etu and Naibi could help care for them, and—"

Clay held up both hands. "Lizzie, Lizzie, slow down."

She fell silent and turned her attention back to the dogs. He watched her, considering her offer. Although the dogs would be an added responsibility, they'd be a reminder of her. And perhaps it would make her rest easier, knowing he had them. He touched her arm and waited until she looked at him.

"I'll take good care of them, Lizzie. I promise."

She rewarded him with a grateful smile that nearly melted him on the spot.

He gulped. "Are you ready for our picnic now?"

She swished her hands together and nodded. She sat cross-legged beside him, but when he reached for the packet of food she said, "Can we read Vivian's letter first?"

"Sure." He removed the envelope from his shirt pocket and slit the flap with his pocketknife. When he unfolded the letter, two newspaper clippings flitted into his lap, one falling crosswise across the other. He reached to retrieve them, but Lizzie's hand shot out and snatched them up. She released a cry of alarm that pierced Clay through the heart.

Chapter Thirty-Four

Lizzie stared at the newspaper clippings, first the article with its bold headline, and then the lengthy obituary. Pa . . . dead? Her hands trembled so badly, the pages rustled. She clenched them tighter and anchored her wrists against her bent knees. Dizziness assailed her, and for a moment she feared she might faint. She took deep gulping breaths. The dizziness passed, but the shock lingered. The papers must be wrong. He couldn't be dead. She was going to live with him.

Clay placed his hand between her shoulder blades and leaned close. "Lizzie, what is it? What can I do for you?" He spoke in a gentle whisper.

A hysterical laugh built in her throat. What could he do? Exactly what he was doing—being nearby, showing he cared. She welcomed his warm palm on her spine and the concern in his eyes. Yet, had she ever felt as alone as she did in those moments? In the years after Mama's death, she'd comforted herself with the knowledge that she still had a father. Pa was out there, so she wasn't truly alone.

Now the illusion was gone.

Tears flooded Lizzie's eyes, making the print in the

newspaper articles swim. She held the pages toward Clay. "This man—Voss Dawson. He's . . ."

Clay scowled briefly at the pages, then understanding broke across his face. "Your father?" He took the clippings from her unsteady hands and examined them.

Lizzie sucked in uneven breaths and hugged herself. No one waited for her in California. She'd burned her cabin to the ground. Her grandmother didn't want her. With a moan, she buried her face in her hands.

"Lizzie?" Clay's voice. Tender. Compassionate. "What are you going to do?"

Lizzie couldn't answer. She had to leave, but where would she go? Lowering her hand, she peered toward town. Maybe one of the businesses in Fort Yukon would hire her. She could rent a room, or perhaps even buy a small house with the money from her furs. Although the plan made sense, she possessed no great desire to pursue it. "I don't know . . . yet."

She waited for him to suggest something. To suggest she stay with him. In the past two days she'd been rejected by her grandmother, watched her grandfather die, and learned of her father's death. She needed him. She needed *someone* to care. She'd told Etu and Naibi the mission was in place to help people in need. Was there anyone more needy than she at this moment? But even as hope rose within her, reality squashed it. The mission was for the village, and she wasn't a part of the village.

Before he could crush her by voicing his inability to offer assistance, she began gathering up their picnic items. "Since I won't be leaving for San Francisco today, I'll return to the village and attend my grandfather's funeral. After that . . ." Her hands stilled, her words falling silent. After that, what would she do?

❧

All my love, Vivian.

After penning the final words, Vivian folded the letter, slipped it inside the waiting envelope, and then leaned her head on the back of the chair and sighed. She fingered the envelope, envisioning its contents. How she prayed Mother would read the love between the lines. Spilling her long-held hurts onto the page, asking her mother's forgiveness for holding herself aloof for so many years, and offering to begin their relationship anew had released a great weight from her heart. And if Mother reached back, she felt certain the joy would make her buoyant. She released a giggle, imagining herself hovering several inches above the ground.

"Miss Vivian?" Aunt Vesta's upstairs maid, Lorena, peeked into Vivian's room from the hallway. "Mr. and Mrs. Stockbridge are back from the doctor. Mrs. Stockbridge asked you to come to the parlor."

Vivian's heart skipped a beat. Aunt Vesta had anticipated positive news on Uncle Matthew's progress, but Vivian was eager to hear what the doctor had said. "Of course. I'll be right down." She scrambled to retrieve her shoes, which she'd kicked off under the desk. As she wriggled her feet into the satin slippers, she held out the envelope bearing the long letter to Mother. "Lorena, would you please post this for me? If it's too late for it to go out today, tomorrow is fine."

"Certainly, Miss Vivian." Lorena curtsied and departed.

Vivian took a moment to smooth stray wisps of hair into place and then hurried to the parlor. Uncle Matthew sat in his wicker wheelchair near the window, and Aunt Vesta perched on a nearby side chair. Vivian paused beside the silk tassels framing the parlor doorway and examined both of their faces. Her anxiety lifted, and she gave a little skip as she entered the room.

"The news is good, isn't it?"

Aunt Vesta laughed, curling her hand over Uncle Matthew's knee. "Ah, so obvious, are we?" She gave her husband a loving look before turning her smile on Vivian. "Yes, the news was very good. Matthew has far exceeded the doctor's expectations already. He says your uncle should make a complete recovery in time."

Vivian steepled her hands beneath her chin and let out a short squeal of delight. She dashed to her uncle and knelt beside his chair, stacking her hands over his on the chair's carved armrest. "Our prayers have been answered, Uncle Matthew! I'm so happy for you."

Her uncle beamed, his blue eyes twinkling. He didn't reply, but Vivian didn't expect him to. Even before his stroke, Uncle Matthew had allowed his wife to do most of the talking. Now that the stroke had stolen some of his ability to bring forth words, he seemed content to communicate as he always had—with smiles and nods.

Aunt Vesta poured Vivian a cup of tea, and Vivian slipped into the chair next to her aunt. "Receiving that excellent report, however, does give me cause for remorse." She handed Vivian the steaming cup, her lips pursed into a self-deprecating frown. "Had I realized he would do so well, I never would have summoned you from the mission in Alaska. I'm sorry, Vivian."

"Please don't apologize." Vivian stretched out her hand and patted her aunt's wrist. She included Uncle Matthew with a smile of assurance. "I'd much rather be here and not needed than not be here and needed."

Uncle Matthew chortled, and even Aunt Vesta released a short laugh. "What did you say?"

Vivian replayed her answer and laughed, too. "I suppose that was confusing. What I meant was if you need me, of course I want to be here. I don't regret making the trip." Had she not come, she wouldn't have had the freeing conversation with her aunt.

Aunt Vesta sat back, cradling her teacup beneath her chin. "And we appreciate your dedication to us, dear, but it does create a dilemma." Her gaze whisked to Uncle Matthew, and he gave a subtle nod. Aunt Vesta continued. "Since your uncle is making such wonderful progress, and I find I can meet his needs quite well on my own, there isn't really a reason for you to remain in Huntington . . . that is, unless you want to."

Vivian blinked twice, uncertain how to decipher her aunt's last statement. "What do you mean?"

"Well, dear, you know you're always welcome here. But we did call you away from a rather noble endeavor—ministering to the poor heathens in that humble village."

Faces appeared in Vivian's memory—little Naibi and Etu, stone-faced Shruh, dignified Taima and delicate Magema. And spunky yet elegant Lizzie, her dear friend. She missed them.

Her aunt set her cup on the marble table next to her chair and smiled at Vivian. "If you want to stay with us, regardless of need, you are very welcome. It would give your uncle and me great pleasure to have you near again. But if you prefer to travel to Oklahoma or return to the mission in Alaska, then we will support your decision and provide travel fare for you." She rose and took hold of the handles on Uncle Matthew's wheelchair, giving it a gentle push across the rose-patterned carpet. "We don't want to detain you from following your heart's call, Vivian." She paused beside Vivian's chair and briefly cupped Vivian's cheek. "You let us know what you prefer, will you?"

Vivian nodded, and her aunt wheeled Uncle Matthew around the corner. Vivian remained in the parlor, sipping her tea, and considering her aunt's comments. *"We don't want to detain you from following your heart's call . . ."* She'd gone with Clay to Alaska to prove her lack of fear both to herself and to her parents. She'd never had a desire to minister in its truest sense, yet she had found pleasure in reaching out to the natives and gaining their trust. In her short time there, she'd grown to love many of them.

Yet, even while she found beauty in the landscape and the people who resided on the rugged frontier, she had to admit she didn't care for the primitive conditions. She held the tea beneath her nose, inhaling the pleasant aroma of cinnamon. She adored the smooth feel of fine porcelain in her hands—hands that were no longer chapped and rough looking. Her body relaxed, cradled by the tufted velvet chair, and her eyes feasted on the hand-painted wall coverings, tasseled draperies, and lovely statuary decorating the parlor.

There was beauty in Alaska, but there was also beauty here.

Vivian took a sip of the spiced, sweet tea, uncertainty stealing the pleasure of indulging in her favorite beverage. She'd sampled and discovered pleasure in two different worlds, but in which did she belong?

༄

Four days after Shruh's death, the village gathered to pay homage to the tribal leader. Clay had observed that funerals in Gwichyaa Saa were ceremonial with unexpected moments of informality. But Shruh's potlatch contained none of the spontaneous lightheartedness of previous services. From beginning chants to ending dances, all of those in attendance—from small children to the elderly—maintained a solemn, reverent demeanor.

Clay stayed close to Lizzie throughout the long day of ceremony. On the walk back from Fort Yukon, he had convinced her to stay in the mission for a while. He'd returned to his decrepit little hut at night. Bugs and other vermin plagued him, but he wouldn't complain. At least Lizzie was safe within the village instead of sleeping on the ground outside the charred remains of her cabin.

Co'Ozhii, to Clay's surprise, had agreed to let Lizzie prepare some of the foods for the potlatch, and Lizzie confided that twice during their cooking sessions her grandmother had spoken to her in something other than a harsh tone. Clay prayed this small softening was the first whisper of peace between the two women. Co'Ozhii kept her distance from Lizzie during the day of the potlatch, but Clay took heart that the older woman hadn't demanded Lizzie leave the village.

Clay wondered if Shruh's death and Co'Ozhii's hesitant acceptance might lead to acceptance from the entire village. His heart pattered with hope every time he considered it. He wanted her in the village. He wanted her in his life. But he hadn't told her so yet. He'd prayed, asking for the Lord's leading on the matter, but as of yet, he hadn't perceived a clear answer.

At the end of the day, when the food trays were emptied of all but crumbs and the dancers ready to collapse in exhaustion, the newly appointed leader of the tribe, Da'ago, stepped forward and raised both hands in the air. Clay recognized the signal. He moved to Lizzie's side as the entire village fell into formation like soldiers on parade. At the front of the surging, singing crowd, six men carried the travois bearing Shruh's hide-wrapped body. Co'Ozhii marched directly behind the travois, two women holding her arms to assist her. Lizzie, as Shruh's granddaughter, should have been at the front, but she waited and joined the last row of villagers.

Lizzie moved stiffly, as if her legs had forgotten how to function. She sent Clay an anguished look. "This is the hardest part—putting him in the ground and watching them cover him up." She swallowed. "It's over then. He's really gone."

Clay linked hands with her, fitting his fingers between hers. "It's only his body they place in the ground, Lizzie. His soul has already gone to his Father." Clay's soul rejoiced, knowing where Shruh now resided. In those brief minutes before the old man closed his eyes for the final time, Shruh had asked Clay to help him find the High One. With Clay's assistance, he'd given himself into God's care. When the time was right, he'd share Shruh's decision with Lizzie. But he hadn't yet sensed her readiness to hear it.

While the leaders chanted their good-bye prayers, Clay offered a silent prayer for each of the people surrounding the grave that one day they would see Shruh again. *Let us all gather in Your house one day, Father. And please . . . please*— longing rose up with such intensity, tears stung his eyes—*let Lizzie be among those welcomed home.*

Chapter Thirty-Five

Lizzie smoothed the blanket into place over the mattress and then sat on the bed, elbows on knees. Vivian would tell her she'd chosen an unladylike pose, but what difference did it make? She wouldn't be living in San Francisco as a lady in her father's house.

She shifted her gaze to the four-drawer bureau standing between the two beds in the little sleeping room. Pa's old bureau fit well in the room, just as the breakfront cabinet—now holding books and supplies rather than dishes—seemed to belong in the back corner of the mission's main room, and her old table and chairs found a perfect place in the corner of the second sleeping room for Clay's use as a desk. Her furniture belonged here. But did she?

A bird's cheerful song interrupted her reflections. With a sigh, she pushed to her feet and scuffed to the window, seeking the singer. But the oiled paper made the view appear murky, out of focus. *Much like my life.* She drew her hand down her face. What was she going to do?

The ringing clang of an iron pan meeting the stovetop alerted her to Clay's arrival. He must be starting breakfast. She should cook for him out of gratitude for the shelter he provided. Quickly, she sat on the edge of the bed, whisked the blue-checked skirt out of the way, and tugged on her moccasins. Then she scurried out the door.

"Let me do that."

He flashed a smile over his shoulder. The man smiled more than anyone she'd ever known. Even when things went awry—when Etu and Naibi fussed at each other or one of the villagers snubbed him—he maintained an even, cheerful attitude. She envied his innate happiness. Although she'd never been one to wallow in despair, she couldn't honestly say she held the same penchant for joy that Clay possessed.

"I'm fine," he said. "I've learned to cook pretty decently since Vivian left, if you don't count my bread. Still can't figure out how to make the loaves rise." He withdrew a speckled egg from a basket on the edge of the stove. "We'll be having a treat this morning. When I fetched water, I spotted a duck nest and helped myself." He cringed. "I feel bad for the mother duck, but I couldn't pass up the chance for fried eggs."

A little bubble of laughter tickled the back of Lizzie's throat. He felt badly for the duck? The giggle emerged, and she quickly covered her mouth, aghast. She should be in mourning. How could she laugh at Clay's antics?

His brows pinched. "Lizzie? What's wrong?"

She sat on the bench closest to the stove and sent Clay a serious look. "I've been here a full week already, and I still don't know what I'm to do. Should I build a new cabin on my land? Or should I buy a house in Fort Yukon or White Horse and seek work?" She hunched her shoulders, wishing she could crawl inside a shell like a turtle and hide from the world. "If I believed my father had told his wife and children about me, then maybe I could have . . ."

322

With a fierce swipe of her hand, she forced the thought away. Each time she considered the obituary with its list of survivors—excluding her name—pain and anger swelled. Contempt filled her voice as she added, "Pa erased his memories of me from his heart. So I must do the same for him." She glared up at Clay, fury making her limbs tremble. "I'm glad I burned the cabin. At least I never have to look at it again and remember the years we lived there together."

Clay looked at her for several seconds, his expression unreadable. Then he placed the egg in the basket, shifted the skillet to the corner of the stove, and sat beside her. He didn't take her hand. She wished he would. She needed comfort—connection.

"Lizzie, you're angry at your father, and you have a right to be. He wronged you by leaving, and he wronged you by never telling his family about you."

I am his family! She jumped up and stormed to the door. Propping her hand on the frame, she stared across the village. Families mingled in yards. Children playing, women stirring cookfires to life, men standing in small circles to discuss the day's plans. A happy scene. A scene in which she had no part. The anger drifted away on a fierce tide of sorrow. "I'll never know how it feels . . ."

Clay moved behind her, so close his breath stirred her hair when he said, "How what feels?"

Her lips quivered. She swallowed hard. "To belong."

Clay took hold of her shoulders and turned her to face him. "Lizzie, you *can* know how it feels. There's a place of belonging waiting for you—there's a Father standing with open arms right now ready to welcome you into His family. All you have to do is lean into His embrace."

She swayed toward him, remembering the bliss of his embrace when he'd run into her yard the day of the fire. She wanted—*needed*—that bliss again. But his hands remained on her shoulders, holding her away from him. She slipped free of his gentle grip and moved to the other side of the bench inside the door of the mission.

"No father wants me. Vitsiy didn't want me. Pa left me behind." Lizzie grated the words, torturing herself with the truth. She waved one hand toward the village. "All of those families out there—none ask me to be a part of their circle. No one wants me, Clay Selby!" Her knees began to quake, but pride stiffened her spine. She wouldn't cower and cry before this man. "And I don't want them."

Clay took two steps toward her, tears glinting in the corners of his gray-green eyes. A sweet, tender smile touched the edges of his lips. "Yes, you do. Or it wouldn't hurt so much to be excluded."

The gently worded admonition stung like a wind-thrown willow branch slapping across her face.

He came ever closer until his knees bumped against the log bench. Close enough that he could touch her if he tried. Her gaze dropped to his hands, waiting for them to lift and reach for her. But they remained at his side. She started to run to the sleeping room, to hide in shame and agony, but he spoke again, sealing her in place.

"Even more than you want them, Father-God wants you."

His statement coiled around her like wild honeysuckle vines encircling a tree trunk with scent and beauty. The sensation of being encompassed was so strong, her senses filled with the sweet aroma of delicate blossoms. A tingle climbed her spine—her body's response to awareness of a presence that hovered just out of sight and reach. She stared at Clay, unable to turn away. Her pulse increased. Tiny, rapid puffs of air escaped her parted lips.

Clay clasped his hands—the way he did when he

prayed—and spoke in a voice so soft, so tender, her heart ached listening to him. "Thousands of years before your birth, God sent His Son into this world to serve as the bridge between Himself and man. Even then, the Father knew one day a woman named Lizzie—White Feather—would walk the earth. Even then, the Father loved you. Even then, the Father longed for you to seek His Son and find your way to Him. All this time, Lizzie, He's been there, waiting for you, loving you."

One hand reached across the bench, his fingers landing softly on her forearm. He slid his fingers downward until he found her hand. His warm, firm fingers took hold, the touch becoming a symbol of Father-God reaching across the separation she'd created . . . and capturing her in a precious bond of love.

Clay's gaze drifted to the open door and returned. He tipped his head, his thumb slipping to her wrist where her pulse raced in an eagerness she didn't quite comprehend. "Lizzie, you live in the shadow of Denali, the High One. Clouds mask its peak, yet you know the mountaintop exists, yes?"

Very slowly, afraid a rapid movement might destroy their moment of intimacy, she offered a single nod.

"How do you know?"

She licked her lips, forcing her clumsy tongue to form an answer. "Because there are days the sun burns the clouds away, and its fullness is revealed."

A smile burst across Clay's face. "That's right—the sun burns the shielding mask away so the High One is revealed." He tugged her hand, drawing her snug against the opposite side of the log. His face only inches from hers, he whispered, "Just as accepting Jesus the Son removes the clouds of doubt and reveals the glory of Father-God." The fervency in his tone and the lovelight shining in his eyes stole Lizzie's ability to breathe. "He wants you for His own daughter, Lizzie. Won't you open your heart and believe?"

He brought up his free hand and smoothed it over her hair. The touch brought back treasured memories from childhood when Pa brushed her hair from her face. A longing for Pa, for a father—for *the* Father—created a quake in the center of her being. She gripped Clay's hand. "I want to be His daughter, Clay. Will you help me?"

With a gentle tug on her hands, he seated her on the bench. He then retrieved his Bible and read to her—verses about sin separating man from God, verses about Jesus submitting to the pain of the cross to serve as a sacrifice for man's sin and then rising to life once more, verses that sent fingers of truth into Lizzie's seeking, needy heart. Realization swept through her—only a Father who loved with His entire being could make such a sacrifice. And He'd sacrificed all . . . for *her*.

Clay finished in the tenth chapter of Romans, verse nine. Lizzie closed her eyes as she listened to his deep, reverent voice recite, " . . . if thou shalt confess with thy mouth the Lord Jesus, and shalt believe in thine heart that God hath raised him from the dead, thou shalt be saved."

Her eyes still tightly closed, her fingers twined together beneath her chin, Lizzie whispered a prayer to the Father confessing her desire to receive Jesus as her own Savior. Love bloomed within her heart—a love as real and immovable as the great mountain Denali. The warmth of acceptance filled her, infusing her entire body with a joy so intense her eyes flew open.

Clay sat before her, his smile swimming through her tears. She laughed—a genuine, delight-filled laugh. The heart-lifting sound trickled into silence as she pondered her ability to laugh. She had no home, no family, no idea what she was meant to do next. Nothing had changed. Yet everything had changed. Instead of facing a bleak future alone, she was loved eternally by Father-God. Tears coursed down her face past her smiling lips. *Thank You, my Father* . . . Never again would she be alone.

Chapter Thirty-Six

Clay reached for Lizzie. The glow on her face and the joyful laughter pouring from her lips communicated the change that had happened beneath the surface. He wanted to celebrate, and it seemed natural to wrap her in his arms. She reached for him at the same time. Her palms pressed firmly against his back as she nestled her head against his shoulder. Their joined hearts beat out a double-thrum of happiness.

"Thank you for showing me the way." Her voice wavered, the words falling on his ears like gentle raindrops from a summer sky. "I'm . . ." She sighed, a wispy expulsion of breath. "I'm at peace." She pulled back, looking at him in surprise. "I'm at peace, Clay."

He nodded, understanding. Although he'd never understand how God calmed His children even in the midst of heartache, he'd experienced it enough to know its reality. "And you always will be. Just look to Him whenever you feel lost, alone, or frightened. He'll always be there."

She opened her mouth to say something else, but the pounding of little feet intruded. Naibi and Etu burst into the mission building. Naibi bounced over to Lizzie and flopped into her lap, but Etu ran straight to the stove and peeked into the empty skillet. He spun to face them.

"You haven't cooked breakfast yet?" He plunked his fists on his hips. "Naibi and I fed the dogs already. Hurry and cook something, Mister Clay!"

Clay laughed. He returned his Bible to the table—Lizzie's table—in his sleeping room and then followed Etu's direction to hurry and cook something. They feasted on fried duck eggs, corn bread, and strips of smoked salmon. Clay might as well have been eating chunks of bark peeled from his ramshackle hut. Lizzie so filled his senses, there wasn't room for anything else.

She'd accepted the gift of salvation through God's Son, which meant they were joint heirs with Christ. He could now pursue a relationship with her without fear of breaking the biblical admonition about becoming unequally yoked with an unbeliever. He wanted to take her in his arms and proclaim his love for her, but how could he do it with two children seated between them, dominating the conversation?

More than Etu and Naibi's presence stilled his tongue. Another barrier rose between them—one that wouldn't leave at the close of the school day. Although the village leaders hadn't rebuked him about Lizzie residing in the mission, neither had they offered any overtures of acceptance. He'd seen Da'ago standing in the center of the village, hands on hips, staring toward the mission, and he suspected the man was trying to decide what to do about Lizzie.

As much as it pained Clay to accept, Lizzie had been ex-communicated by virtue of her mother's expulsion from the village. Shruh had encouraged his wife to make peace with Lizzie, but Co'Ozhii—still mourning—remained aloof. It was only a matter of time before the leaders gathered for a meeting, and unless Co'Ozhii requested a reversal of the ban, they would insist Lizzie leave. Where would she go?

If she leaves, Father, it will take every bit of willpower I possess not to go, too. She's embedded in my heart now. I'll be lost without her.

Across the table, Lizzie laughed at something Naibi said and then leaned down to give the little girl a one-armed hug before picking up her fork again. She looked so relaxed—completely at ease. Helplessness coupled with frustration pinched Clay's chest. If she wanted to stay, she should have the freedom to do so.

The key to Lizzie's acceptance in the village lay with Co'Ozhii. The woman's time of deep mourning would last for another two weeks. Until then, he shouldn't bother her. But the moment it was considered appropriate to visit her, he intended to knock on her door and make his most heartfelt plea on Lizzie's behalf.

He pushed away from the table. "Breakfast all done?" The children nodded. "Good. Naibi, fetch a bucket of water. Etu, empty the scraps into the slop bucket. Then Missus Lizzie"—he sent a smile in her direction—"will sweep up our crumbs while we wash the dishes."

The children scampered to obey. And while they completed their chores, working together companionably, he did his best not to imagine them as a family.

———

July faded into August, and the sun's bright face chose to hide a little longer each night. Clay appreciated the change. Although he'd tried to patch his little bark hut, large gaps between strips of wood remained, and the sunlight pouring through held sleep at bay. Having a few more hours of dark ensured more rest. Rest he needed after the weeks of too little sleep.

The sunlight hours were changing, but the villagers remained stubbornly the same. Every Sunday he planned a service, and every Sunday he preached to three people—Lizzie,

Etu, and Naibi. Every day, he left the door wide open so any of the villagers could wander in and join the lessons. But only Etu and Naibi attended school. The natives seemed to have lost their curiosity about him—they ceased to gather when he washed his clothes in a tub in the yard or soaped his face to shave, and they prevented their children from scampering close when he sat on the stoop and played his accordion.

Daily he watched, eager and hopeful, for a passing trader or trapper to deliver a letter from his father. He prayed Pa would offer the advice he needed to turn the villagers' eyes toward heaven. But the letter didn't come, and day by day his feelings of failure grew.

Lizzie assured him he was a fine teacher—she'd taken to assisting in the classroom, teaching the children the things they would have learned from their parents if they'd lived—but he shrugged off her compliments. Naibi and Etu weren't happy with Tabu, and Tabu didn't care about seeing to their needs. But if they'd been placed in a different home, he doubted they'd have been able to come to the mission at all.

He'd told Lizzie she'd always have peace, and he witnessed the peacefulness in her blue eyes and relaxed demeanor. But he battled an increasing despondence as days marched on with the villagers avoiding the mission building. The only thing that gave him pleasure was having Lizzie near. In the evenings, they took walks in the woods. He didn't even mind swatting mosquitoes if it meant having Lizzie to himself for a while.

She, like he, was waiting for the tribal leaders to visit, but in childlike faith, she said, "If they send me away, I won't go alone. My Father goes with me, and He will keep me from being lonely." Clay gloried in her confidence, but he wished he felt as secure. His love for her grew deeper with each hour they spent together.

On the morning of August eleventh, Clay dressed in his black preaching suit, tamed his hair with macassar oil, and drew in a fortifying breath. Four weeks had passed since Shruh's body was laid in the ground. He could now visit Co'Ozhii. Etu and Naibi would come for school, but he intended to release them early so he could visit the woman before the evening mealtime hour.

He walked across the dewy ground to the mission. The door stood open in invitation, signifying Lizzie was up. His pulse beat like a hummingbird's wings in anticipation of seeing her again. The effect this woman had on him . . . Surely God wouldn't let these feelings grow only to take her away, would He?

Lizzie stood at the cookstove greasing a black iron skillet, dressed today in her buckskin tunic and leggings. Her hair hung in neat braids alongside her dusky face, and she hummed a hymn he'd played the previous Sunday on his accordion. Her beauty, as always, made his breath catch, and the sight of her at the cookstove, looking every bit like she belonged there, brought an immediate prayer from his heart.

Father-God, let them let her stay. She's content here . . . happy. And I love her. I love her more than I ever imagined possible. Please let her stay.

She turned and looked him up and down, a shy smile on her rosy lips. "How fine you look."

He mimicked her leisurely perusal by allowing his gaze to travel from the fringed hem of her leggings to the beaded neckline of her tunic. "As do you."

She ran her fingers down the length of one braid, seeming to trace the strip of leather woven into the dark strands of her hair. "I must be Athabascan today."

Clay nodded, approving her choice of clothing.

Her chin lifted, a hopeful glint lighting her blue eyes. "We will know by day's end, yes?"

They'd discussed Clay's intention to visit with Co'Ozhii, and Lizzie had counted the days with him. Unconsciously, he ran his hand over his slicked-back hair, checking to see if the unruly strands remained in place. "I'll visit her after the children are done with their lessons."

Her brow pinched, a slight movement. "*I* will see her after the children are done."

Clay crunched his brow tightly and moved beside the stove. "Lizzie . . ." He interjected a gentle warning into his tone.

She shook her head, her braids flopping. Her jaw jutted into a stubborn angle. "She is *my* grandmother, Clay. And she has cast *me* from her life. I must be the one to talk to her." An ornery twinkle appeared in her eyes. "But you may come if you'll be quiet and let me talk." Her expression changed from impish to pleading. "You will honor my desire?"

Clay bit the inside of his lip. He'd planned this visit for weeks. Lying awake in the bark hut, he'd practiced the speech in his head so many times he could recite it in his dreams. He'd always envisioned going to Co'Ozhii on his own, convincing the woman to bend her stubborn pride and welcome Lizzie into her life. *He* wanted to be the one to bring peace between Co'Ozhii and Lizzie.

He gave a start, realization descending like a log beam on his head. What a selfish plan. He hung his head, asking God to speak His will into his heart. A whisper of peace floated on the fringes of his mind. Months ago, Lizzie had insisted he not intrude in her relationship with her grandmother. She'd set aside her stoic stubbornness in exchange for gentle persuasion, but maybe it would be best for him to abide by her wishes.

He drew in a deep breath, releasing it along with the selfish pride that made him want to run ahead of Lizzie and pave the way. "All right. You talk to her. I'll go with you to offer my support, but I'll stay quiet unless you ask me to speak."

She caught his hand and gave it a squeeze. "Thank you, Clay. I've been praying and asking Father-God to make the way to peace. Even if He says no, I will accept His will. You see . . ." Tears glimmered in her eyes. "I wanted to be with Pa, but God brought me to Himself instead. What He has for me is what is best for me. I will trust Him."

∽

"You may come in."

Lizzie's heart cheered at Co'Ozhii's invitation, but she managed to maintain a composed posture as she followed her grandmother into the little cabin. To her relief, the smell of sickness that had hung in the air was gone, but dark shadows shrouded every corner. Co'Ozhii hadn't pinned back the furs covering the windows. The gray cast gave the room a gloomy feel, and Lizzie battled a feeling of melancholy as she slid into the chair Co'Ozhii indicated.

The older woman grunted at Clay and pointed silently to a third chair in the corner. He dragged it to the table, but he waited until Co'Ozhii dropped into her chair before seating himself.

Co'Ozhii sent Lizzie a wary look. Although she appeared less haggard than the day of Vitsiy's funeral, a sadness seemed to penetrate her being. Lizzie recognized the haunting look of loneliness, and her heart turned over in sympathy. *My Father-God, open my grandmother's heart to You so she might know the joy of Your ever-presence.*

"You have come to speak. So speak."

Although no kindness tempered Co'Ozhii's tone, Lizzie chose not to take offense. In the past, Lizzie had spoken coldly to Clay to mask her true feelings. No matter how Co'Ozhii behaved, she would show Vitse respect and compassion, loving her the way God loved her. Lizzie had glimpsed evidence of God's love in Clay's actions. Perhaps Vitse would see God if Lizzie chose gentleness.

Lizzie lapsed into Athabascan. "When last we spoke, I told you I would trouble you no longer because I planned to go to my father in California." The sharp sting of loss had lessened over the past weeks, but a residual pain remained, like a bruise that lingered far beneath the skin. Lizzie swallowed a lump of sadness and continued. "I come now to tell you I am not able to go to Voss Dawson. He . . . he died, just as Shruh died. No home waits for me in California."

She paused, waiting to see if Co'Ozhii would offer a condolence. But the woman sat in stone-faced silence. Lizzie shot Clay a quick look. His tender smile encouraged her to continue.

Shifting slightly in the chair, she crossed her ankles and looked directly into her grandmother's face. "Mother is gone. Voss Dawson is gone. Shruh is gone."

A muscle twitched in Co'Ozhii's jaw, the only indication she listened to Lizzie.

"You are the only family I have left. I do not wish to remain separate from you, Grandmother. You brought my mother into this world. You nursed her and taught her and loved her."

A single tear formed in the corner of Co'Ozhii's eye. The woman blinked, but the moisture didn't disappear.

"She hurt you when she married my father, but leaving you hurt her, too. She never stopped loving you or Grandfather. Her final wish, a wish made as she lay with death waiting to steal her away, was for reconciliation with you." Lizzie inched her hand across the table and placed it, ever so gently, on top of Co'Ozhii's wrinkled hand. Co'Ozhii stiffened, but she didn't pull away. Heartened, Lizzie went on softly.

"My mother's wish is also my prayer, Grandmother. Might peace blossom between us? Can you forgive my white blood and see my mother in me?" Her hand still cupping Co'Ozhii's, Lizzie fell silent. She'd made her request. Now it was up to Co'Ozhii to accept or reject her only grandchild. Lizzie continued to pray, even while she waited, for her grandmother to choose peace.

Moments passed. Outside the cabin, voices chattered and dogs barked. A bush growing along the cabin's stone foundation, teased by a breeze, *skritch-skritched* on the rough log wall as if counting the seconds. And still Co'Ozhii didn't speak. But Lizzie sat patiently in silence, taking hope from the fact Co'Ozhii hadn't yet pulled her hand from Lizzie's light grasp.

Suddenly the woman jerked and pinned her gaze on Clay. "Clay Selby, the day my husband's spirit left his body . . . you spoke to him."

Clay looked at Lizzie, as if seeking her permission to reply. Lizzie offered a quick nod, and he turned to Co'Ozhii. "Yes."

"What words did you say to one another?"

Clay folded his hands on the tabletop. "Shruh asked me how to find the way to the Father. He knew his time here was almost gone. He said he did not wish to step into the next world without assurance. So I told him how to have eternal life with Father-God."

Lizzie's heart sang with the realization that her grandfather now abided with the Father. Just as she would one day reside with the Father. And on that day, she would have the chance to know Vitsiy, in Heaven.

Co'Ozhii made a face. "Did you tell him this assurance would come if I made peace with my granddaughter?"

Clay shook his head. "Human relationships might bring

temporary happiness and comfort to us here on earth, but only a relationship with Jesus brings the assurance of eternity with the Father."

His gentle voice, the same tone he'd used when sharing the truth with Lizzie, embraced her once more with warmth. She closed her eyes and offered a prayer for her grandmother to accept the truth that now lived in her own heart. She continued to pray while Clay explained, in simple terms, the way to find everlasting peace.

When he'd finished, Lizzie dared peek at her grandmother, her heart pattering in hope. But no joyful spark lit Co'Ozhii's eyes. Instead, she released a heavy sigh. The untidy tufts of her gray hair, chopped short as a sign of mourning, fluffed out as she shook her head sadly.

"The way of your God, white man, is unknown to me. I do not understand it." She slipped her hand from beneath Lizzie's and rose. Her unsmiling gaze shifted from Clay to Lizzie and then drifted to the darkened corner of the cabin where Shruh had lain the last days of life. She shuffled to the corner, her gait slow, her shoulders bending as if she carried a burden. Lizzie squinted through the feeble light, trying to determine what her grandmother was doing.

Still bent forward with her back to them, Co'Ozhii rasped in a tired voice, "But I will honor my husband's words to me on the day his spirit left. He wished for peace between us, White Feather, so . . ." She turned and moved toward them, stepping from the darkest shadows into murky gray.

Lizzie clapped her hand over her mouth to hold back her cry of joy. Vitse wore the coat Lizzie had so painstakingly crafted.

Chapter Thirty-Seven

Clay followed Lizzie into the sunny yard outside Co'Ozhii's cabin, his heart light as he observed Lizzie's skipping footsteps and beaming smile. He wished he could scoop her into his arms and celebrate this moment of victory with a kiss. But other Gwich'ins milled about in the village's common area, so he pushed his hands into his pockets and offered a smile of congratulations instead.

Lizzie walked alongside him, her hands clasped in front of her as if she held tight to her new bond of harmony with her grandmother. Her eyes, bright with wonder, scanned the skies. A short, joyous giggle left her lips. "Peace, Clay . . . at last we have peace, my grandmother and me. And now my prayer is that this peace will spread across the village."

Clay nodded. Co'Ozhii had told them she planned to call a special meeting with the tribal council later that evening to recommend ending Lizzie's excommunication. In a few short hours they would know whether Lizzie would be welcomed or ostracized. Looking into Lizzie's trusting face now, he could do nothing less than believe her time of acceptance drew near.

"Vitse still resists the Father," Lizzie went on, her tone taking on a wistful quality that tugged at Clay's heart, "but I will speak to her often and share with her how I hold Him inside of me, how He brings me joy." She crossed both palms over her heart and beamed at Clay. "She will come to believe. My Father-God will answer my prayer."

Her confidence spurred his confidence. He'd prayed so often for the people of this village to come to the mission he'd nearly worn out the words. Why hadn't God answered his prayer? God knew how much he wanted to remain here, serving the people and bringing change into their souls, so why didn't He light the fire of desire in their hearts?

As they neared the mission building, Lizzie pointed ahead. "Someone has been here and left something behind."

Clay squinted against the descending sun. A white rectangle of paper, tacked to the building's doorframe, flapped gently in the light breeze—an envelope. Anticipation pushed him into a trot, and he closed the distance quickly. He yanked the envelope loose and, his hands shaking, turned it over to look at the handwriting. With a grin, he waved it at Lizzie. "It's from my father!"

Lizzie hustled to his side, her eyes alight with eagerness. "Open it."

Clay's hands turned clumsy as he slit the envelope and removed a small square of paper, folded in half. His elation dimmed momentarily. He'd expected a lengthy letter, citing suggestions and offering support. He shot Lizzie a puzzled look before tucking the empty envelope into his pocket and unfolding the paper. His brows crunched as he read the single-sentence message. He shook his head, trying to unfuzz his brain, then read it a second time. Despite himself, he smiled, then guffawed, and finally let loose with a long, self-deprecating belly laugh.

He held the paper high and shook it. The paper's crinkling sound emulated laughter. Clay snorted. "Pa . . . you rascal. Trust you to get to the heart of the matter."

Lizzie stared at him, concern marring her brow. "Clay?"

Without replying, he handed her the short letter, then strode away several feet, scuffing his toes against the hard ground and shaking his head while bubbles of laughter continued to escape his lips.

Lizzie read Pa's advice out loud. " 'Son, the church isn't a building. Love, Pa.' " She refolded the letter and gazed at him with a puzzled expression. "What does it mean?"

Clay returned to her side and plucked the letter from her hand, his father's wisdom making him feel both foolish and grateful at the same time. "It means I've had my focus in the wrong direction all along." He paced back and forth, gesturing to the fine mission built of sturdy logs. "I was so determined to complete the building I lost sight of what really matters—serving people." He swung to face her. "I've prayed and prayed for the people of Gwichyaa Saa to come and sit on those benches and hear me preach . . . but I should have been going to them."

A lump filled his throat. How shortsighted he'd been. How much time he'd wasted. He looked at the fine structure again, recalling the way his chest had swelled with pride when he'd examined his craftsmanship. The remembrance shamed him. *I came to do Your will, but I got so caught up in my own plans, You were pushed aside. Father, forgive me.*

To Lizzie, he said, "The church doesn't reside within a building, but within the hearts of God's people. And that's what I came to teach, Lizzie. I hope this building will one day be the place we gather to worship together, but I'm no longer going to wait for them to come to me. I'll go to them, the same way my pa did when I was a boy. Door to door, serving them in any way I can. And I'll grab every oppor- tunity to tell them of God's love." Determination stiffened his spine. *One heart at a time . . . that's the way the message of truth spreads.*

He clamped his hands over her shoulders, rejoicing in the way her hands rose to grasp his wrists. Peering directly into her attentive face, he made a vow. "I'll push my pride out of the way and follow the leading of the Spirit. If I allow Him to work through me, we'll see change, Lizzie. I *know* we'll see change."

"And I'll help you, Clay Selby."

Her immediate promise of support sent a shaft of joy through Clay's soul, but a worrisome thought cast a shadow over his delight. The uncomfortable fear that had pestered him at night had to be addressed, and this seemed a good time. He led Lizzie to the stoop and sat, pulling her down beside him.

"Lizzie, I have to know something. Will you answer me truthfully?"

None of her former rebellion or distrust flared. She gave a quick nod.

He drew a steadying breath, fearful of the answer yet needing to know. "You've made peace with Co'Ozhii and you said you would pray to be accepted into the village. But . . ." His mouth felt dry. He swallowed and continued. "Do you truly want to live in the village, or are you hoping to stay because you have no place else to go?"

If she chose the village out of desperation rather than a real desire to live there, he feared she might also lean on him because she had no one else. He loved her and wanted her permanently in his life, but he needed her to feel the same way about him. His pulse pounded like a drumbeat in his ears while he waited for her reply.

Lizzie sucked in her lips. She sat for several seconds, her fine brows pulled together in a manner of deep reflection, and then a smile—a knowing smile that spoke of an inner decision being reached—graced her lovely face. She placed her hand over his, slipping her fingers between his to link them together.

"Clay, I've lived my entire life on the other side of those trees, knowing the village existed but never being a part of it. When I was a little girl, I had no need for the villagers. I had Mama and Pa, and I was happy. But then Pa left, and Mama died, and I was alone." Pain briefly puckered her lips, but then peacefulness washed over her countenance. "During those lonely years I pined for the village even while resenting it. I honored their ban against me even while inwardly hating them for rejecting me."

Her fingers tightened, and Clay placed his other hand over hers. She offered a quick, appreciative smile before continuing.

"And then you and Vivian came along. You showed me friendship and affection even when I didn't know how to reach back. You touched my heart."

A flutter moved through Clay's chest—his heart's reaction to her sweetly spoken words.

Lizzie angled her head, peering at him with a pensive look. One braid framed her cheek, the tip of the other brushed Clay's knuckles. Her blue eyes shimmered with an emotion that held him in place as effectively as a tether—a tether he had no desire to escape.

"You told me once that these people were your people, all created by the hands of the same Father-God. I didn't understand, but now I do. I want the villagers"—she bobbed her chin in the direction of the village, one bright tear trailing down her cheek—"to know the peace and joy I now

342

know. I want to be to them what you were to me—a living, breathing example of God's presence."

She shifted to face him again. Her tear-damp face glowed with an inner love that heightened her natural beauty. Clay's breath caught in his throat as he gazed at this woman—this lovely, open, strong-willed Athabascan woman who now shared his passion for changing souls.

"More than anything else, I want to stay here . . . to abide in this village with my people and with you. But—" Her gaze dipped downward, her thick braids falling to swing gently above her lap. "If the council says no, I will honor them and go. God will make a place for me." She lifted her head, once more looking him full in the face. Peace and confidence shone in her sky-colored eyes. "But I will never stop praying for Grandmother and my tribesmen to discover the love of my Father-God."

Her answer, even more than Clay had hoped to hear, lifted him to a new height of delight but then plummeted him to fearful despair. Lizzie's words told him she loved him and wanted a life with him. If he asked her to be his wife, he knew she would accept—he saw the truth in her eyes. But he didn't yet have the freedom to ask. Not until they knew what the future held.

No matter what the council decided about Lizzie, he would stay in Gwichyaa Saa and minister to the villagers, as he'd been sent to do. They were the people entrusted to him by God, and he wouldn't fail his Father by turning his back on them.

You sent me here for a purpose, Father, and I discovered more than I expected by falling in love with Lizzie. She loves You, too, and wants to serve You. Will You open the doors so she can serve right here, at my side, as my helpmeet and partner in the ministry to which You've entrusted me?

"Clay?" Lizzie's whisper interrupted.

He looked at her, but she was looking ahead, toward the village. He shifted his attention, and his tongue suddenly seemed stuck to the roof of his mouth. Da'ago and three other elders moved in a solemn procession toward the mission.

Clay squeezed her hand, which still nestled between his. "Whatever they say, we'll accept it as God's will."

Lizzie nodded, her face serene.

Clay rose, giving Lizzie's hands a gentle pull that brought her up with him. "Come. Let's go meet them."

Chapter Thirty-Eight

TWO YEARS LATER

Lizzie sagged in exhaustion—had she ever worked so hard?—but she held out her eager arms. "Let me hold her."

Vivian set aside the soft cloth she'd used to bathe the squalling baby. "Just as soon as I wrap her up. Maybe she'll stop complaining if we get her warm."

Lizzie watched Vivian swaddle the squirming little girl in a caribou hide, her arms itching with impatience. *Hurry, hurry,* her heart begged. She'd hardly been given a glimpse of the newborn before Co'Ozhii handed her to Vivian to be cleansed.

Vivian laughed, the sound nearly swallowed by the baby's unhappy wails, as she placed the bundle in Lizzie's waiting arms. "She certainly is a noisy one. She must have quite a bit of her papa in her."

Lizzie peered into the red, wrinkled face of her firstborn

345

child. A love more all-encompassing than anything she could imagine swelled in her heart. Surely it would burst, so great was her joy. She touched the tiny rosebud mouth, and the hiccupping wail abruptly stopped. The little lips sucked fiercely on Lizzie's finger for a few seconds and then, with a few shuddering sobs, the baby closed her puffy eyes, and she fell asleep.

Lizzie lifted her head and sought Co'Ozhii, who'd moved to the foot of the bed and stood gazing at the mother and daughter, her lined face creased with a smile. "A girl, Grandmother, just as we wanted." She shifted her attention again to the baby nestled in the crook of her arm. Tears welled in Lizzie's eyes. So tiny and innocent, created by the love she and Clay shared. Clay needed to meet this little girl. She flicked a pleading glance at Co'Ozhii. "Bring Clay in now?"

Co'Ozhii had insisted Clay stay away during the birthing. She'd placed Vivian as sentinel on the doorstep to be certain he didn't try to sneak in. But now that the baby and Lizzie were presentable, it was time for the new father to meet his baby daughter. Co'Ozhii shuffled to the window and threw it wide, allowing in the sweet breeze of early fall. She called, "*Yuxudz xidinuxdal*—you come in!"

Moments later, footsteps pounded and the sleeping room door flew open. Clay, Naibi, Etu, and Vivian's husband spilled into the room. Co'Ozhii clucked in disapproval and stepped into their pathway, holding back all but Clay. He dashed to the bed and sat gingerly on its edge, his eyes locked on the little face peeking out from the fur blanket. Lizzie experienced a second rush of tears, witnessing Clay's wonder.

"A girl?" he said on a breathless note.

Lizzie nodded, her gaze flicking from Clay to their daughter and to Clay again. "Our Nayeli is here." They'd chosen the Kiowa name meaning "I love you." Lizzie chuckled softly. "But our next baby will be Judson. She'll need a brother to watch over her."

"Or maybe" —Vivian inched past Co'Ozhii, drawing her husband, Leonard, by the hand—"she'll have a strong, brave boy cousin to watch over her instead."

Clay aimed a startled look at his stepsister and brother-in-law. "You—already?"

Leonard wrapped his arms around Vivian from behind, smiling at Clay and Lizzie over Vivian's head. "Already. I suppose we don't wait for anything, do we?" He placed a kiss on Vivian's temple.

"I suppose you don't," Clay said with a laugh. He winked at Lizzie, and Lizzie smiled in reply.

They'd wondered if Vivian was rushing into things when she wrote about falling in love with Leonard Warren, a schoolteacher she'd met at church in Massachusetts. Only two months after meeting, the two exchanged vows at the chapel on the Kiowa reservation with Clay's father officiating the ceremony and Vivian's mother standing up beside her daughter.

When Leonard expressed a desire to use his teaching abilities in a mission setting, Clay's father and stepmother suggested the pair join Clay and Lizzie in Alaska. Lizzie had rejoiced in having her dear friend close by once again, and the newly married couple eased much of the work load, allowing Clay to travel to several other villages to share about Father-God. Lizzie sometimes wondered how she and Clay had managed an entire year without their assistance.

Lizzie caught Vivian's hand and gave it a tight squeeze. "Congratulations, Vivian and Leonard."

Naibi and Etu tried to sneak past Co'Ozhii for a peek at the baby, but the sharp-eyed woman swooped down on them. "Out, out," she scolded, pointing to the door. "Children out. White Feather and baby must sleep." She waved her arms, shooing the two crestfallen children out the door. She whirled on Vivian and Leonard, her gnarled fists on her hips. "You go, too. Leave the mother, father, and baby alone."

Vivian giggled. "We'll go." She tipped forward, bestowing kisses on first Lizzie's cheek and then Clay's. "She's beautiful, reflecting the best of both of you." Then, hand in hand with Leonard, she scurried out the door.

Co'Ozhii followed, pausing in the doorway. She peered back for a moment. Tears winked in her deeply lined eyes. "*Ngp'adist'a*—all of you."

Lizzie touched her lips with her fingers and flicked an imaginary kiss in her grandmother's direction. "We love you, too, Vitse."

With a gentle nod, Co'Ozhii closed the door, sealing away Lizzie, Clay, and their little daughter from the rest of the world.

Clay sighed, peering down contentedly at the sleeping baby in his arms. "Vivian was right—I see both of us in Nayeli. She has your beautiful skin, my light brown hair, your heart-shaped face . . ." He slipped his finger beneath the baby's tiny hand. Perfectly formed, minute fingers gripped him in return. He grinned. "And my long fingers. She'll be an accordion player. I just know it."

Lizzie chuckled softly. "Perhaps we should wait a year or two before you begin lessons."

"No more than two," Clay teased.

Lizzie watched her husband rock their daughter, his dear eyes glittering with unshed tears. Had her father held her in his arms and smiled at her in this way when she was born? The musing brought no sting of pain. Knowing she was loved unconditionally and forever by Father-God had replaced the hurt of her earthly father's abandonment.

She reached up and cupped the baby's head, joining the three of them together. "Clay?"

"Hmm?" He seemed unable to take his eyes off his daughter.

"I'm very sleepy."

His concerned gaze zinged to meet hers. "Do you want me to go?"

She shook her head. "No. I want you to pray with us before I fall asleep."

Clay's tender smile warmed her from the center of her soul. He lay little Nayeli in the crook of her arm and then slipped to his knees beside the bed. She closed her eyes as Clay's deep voice addressed their Father. He thanked God for the new life He'd entrusted to them and asked for wisdom in guiding Nayeli to a relationship with her Father-God one day. He asked health and strength for the tiny babe growing in Vivian's womb.

"We praise You, our Father, for the opportunity to serve You here together. We thank You for the precious gift of family. May we abide—ever, always—joyfully and peacefully in the shadow of Your wings. Amen."

He opened his eyes and leaned forward, his lips meeting hers in a kiss salty from happy tears. He then delivered a kiss on their daughter's fuzzy head. Very gently he tucked the blanket beneath Lizzie's chin. "Sleep now, little mother," he whispered, his voice as soft as the cottonwood seeds that floated on the summer breeze.

Lizzie gave a contented sigh and allowed her eyes to drift closed. She slipped away to sleep, thanking the Father for the gift of Clay's love and dreaming of the blessings yet to come.

Acknowledgments

Mom, Daddy, and Don—our time together in Alaska lives on in my heart as one of my most treasured memories. I'm so grateful for the family with which God gifted me.

Judith Miller, Nancy Moser, and Stephanie Whitson—thank you for your suggestions when brainstorming this story. Thank you also for the sweet time of fellowship.

My amazing critique group—thanks for taking these mad dashes through manuscripts with me and for being my friends. You are appreciated.

Aunt Vivian—thank you for letting me borrow your name.

Charlene and the wonderful folks at Bethany House—thank you for sharing this ministry with me. I thank my God upon every remembrance of you.

Finally, and most importantly, *God*—thank You for gifting me with the desire to put words on paper and opening the door to a writing ministry. I stand in awe of You! May any praise or glory be reflected directly back to You.

About the Author

KIM VOGEL SAWYER is the author of more than twenty novels, including many CBA and ECPA bestsellers. Her books have won the ACFW Carol Award, the Gayle Wilson Award of Excellence, and the Inspirational Readers Choice Award. Kim is active in her church, where she leads women's fellowship and participates in both voice and bell choirs. In her spare time, she enjoys drama, quilting, and calligraphy. Kim and her husband, Don, reside in Central Kansas, and have three daughters and nine grandchildren.

www.kimvogelsawyer.com